POUL AND KAREN ANDERSON

The King of Ys 1: Roma Mater

GRAFTON BOOKS

A Division of the Collins Publishing Group

LONDON GLASGOW
TORONTO SYDNEY AUCKLAND

Grafton Books
A Division of the Collins Publishing Group
8 Grafton Street, London W1X 3LA

A Grafton UK Paperback Original 1988

Copyright © Poul and Karen Anderson 1986

ISBN 0-586-07341-8

Printed and bound in Great Britain by
Collins, Glasgow

Set in Times

Gratillonius felt no fear. He had a task before him which he would carry out, or die; he did not expect to die.

In the middle of the court grew a giant oak. From the lowest of its newly leafing branches hung a brazen circular shield and a sledgehammer. Dents surrounded the boss, which showed a wildly bearded and maned human face.

Gratillonius sprang to earth, took hold of the hammer, smote the shield with his full strength. It rang, a bass note which sent echoes flying. Eppillus gave him his military shield and took his cloak and crest before marshalling the soldiers in a meadow across the road.

The priestess of Ys laid a hand on Gratillonius's arm. Never had he met so intense a gaze, out of such pallor, as from her. In a voice that shook, she whispered, 'Avenge us, man. Set us free. Oh, rich shall be your reward.'

It came to him, like a chill from the wind that soughed among the oaks, that his coming had been awaited. Yet how could she have known?

The storehouse door crashed open and Colconor strode forth. He had outfitted himself well for a barbarian – conical nose-guarded helmet, scale coat reaching to his knees, calf-length leather boots reinforced with studs. His left hand gripped a small round shield. The longsword shone dully in his right.

Also by Poul Anderson

This tale is all for
Astrid and Greg
with our love

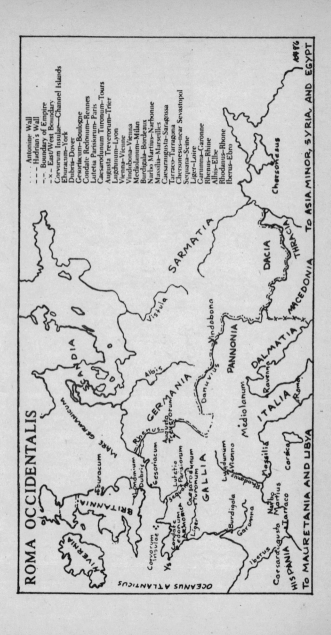

ROMA OCCIDENTALIS

.... Antonine Wall
---- Hadrian's Wall
--- Boundary of Empire
--x-- East/West Boundary
Corvorum Insulae—Channel Islands
Eburacum—York
Dubris—Dover
Gesoriacum—Boulogne
Condate Redinum—Rennes
Lutetia Parisiorum—Paris
Caesarodunum Turonum—Tours
Augusta Treverorum—Trier
Lugdunum—Lyon
Vienna—Vienne
Vindobona—Vienna
Mediolanum—Milan
Burdigala—Bordeaux
Narbo Martius—Narbonne
Massilia—Marseilles
Caesaraugusta—Saragossa
Turraco—Tarragona
Chersonesus—near Sevastopol
Sequana—Seine
Liger—Loire
Garumna—Garonne
Rhenus—Rhine
Albis—Elbe
Rhodanus—Rhone
Iberus—Ebro

Luguvalium–Carlisle
Isurium–Aldborough
Eburacum–York
Mona (1)–Man
Mona (2)–Anglesey
Deva–Chester
Viroconium–Wroxeter
Lindum–Lincoln
Glevum–Gloucester
Isca Silurum–Caerleon
Segontium–Carnarvon
Abonae–Sea Mills
Aquae Sulis–Bath
Borcovicum–Housesteads

Isca Dumnoniorum–Exeter
Vectis–Wight
Venta Icenorum–Caister St. Edmunds
Venta Belgarum–Winchester
Anderida–Pevensey
Rutupiae–Richborough
Dubris–Dover
Durnovaria–Dorchester
Camulodunum–Colchester
Calleva Atrebatum–Silchester
Corstopitum–Corbridge
Sabrina–Severn
Tamesis–Thames

BRITANNIA

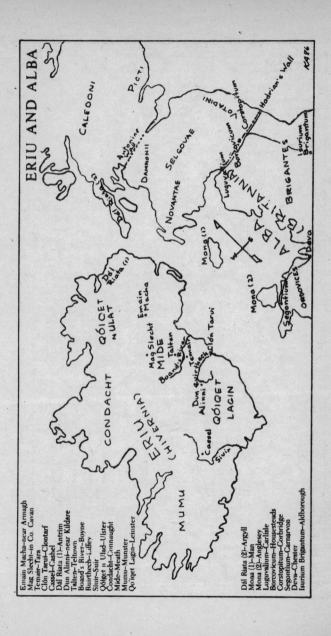

ERIU AND ALBA

Emain Macha—near Armagh
Mag Slecht—in Co. Cavan
Temair—Tara
Clón Tarui—Clontarf
Cassel—Cashel
Dál Riata (1)—Antrim
Dun Alinni—near Kildare
Tailten—Teltown
Boand's River—Boyne
Ruirthech—Liffey
Siun—Suir
Qóiget n Ulad—Ulster
Condacht—Connaught
Mide—Meath
Mumu—Munster
Qóiget Lagin—Leinster

Dál Riata (2)—Argyll
Mona (1)—Man
Mona (2)—Anglesey
Luguvalium—Carlisle
Borcovicum—Housesteads
Corstopitum—Corbridge
Segontium—Carnarvon
Deva—Chester
Isurium Brigantum—Aldborough

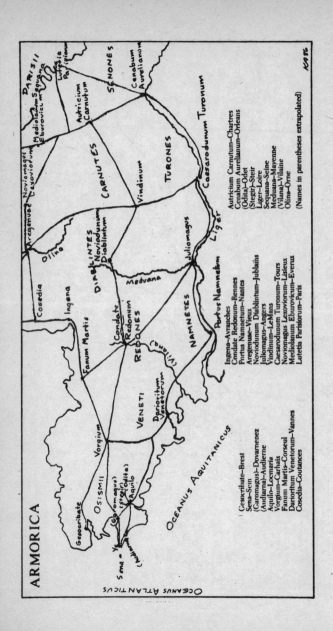

ARMORICA

OCEANUS ATLANTICUS

OCEANUS AQUITANICUS

DARISII
SENONES
Lutetia Parisiorum
Mediolanum Segusia
Eburovices
Autricium Carnutum
Canabum Aurelianum
Aregenua
Noviomagus Lexoviorum
Olina
CARNUTES
Caesarodunum Turonum
Noviodunum Diablintum
DIABLINTES
Vindinum
TURONES
Meduana
Liger
Condate Redonum
REDONES
NAMNETES
Portus Namnetum
Juliomagus
Fanum Martis
Ingena
Cosedia
Darioritum Venetorum
VENETI
Vorgium
OSISMII
(Gobaeum)
(Stalir)
Aquilo
Sena=Y
(Uxantis)
Gesocribate

(Odita)—Odet
(Steglr)—Steir
Liger—Loire
Sequana—Seine
Meduana—Mayenne
(Vilana)—Vilaine
Olina—Orne

(Names in parentheses extrapolated)

Autricum Carnutum—Chartres
Cenabum Aurelianum—Orleans

Ingena—Avranches
Condate Redonum—Rennes
Portus Namnetum—Nantes
Aregenua—Vieux
Noviodunum Diablintum—Jublains
Juliomagus—Angers
Vindinum—LeMans
Caesarodunum Turonum—Tours
Noviomagus Lexoviorum—Lisieux
Mediolanum Eburovicum—Everux
Lutetia Parisiorum—Paris

Gesocribate—Brest
Sena—Sein
(Garomagus)—Dovarmenez
(Audierna)—Audierne
Aquilo—Locmaria
Vorgium—Carhaix
Fanum Martis—Corseul
Darioritum Venetorum—Vannes
Cosedia—Coutances

KAPC

PROMONTORIUM GOBÆUM

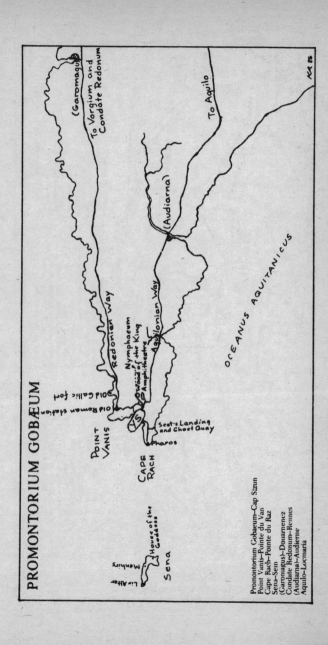

Promontorium Gobaeum–Cap Sizun
Point Vanis–Pointe du Van
Cape Rach–Pointe du Raz
Sena–Sein
(Garomagus)–Douarnenez
Condate Redonum–Rennes
(Audiarna)–Audierne
Aquilo–Locmaria

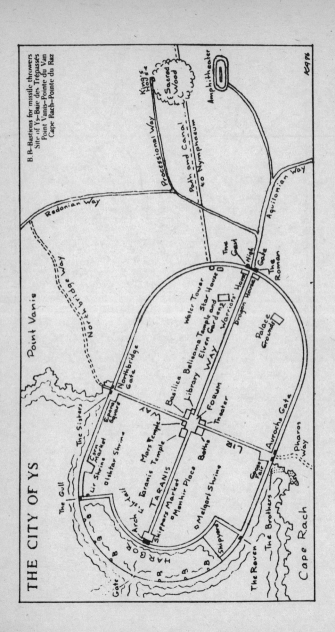

THE CITY OF YS

B. B.—Bastions for missile throwers
Site of Ys—Baie des Trépassés
Point Vanis—Pointe du Van
Cape Rach—Pointe du Raz

Point Vanis

Redonian Way

Northbridge Way

The Sisters

The Gull

Gate

HARBOR

Arch

Corn Market

Ishtar Shrine

Lir Shrine

Mars Temple

Taranis Temple

TARANIS

Skippers Market

Menhir Place

Baths

Melqart Shrine

Shipyard

The Brothers

The Raven

Cape Rach

Northbridge Gate

Epona Square

Basilica

Library

Belisama Temple and Elven Garden

Water Tower

Star House

Warriors' Way

WAY

FORUM

Theater

Goose Fair

Auroch Gate

Pharos Way

Dragon House

Palace Grounds

Processional Way

Path and Canal to Nymphaeum

Sacred Wood

King's Hog

Amphitheater

Aquilonian Way

The Crawl

High Gate

The Roman

K.A.96

I

1

At noon upon that Birthday of Mithras, the sun blazed low in an ice-clear heaven. As Gratillonius looked south, he saw its brilliance splinter into rainbow shards amidst his eyelashes. Hills afar, ditch and earthworks nearby, terraced fields below, lay whitened and still. Smoke rose from Borcovicium fort and the settlement huddled against its ramparts, but so straight that it scarcely marred the purity. When he turned his gaze north, there was nothing of man save the shadow of the Wall, huge and blue, down a cliff whose own shadow filled the hollow underneath. Heights beyond were dark with forest in winter sleep. Light flashed starlike off icicles. A few crows aflight set their blackness against his breath, their distant cawing against his heartbeat, and that was all that stirred.

For a moment he felt wholly alone. The summer's warfare was not only past, it was unreal, a dream he had had or a story told him in his childhood, fading out of memory – but what, then, was real?

A glance right and left brought him back. Four-square, the murky bulk of a tower blocked off most westward view; but eastward, vision ran along the walkway past the two intermediate observation turrets to the next mile-castle, and the next, until the Wall swung under the horizon: fifteen feet from base to battlements, seventy-seven miles from sea to sea across Britannia. Metal made small fierce gleams where men stood watch down that length. Cloaks and drooping standards splashed their colours athwart its grey. Below them, some two hundred Roman paces from him, the legionary base rose in a gridiron of streets and lanes which seemed doubly severe next to the paths twisting between houses in the vicus. Everything he saw belonged here.

And so did he. His body rested easy under helmet, mail, greaves. Beneath them, his tunic hung lower than the skirt of studded leather straps; a scarf protected his neck from chafing by armour; woollen half-breeches, stockings inside the hobnailed sandals, fended off the season; all was familiar. Sword at hip, stick cut from the mainstem of a grapevine, were as much limbs of his as were arms and legs. Because the day was holy, he had not yet taken food, nor would he until the Mystery at eventide, and hunger somehow spurred awareness of his own strength. The chill in the air made it feel liquid, it bathed him within and without. And now trumpets sounded, echoes rang, high noon had come.

To most in the army, that signalled no more than a change of guard. It called Gratillonius to prayer. He faced the sun again, removed his helmet and set it on the parapet. A scarlet horsehair crest, attached for the round of inspection which he was on, scratched his wrist and scritted. He raised his arms and began the office – softvoiced, because such was seemly and it would be his heart that the God heard – 'Hail, Mithras Unconquered, Saviour, Warrior, Lord, born unto us anew and forever – '

'Centurion.'

At first he barely noticed, and did not imagine it meant him. ' – hear us, You Who did slay the Bull that Its blood might make fruitful the world. You Who stand before the Lion and the Serpent – '

'Centurion!' yelled in his ear.

Rage flared. Had the contumely of the Christians swollen to this?

An instant before snatching his vinestaff and giving the intruder a slash across the mouth, Gratillonius checked himself. It behoved an officer both of the Halidom and of Rome to curb a temper he knew was too quick, not profane his devotions with violence. He shot a glare which made the fellow step back alarmed, and continued.

The words were soon finished. It was as well, he thought, when anger seethed in him. He turned to confront the stranger, and beheld insignia of the Sixth Victrix. His mind sprang. Although that legion was based at Eboracum, closer than either of the other two in the island, it had not joined them against Picti and Scoti raging down from the north, but stayed behind. Supposedly that was to stand off any Saxon raiders. However, some few of its men had accompanied Maximus as bodyguards, couriers, confidants.

No matter yet. Gratillonius picked up the stick that marked his rank, tucked it under an elbow, and rapped forth: 'Attention! Have you no better manners than to interrupt a man at his worship, soldier? You disgrace your eagle.'

The other stiffened, gulped, abruptly recovered and answered, 'I beg the centurion's pardon. No bishop ever told me this is a time for services. I had my orders, and only supposed the centurion was deep in thought.'

Insolent knave indeed, Gratillonius knew. He sagged a little, inwardly. Of course he was dealing with a Christian. Most legionaries were, these days, or pretended to be. This very year the rescript had arrived that banned the old faiths, along with tales of how the authorities were despoiling Mithraic temples first. Men at war on the uttermost frontier paid scant heed, and Maximus knew

15

better than to enforce such a decree . . . until today, when the immediate danger was past?

Within Gratillonius, his father drawled anew, 'Son, you're too rash, you always court trouble. No sense in that. She'll come on her own, never fear. Better just court girls.' A curious tenderness followed. Gratillonius must even quell a smile as he said:

'I should take your name and remand you to your unit for punishment drill, if not a flogging. But since you admit ignorance, I'll be merciful. What do you want?'

An awakened caution replied. 'Mine is . . . the honour of addressing Gaius Valerius Gratillonius, centurion of the Second . . . is it not? I asked the squad where you were.'

'Which is here. Speak on.'

The messenger donned importance. 'The Duke of the Britains sent me. You are relieved of your regular duty and will report to him at once in the praetorium.'

'The Duke? What, not at Vindolanda?' Gratillonius was surprised. The old fort and settlement, close by but somewhat behind the Wall, was where the grand commander had generally stayed when in this area.

'He is making a progress of inspection and . . . other business, it seems. He summoned you by name.'

What could that mean? A mission? The blood thrilled in Gratillonius.

2

The close-packed buildings of the strongpoint shaded streets and turned the lanes between into tunnels of cold and gloom. Nonetheless several men were passing time off watch with a dice game on the verandah of their

16

barrack. But they were Tungri, auxiliaries such as formed the permanent garrisons of the Wall; regulars only arrived in emergencies like this year's. Well wrapped in furs, the barbarians doubtless found the dry air a blessed change from their native marshlands. Their speech went croaking and hawking through a quiet otherwise broken by little more than footfalls, although those rang loud enough on frozen earth.

Entering on the west, Gratillonius must pass the headquarters block standing sheer around three sides of its courtyard. He halted to salute the basilica, for it held the legionary shrine and standards: not his legion, true, but equally Rome's. The sentries saluted him in their turn. The smartness of it pleased, now when the Tungri had reminded him of the slovenly ways he found when his vexillation first came here. Maximus had done marvels in restoring discipline. To be sure, Gratillonius thought, the long campaign helped; poor soldiers were apt to become dead ones.

Memory ranged across the months that were past: the march up country through springtime rains to a stone wonder he had never seen before; settling in, getting to know the hills and heaths, exploring what often sleazy pleasures the civilian villages had to offer; shamefaced purification before he sought the Mithraeum, but then, for no good reason that he could see to this day, his elevation in grade – well, they said he had fought valiantly, but that hardly sufficed, and most likely it was that pious Parnesius had recommended him to the Father, and after all, the congregation had grown so pitifully small –

The warring itself was somehow less vivid. It had been an endlessness of expeditions from this base to seek whatever band of painted Picti or gaudy Scoti had been reported, of weather wet or hot, of troubles with supply trains and troubles among the men such as a centurion must handle, of having them shovel trenches and ramparts for encampments they would demolish the next dawn, of finally – most times – coming upon the enemy and going to work, of the dead afterwards and the wounded, the wounded . . . You did what you and the surgeons could for your own, and tried to keep your men from being needlessly cruel when they cut the throats of tall dark highlanders and fair-skinned warriors from over the water. There was no safe way of bringing prisoners to a slave market, and you could not risk that any would recover from his injuries. You had seen too many home-steads plundered and burnt, slain men, ravished women who wept for children carried off because the Scoti did do a brisk trade in slaves; and this was not only north of the Wall, among tribes friendly to Rome, but south of it, in territories thinly peopled but still subject to Caesar. The foe came around every defence in their leather coracles. So as leaves withered and fell. Gratillonius killed his last opponent (hail rattled on helmets; its pallor across the ground made blood spurt doubly red) and Britannia lay at peace. But thus it had been again and again in the past, and surely would in the future.

He curbed his mind, squared his shoulders, and strode onward. Forebodings were foolishness. The truth was that Maximus had prevailed, had reaped so widely among the wild men that they would not soon come back, and had something to tell an infantryman who was chafing at the sameness of garrison life. What better omen than getting that word on the holiest day of the year?

The praetorium was almost as large as the principia. When Gratillonius identified himself, the guard called a man to guide him. Inside, the warmth of a hypocaust radiated from tiled floors; frescos on the walls glowed with flowers, fruits, beasts. Homeric Gods and heroes; more servants than soldiers passed by. But such was usual, Gratillonius knew. His own commandant's house in the base at Isca Silurum made this one on the far frontier look impoverished. Maximus had the reputation of living austerely wherever he was.

Another legionary of the Sixth stood at a certain door. Upon learning who had appeared, he opened it and waited at attention until bidden to speak. 'Gaius Valerius Gratillonius, centurion of the seventh cohort, Second Legion Augusta,' he then announced, and gestured the newcomer in. The door closed. Gratillonius saluted.

Light, straggling bleak through a glazed window, got help from lamps. It showed lavishness neglected. Two men sat at a table whereon were beakers, bescribbled notebooks of thin-scraped wood, a map drawn on parchment, an inkwell and quill, a waxed tablet and stylus. One man, big, young, freckle-faced, was clearly a native. He had donned Roman garb for this occasion, but a moustache flared, his ruddy hair was bound in a knot, a golden torque gleamed around his neck. His companion, whom Gratillonius knew by sight, was the Duke of the Britains.

Magnus Clemens Maximus hailed from the uplands of Hispania Tarraconensis. It showed in his height and leanness, hatchet features, olive skin, hair stiff and black and slightly grizzled. It also softened his Latin as he said, 'At ease, centurion. Take off your cloak and helmet.' The steel of him was in his voice, though, and his eyes were always probing.

To the tribesman he added: 'This is the officer whom I have in mind to lead your escort.' To Gratillonius: 'You have the honour of meeting Cunedag, a prince among the Votadini and Rome's loyal ally. Your assignment will be to accompany him and his following to the Ordovices, on your way back with your century.' Smiling: 'Look well, you two. I trust you both like what you see.'

Gratillonius sped through memory. Dwelling north of

19

the Wall, the Votadini had formerly been subjects and, after the tide of empire ebbed southward, had stayed on reasonably good terms. Indeed, their leading families claimed Roman descent and often bestowed Roman names. He had not met Cunedag before, but had heard of him as a useful warlord throughout the year's campaigning.

The chieftain's gaze searched over the centurion. It found a man of twenty-five, medium tall for a Briton – which made him overtop most Italians – and robustly built. The visage of Gratillonius was broad and square, clean-shaven, with craggy nose and wideset grey eyes. His complexion was fair, his close-cropped hair auburn. He moved like a cat. When he spoke, the tone was deep and rather harsh.

'You have won a high name,' said Cunedag in his own language. 'I think we shall travel well together.'

'Thank you, lord. I will do my best,' replied Gratillonius. He used the tongue of the Dumnonii, which was not too alien for the Northerner to understand and chuckle at.

'Good,' said Maximus, sensing the accord. 'Prince, we have talked a long while and you must be weary. The centurion and I have matters to discuss which can scarcely interest you. Why do you not seek your guestroom, or whatever else you like, and rest until we meet at the evening meal?'

Cunedag, an intelligent barbarian, took the hint and uttered a stately goodbye. A gong summoned an attendant to lead him out and a second man to bring Gratillonius a goblet of wine and water. The officer took the vacated stool at his commander's word and peered across the clutter on the table. His pulse drummed anew.

Maximus stroked fingers across his prow of a chin. 'Well, soldier,' he said, 'you must be wondering how I even knew who you are, let alone found a rather special task for you.'

'The Duke surely has many ears,' Gratillonius ventured.

Maximus shrugged. 'Fewer than he could use. In this case, you've become a friend of Parnesius, and it happens that I am acquainted with his father and have kept my eye on the son. Parnesius praised you to me: less your valour, which any dolt could show, but skill and coolness overriding a temperament hot by nature, a talent for improvising, a gift of leadership.' He sighed. 'That is a gift, you know, a mystery. God's hand touches a man, and that man turns into one whom others will follow though it be past the gates of hell. Would I had more like that to follow *me*!'

A chill tingle passed through Gratillonius. The provinces of the Empire bred men who claimed the purple by right of the sword, and Britannia was among them. Here the legions had first hailed great Constantinus, almost a hundred years ago. More recently there had been Magnentius, rising in Gallia but born in Britannia and supported by Britons; his failure and its terrible aftermath need not discourage later dreams. As warfare ended and winter closed in, legionaries had time to think, wonder, mutter . . . fifteen years was a long time to keep as able a leader as Maximus off on the frontiers . . . he declared that he held the Sixth in reserve at Eboracum against Saxon attack, and maybe this was true, but it was likewise true that the Sixth had come to be his adoring own . . . the real rulers of the West were not the co-Emperors but a barbarian, a woman, and a churchman . . . the hour might be overpast for putting a man of proven metal on the throne . . .

Maximus's voice levelled. 'I've kept your detachment, together with that from the Twentieth and all the sundry oddments, on the Wall to make sure our pacification was nailed down. The Picti wouldn't worry me by themselves. Their little quarrelsome packs will never do more alone than snap up some loot, take a drubbing, and scatter back to lick their wounds. But lately the Scoti have been leagued with them, and – the Scoti are a different breed of wolf.' He scowled. 'Somebody in Hivernia has been behind the last onslaught, somebody powerful and shrewd. I would not have put it past him to deliver a surprise blow just when we thought we were safely finished.'

Maximus tossed off a laugh and a swallow from his cup. 'Well, he didn't. Now he couldn't possibly before spring, and one may doubt he'll care to try again that soon. So the vexillations can return to their legions: a cold trek, but not one that I think they'll mind. On your way, Gratillonius, I want you to guard Cunedag on his. At Deva you and your century will part company not only with the Valeria Victrix troops, but with your fellows of the Augusta. Proceed with Cunedag into Ordovicia, stop where he wants, and do whatever is necessary to establish him.'

'Would the Duke explain why?' Gratillonius requested.

'It won't likely be a severe task,' Maximus said. 'I have had negotiators there, and on the whole, the clans will welcome him. See here. Stationed where you are, you must know how law and order have been breaking down in those parts, leaving people well-nigh helpless before the Scoti, not to mention home-grown brigands. I can't have that sort of thing at my back when – ' He broke off. 'Cunedag possesses a fairly sound grasp of both military and political principles. He'll take charge. Your century shouldn't have a great deal to do, nor need to linger long, before it can return to Isca Silurum.'

'I understand, sir,' Gratillonius said. 'In part.'

'Never fear, you'll know more before you leave. Half a

dozen men, both Roman and tribal, are set to instruct you. Meanwhile,' and Maximus smiled, 'you can get to know Cunedag better this evening at supper.'

Gratillonius stiffened. He must summon up as much of himself as he had ever needed in combat in order to say: 'I regret that I cannot accept the Duke's invitation.'

Maximus raised his brows. 'What?'

'Sir, this day is sacred. I may only take part in the feast of the God.'

'Oh.' Maximus was silent for a space. When he spoke, it was like the winter outside. 'I had forgotten. You are pagan.'

It prickled in Gratillonius's armpits. 'Sir, I do not worship Jupiter, if that's what you mean.'

'But Mithras. Which is forbidden. For your soul's good, understand. You'll burn for ever after you die, unless you take the Faith.'

Gratillonius bridled. 'The Duke has not yet seen fit to close our temples.'

Maximus sighed. 'As you will, as you will. For now, at least. After all, Parnesius is obstinate too. But he serves Rome well, like you and, I dare hope, me. Come, let us drink to the well-being of our Mother.'

The wine was excellent, unlike what was issued the troops. Yet its sweetness dimmed on Gratillonius's tongue as Maximus frowned, lowered his beaker, stared into the shadows that filled a corner, and murmured: 'Little enough well-being is hers any longer. You've never seen Rome, the City, have you? I have. Our Mother is fallen on evil days. There are more ghosts than living folk in her streets, and the Emperor reigns from Mediolanum, Augusta Treverorum, or . . . anywhere except poor, plundered Rome. The Emperor of the West, that is. No, today the joint Emperors of the West, the first a plaything of his Frankish general, the second of his mother, and the

West divided between them. And even the Augustus of the East feels Constantinople tremble beneath him. It is but four or five years since the Goths rode down the Romans at Adrianople. Have you heard about that, centurion? The Emperor Valens himself died on the field. His successor Theodosius must needs buy the alliance of those barbarians, Arian heretics, those that are not still outright heathen – ' He straightened. His voice clanged forth: 'By the Great Name of God, Rome shall not suffer this! Mother, your hour of deliverance draws near.'

Then immediately he was again the self-contained man whose patience had forged victory. He raised his cup, sipped, regarded Gratillonius over the rim, and smiled afresh before he said, 'Be not alarmed, centurion. I've no wish to scare off the few trustworthy men left me. Rather, I've work in mind for you, more challenging and more glorious than the mere delivery of a leader and his warriors to some ragged hillfolk. Indeed, that assignment is essentially a final test of you. If you carry it off as well as I expect – '

Leaning forward: 'I've made inquiries about you, of course, since Parnesius's mention of you drew my attention your way. Now I wish to talk freely with you, explore what sort of *person* you are.'

'A very ordinary soldier, sir,' Gratillonius replied uneasily.

Maximus laughed, straightened on his stool, crossed shank over knee. Such putting aside of dignity, by the Duke himself, caught at Gratillonius's heart. Eagerness rekindled in him. 'Oh, no, you don't, lad!' Maximus crowed. 'You'll never make that claim stick, not after this summer. And I hear you did well in the South, earlier.'

'That was nothing unusual, really, sir. Sometimes Scoti or Saxons came visiting, and we went out to meet them. Otherwise it was plain patrol and camp duty.'

'Um-m, I've heard of a fire in town, and a young legionary who risked his life to rescue the children from a burning house. I've also heard how that same fellow gets along well with natives, whether they be his familiar Silures and Belgae or the half-tame dwellers in these parts.'

'Well, I'm of Britannic blood myself, sir.'

'Unusual – No, you are a regular, of course, not an auxiliary. Almost a namesake of the Emperor Gratianus.'

The centurion felt his muscles grow tense. Likening his family to that Scythian-loving sluggard! 'Pure chance, sir,' he stated. 'My folk are Belgae, living near Aquae Sulis since before Claudius. Naturally, we've long been civilized, and a forebear of mine gave the name a Latin form, but we've kept our ties to the land.'

Maximus seemed a trifle amused. 'Have you no ancestors who were not Belgae? That would be strange.'

'Of course there were some, sir. Soldiers stationed in Britannia, Italians, a Dacian, a Nervian. And a couple of Gauls, though they were female, brides brought home.'

Maximus nodded, once more grave. 'Sound stock throughout. You are of the curial class, I understand.'

Gratillonius grimaced. Maximus hastened to bespeak happier matters: 'Your grandfather had a distinguished military career, did he not? And your father went into trade out of Abonae, and prospered. That took real seamanship – those tides in the estuary – and fighting skill, too, when pirates infest the waters.'

The Duke must have queried Parnesius closely indeed, to dig out things casually related over a span of months. The voice quickened: 'His main business was with Armorica, true? And he took you along on his voyages.'

'Well, between the ages of twelve and sixteen, when I joined the army, I used to go with him, sir,' Gratillonius replied.

'Tell me about it.'

'Oh, we'd coast along Britannia, taking on cargo here and there, then cross over to a Gallic port – maybe as far east as Gesoriacum – and work our way west, stopping off to trade. Sometimes we'd leave the ship and travel inland to markets in places like Condate Redonum or Vorgium – ' Gratillonius shook himself. Those joyful years were far behind him and his father both.

Maximus's tone sharpened. 'Did you ever visit Ys?'

'What?' Gratillonius was startled. 'Why . . . why, no. Does anybody any longer?'

'We shall see. You appear to have an ear for language. Did you acquire fluency in any Gallic tongues? I'm interested especially in whatever they use on the western end of Armorica.'

'I got along, sir. That was quite a while ago, and I haven't returned since.' Gratillonius began to realize what Maximus was driving at. The hair stirred on his neck and arms. 'But I ought to regain it pretty quickly. Those dialects aren't too different from the southern Britannic, and I had a Dumnonic nurse when I was small.' Awkwardly: 'She stayed on in the house for my younger siblings, and we used to talk in her speech, she and I, till I enlisted – and afterwards, when I was home on leave. I do hope old Docca is still alive.'

The wistfulness flickered out, for Maximus was saying low, while he stared before him as if his vision could pierce the wall and fly away over Europe: 'Excellent. The Lord is gracious to me, a sinner. It may actually be Providence that you are an infidel; for there could be things yonder that are not for a Christian man to deal with.'

A fire leapt up in the breast of Gratillonius.

Once the temple had not been as far as it now was from a vicus of several hundred veterans, artisans, merchants, innkeepers, harlots, wives, children, hangers-on, a settlement akin to the rest that clustered south of the Wall, from sea to sea, within a mile or a few of each other. But nearly two hundred years had passed since Caledonic invaders laid the Borcovicium region waste while Rome writhed at war with itself. After Severus restored things, rebuilding was done farther uphill, next to the military base. Perhaps in awe, the reavers had spared the Mithraeum. Thus it stood alone on a knoll near the ditch, only brush surrounding its temenos. Northward, darkness rose like a tide towards the battlemented horizon the Wall made; southward, the ground rolled off in ridges which the setting sun reddened. Frost creaked underfoot, voices mumbled through smoke signals of breath, silence everywhere else deepened with cold.

Arriving early for the service, Gratillonius found Parnesius among those who waited outside. His friend was wrapped in a cloak but had not drawn the hood over his black hair. It curled back from his forehead to show the tiny brand of initiation which Gratillonius also bore, both now faint; hot iron had made larger and deeper marks on their bodies when they first entered the army. Beneath the religious sign, Parnesius's eyebrows formed a single bar over his jutting nose. 'Hail,' he said, more cheerfully than might be suitable at this hour. 'How went it with the Old Man today?'

They clasped forearms in the Roman manner. 'Lad, you're all aquiver,' Parnesius exclaimed.

'How I wish I could tell you,' Gratillonius replied. 'It's – oh, wonderful – but he made me vow secrecy for the time being. When I can talk, when actual operations are in train, then I'll be far from here.'

'Well, I'm glad to see you're glad. Although – Come.' Parnesius plucked at the other's mantle. 'Step aside for a bit, shall we?'

More men were climbing the trail hither. While they numbered under a score, they were of many sorts, not only soldiers but workmen, serfs, slaves. Rank on earth counted for nothing before Ahura-Mazda.

As it did not before the Lord of the Christians . . . but they welcomed women to their services, passed fleetingly through Gratillonius. His father, his brother, himself followed Mithras; but his mother had been Christian and so, by amicable agreement, were his sisters raised. Could that alone be the reason why Christ was triumphing?

He thrust the thought away and followed Parnesius off as he had followed this comrade in arms, and the still more experienced Pertinax, on days when they could 'take the heather' – fare off with a native guide to hunt, fish, be at ease in clean and lonesome country. 'What have you to say?' he asked. 'Time's short.' Because the service was conducted on sufferance, military members had better be in their quarters by curfew.

Parnesius looked off and beat fist in palm. 'I'm not sure,' he answered roughly. 'Except . . . I couldn't help getting hints when he quizzed me about you. And . . . Pertinax and I have had an offer . . . but we'll stay on the Wall, we two. You're going south, aren't you? Not just back to Isca, but on to Gallia.'

Gratillonius swallowed. 'I'm not supposed to say.'

'Nevertheless – ' Parnesius swung about and seized him by the shoulders. His gaze probed and pleaded. 'He wouldn't have told you outright, but you must have a fair idea of what he intends. You must be aware you're to guard his back while – Well, what do you think about it? The next war will mean a great deal more than this last one, you know. Don't you?'

'I am . . . a soldier,' Gratillonius answered most carefully. 'I follow my orders. But . . . an Emperor who is a soldier too might be what we all need.'

'Good!' cried Parnesius, and pummelled him lightly on the back. 'And here in the North, Pertinax and I'll hold fast. Ho, I see him coming. Hail, Pertinax!'

But then the Father appeared, and men ranked themselves for the ceremony.

The Mithraeum was plain and low. It could not hold even as many as the remnant who were gathered. However, it was not meant to. The junior initiates, Ravens, Occults, Soldiers, did not attend the holiest of the rites. They joined their seniors in hymning the sun as it departed.

Flame glimmered across a green southwestern heaven, and went out. More and more stars gleamed forth, and lights along the blackness of Wall and fortress. Elsewhere the world sheened phantom grey. The song ended. The three underling ranks formed their squad and saluted while Lions, Persians, the Runner of the Sun, and the Father whom he attended went inside.

There was no space for a pronaos. There was, though, a vestibule, where Gratillonius and his fellows changed into their sacred garb. For him it was robe, mask, and Phrygian cap, because in the past year the elders had promoted him to Persian. Solemnly, they entered the sanctuary.

Lamplight amidst restless shadows picked out the altars that jutted into the narrow nave. At the end of the chamber, reliefs depicted Mithras slaying the Bull and His cosmic birth with the signs of the zodiac around. The stone was pierced so that illumination behind created the halo about his head. Flanking were the graven Dadophori, the brother figures, one with torch held high, one with torch down and guttering out. It was very quiet. After the chill outside, air felt merely cool. The sweet smoke of pine cones breathed through it.

The celebrants crossed the floor of oak planks and birch logs to their benches along the walls. The Father took his place before the Tauroctony. He was an aged man, as was the Heliodromos who served him. Their deaths would surely spell the end of worship here.

Gratillonius raised up his heart. However men blundered, Mithras remained true to His world; and meanwhile he, Gratillonius, had his own victory ahead of him.

II

Imbolc marked the season of making ready for the year's work, the lambing that would soon begin, spring sowing later, fishing whenever Manandan and the merfolk would allow. People took stock of what supplies remained in household and farmyard. On the coasts they gathered seaweed to cut up and strew on their fields, as well as shellfish when the tide of Brigit stood at its lowest. Yet the day itself and the vigil of the day were hallowed. Along the shores of Condacht and Mumu, live periwinkles or limpets were buried around each house for luck on strand and water. Many tuaths elsewhere did no work that called for the turning of a wheel, such as carting; it might bewilder the sun on his homeward course. Families wove new talismans of straw and twigs and hung them about dwellings for protection against lightning and fire. They celebrated the eve with the best feast their stores could provide, putting some outside for the Goddess, Who would be travelling that night, and grain for Her white cow. They reckoned, however, that Brigit was also pleased if the food went to the needy, or to those parties of youths and maidens that carried Her emblems from home to home across the land – as long as the gift was given in Her name.

Anxiously they watched for weather signs. Rain was welcome, to soften the ground and hasten growth of new grass; but storms were ominous, and if the hedgehog did not appear, that meant he was keeping his burrow in expectation of more winter followed by a hard summer. This year, what happened was so shifty across Ériu that no one knew what to await. Wisewomen said it portended strange doings and great changes; druids generally stayed silent.

On Temir was the most splendid of all festivals, for it was the King's, and Niall maqq Echach bade fair to become the mightiest since Corbmac maqq Arti, or even to outreach that lord. Not only his household and following were on hand, learned men, ollam craftsmen, warriors, their women and children; not only free tenants of both his and theirs, and families of these, from end to end of Mide; not only kings of the tuaths over whom he held sway, and their own attendants and underlings. From Condacht, whence the forebears of Niall had sprung, came many to greet their kinsman. From Mumu, where he had friends, came not a few. From the Lagini came some, more in hopes of mildening him towards themselves than in love. From the Ulati, alone among the Fifths, came not a man, unless it be a few outcasts begging. But then, in Emain Macha they held a revel too, which they said was as royal and sacral as this.

Throughout the day of the vigil Niall had been taken up with welcoming his guests as they arrived, in such ways as became their standings and his. Now at eventide he would open the festivities.

Bathed and freshly clad, in stately wise he walked from the King's House to the point where the southward-running of the Five Roads to Temir came up on the hilltop. There his chariot awaited him. Its matched grey horses snorted and pawed; Cathual the driver must keep tight reins. Niall mounted easily. When the wheels groaned into motion, he stood steady amidst the rocking and jouncing. His spear swayed like a ship's mast. Sunlight streamed level to make its head shine as if newly bloodied.

From here Niall saw widely over his domains. Down along the road clustered the booths and tents of lower-ranking folk for whom the buildings had no space. Many were striped in colours, and pennons fluttered above some. On the next summit loomed the hill fort sacred to Medb. Heights round about were still bright, but hollows were filling with shadow. Though leafless, forest hid Boand's River to the north; yet the air, damp and turning chill, bore a sense of Her presence among the spirits that thronged nigh. Westward land dropped steeply to the plain, its pastures winter-dulled, save that mists had arisen to beswirl them with molten gold. The sun cast the same hue on clouds above that horizon, with heaven violet beyond them. Ahead of Niall bulked the Great Rath, its lime-whitened earthwork and the palisade on top likewise aglow.

People crowded the paths to watch him and his guards go by. Men's tunics and cloaks, their breeches or kilts, the gowns of women were vivid in red, yellow, blue, green, orange, black, white; gold, silver, amber, crystal, gems glistened around brows, throats, arms, waists; spears, axes, drawn swords flashed high in reverence; on shields, round or oval, the painted marks of their owners twined or snarled or ramped. Children, dogs, pigs ran about among the grown and joined their clamour to the shout that billowed for the King.

Well did he seem worthy of hailing. His chariot of state bore bronze masks on the sides; the spokes of its two wheels were gilded; at either rail hung the withered head of a Roman, taken by him in the past summer's warfare. Cathual the charioteer was a youngling short but lithe and comely, clad in tunic of scarlet; headband, belt, and wristlets were set with silver. From the shoulders of Niall swung a cloak of the finest wool, striped in the full seven colours permitted a king; his undershirt was of Roman silk, his tunic saffron with red and blue embroideries; rather than breeches he wore a kilt, dark russet to show off the whiteness and shapeliness of his legs, with shoes of kid on his feet. His ornaments outweighed and outshone all others.

Finest to see was himself. At some thirty years of age, after uncounted battles against men and beasts, Niall maqq Echach remained without any flaw that might cost him his lordship. Taller than most he reared, wide in shoulders and slender in hips, skin fair even where weather had touched it and not unduly shaggy, wildcat muscles flowing beneath. Golden were his long hair and moustaches, his close-trimmed beard. His brow was broad, his nose straight, his chin narrow; eyes gleamed fire-blue.

Behind the chariot paced his hounds and his hostages, the men's attire revealing his generosity. They wore light golden chains, that everyone might know them for what they were, but strode proudly enough; their position was honourable, and most times they went unhampered. Behind them, and also in front of the chariot, walked his warriors. Closest to him were the four bodyguards and the gigantic champion, bearing helmets and dress shields of polished bronze; but the rest were hardly less brilliant, in tunics like their master's, axes glimmering and spearheads nodding on high.

Folk cheered themselves hoarse to see the power of King Niall. Few were so close as to make out the grimness upon his lips, the bitterness in his face.

The procession turned where a gate stood open in the Great Rath and a bridge had been laid down across the ditch. It went over the lawn within, past the lesser enclosure of the Royal Guesthouse and the embanked mound whereon rose the King's quarters. A ways farther on, it halted. There the Mound of the Kings lifted itself athwart the outer palisade.

Niall did not dismount and climb its grassy slopes. That

34

was only done when a new King was taken. Then he would stand on the sacred slab at the top, make his three turns dessiul and widdershins, receive the White Wand, invoke the Gods. On this holy eve, Cathual guided the chariot past the Phallus below, five lichenous feet of standing stone. A fighting man stationed at that menhir swung a bullroarer to proclaim that this was truly the King who came by.

The procession went on, out of a northern gate, past other stones to which Niall dipped his spear, past the Rath of the Warriors, between the small mounds Dall and Dercha, on to the Feasting Hall. Niall's Queen, his sons, his counsellors, their chief servants stood waiting. Cathual drew rein and the overlord sprang down. He gave his weapon to the charioteer and first greeting to the druid and the poets, as was seemly. Thereafter he received the salutations of the others according to their status.

'Now we've a time to wait,' he said. 'Is it a good sign that we are free of rain the while?'

'It is that,' answered the druid, Nemain maqq Aedo, gravely, 'but other signs have been such that you will be wise to sacrifice more than is wont tomorrow.'

Niall scowled. 'I did so last year, at both Imbolc and Beltene, and meagre gain did we have of it.'

Some people looked aghast at this defiance of the Powers. Nemain simply raised his hand. He was gaunt, snowy-bearded, his eyes dimmed by years and by peering into mysteries. Unlike everyone else, he wore a plain white robe and blue cloak; but his staff was carved with potent ogamm signs. 'Speak not rashly, dear heart,' he said. 'If you failed to overrun the foe – then, sure it nonetheless is that you brought home alive yourself and most of the men, with not so little plunder. Would it not have been easier, now, for the Mórrigu to let you lie raven-food under the Roman Wall? The signs I have read, in stars and staves and secret pools, are signs of mighty deeds, of a world in travail with a new birth. Give freely, and receive back honour.'

Flame flickered up through Niall's sullen mood. 'Warfare already again this summer?'

'That is as may be. Thus far the red wind only whispers, and I know not from what quarter it is blowing.'

Niall's glance flew about, south towards the Lagini, north towards the Ulati, east towards Alba across the water, which the Romans called Britannia. There it lingered.

Breccan, his eldest son, advanced. 'Father, dear,' he cried, 'you'll be taking me along, will you not?'

Niall turned and regarded him. The sun had just set, but light remained in heaven to make the boy shine forth against a world going dun. Breccan was tall for his fourteen years but not filled out; his limbs thrust spidery from the garments that covered his slip of a body. The hair tumbled flax-white past huge blue eyes and a face whose beauty was redeemed from girlishness by the down on its upper lip. Yet he moved with a certain coltish grace; few could match him in a race afoot or on horseback; he was fierce in the games that his kind played and in practice with weapons.

'You are a stripling,' Niall said, though he smiled more kindly than he had done since his return. 'Be patient. You'll be winning fame aplenty in due course.'

Breccan swallowed, stood his ground, and said stoutly, 'Seven years it's been since I took valour. You told me then that I should have to wait no longer than that.' He appealed to the Queen. 'Mother, did he not indeed?'

She, who was in truth his stepmother but had always got along with him, smiled in her turn. 'Niall, darling,' she said, 'I remember you promised he should – fare

36

widely, those were your words – after seven years. And did not yourself do the same?'

Niall's countenance darkened. She made a mistake when she reminded him of his own stepmother and how Mongfind schemed his destruction for the sake of her sons by his father.

Laidchenn maqq Barchedo spoke softly: 'It is to the glory of the King when someone recalls his exploits. This is also true of deeds done together by brothers among whom there was faith.'

For a heartbeat Niall's mouth tightened. But he could not gainsay an ollam poet, who moreover was a guest and the former pupil of his foster-father. Nor did the man from Mumu intend anything but good. He merely called to mind that the sons of Mongfind had themselves never conspired against Niall but had become his trusty followers; and that he had no right to suspect his wife of urging Breccan into early battle, to get him out of the way of her sons.

The King eased. 'We shall see,' he told the boy. 'Do you begin by learning how to wait. You will do enough of that in war.' Suddenly he grinned. 'And likewise you will know chills, rains, mud, growling belly, weary feet, grumbling men, and baggage trains gone astray. Not to talk of dripping noses, runny guts, and never a woman for your bed!'

Gladness went through listeners like a wave. For the first time since coming back to Ériu, himself seemed cheerful. Well, this was the eve of Brigit, and She a healing Goddess.

Meanwhile guests had come crowding about. Men gave their weapons into the care of attendants, for it was gess to go armed into this house. The very eating-knives must be solely in the hands of the servers who would carve the joints. Their shields the men turned over to the steward.

Aided by household staff, he bore them inside. There the royal senchaide directed where they should hang, in order of dignity, so that each owner would go straight to his place without scrambles or quarrels. It took a knowledge of lineages and histories through long generations. Dusk had deepened before all was ready and a horn blew invitation.

Magnificent was the Feasting Hall on Temir. The earthwork that sheltered it was not round but seven hundred and fifty feet in length, ninety feet in width; and the building left scant room between. Although it had stood for more than two years, and would be torn down this year before a new one was raised for the next Harvest Fair, it did not much show wear. Peeled upright poles making the walls were still bright, ties and chinking still solid; winds had not disturbed the intricately woven patterns of the thatch.

Within, the double rows of pillars upholding that high roof would be reused, as great as they were and as thickly carved with magical figures. Lamps hanging from the rafters and a fire in a pit at the middle gave light to see by, reflecting off gold and burnished bronze. Down the length of the nave, servers stood ready to carve the meat that kitchen help were bringing in from the cookhouse. Guests took benches along the aisles, before which were trestle tables bearing cups of mead. Foremost, at the centre of the east side, was Niall's place, flanked by the men of greatest honour. Fifty guards stood in attendance, also disarmed but their shields and helmets asheen in unrestful shadows.

The Queen and other women sat opposite. Unlike most homes, at Temir it was not usual for them to join the men at feast. Instead, they dined in the Royal Guesthouse. This, though, was time sacred to a female God and to the fruitfulness of the coming season. Besides, some of them flaunted scars from battles, and had brought back several of the skulls which stared emptily from the walls. Medb Herself could take pride in celebrants like these.

The surf-roar and clatter of people finding their seats died away. Looks went to the King's companions. Before anyone touched food here, always a poet spoke.

Laidchenn stood up, rang the chimes on the baton that declared what he was, lifted from its carrying case a harp he had already tuned, and cradled it in his left arm. There had been no question but that he would take the word, among those poets who were present. Not only was he a visitor from afar, he was from the school of Torna Éces. A barrel-chested man with bushy red hair and beard, richly but a little carelessly clad, he did not seem one who could call forth such icy-sweet notes as he did. Power pulsed in his deep voice when he looked straight into the eyes of Niall and chanted:

> 'Lúg, bright God, of war the Lord,
> Long-Arm, hear my harp!
> Hark to tales that I will tell,
> Talking unto all.

> 'Heaven sees how Temir's holy
> Hilltop now bears Niall,
> Never conquered, as its King,
> Keeping warlike watch.

> 'See him seated in his splendour.
> So it was not once.
> Well that men should know how much
> Might wrung wealth from woe.'

A happy sigh went over the benches. Listeners knew they were about to hear a grand story.

And Laidchenn told it; and those who had heard it

often, growing year by year, found newness, while others found wonder.

Niall, sang the poet, Niall, descendant of Corbmac maqq Arti, son of Eochaid maqq Muredach who was called Magimedon – Niall was born of dark curly-haired Carenn, a princess whom his father had carried away from Alba. In those days his grandfather still ruled. Eochaid had a wife named Mongfind, daughter of a tuathal king in Mumu, who was a witch and a ruthless woman. She bore him four sons, Brión, Féchra, Alill, and Fergus. Because Niall showed early promise, Mongfind plotted to do away with him, lest he succeed to lordship instead of Brión or a brother of Brión. She had him carried off, a small boy, while his father was gone warring. When Eochaid returned, Mongfind persuaded him that the loss was due to Carenn's carelessness, and Eochaid let Mongfind make a menial slave of his erstwhile leman.

But Torna, great poet in Mumu, knew by his arts what had happened, and foresaw what was in Niall. He rescued the child and fostered him. When the early signs of manhood were upon Niall, Torna sent him back to reclaim his own. Eochaid, now King, joyously received this son he had thought lost, and Carenn was released from her bondage.

Once Eochaid wished to test the five youths. A blacksmith's shop caught fire, and he commanded them to save what they could. Brión fetched out the chariots, Alill a shield and sword, Féchra the forge trough, Fergus merely some firewood; but Niall rescued anvil, block, sledges, and bellows, the heart of the smith's trade.

On another time when they were hunting and had grown sorely thirsty, they came upon a well deep in the forest. However, its guardian was a hideous old hag, who would give a drink to none unless he lie with her. No son of Mongfind could make himself do that; at most, Brión achieved a hasty kiss. But Niall led her aside and laid her down. Then rags and shrivelled skin fell from her, she came forth radiant in youth and beauty, for this was the Goddess Who bestows sovereignty. Afterwards Niall made his half-brothers pledge fealty to him before he would let them drink. They abided honestly by that, and Brión presently fathered a line of chieftains.

But meanwhile Mongfind lived and schemed. Through her magics – and, no doubt, kinsmen in Mumu of whom Eochaid had need – she kept him from putting her from him. Upon his death, she succeeded in having her brother Craumthan maqq Fidaci chosen as his successor.

He, though, proved to be no clay for her moulding, but instead a man who laid a firm grip on the land and warred both in Ériu and across the waters. After years, despairing of aught else, Mongfind sought to poison him. He required that she drink first of the cup she proffered; and so they both died. Spells were still cast on certain nights to keep quiet the ghost of Mongfind the witch.

Throughout this time, Niall had been at the forefront of battles. In council his words were shrewd, later wise. It was upon a tenant's daughter, Ethniu, that he begot his eldest child, Breccan; but she was lovely and high-hearted, and everybody mourned when she died in giving birth. Niall soon married well – behold how his sons by the Queen are already shooting up! Thus after the death of Craumthan four years ago, it was no surprise when the Mide men chose him to be their King.

And he has wrought deeds that will live in memory as long as valour is cherished. Besides much else closer to home, he has harried the coasts overseas, bringing back huge booty. When the Cruthini of Alba, whom the Romans call the Picti of Caledonia, threatened the settlement of Dál Riata, Niall made alliance with its mother kingdom for its rescue; then, having cast the Cruthini back, he made alliance with them in turn. In Ériu, too, he called warriors to him from far beyond the bounds of Mide. No vaster hosting has been seen since the Cattle Raid of Cóalnge, than when the men of tribes conjoined roared down to the Wall of Rome.

And this time it was not Cú Culanni who stood alone in defence, it was Cú Culanni reborn at the van of attack. Many a Roman soldier sprawls headless in the heather, many a Britannic estate lies plundered and burnt, many a slave has gone to market and today herds sheep or grinds grain for a worthy master; and if the Wall of Rome still stands, why, the more glory to reap when we return!

> 'Never shall the hero Niall
> Kneel to any other.
> Witness, all You Gods, my words,
> Aware I tell the truth.'

The last notes shivered away. Cheers thundered from benches to ridgepole. The King took from his arm a heavy coil of gold. Standing up, he put it in the hands of Laidchenn. 'Have this of me in token of thanks,' he said amidst the din, 'and let me ask of you that you abide with me a long while – for ever, if I may have my wish.'

Flushed, breathing hard, eyes asparkle, Niall sat back down. The druid Nemain stroked his beard and murmured, 'Your fame grows by leaps, darling.'

Niall tossed his head. 'What a poet says is true. He may find fresh words for the clothing of truth – but – you would not be denying that I wedded the Goddess of the land, would you?'

'I would not,' replied Nemain, 'nor speak against anything I have heard tonight; for indeed truth is a lady who has many different garments to wear. I would simply lay caution upon you. Not qualm, only caution, for sadly would we miss our lord should he fall, and worst if it was needlessly.'

Niall did not hear. Again his head was aflame with dreams. Long though the nights still were, he did not look for much sleep in this one, if any; for among the gessa laid on a King of Mide was that sunrise must never find him in bed on Temir. It did not matter. He *was* the King.

As host, he should make a speech of welcome. Rising, he lifted his goblet – Roman glass, loot from Alba. Out of full lungs, he shouted: 'It's glad I am to see so great and fair a company here, and glad Herself must be, and every God. If I name not the kings and nobles among us and their honours, it is because dawn would break well before I was done. Let us instead make merry, let us no more grieve over our losses or brood on our wrongs, let us look ahead to a year of revenge and victory!'

III

His father's house felt strangely empty to Gratillonius.

Or not so strangely, he thought. When he arrived the evening before, joy was too tumultuous for him to pay close heed to his surroundings. Notified in advance, Marcus had had a feast prepared for his soldier son. The food was local, fish and meat and dried garden truck, but seasoned with such things as pepper and cloves, scarce these days, while the wines were from Burdigala and Narbonensis, not a mediocre Britannic vineyard. If the tableware was of poor quality and the attendant an untrained yokel, talk between the two men made up amply for that. When it turned to Gaius's older brother it grew evasive – Lucius was 'studying in Aquae Sulis; you know what a bookish sort he's always been, not like you, you rascal' – but then the news quickly came that his youngest sister Camilla had married an able farmer, Antonia and Faustina continued happy in their own homes, and another grandchild was on the way. And his old nurse Docca had earlier hugged him in arms crippled by rheumatism, and he learned that three or four more of those who had been dear to him in boyhood were still above ground.

Soon after supper weariness overwhelmed him and he went to bed. It had not been any route march to get here, only a few miles from Isca to the Sabrina, a ferry ride across the broad rivermouth, and a little way inland beyond that. He had, though, been at work since dawn preparing, as he had been for days previously. It won him an early enough start that he could justify spending two nights at home before he began his journey in earnest.

Thus he awoke ahead of sun and household. When he got up, the air nipped and the floor was cold. He recalled that the place had been chilly yesterday too, nothing but a couple of charcoal braziers for heat; he had avoided asking why. Fumbling his way through murk, he drew aside a curtain that, as spring approached, had supplanted shutters. On the leaded window, bits of leather were glued over three empty panes. The glass must have been broken in some accident or juvenile mischief. Why had his father, who always took pride in keeping things shipshape, not had it replaced?

Sufficient moonlight seeped through for Gratillonius to use flint, steel, and tinder. When he had ignited a tallow candle, he dropped the curtain back to conserve warmth and took care of his necessities. Clad in tunic and sandals, candlestick in hand, he padded forth in search of all he remembered.

The house reached shadowy around him. It had grown, piece by piece, for almost two hundred years as the family prospered; but his grandfather had been the last to make any additions. Doors were closed on this upper storey, though only he and Marcus occupied bedrooms. (Once the hall was a clamour of footfalls and laughter.) Well, no sense in leaving chambers open when servants were too few to keep them dusted.

Gratillonius went downstairs. The atrium was still elegant, peacock mosaic on the floor and Theseus overcoming the Minotaur on a wall. Colours glimmered where the candlelight picked them out of darkness. However, most of the heirloom furniture was gone. Replacements were conscientiously built, but by carpenters, not artists.

An ebony table was among the few ancestral pieces remaining. Upon it lay several books. They were copied on scrolls, not bound into modern codices, because they too had been in the family for generations. Gratillonius's

45

left hand partly unrolled one. A smile passed faint over his lips. He recognized *The Aeneid*. That he had enjoyed reading, along with other hero stories, as he did hearing the songs and sagas of the Britons from those backwoods folk who knew them yet – and did emphatically not enjoy Fronto and other bores he was supposed to study so he could become a proper Roman. Learning Greek turned out to be impossible for a boy who could be rambling the woods, riding, swimming, boating, fishing, playing ball or war with his friends, alone in the workshop making something – later, hanging around neighbour Ewein's daughter Una – Finally his tutor gave up.

Lucius was different, of course. Their mother had been proud of him.

Sadness tugged at Gratillonius. He left the atrium, went down a corridor to the west wing, and opened a door he knew well. Behind it was a room Julia had used for sewing and such-like lady's work. And for prayer. Her husband let her have a fish and Chi Rho painted on a wall. Before them each day, until a fever took her off, she humbly called on her Christ.

Gratillonius's free hand stroked the air where her head would have been were she sitting there. 'I loved you, mother,' he whispered. 'If only I'd known how to show it.'

Maybe she had understood anyway. Or maybe she now did in whatever afterworld had received her.

Gratillonius shook himself, scowled, and went out. He wanted to inspect the kitchen and larder. That wasn't supposed to be any concern of his. But every soldier developed a highly practical interest in grub. Though supper had been fine, what were ordinary meals like, in this house where they couldn't pay to fuel the furnace? Gratillonius meant to make sure that his father was eating adequately, if perhaps frugally.

He should have looked into that on earlier visits. Even before he enlisted he was aware of a pinch that strengthened year by year. But his awareness was only peripheral, as stoic as his father was and as lost as he himself was in his dreams of Una, the lightfoot and golden-haired – until she perforce married elsewhere, and he flung himself into the army – She no longer haunted him, much. He should have become more thoughtful of his own kindred.

Yet regardless of Isca's nearness, his appearances here had been infrequent, the last one three years back. And they had been short. He'd spent most of his furlough time ranging the Silurian hills, forests, remote settlements where men were friendly and girls friendlier; or else he'd be off to the baths and frivolities of Aquae Sulis, or as far afield as smoky Londinium. The recollection hurt him, on what might well be his last sight of home and these people, hurt him both with guilt and with a sense of having squandered a treasure.

When he had finished his tour, the sky showed wan through glass. The cook and the housekeeper yawned their way forth, too sleepy to greet him. He could forgive that in the former, who had been here longer than he could recall, but the latter was a young slattern. Gratillonius considered giving her a tongue-lashing for insolence. He decided against it. She would merely be the surlier after he was gone. Besides, maybe she was the best Marcus could find. The older man had bespoken a dearth of good help. Not only was the countryside population dwindling as small farms were swallowed up by plantations or abandoned altogether by owners whom taxes and weak markets had ruined. Those folk who stayed were generally bound by law to the soil, and serfs seldom raised their children to much pride of workmanship.

As he re-entered the atrium, Gratillonius met his father coming from upstairs, and was especially filial in his salutation. 'Good morning,' replied Marcus. 'I hope you slept well. Your old bed is one thing I've managed to keep.'

Touched, Gaius gave him a close regard. The dawnlight showed a face and form resembling his own; but Marcus's hair was grey, his countenance furrowed, the once powerful body gaunt and stoop-shouldered. 'Thank you, sir,' Gaius said. 'Could we talk today . . . privately?'

'Of course. You'll want a walk around the place anyway. First, though, our duties, and next our breakfast.'

They went forth together on to the verandah, sought its eastern end, lifted arms and voices to Mithras as the sun rose. It stirred Gaius more than rites in a temple commonly did. He paid his respects to the God and tried to live by the Law, because that was upright, soldierly, everything this man at his side – and this man's stern father, once – had tried to make him become. But he was not fervent about it. Here, somehow, a feeling of sanctity took him, as if borne on those rays bestorming heaven. Tears stung his eyes. He told himself they must be due to the wind.

Everydayness came back. The men spoke little while they had their bread and cheese. Afterwards they dressed against the weather and left the house. 'Let's begin at the stable,' Marcus suggested. 'There's a colt you'll appreciate.'

Gaius looked about him more closely than yesterday. The house stood firm beneath its red-tiled roofs, and likewise did the farm buildings to either side, around a cobbled courtyard. But he saw where whitewash had flaked from walls, the cowpen and its barn gaped almost empty, a single youngster went to feed pigs and chickens where formerly the grounds had roared with life.

The wind shrilled and plucked at his cloak. He drew

the garment tight against those icy fingers. Northwards he saw the land roll in long curves to the woods where boys went – sometimes in defiance of orders from parents who feared Scoti might pounce from the river and seize them for slaves – and where Gwynmael the gamekeeper had taught him how to read a spoor and set a snare. Closer in, the acres were cleared, but most had gone back to grass and brush, still winter-sere, although quickened by the faintest breath of new green. Through an apple orchard he discerned a cultivated field, dark save where wind-ruffled rain puddles blinked in the sunshine. Rooks and starlings darted above, blacker yet. A hawk high overhead disdained to stoop on them. Its wings shimmered golden.

A thought struck Gaius. 'I haven't seen your steward, Artorius,' he said. 'Has he died?'

'No – '

'Good. He used to tell me wonderful stories about his days as a legionary. That was what started me thinking I'd want to enlist, myself.' Gaius forced a laugh. 'After I did, I discovered what a liar he'd been, but no matter, he's a grand old rogue.'

'Too old. Nearly blind. I retired him. He's moved in with a son of his.'

'Um, who do you have now?'

Marcus shrugged. 'Nobody. Can't find a competent man and couldn't afford him if I did. I'm my own steward. The villa's no longer so big or busy that I can't handle it.'

They neared the stable. A hound sprang forth, baying, until a word from Marcus brought it to heel. A white-haired man shuffled out behind the creature. He stopped short, blinked, squinted, and quickened his pace. 'Why, bless my butt if that's not the young master!' he cried in Belgic dialect. 'We'd heard you were coming, but I thank the Gods just the same. Welcome, lad, welcome!'

Gaius took a hand gnarled into a set of claws, regarded

a visage withered and well-nigh toothless, and remembered how Gwynmael had drifted like a shadow down forest paths till his bow twanged and the arrow found its mark. He hadn't been nearly this aged three years ago. Well, Gaius thought with pain, you grow old, suddenly you can't run fast enough, and Time the Hunter overtakes you in a pair of leaps. 'Are you working here?' he asked in the vernacular.

'So 'tis, so 'tis. I'm no use any more for chasing off poachers or bringing back venison. But your dad's a kindly sort and lets me pretend to earn my keep being his head groom. That's easy, because except for a boy I'm the only groom, heh, heh. Not that I could've carried on in my real job after our woods got sold off.' In his shock at hearing that, Gaius hardly noticed when Gwynmael fondled the hound's ears and said, 'Splendid dog, eh? Remember Brindle, what coursed the stags so well? Here's a pup from the last litter she bore. Too bad we can't let this 'un do what his blood meant him for.' Taking the centurion's elbow: 'But come inside, young sir, come in and look at what we got in a stall. Juno foaled him last summer, and if he don't live up to his promise, why, he's the biggest braggart in horsedom.'

The stable was dim and warm, smelling sweetly of hay and animal, pungently of manure. Gaius stopped to stroke the two beasts he knew, mare and gelding – their noses were silk-soft, and Juno whickered for pleasure – before he went on to the stallion colt. That was indeed a superb creature, like a cross between flesh and wind. 'Epona Herself 'ud be glad to ride him when he's full-grown,' Gwynmael said. He had never made any bones about his devotion to the ancient Gods of the Belgae.

'What sire?' Gaius asked.

'Commius's prize stud,' Marcus told him.

'Really? Commius the senator? He must have charged you a pretty solidus.'

'He did, but I should profit eventually. You see, I think I can fence in most of what land we have left, take out the scrub, sow pasturage, and breed horses. Blooded horses, for riding. Skilled help may not be too hard to come by in that business: veteran cavalrymen from the eastern provinces, especially, or their sons.'

'But who could pay the price you'd have to set?'

'The army. I may have swallowed the anchor, but I still get word from overseas, as far as Constantinople. Given the new Asiatic saddles, horsemen are the soldiers of the future. Cataphracts could roll the barbarians back – though we won't get them in Britannia during my lifetime. However, I expect we'll begin to see more and more cavalry in Gallia, and here I'll be, prepared to export.' Marcus's smile turned grim. 'Also, rich men everywhere will want fast mounts in case of raiders or uprisings.'

His moods gentled. He touched Gaius's arm. 'I'll need this fellow for breeding,' he murmured, 'but I'll set aside the best of his get for you.'

The son gulped. 'Thank you,' he said unsteadily. 'I'm not sure whether – oh, we have to talk about all this.'

They went out and set off towards the Roman road. Little used, the wagon track alongside which they walked was not very muddy. Rounding the orchard, Gaius saw two men, no more, at work in the grainfield. They were ploughing with ards drawn by cows. Gaius halted. 'Where's the proper gear?' he wondered.

'Sold, like much else,' Marcus replied.

Keen as its coulter there rose before Gaius the memory of a wheeled mouldboard plough and the mighty oxen that pulled it. Rage rose acid in his throat. 'But this is wrong, wrong!'

'Oh, the villa hasn't enough land under cultivation to need better equipment.'

'You've sold . . . still more? Besides the woods?'

'Had to. They slapped an extra assessment on me for waterworks, after Tasciovanus went bankrupt, Laurentinus suicided, and Guennellius disappeared – ran off to Londinium and is hiding in its proletary, some say.'

'Who bought your land?'

'Commius. Who else?'

Fury lifted higher. Commius the gross, Commius the crooked, Commius the unmerciful squeezer of tenants, servants, slaves. Commius who bought his way to senatorial rank – everybody knew that was a question of bribing the right people – and thus escaped the burdens of the curials, Commius who thereupon had the gall to boast how public-spirited he was because he maintained a theatre, whose pornographic shows must swell business at the whorehouse everybody knew he owned –

'Calm down,' Marcus advised. 'His sort, they come and go. Rome's had them since first the Republic began to rot, if not earlier; but Rome endures, and that is what matters.' When he grinned, his leathery face looked, briefly, wolfish. 'In fact, last year, at a series of council meetings, I had the pleasure of frustrating him. He wanted to close our Mithraeum as the Emperor had decreed. I got my friends behind me and we agreed that if that was done, we'd see to it that his precious theatre was shut down too. Those plays pretend to show myths of the ancestors, you know, and we'd claim this made them not "educational displays" but pagan ceremonies. An Imperial inquiry would have turned up more about his affairs than he could well stand – investments in commerce and industry such as are forbidden a senator, for instance. He stopped calling for any religious prohibitions. It was marvellous, seeing him flush red and hearing

52

him gobble. The God does send His faithful a bit of fun once in a while.'

But the God's faithful die or fall away, year after year, and ever fewer take their places, Gaius thought.

The sombreness dampened his wrath. 'At least you've lowered your tax by selling off,' he ventured, 'and with this horse-breeding scheme you may win back to something better . . . for Lucius and the grandchildren he'll give you.'

Marcus's mouth drew tight. They trudged on in silence, except for the wind. Finally the father said, tonelessly, looking at the far hills: 'No. I didn't tell you earlier because it would have spoiled our evening. But Lucius has turned Christian. He's studying under the bishop in Aquae Sulis, with the aim of becoming a churchman too. He talks about celibacy.'

Gaius's feet jarred to rest. Emptiness grew from his heart until it engulfed him. 'Not that,' he whispered.

Marcus stopped likewise and squeezed his shoulder. 'Well, well, don't take it overly hard. I've learned to live with it. We've stayed on speaking terms, he and I. It *was* his mother's religion, and is that of his sisters and their husbands and . . . Maximus, who cast back the wild men . . . I can't blame him greatly. If he'd waited till I died, he'd have been trapped in the curial class himself. Taking Christian holy orders now is his way out of it.'

Out! thought Gaius. The army was another way, and he had chosen it, although that would not have been allowed if he were the older boy. Since Diocletianus, a son and heir must follow in his father's occupation. The law was frequently evaded, but the curials – the landowners, merchants, producers, the moderately well-off – were usually too noticeable. Once it had been an honour to belong to their class. They were the councillors and magistrates; they did not endow the grandiose spectacles that Caesars and senators and ambitious newly rich did, but they underwrote the useful public works. That had been long ago. The burdens remained; the means were gone.

'I hoped to be free of it myself, you know,' Marcus was saying. 'That's why I went into sea traffic. High profits for men who didn't mind the risk. Your grandfather approved – and he was a man of duty if ever there was one – and got me started. But at last . . . well, you know. It had taken all my father's influence, and a stiff bribe, to get permission for me to become a navicularius when I wasn't the son of one. Then your uncle, my older brother, died, and the guild was only too happy to "regularize" my status. That laid this estate on me. It's devoured everything I had.'

'I do know. But I've never quite understood how.'

'I didn't explain because I didn't want to whine at you, who were young and had neither gift nor wish for this kind of thing. I did have my good, quiet Lucius, who was supposed to inherit anyway. It's the taxes and assessments. You'd think, as debased as the money is, coin wouldn't be hard to find. But that's not so, we're more and more going over to barter, and meanwhile the Imperium wants its cash. The taxes in kind, they get higher all the time too, as the number of farmers shrinks. In my seafaring days I was a sharp bargainer, you may recall; but I don't have Commius's talent for grinding wealth out of the poor underneath me.'

Abruptly Marcus lifted his head, glanced at Gaius through crow's-footed eyes, and laughed. He might almost have been standing at the prow of his ship as a gale blew up. 'At ease, boy, at ease!' he said. 'You're safe. The law will scarcely haul a battle-proven officer back to the farm, especially when you're known to none less than Duke Maximus. He'll probably get you senatorial rank. As for this place, why, if my plan pays off, I should have a chance of joining forces with my sons-in-law after they inherit. Between us, we might yet put together a villa that will last.'

'But if you fail to?' Gaius breathed.

'I won't consider that till it's upon me, which the God forbid. At worst, I'll never do what too many broken curials have, slunk off under changed names and become underlings, even serfs. No, your old man will die a Gratillonius.'

'I would help you if I could. I hope you know that, father. But . . . I'm bound afar, and what will happen to me I cannot foresee.'

'Let's go on,' said Marcus. A while of walking passed until he remarked, 'You've told me nothing but that you're off to Gallia on a special mission for the Duke. Crossing the Channel before equinox – Did he give you the funds you'll need to persuade a skipper to take you?'

Gaius smiled. 'Better than that. A writ letting me commandeer a naval transport. And I mean to cross by the shortest way, from Dubris to Gesoriacum, where one can scarcely get lost in anything less than an oatmeal fog. Cutting out that hazard makes the added overland travel worthwhile.'

'Then your march will take you through Londinium,' said Marcus, also trying to lighten the mood. 'Give the fleshpots a workout for me.'

Gaius shook his head. 'We won't stop after today, except for sleep. We've this breadth of Britannia to cross, and then it's more than four hundred miles over Gallia, and . . . the task is urgent.'

Marcus squinted into the wind. Some distance off, Gaius's legionaries had pitched their tents in a vacated field. That was all they had done, being too few for the labour of constructing a standard camp, but they had done it properly. The leather was drawn so taut over poles and guys that the air got no purchase on it but must be content with flapping a banner.

Metal gleamed on statue-like sentries. Men detailed to camp chores were in plain tunic and trousers, but neat. The rest were outside in full battle dress, drilling. When they hurled their javelins, it called to mind a flight of bright birds. Tethered pack horses stood placidly, used to the sight, but the centurion's mount and remount, more spirited, stirred as if impatient for action.

'Four tents,' Marcus counted. 'Thirty-two men, eh? Not much.'

'I chose them carefully, the best I have who aren't bound to wives. Most are Britons; we'll understand each other's thinking. I didn't order them to follow me but offered them the privilege of volunteering. They're eager. Over-eager, maybe, but I think the march will shake them down into a crack unit.'

'Still, I can hear in your voice you'd have preferred a larger force.'

'Maximus sent direct word to my commandant that I was to have no more than this. He . . . can't spare many.'

'So I've been suspecting . . . But he obviously doesn't expect you'll meet serious opposition.'

'No. Yonder fellows will be my bodyguards and, um, the presence of Rome. That should suffice.'

'Where?'

'Father, I'm not supposed to tell – '

'Four hundred-odd miles of Gallia. Not south, because that's where the main action will be. Also, your experience has been with Armorica, as Maximus must know. Westbound, you'll fetch up at Gesocribate, or else fairly close. But Gesocribate already has an ample Roman presence. And I don't think the Duke of the Armorican

56

Tract would welcome troops dispatched by the Duke of the Britains – certainly not before he knows which way the cat is going to jump. Therefore he's doubtless not been informed, nor is he meant to get the news until too late for him to do anything about it.' Marcus nodded. 'M-hm. Your task is to secure a critical area and thus help assure that Armorica will stay safe – for Maximus.'

Gaius's bark of laughter flushed a hare from a briar patch. It lolloped off as if a fox were at its tail. 'Father, you're too shrewd!'

'I told you I get word from outside.' Marcus bleakened. 'For some time, now, I've caught the smell of war on the wind, stronger and stronger. Civil war. Maximus will get the Britannic legions to hail him Augustus. The Sixth may be doing it in Eboracum at this very hour. He'll cross to Gallia and try for the throne.'

'Wait, wait! He didn't say that to me. He said only that affairs of state are approaching a crisis and Rome will need a loyal man in Armorica.'

'Loyal to him. You're not stupid. You know what he meant.'

'He is . . . a valiant leader, father. And intelligent and just. Rome perishes for want of right governance.'

'Those sound like words you got from him,' Marcus said, low in his throat. 'Oh, we could do worse. Provided the struggle doesn't wreak the kind of harm the last such did, or give the Northfolk their chance to invade.'

Gaius recalled Parnesius. 'The Wall will abide, I swear.'

'Scoti sail past it. Saxon galleys sweep in from the eastern sea.'

'Against them – Rome will have new help.'

Once more they halted. Marcus's gaze probed like a sapper's spade. 'That's your task,' he said finally.

Gaius swallowed hard and nodded.

'I believe I know where. I'd liefest hear it from your

lips, son. Mithras be witness that I'll keep the secret.'

Gaius thrust the name forth. 'Ys.'

Marcus drew a sign before him, the Cross of Light that marked the shield of his warrior God. 'That's an uncanny place,' he said.

Gaius mustered courage. 'It's been left alone so long that all sorts of wild stories about it have sprung up. What do we know for certain? What do *you* know, father?'

Wind roared and whistled. Clouds were appearing over the horizon. Their shadows raced across winter-grey hills and the few springtime-wet croplands. A solitary willow nearby lashed its withes around. At their removes, the manor house and the soldiers' camp looked very small. The hawk wheeled scornful overhead.

Lines deepened in Marcus's brow and beside his mouth. 'I was never there myself,' he said. 'I did speak with Britannic and Gallic captains who'd called. But they were just three or four, and none had done it more than once. The Ysans don't seem to want any trade with the outside that they don't carry on for themselves. No more involvement of any kind with Rome that they can avoid. Not that they act hostile. My talkmates said the city is still more wonderful than they'd heard, Ys of the hundred towers. But even in the joyhouses there was always . . . an otherness.'

'It's a foederate of ours,' Gaius reminded.

'After a fashion. And only in name for – what? These past two hundred years? When did the last Roman prefect leave?'

'I'm not sure.' Gratillonius straightened. 'But I will be the next.'

'Keeping Ys neutral, at least, and a counterweight to people elsewhere in Armorica who might otherwise side with Gratianus and Valentinianus against Maximus.'

Gaius responded louder:

'And, I hope, taking a more active part than hitherto in measures against pirates. Ysan commerce has shrunk with Rome's. From what little I recall or could find out these past months, Ys trades mainly with its Osismiic neighbours, overland; but once it was the queen of the Northern seas. I should think it'd welcome guidance in rebuilding security and commerce. Father, I don't see how any living city can be the kind of witch-nest those rumours tell of. Give me a few years, and I'll prove as much to the world.'

Marcus Valerius Gratillonius smiled, more in pride than in pleasure. 'Good for you, son. Sink or sail, you're a Roman!'

And how many such are left? he did not ask. Men who have hardly a drop of blood in them from Mother Rome, and who will never see her whom they serve. Can she hold their faith, today when new Gods beckon?

IV

1

It was good to be on salt water again. Gratillonius braced himself at the taffrail of the transport, near a swan's-head figure that decorated the after section, and looked happily about. Forward of him was the deckhouse, on top of which two men strained to hold their steering oars against seas running heavy. It hid from Gratillonius the main deck, with lifeboat, cargo hatch, crewmen, and his soldiers. The mast rose over it. Square mainsail and triangular topsail bellied against swift grey clouds and malachite waves. Gratillonius could also glimpse the spar that jutted out over the prow and the artemon sail it bore.

No other craft was in sight. Their whiteness dulled by spindrift, the cliffs of Britannia were sinking under the horizon, though he could still make out the pharos that loomed over Dubris. Ahead, hillscape was shouldering out of Gallia, likewise vague and distance-dimmed.

The ship rolled and bounded like a live creature. Waters rushed, boomed, clashed. The wind skirled and flung briny spatters across his lips. Timbers and rigging creaked. Gratillonius's muscles rejoiced in the interplay that kept him erect. Tomorrow he'd be on the road again, and that was good too, because he'd fare through country new to him until he reached magical Ys. But Mithras be thanked that first he got this brief voyage.

He laughed aloud at himself. Had the Gods really carved out a strait at the Creation in order that Gaius

Valerius Gratillonius could have a day's worth of feeling like the boy he once was?

The captain strode around the deckhouse. His blue uniform was hidden beneath a cloak he hugged to him in the cold. Approaching, he said through the noise: 'Come forward with me, Centurion. A fight's brewing between your men and mine.'

'What? How?'

'Several of yours are miserably seasick, and when one of them puked on the deck, the sailors didn't want to clean it up. Then they started mocking those landlubbers.'

Gratillonius bridled. 'What kind of discipline do you have in the fleet?'

The captain sighed. 'They resent being forced out this early in the year, in this tricky weather. I do myself, frankly, but I realize you have your orders, whatever they are. Now do come along. It'll work better if we both take charge.'

Gratillonius agreed and accompanied the other. On the broad expanse around the mast, men stood at confrontation. They were not all there were in their units. Some deckhands would have been flogged if they left their duty stations – though they too gibed and made obscene gestures. Half the legionaries huddled shivering, turned helpless by nausea. The rest had reflexively formed a double rank; their weapons were stowed but their fists were cocked. The sailors bunched loosely, about an equal number. They were not professional fighters. The garrison commander had ruled that the danger of Saxons was so slight at this season that he wouldn't subject any of his too few soldiers to the real hazard of the crossing. However, each crewman bore a knife, and fingers had strayed to hilts.

Quintus Junius Eppillus stood before his troops, growling at a sailor who appeared to be a leader. Eppillus was a stocky, paunchy man in his forties, big-nosed, bald on top, a Dobunnian with considerable Italian in his bloodlines, Gratillonius's appointed deputy. His Latin came hoarse: 'Watch your tongue, duckfoot. The bunch o' you watch your tongues. You're close to insulting not just us, but the Augusta.'

The sailor, a tall redhead, leered and answered with a thick Regnensic accent: 'I wouldn't do that. I only wonder why your legion allows fat swine like you in it. Well, maybe they've got tired of sheep, and pleasure themselves now with swine.'

'Take that back before I remove some o' those rotten teeth from your turnip hatch.'

'Very well, I'll take it back. You're not swine. It's just your fathers that were. Your mothers were whores.'

Cynan, who was young and of the still half-wild Demetae, yelled a battle cry. He broke from the army rank and threw himself on the sailor. They went down together, to struggle for possession of the knife and each other's throats.

'Stop!' Gratillonius roared. 'Eppillus, break that up! Nobody else move!'

The legionaries who were standing froze. The captain grabbed a belaying pin and bloodied a head or two among his tars. They retreated in confusion, babbling excuses and pleas for mercy. Eppillus gave the combatants a couple of efficient kicks. They separated and crawled to their feet, gasping, spitting, and shuddering.

'Attention!' Gratillonius barked. He lifted his vinestaff of authority, which seldom left him. 'Captain, I want that man of yours whipped.'

'Five lashes,' the skipper agreed. 'The rest of you bless whatever saints you know about. Hop to it!' The redhead was immediately seized. He didn't resist, doubtless realizing he was lucky to escape with nothing worse. The captain turned to Gratillonius. 'We'll make the same example of your fellow, eh?'

The centurion shook his head. 'No. He must be in shape to march. But we can't have this kind of conduct, true. Keep still, Cynan.' The vinestaff cut a crimson line over the youth's cheek. 'Go to the horses and stay there till we land. The rest of you who were involved, except the deputy, hold out your right arms.' He gave each wrist a blow that raised a welt but would not be disabling. Eppillus possibly deserved punishment too, but not enough to make it worthwhile compromising his dignity.

Fingers plucked at Gratillonius's ankle. He glanced down and saw that his follower Budic had crawled to him. The youngster's ash-pale hair fluttered around eyes hollowed by misery. He lifted a hand. 'Here, sir,' he mumbled.

'What?' asked Gratillonius.

'Strike me, sir.'

'Why, you didn't do anything.' Gratillonius smiled. 'You were too upchucking sick.'

The blue gaze adored him. 'But . . . I might have . . . when that . . . that sailor said what he did . . . about our legion. And surely I failed my centurion, me, useless when he needed his men. Please, sir. Make it right.'

Gratillonius quelled an impulse to rumple those locks, as if this were one of his small nephews. 'It is already right, soldier. Just remember and learn.' He paused. 'Oh, and be sure you shave before we march tomorrow. I want this outfit smart.'

Adminius snickered at his comrade's discomfiture. 'Spruce,' he said, 'not peach-fuzzy. I'll guide yer 'and if it's been so long you've forgotten 'ow.' He was from Londinium, given to teasing country boys like the Coritanian Budic.

Stripped and triced to the stays, the deckhand choked

63

off screams as the lead-weighted cords of the whip reddened his back. Cynan slunk down the hatch. Gratillonius gave the captain a discreet grin and muttered, 'Fresh air's the best medicine against seasickness. He'll be where it's warm and stale.'

'You're sharper than you look to be,' the captain said. 'Uh, best we absent ourselves for a while, you and I.'

'Right. Let them regain control on their own. It takes hold firmer, that way.'

The commanders sought the captain's room within the cabin. There he lifted a flagon from its rack and offered wine, thin sour stuff that didn't call for watering. 'Military honour isn't high in the fleet,' he admitted, 'and it drops year by year. I can't blame the men too much. Time was, you may know, when Rome had a navy in these parts. Now there's just some tubs like this one, that the Saxon galleys can sail or row rings around. They land anywhere they will, the heathen do, and when next we pass by, all we find is ashes and corpses. That wears the spirit away, I can tell you. How do the inland legionaries feel?'

'Not so badly,' Gratillonius replied. 'We did win our war last year, and afterwards my particular detachment had fun getting a new chief installed among the Ordovices. No one objected to him, so we'd nothing more to do than hike around in the hills showing the eagle and proclaiming the news officially. People were delighted to see new faces, and laid themselves out to be hospitable.'

'The girls especially, I hope?'

Gratillonius laughed. 'Well – Anyhow, we came back to Isca Silurum and settled into winter quarters. It's our home, you know; has been for hundreds of years. The older men generally have wives and children in town, and the younger men are apt to acquire their own after the usual pleasures of courtship. On furlough, you can reach Aquae Sulis in a day, baths, foodshops, joyhouses, theatres, games, social life, even learned men for those who care to listen. It's no Londinium, but still, in season you'd think half the world was jostling through its streets.' He drank. 'No, a man could do worse than join the army. Not that we don't keep the troops in line. They gripe. But they'd be appalled if we let their . . . strength fall away from them.'

The captain gave him a narrow stare and said low, 'From time to time the legions raise up an Emperor. That must be a heady feeling.'

Gratillonius veered from the subject. The communities where he had sometimes overnighted, on his march through Britannia, were abuzz with rumours about Maximus, like beehives which were being toppled. He didn't want to give any hint of confirmation, most particularly not to this man who would often be crossing the Channel. If the governors of Gallia got sufficient advance warning to mobilize, the fighting could become disastrous.

'I trust we'll make port before dark,' he said. 'I wouldn't care to spend the night hove to.'

'The wind's not from too bad a quarter, though stiffer than I like. You talk as if you've been a mariner yourself.'

'Oh, more of a supercargo, on my father's ship when I was a boy. We called two or three times at Gesoriacum. But that was years ago.'

'And a kid would scarcely see much. Can you stay over? The circus is small, but gets a canvas roof in bad weather, so it may be open tomorrow. Pretty good spectacles, not like those wretched bear-baitings which are the best we see in Dubris. In Gesoriacum they know how to stage an animal fight, and once I saw actual gladiators.'

Gratillonius grimaced. 'No, thanks. Torture and killing, for the amusement of a lot of rabble who'd loose their bowels if they saw teeth or a sword coming at *them* – I don't even permit my men to draw blood when they must touch up the horses.'

'I hope you're not so soft-hearted in combat,' said the captain, miffed.

'No insult intended. Anyhow, I can't stay. We've got to be off in the morning.'

'Really pressing business, eh? Well,' said the captain as his irritation passed, 'I know a whorehouse in town that keeps late hours.'

Gratillonius smiled. 'Again, no, thanks. It's the hostel and an early bed for me.' He grew serious. 'Also, frankly – and, again, no offence – I'm trying to stay clean. Aside from prayers, it's the only chance this trip gives me to honour the God.'

'Why, you could've stopped off at any church or shrine along the way.'

Gratillonius sighed. 'The Mithraeum in Londinium was closed – closed for ever. Does Gesoriacum have one any more?'

The captain sat straight, or as straight as the heeling ship would allow. His eyes bulged. 'What? You're joking!'

'Certainly not. I serve Mithras. Doubtless you serve Christ. What matter, as long as we both serve Rome?'

The captain made a V of two fingers and jabbed them in Gratillonius's direction. 'Out!' he shrilled. 'Go! It's unlucky enough having a pagan aboard, without sitting here and drinking with him. If you weren't an officer on a mission, I swear I'd have you thrown overboard. Don't think I won't report you when I get back. Now go! Out of my sight!'

The centurion did not argue, but rose and went forth on to the deck, into the wind.

2

Dusk was falling as the ship glided between jetties and docked at the naval wharf. The soldiers collected their gear and tramped down the gangplank under the stares of the crew. Gratillonius had them wait in formation while the horses were unloaded, a process which called forth words that sizzled. In the meantime he queried the harbourmaster, who had come from his office to watch this unseasonal landing, about accommodations for the squadron. To his relief, he learned that most of the garrison were away on joint manoeuvres with those of two other towns. Their barracks would thus have plenty of available beds.

Marching his men there, he found the prefect of the cohort that had stayed on guard and presented his written orders. They declared that he was on a mission of state, as directed by the Duke of the Britains, with rights to food, lodging, and whatever else his band required along the way. The prefect refrained from asking questions. These days there were many curious comings and goings. His only inquiry was: 'Do you require a room for yourself?'

Gratillonius shook his head. 'I think I'll put up at a hostel, and return about sunrise to take your guests off your hands.'

The prefect chuckled wryly. 'You may as well be comfortable.'

Gratillonius made somewhat of a nuisance of himself, seeing to it that his men would have decent quarters and, though it was well past the regular hour, an adequate meal. Not until they were seated in the mess – complain-

67

ing about food meant for auxiliaries from some forsaken far corner of the Empire – did he leave. It was quite dark then, but the prefect assigned him a guide with a lantern. The wind had chased most clouds away before lying down to rest, letting stars and a partial moon add their light. Air was cold, breath smoked and footfalls rattled, but a breath of spring softened it and leaf buds were pale upon trees.

The inn for official travellers was a two-storey building, its tile roof rime-whitened. A stable and a shed flanked the courtyard in front. It stood outside the city, on a highway leading south. Beyond that pavement reached cropland, out of which remnants of two houses poked ghostly. Like many other Gallic cities, Gesoriacum had shrunk during the past several generations, cramping itself within its defences. Walls, towers, battlements gloomed under Draco and the Milky Way.

Passing by the stable, Gratillonius heard a noise that brought him to a halt. 'What on earth?' He listened closer. Someone behind the door was weeping – no, more than a single one. The sounds were thin. His skin crawled. He did not think he had ever before heard such hopelessness.

The door was merely latched. He opened it. Murk yawned at him. The sobbing broke off in wails of terror. 'Come along,' he ordered his escort. 'Be careful about any hay or straw, of course.'

'Don't hurt us!' cried a child's voice. 'Please don't hurt us! We'll be good, honest we will!'

He followed the words without difficulty. This was Belgica, whence the forebears of his own tribe had come to Britannia, and language hadn't changed much on either side. Fair-skinned and flaxen-haired, the children might have been playmates of his boyhood.

They numbered five, three boys and two girls, their

ages seeming about nine or ten. They were dirty and unkempt, but not too poorly clad; two of them sported brightly coloured wool scarves that their mothers must have given them at the farewell. Some horses in the building kept it warm. But it had been altogether dark here, and the children were penned in a stall. Slats nailed around and over it confined them, and made it impossible for them to stand upright.

Lanternlight glistened off tears on cheeks and, elsewhere, caused shadows to dance monstrous. Gratillonius hunkered down. 'Don't be afraid,' he said, as gently as the tightness in his throat allowed. 'I won't hurt you. I'm your friend. What can I do for you?'

A girl's skinny arms reached out between the bars. He took her hands in his. 'Oh, please,' she stammered, 'will you take us home?'

He couldn't help it, his voice harshened. 'I'm sorry. I'm very sorry. I can't – now – but I will see if there is anything I can do, sweetheart. Be brave, all of you.'

'You're not Jesus?' came from a boy. 'I heard Jesus is the God in the city. I heard He is kind.'

'I am not He,' Gratillonius said, 'but I promise Jesus will always watch over you.' He kissed the hands he held, rose, and turned his back. 'Goodnight. Try to sleep. Goodnight.' The wails broke out anew as he left the stable and shut the door.

'New-taken slaves, sir,' the escort observed.

'That's plain to see,' Gratillonius snapped. He strode quickly to the hostel and thundered its knocker.

Candleglow spilled around the ruddy man who responded. 'What do you want?' he asked. Gratillonius was in civil garb. 'It's past suppertime.'

'I'll have supper regardless,' Gratillonius snapped. 'For your information, I'm a legionary officer travelling on

69

Imperial business. Furthermore, I'll have an explanation of those kids caged outside.'

'Oh.' The manager thought for a moment, then jerked his thumb over his shoulder. 'He's in there, he can tell you better than me. Come in, sir.' He didn't require credentials, doubtless reckoning that the soldier who had accompanied the stranger was sufficient.

Gratillonius bade that man farewell – be courteous to subordinates who deserve it, more even than to superiors – and followed the hostelkeeper into a long room feebly lit by candles. Their burning tallow filled it with stench, like an announcement of the poverty into which the Empire had fallen. Four guests sat benched around one of several tables. 'Hail,' called a portly fellow. 'Welcome.' Judging by his robe and the rings that sparkled on his fingers, he was the leader of his companions, who wore ordinary Gallic tunics and breeches. They were having a nightcap.

Gratillonius ignored the greeting. The manager asked him to register – name, rank, avowal that he was on an errand of the state – before taking a pair of candles and guiding him on upstairs. 'We don't get many so soon in the year,' he remarked. 'You say you're of the Second Augusta? Isn't that off in Britannia? Well, well, these be uneasy times, and me, I know to keep my mouth shut. Here you are, sir. I'll go after my wife. Can't make anything fancy, I'm afraid, but we do keep a kettle of her good lentil soup on the hob. We'll get you something pretty quick, sir.'

He left Gratillonius a light and departed. The centurion glanced around the room. Little was in it but a water jug, basin, chamber pot, and a pair of narrow beds. At this slack season, he'd be alone. He unpacked the small bag he had carried, stripped, scrubbed as well as he was able, dressed anew, and said his prayers – well after sunset, but better than not at all.

When he returned downstairs, the portly man called to him again: 'Hoy, there, don't be so aloof. Come have a drink with us.'

Briefly, Gratillonius hesitated. But . . . he had sought here not for the sake of comfort, as the prefect supposed, but in hopes of picking up more gossip, a better feeling for how things were, than he could likely get in barracks. Parts of the Continent were devastated or in upheaval, while he had scant exact information. 'Thanks,' he said, and took a place beside the inviter. A youth, son or underling of the keeper, scuttled forth with a cup, and he helped himself from the pitchers on the table.

'My name's Sextus Titius Lugotorix,' the portly man said. 'My attendants – ' He introduced them. They were a ruffianly-looking lot.

'Gaius Valerius Gratillonius, centurion, on special assignment.'

Lugotorix raised his brows. Seen close up, his face carried a gash of a mouth and eyes that were like two hailstones. He smelled of cheap perfume. His affability was undiminished. 'My, my, you're the silent one, aren't you, friend?'

'Orders. What are you doing here?'

'I'm a publican.'

'I thought so.'

'We were delayed – some bumpkins got obstreperous and we had to teach them a lesson – and didn't reach Gesoriacum till the gates had closed for the night. I suppose you walked around the city wall, from the military post? It wasn't worthwhile persuading the guard to let us in, when this hostel is so close by.' Lugotorix winked and nudged Gratillonius. 'And free.'

'I didn't know your business entitled you to government accommodations.'

'The governor has authorized me. Specifically authorized me.' Lugotorix rolled a pious glance ceilingwards. 'After all, the state must have its internal revenue.'

'Those youngsters in the stable – you're dragging them to the slave market?'

A man laughed. 'Not exactly dragging,' he said. 'Give the little buggers a taste of the whip, and they run along so fast their leashes nearly choke 'em.'

Lugotorix peered at Gratillonius. 'Did you take a look? Well, don't get mawkish, my friend.' He drained his goblet and refilled it. A certain slurriness suggested he was a bit drunk. 'They weren't abused, were they? Properly fed, I swear, and you saw for yourself they have a warm sleeping place and clean straw. Why damage the merchandise? Not that it'll fetch much. Hardly worth the trouble of collecting and selling. But I'm a patriot like you, Centurion. I feel it's my duty to the state to crack down on tax delinquents. I'm very patient, too, especially considering that this is my livelihood and I have mouths of my own to feed. I give those families plenty of time to find the money. Or if they can't, I'll take payment in kind, cattle or grain or whatever, marked down no more than necessary to compensate me for the added inconvenience. But they snivel that they'd starve. What can I do then but confiscate a brat? It helps keep the rest honest. If you let somebody evade his taxes, soon you must let everybody, and the government will have no more internal revenue.'

'What will become of the children?' Gratillonius asked slowly.

Lugotorix shrugged. 'Who knows? I pray they'll land in nice Christian homes and learn the Faith that will save their souls. See what a good work is mine in the sight of God! But I do have to take the best offer I get, you realize, or else how could I meet my own obligations to the state? And whelps like that don't command any large price. They have to be housed and fed for years, you know, before they're grown to field hands or maidservants or whatever.'

A man leered. 'Got a whorehouse in town where some of the customers like 'em young,' he said.

'I don't approve, I don't approve!' Lugotorix maintained. 'But I must take the best price I can get. Besides, those rustic brats are seldom pretty enough. We may have one this time, but believe me, she's a rarity.'

Her hands had lain in Gratillonius's.

He gulped his wine more fiercely than it deserved. The Empire still did fairly well by its officers, most places. In return, his immediate duty was to sound out these people. They must travel rather widely and hear news from farther yet.

'Well, never mind,' he achieved saying. 'Look, I'm bound west to Armorica. I can't tell you more. Now I have, um, been out of touch. If you can give me some idea of what to watch for along the way, I'll be grateful. So will . . . Rome.'

Flattered, Lugotorix rubbed his chin and pondered before he replied: 'We don't hear much from those parts. Courier service across them has got precarious, at least for private messages. Official dispatches have nearly absolute priority, and I understand they aren't too sure of getting through any more. I actually know better what's been happening in Massilia than in Baiocassium, say . . . You shouldn't have trouble here in Belgica. It suffered little from the Magnentian War, and the Germanian province eastward has stayed quiet too – good Germans, those, not Hun-like Franks. You should find Belgica easy;

73

and, if I do say so myself, it's concerned citizens like me who keep it that way. But beyond, as you enter Lugdunensis – my information is that the more west you go, the worse conditions get. I trust you're not alone?'

'No, I have soldiers with me.'

'Good. Just the same, watch out. I don't *think* the Bacaudae would attack a military unit, but you never know, these days. The word I have is that they're growing ever more brazen.'

Gratillonius searched his memory. He had encountered the word before, but only the word, and that was back when troubles were a not quite real thing that happened to somebody else. 'Bacaudae?' he asked. 'Bandits?'

'Worse than bandits,' Lugotorix said indignantly. 'Rebels. Men, if you can call them men, who've fled their obligations, gone into the woods, and don't just live by robbery and extortion – no, they have some kind of organization, they call themselves "Bacaudae" – "the Valiant" – and they war against the very state. Wolves! Vermin! Crucifixion would be too good for them, if we still did it.'

'It was not too good for your Saviour, was it?' Gratillonius murmured.

Luckily, perhaps, that was the moment when the boy carried forth his meal. He ordered it put on a different table, and made clear that he wanted to eat by himself and go to bed immediately afterwards. Lugotorix quacked a few questions – what was the matter? – but, getting no response other than a glower, soon quit.

There was no more to learn from him, Gratillonius thought, and so there was no need to spend more time at his board. Nothing could be done for the children except to beseech that Mithras – or Christ, or whatever Gods had stood over their cradles – would at last receive their weary spirits. The faith of Gratillonius was pledged to the man who could save Rome. Later that man would set about restoring her true law, making her again the Mother of all.

3

The military highway dropped well south before meeting one that bore west, but pavement offered faster going than most secondary ways in this rainy month. Gratillonius set no fixed daily goals. He took his men as far as they could make it under the given conditions without becoming exhausted. That usually meant about thirty miles, since they were spared the labour of constructing a wall and ditch at the end. It took a gauging eye to know when he should call a halt, for he was on horseback. He would have preferred to share the footwork, but dignity required he ride, as it required a private tent. The men expected it and didn't mind.

They made a brave sight on the march. Gratillonius ranked them four abreast so they wouldn't be slowed by any civil traffic they met. To spare hoofs without the trouble of sandalling them, he rode on the gravelled sidestrips when those were provided, while three men at the rear led the pack horses. On the highway, Eppillus named a different man each day for the honour of striding in the van, holding the standard on high and with the bearskin over his armour. Everybody wore full battle gear; in sunny weather, light flashed off helmets, mail, javelin heads, the oiled leather of shield facings. Gratillonius displayed silvery coat and greaves, together with crest athwart his helmet and cloak flowing away from his throat, both as vivid a red as the eagle banner. Hobnails crashed down in drumlike unison, but the lines were not rigid, they had that subtle wheatfield ripple that bespeaks men whose trade is war.

At first they travelled through country such as Gratillonius had heard described. It was smooth terrain, grazed by livestock or worked by gangs of cultivators. Aside from woodlots, trees were few. Hamlets generally amounted to a pair of long houses, half-timbered and thatched, divided into apartments for the dwellers and, in winter, their beasts. Carts trundled along the roads, driven by men in smocks and wooden shoes. Other passers-by rode mules, or walked carrying baskets or tools. What few women appeared were afoot but seemed unafraid. When they saw the squadron, people gaped, then often waved their hats and cheered. Every fifty or sixty miles the highway passed through a small town. This country lay at peace.

Yet Gratillonius noticed how hastily those towns had been walled of late, with anything that came to hand, even tombstones and broken-up monuments. And they had shrunk. Deserted buildings on the outskirts, stripped of everything valuable, were crumbling into grass-grown hillocks. The inhabitants looked poor and discouraged, save those who sat in taverns getting drunk. On market days the forums remained half empty. As for the hinterlands, the farmers ate better, but most of them were serfs. Or worse; Gratillonius remembered the publican. Whenever he passed a villa – a fundus, they called such an estate in Gallia – or a latifundium, a plantation which had devoured many a farm, he thought a malediction.

He would have liked commandeering fresh rations from those places as the need arose, but that was too chancy. Instead, he levied on military warehouses. Sometimes he had trouble getting what he wanted, because the garrisons were composed of alien auxiliaries with their own ideas about diet. His requirement was for what would keep in this wet climate, while being nutritious and easy to prepare: parched grain, biscuit, butter, cheese, dry sausage, preserved meat, beans, peas, lentils, pickled cabbage, dried apples, raisins, wine. That last was apt to be poor, and the water that would dilute it to be muddy, but beer was too bulky for what you got out of it. Not that he allowed drunkenness. However, it was wise to let the men have a treat at day's end, while supper cooked or in their tents if rain forced a cold meal.

The first night out was mild. They pitched camp in a pasture and grinned and winked at some towheaded youngsters, driving cattle home, who stopped to stare timidly. Gratillonius ordered a kettle of warm water brought him when it was ready, sought his shelter, removed his armour, and sighed in relief. Give him a scrub and change of linen, and he'd be ready for a drink himself. He insisted the troops keep clean too, but if he bathed out in the open among them, it would be bad for discipline.

Budic carried the water in, set it down by Gratillonius's bedroll, and straightened. He could stand upright in an officer's tent, though his blond hair brushed the leather. He saluted. 'Sir,' he said in a rush, 'may I ask a great favour?'

Gratillonius laughed. 'You may. You won't necessarily get it.'

'If . . . the centurion would allow me an extra ration of bread and cheese . . . and if, when the chance comes, we would lay in some kippered fish – '

'Whatever for?'

It was getting dim in here, despite the flag being folded back. Did the boy blush? He certainly gulped. 'Sir, this is Lent.'

'Lent. Ah. The long Christian fast. Are you sure? I've

gathered the Christians can't agree among themselves how to calculate the date of their Easter.'

'I didn't – didn't think, I forgot about it, in all the excitement of departure, and then on the march I lost track of time. But that terrible happening on the ship, it shocked me into recalling – this, and all my sins, like lust when I see a pretty girl or anger when some of the men bait me – Equinox has just passed, with the moon new. Lent is already far along. Please, sir, let me set myself a penance, and also do right in the Faith.' Budic swallowed again. 'The centurion is not a Christian, but he is a pious man.'

Gratillonius considered. He wanted everybody fit, not weakened by a growling belly; and special privilege might well cause discord. Yet this was a deprivation, not a luxury. He doubted others would want it, he having picked men he knew weren't holy-holy sorts – men who, Christian or Mithraist, would not feel uneasy about there being no observance on the Sundays that both religions made their sabbaths. Budic he hadn't known so well, the lad being newly enlisted, an orphaned rustic; but Budic had fought like a wildcat beyond the Wall, been a good if perhaps overly earnest trailmate on the way home, and would have been crushed if his leader had passed him over for this expedition. Young, strong in spite of his gangly build, he should get along, no matter his curious practice. Maybe he was so fervent because Christians were scarce where he came from, and other children had jeered at him. Maybe he enlisted partly in hopes of finding friends.

'You may, if it's that important to you,' Gratillonius decided. 'Just don't act sanctimonious if nobody else follows your example. Go tell the cook.'

'Oh, sir!' Adoration blazed forth. 'Thank you, sir!'

Presently Gratillonius emerged to find the squadron at

ease except for sentries and kitchen detail. The campfire crackled, raising savoury fumes out of a pot suspended above. A low sun gilded the earth. Grass was dry enough to sit on, but several men, with goblets in hand, stood clustered before Budic and teased him.

'You mean you didn't think to get a special dispensation?' asked Adminius. 'Why, the bishop was 'anding 'em out like 'otcakes at a love feast. Dibs on yer porkchops.'

Cynan sneered, which made the mark of his punishment writhe on that cheek. It marred his dark handsomeness, and must still hurt, but should heal soon. Probably he wasn't quite over his resentment. Those Demetae were inclined to be broody sorts. 'I suppose somebody among us may as well get in good with Jesus,' he said, 'though I hear this countryside is still blessedly free of Him.' He heard Mass when that seemed expedient, but made no bones about reckoning the faith one for women and soft city dwellers. Himself, he sought the temple of Nodens when he could.

'Can't stop and dicker with any cleric we might come across.' Adminius's thin features split in a gap-toothed grin. 'Tell you wot, though, Budic. If we do meet one, I'll 'elp you grab 'im up and sling 'im over a 'orse, and 'e can oblige you as we travel.'

The youth reddened. He doubled his fists. Eppillus's burly form pushed close. He had sensed trouble brewing. 'That will do,' the deputy rumbled. 'Leave off the jibes. Every man's got a right to his religion.'

The tormentors drifted away, a little abashed, to mingle with their comrades. 'Thank you,' Budic said unevenly. 'I, uh, may I ask what your belief is? I've never seen you at . . . our services.'

Eppillus shrugged. 'I follow Mithras, same as the centurion and two others amongst us. But I admit that for luck I look more to a thunderstone I carry.' It was a piece of flint in the form of a spearhead, found near a dolmen many years ago. He chuckled deep in his hairy breast. 'Could be that's why I've never made better than second grade in the Mystery. But I'm too old to change my ways, when there's no wife to badger me out of 'em.'

'I thought . . . you would be married.'

'I was. She died. Two kids, both grown and flown the nest. I've got my bit of a farm still, back near Isca, and when my hitch is up – couple years to go – I'll find me a nice plump widow.' Eppillus grew aware of Gratillonius, who had stood quietly listening. 'Oh, hail, sir. Budic, don't stand there like a snow man in a thaw. Go get the centurion his wine.'

Gratillonius smiled. On the whole, this episode seemed to bode well.

4

The land began to rise after they crossed into Gallia Lugdunensis. Roads must curve, climb, swing back down again, around and over hills that were often steep. Nevertheless, the legionaries continued day by day to eat the miles.

Or the leagues, which were what waystones now measured. Unlike Britannia, Gallia had reverted from Rome's thousand paces to the larger Celtic measure. Gratillonius didn't know just when or why that had happened. But he did know that the Gallic provinces, together with the Rhenus valley, had been the richest, most populous and productive territories in the Empire. What they wanted, they could likely get – including a new Emperor?

Certainly this land clung unhindered to its own old ways. Cynan had been right; Christianity was a religion for towns. Frequently Gratillonius spied a cella, a Celtic temple. Even smaller than a Mithraeum, it consisted of a single square room surrounded by a porch. Public rites took place in the temenos outside; the chamber could barely hold one or two persons who had some special need of their Gods.

Now and then the legionaries passed a hill fort, earthworks raised on a height before ever Caesar arrived. Most were deserted, their outlines time-blurred, but Gratillonius observed that some had lately been refurbished, refuges against the failure of everything Roman.

Spring rolled northwards apace. Trees leafed, hawthorn hedges bloomed white, wildflowers bejewelled meadows gone intensely green, larks jubilated aloft. Where fields lay under cultivation, the first fine shoots thrust out of furrows and orchards were riotous with blossom. Views became splendid from the ridges, down over dappled valleys where rivers gleamed and clanged in spate. Rain turned into scattered showers after which rainbows bridged the clouds. Most days were clear, warm, full of sweetness. They grew swiftly longer too, which made for better time on the road, although Gratillonius liked the gentle nights and would sometimes stroll from camp to be alone with the stars.

Speech changed across the country, shifting from dialect to dialect until you could say that Caletes and Osismii spoke distinct languages. However, he could always make himself understood, whether or not anybody knew Latin – which many farmers, who never went more than a few miles from their birthplaces, did not. Barely enough commerce still trickled along that he could obtain information about conditions ahead. Thus advised, he twice took shortcuts over local roads that were adequate. The gravel on them was washing away and not being replaced, but in dry weather they still served.

That neglect was a sign of much else. The farther west the men came, the more desolation they saw. At first it was not unlike parts of Britannia, vacant huts, acres gone back to weeds, squalid serf shacks well away from the mansions of the honestiores, towns listless and half empty. The larger towns had garrisons, which saw to such things as the maintenance of bridges, but these were auxiliaries from as far away as Egypt, foreign alike to Roman and Celt, generally sloppy. Or, worse, the troops were laeti, Germanic or Alanic barbarians who had forced their way into the province and carved out settlements for themselves: men surly, shaggy, fierce, and filthy, on guard more for the sake of their own kin than for the Empire to which they gave nominal allegiance.

Thirty years had passed since Magnentius failed in his try for the throne. The ruin left by the war was not yet repaired, nor did it seem likely ever to be. Why? wondered Gratillonius. Nature was no less generous here than erstwhile: rich soil, timber, minerals, navigable rivers, fructifying sunshine and rain. The Gauls were an able race, to whom Rome had brought peace, civilization, an opening on the rest of the world. Her armies and navies easily kept prosperity unplundered by outsiders. In return she asked for little other than loyalty, obedience to laws that were more tribal than Roman, a modest tribute so the engineers and soldiers could be paid. Gauls grew wealthy, not only from agriculture and mining but from manufacturing. Art and learning waxed brilliant in their cities. Gallia became the heartland of the Empire. Why could she not now recover? What had gone wrong?

Gratillonius didn't ask his questions aloud. The men were already oppressed by what they saw. In camp they didn't sing or crack jokes, they sat wistfully talking about their homes. The centurion heartened them somewhat with a speech on the marvels awaiting them at Ys, but he was hampered by the fact that he didn't know just what those were.

The more they marched, the grimmer it was. The road ran near the coast. Saxon raiders had been coming yearly out of the sea, in ever greater fleets whose crews would go ravaging far inland. The Duke of the Armorican Tract could do little to check them. His forces were depleted, and the shore forts had never been as tightly interlinked as those of Britannia. If a detachment was not simply too small to fight a barbarian swarm, it was seldom fast enough to catch them before they had wrought their havoc and were off elsewhere. They took care to demolish message towers, so that Roman signals of fire by night and smoke by day were no longer visible at any very useful distance; it looked to Gratillonius as if the army had given up attempts at rebuilding.

Otherwise the Saxons were as insensate as wildfire. They slaughtered men, ravished women, made quarry of children. Having clumsily sacked, they burnt. Were a place too poor to rob, they kindled it anyway, for sheer love of destruction. Gratillonius came upon ash heaps that had been houses, buildings of brick and stone rooflessly agape, towns where a few who fled had returned to squat in the ruins and tell their tales of horror, defensive walls broken and never repaired, orchards chopped down, fields charred, harbours empty of their fishing boats. He glimpsed livestock skeletons, strewn human bones which nobody had come back to bury, wandering beggars who had once had homes, three or four women who had gone mad and went about unkempt, ragged, and gibbering. Wild dogs were more dangerous than wolves. One rainy day at the remnant of a manor house, he saw a peacock dying of chill and starvation, its tail dragged down in the mud, and wondered why the sight moved him so.

Scoti out of Hivernia had been arriving too. They were

fewer in number than the Saxons, not as wantonly cruel, and their leather coracles could hold less loot than German galleys. They did their share of damage, though, especially by carrying off able-bodied young captives for slaves.

Not every stronghold had fallen, not every farm stood abandoned. A measure of civilized life went on, however wanly. The land itself was beautiful, wide beaches, long hills and dales whose grass rippled and trees soughed in the wind off the sea. Birds filled heaven, gulls, gannets, cormorants, ducks, geese, swans, cranes, herons, a hundred smaller sorts and the eagle high above them. Fish flashed in every stream, bats and swifts darted about at dusk while frogs croaked in chorus, lizards basked on sunny rocks. Squirrels streaked like meteors, hares bounded off, deer browsed in the distance. At least wildlife was coming back.

At Ingena Gratillonius planned to turn south of west, inland, towards Vorgium. There he would collect fresh supplies and have the men put their equipment in top form before the last leg of their journey. The military commander, a grizzled Italian, counselled him against it.

'Yonder's only a husk, scarcely a village, after what the Saxons did to it – Osismiis, that was once the finest city in Armorica, after Ys,' he said. Gratillonius felt a slight shock at hearing how the Roman name had fallen out of use, even for this man. 'A few Mauretanians stationed there yet, but they don't keep proper stores, they rely on outside supply mostly. No, I'd say you should head south from here to Condate Redonum. It's about your last chance to restock, if you're bound west. I suppose you've business among the Veneti?'

'Farther north,' Gratillonius evaded.

'Well, then, first proceed to Fanum Martis. Don't bother exchanging courtesies with the garrison, they're a lot of scruffy Egyptians. It's a detour, but you'll make better speed, because you'll have trunk roads to there and then down to Redonum. Thence it's secondaries, but gravelled and well kept up, because the Osismii and sometimes the Ysans use it for their wagons. A good deal is through wildwood, but you should have no trouble; I scarcely think Bacaudae will jump Roman regulars. At the coast you'll come to Garomagus – m-m, the ruins of Garomagus – and from there another good secondary road will take you down to the maritime station near Ys. That's ruined too, been ruined for a long time. However, I hear the Ysans maintain the roads through their hinterland, and they should certainly allow you passage, if that's the way you're going.'

A thrill passed through Gratillonius. 'I've heard tell about Ys,' he said carelessly. 'Things hard to believe. What's it like in truth?'

The commander frowned. 'Who knows, any more? A city-state on the west coast. I've never been there, but people say its towers are the eighth wonder of the world.'

'Surely you know more, sir.'

The commander scratched his head. 'Well, let me think. I've heard it began as a Carthaginian colony, back before the Celts arrived. The colonists interbred first with the Old Folk, those who're said to have raised the great stones, and afterwards with the Osismii. They grew prosperous on trade. Julius Caesar made a foederate of Ys, but relations were never close and the last Imperial resident departed, oh, one or two hundred years ago, I guess. Ys no longer even pays tribute. Lately the Duke asked it to cooperate in the defence of Armorica. I hear the answer he got – in polite words, no doubt – was that by patrolling its own waters Ys was doing the best possible service to Rome. He hasn't the manpower to enforce anything on the city; it's well protected by its wall and

85

there'd be no way to close its sea lanes. Besides, maybe the Ysans are right. I don't know. I told you I've not been there myself.'

'Few seem to. Odd. I should think curiosity alone – '

The commander pressed lips together. 'I should too, now you say it. But that isn't the case. I never wondered much about Ys either, even when I was young and lively. You see practically no mention of it in any records. I've read Caesar and Tacitus and Plinius and – and many more – and nowhere have I found a word about Ys, not in the *Gallic War* itself, though native tradition insists Caesar paid a visit in person.' He sighed. 'Christ and all angels help us, there's something damnably strange about Ys. They have a grisly kind of royal sacrifice, and nine witch-queens who go out on a desert island and work black magic, and – Well, I don't want to talk about it. I've troubles aplenty as is.'

Gratillonius did not pursue matters.

At sunrise he led his men onward. After two days they came to Fanum Martis, where the tower dedicated to the war God loomed huge and empty above houses, many of which were also deserted.

There they swung south. In that direction they found ample traces of former habitation. Armorica had once been thriving and well populated, except for the heavily forested interior; but little remained. Land rolled gently, taken over by grass, brambles, young trees. Often the travellers spied megalithic monuments. Gauls said Gods, or elves, or wizards, or the Old Folk had raised those gaunt menhirs, solitary or in cromlech circles, those massive dolmens and passage chambers. Once the party made camp by one of the latter. Gratillonius took a torch inside and came upon relics of a family who had sheltered there – a well-off family, whose glassware gleamed while furniture decayed and silver corroded on the earth. He wondered what had happened to them. Thieves had not dared enter this haunted place afterwards. Gratillonius left the things where they were, out of respect for the dead, and did not mention them.

None of his followers had volunteered to accompany him, though he knew they would have done so if asked. Gratillonius was not himself afraid. He didn't think Ahriman would deign to employ mere spooks, and in any event they must flee from the light of Ahura-Mazda which Mithras bore. He could not understand why otherwise rational people had all those vague superstitions about Ys.

Next morning the soldiers rose at first light as usual, paid their various devotions, got a meagre breakfast, struck camp, and marched. They reached Condate Redonum before noon.

This riparian city too had withdrawn behind fortress walls; but those were unbreached, the houses within unplundered, if dirty and dilapidated. More life flowed over the cobbles, between buildings and across the forum, than Gratillonius had seen for some time. After passing through areas where folk tended to be dark-haired, here he found them again generally fair, as well as robust and rather tall.

Most were local Redones, but quite a few were Osismii come from the west to market. Gratillonius observed the latter with special interest; their country bordered on Ys. The men ran to sweeping moustaches and hair in long braids. Their clothing was of good stuff and frequently fur-trimmed. They carried themselves boldly. Gratillonius recalled that the honestiores had never taken root among them, nor had there ever been many curials to grind between the millstones.

In contrast, the garrison appalled him. It was mainly of Frankish laeti. They were big men, armoured in conical

87

helmets and leather reinforced with iron rings. Sword and francisca, the dreaded throwing-axe, were their principal weapons; shields were small and round, garishly painted. They swaggered about pushing others out of the way, daring anybody to defy them.

Gratillonius sought the military prefect at headquarters. That Iberian could only say, 'I'm sorry. I'll see to it that you get what you need, of course, but in this confusion it may take a little time, and meanwhile I urge you to camp well away from town. Our people have got used to the Franks, if not exactly liking them, but your men could too easily get into a fight. You see, it happens they're holding one of their festivals tonight.'

'Hm-m. Drunk and rowdy.'

'To say the least. They're heathen, did you know? They'll swill themselves into madness and believe they're inspired by Mercurius – Wotan, they call Him, chief of their Gods.' The officer grimaced. 'It won't be as bad as the quarter days. Then they go out in the country and make human sacrifices. True, that does take them out of town. Redonum won't be safe tonight. But what can we do?'

Gratillonius thought furiously that he knew very well what *he* could do. Still, he must not lose men in the chastising of Franks . . . who were allies against barbarians from outside . . . His mission lay before him, in glorious Ys.

Next day his troop marched westward.

V

At midnight the Nine left the House of the Goddess and
set forth. They bore no lanterns, for the moon was nearly
full and the sky clear. Their weather spell had seen to
that. But there was a wind, whistling and cold from the
east, over the island and away across Ocean. This too was
the will of the Nine, for it was such a wind as rode with
the souls of many among the dead. The Gallicenae would
need every unseen power they could raise to strengthen
them in that which they were about to do.

Sena was small, flat, treeless. Moonlight lay hoar on
harsh grass, darkling on rocks, ashimmer on tide pools
and the kelp strewn around them. It frosted the manes of
waves as they rolled and tumbled, it made white fountains
where they crashed on outlying reefs and rocks, it glimmered off the coats of seals that swam along as if following
the procession. It drowned most stars; those that were left
seemed to flicker in the wind.

The women walked slowly, silent save when a cloak
flapped or a pebble gritted underfoot. The wind spoke for
them. Forsquilis led. She stared before her, blind and
deaf in trance. Vindilis and Bodilis guided her by either
arm. They were those who could hold themselves steadi-
est when next to such a vessel of strangeness. The other
six followed in file. Quinipilis was in front, as befitted the
oldest, the presiding one. Fennalis came after, and then
her daughter Lanarvilis, then Innilis, then Maldunilis.
Last was Dahilis, who crowded a little as if the bulk ahead
could somehow shield her from the terrors that prowled
about. A covered firepot she carried glowed out of
airholes like red spider eyes.

It seemed long, but was not, until the Queens reached the Stones. Those two pillars, rough-hewn and raised by the Old Folk, stood close together near the middle of the island. The beak of the Bird, the more pointed head of the Beast – vague resemblances – were some two man-heights aloft. Vindilis and Bodilis helped Forsquilis in between them. They engulfed her in shadow; hardly any of her was now to be seen other than the manyfold linen windings of her headdress, phantom-wan. She laid her palms against the rock and stood motionless except for quickened breath.

The rest ranged themselves in a circle, Quinipilis facing the seeress. The aged woman lifted her arms and countenance on high. 'Ishtar-Isis-Belisama, have mercy on us,' she called in a voice still strong. 'Taranis, embolden us. Lir, harden us. All Gods else, we invoke You in the name of the Three, and cry unto You for the deliverance of Ys.'

Her prayer used the ancestral speech because of its sacredness and potency, but thereafter she returned to the vernacular: 'Forsquilis, Forsquilis, how go you, what find you?'

The priestess between the Stones answered like a sleepwalker: 'I go as an owl. The treetops beneath my wings are a net wherein the moon touches buds and new leaves with argent. It is lonely being a spirit out of the flesh. The stars are more far away than ever we knew; the cold of those vastnesses comes seeping down over the world, through and through me.

'I see a glade. Dew sparkles on grass around a camp where a fire burns low. Metal gleams on its guardians. I glide downward. The forest is haunted tonight. Do I glimpse the antlers of Cernunnos as He walks amidst His trees?

'They are soldiers, yon men, earthlings only, naught in them of fate. Am I misled? Did the Gods not hear us or

90

heed us? Oh, surely these men are bound hither and surely that is a sign unto us. Yet – Bewildered, I flutter to and fro in the air.'

Suddenly her voice came alive: 'A man steps forth from darkness. Was it him that I espied under the boughs? Sleepless, he has walked down a game trail to sit by a spring and love the sky. Sleepless – he knows not why – but I know him! Now when he is drawn this near, his destiny has reached out of the future and touched him.

'He feels it. He looks upward and sees my wings beneath the moon, the moon that turns his eyes to quicksilver. The dread of the mystery in him comes upon me. I fly from his terrible gaze. It is he, it is he, it is he!'

Forsquilis shrieked and fell. Quinipilis stood aside while Bodilis and Vindilis pulled her out into the open and stretched her carefully on the ground. The rest clustered about. Between dark cloaks and blanched headwraps, most visages were paler than was due to the light.

Bodilis knelt to examine the unmoving woman. 'She seems in a swoon,' she said.

Quinipilis nodded. 'That is to be awaited,' she replied. 'Our Sister has travelled along weird ways. Cover her well, let her in peace, and she should arouse soon.'

'Meanwhile, what shall we do?' asked Lanarvilis.

'Naught,' quavered Maldunilis, her wonted placidity torn apart. 'Naught save abide . . . abide that moment.'

'Surely *something* else,' was Innilis's timid thought. 'Prayer?'

Fennalis stroked her hand, responding, 'Nay, I think not. We have held rites since sunset. It were not well to risk the Gods growing weary of us.'

Bodilis said slowly: 'Hold, Sisters. Belike those same Gods have given us this pause. We can think on what our wisest course may be.'

Wrath flared in Vindilis. 'What mean you?' she cried.

'We held council and made decision at equinox. We cast our spells and tonight we know they've wrought well. What else remains but to curse Colconor?'

'That . . . that is such a dreadful thing,' Dahilis dared say. 'Mayhap we shouldn't – '

Vindilis turned on the girl as if to attack. 'You dare?' she yelled. 'Has he won your heart, little traitress?'

'Please, darling, please,' Innilis begged. She tugged at the sleeve of the older woman, whose anger thereupon abated somewhat.

Dahilis helped by blurting, 'I meant no cowardice, in truth I did not. It was but that Bodilis said – oh – '

'Bodilis said,' declared that one, 'we should take heed this last time ere we do what cannot be undone. Magic is ever a two-edged sword, ofttimes wounding the wielder. I loathe Colconor as deeply as do any of you, my Sisters. But we have called his death to him. May not that be enough? Need we hazard more?'

'We must!' Lanarvilis exclaimed. 'If we stand by idle at this pass, well shall we deserve it that our whole enterprise comes to grief.' She crooked her fingers aloft like talons. 'Also, I want my share in the death.'

Vindilis hissed agreement.

'Calm, Sisters, calm, I pray of you,' urged Fennalis. 'I've no wish myself for black sorcery. Yet if 'tis needful, 'tis needful.'

'I believe it is,' Quinipilis told them. 'Forsquilis is most profound in the lore, aye, but over the years that have been mine I've had to do certain deeds, and watch others done. You, Bodilis, are wise, but it is the wisdom of your books and philosophers. Bethink you. Thus far we have at best brought a man who *may* prevail, and thereafter prove a better King than Colconor.'

'He could never prove worse,' whispered gentle Innilis.

'This man may choose not to fight,' Quinipilis went on.

'If he leads soldiers, he is on duty he would be reluctant to set aside. If he does fight, he may lose. I doubt me Colconor's strength has much dwindled since he won the crown.'

Bodilis nodded thoughtfully. 'True. If then the soldiers slay him who killed their comrade, why, we would be rid of the monster, but how shall we have a new King? The sacred battle may never be of more than one against one. Ys beholds too much desecration already. I believe that is why the powers of the Gallicenae are fading and failing.'

'Oh, nay,' Innilis shuddered and crept close to Vindilis, who laid an arm about her waist.

'Fear not, my sweet,' Vindilis assured her. 'We will cast our spell in righteousness, that the hero shall indeed take lordship and redeem us.'

Dahilis clasped her hands together. 'The hero!' Her eyes shone.

Forsquilis groaned, stirred, looked up with merely human sight. Her colleagues aided her to sit, chafed her wrists, murmured comfort. Finally she could rise.

'Feel you that we should go on as we've planned?' Quinipilis asked. 'And if you do, have you the strength?'

The witch straightened. Teeth gleamed between lips drawn thin. 'Yea and yea!' she answered. 'Wait no more. Our might sinks with the moon.'

The Nine had, earlier, brought wood and laid it on a blackened site near the Stones. Dahilis had had the honour of carrying the fire: for the Sisterhood had agreed, upon Quinipilis's proposing, that Dahilis, youngest and fairest of them, should be the bride of the new King's first night. She prayed to Belisama while she emptied glowing charcoal on to kindling. The wind made flames leap quickly.

From under her cloak Forsquilis took a silver vessel whence she dusted salt across every palm. The Queens licked it up in the name of Lir. Quinipilis called on Taranis while she drew forth a knife, nicked her thumb, and flung drops of blood on to the fire. They spat when they struck the coals. Each by each, the Sisters passed before her and made the same sacrifice.

They joined hands around the blaze. It roared, streaming and sparkling on the wind. Red and yellow unease below, icy white above, were all the light there was; everywhere else reached blindness. Sang the Nine:

> 'Winter wolf and sheering shark,
> Whip and tautened traces,
> Shame by day and fear by dark,
> Hobnails down on faces,
> Worms at feast in living hearts,
> Dulled and rusted honour –
> From his spirit, let these parts
> Rise to curse Colconor!

> 'May he fall as falls a tree
> When its roots are rotten
> And a wind whirls off the sea,
> Angry, Lir-begotten.
> Lord Taranis, in Your sky
> Hear the tempest clamour.
> Long those poisoned boughs reached high.
> Smite them with Your hammer!

> 'Belisama, may our spell
> Make You come and take him
> Down to doom, and there in hell
> Evermore forsake him.
> Hitherward his bane we draw
> In this vengeful springtime.
> Stranger, heed the holy Law
> All throughout your King time.'

Aboard their boat at the dock, looking beyond the House, the fishermen who had brought the Nine hither saw the fire. They did not know what it portended, they had only obeyed when called upon, but they shivered, muttered charms, clutched lucky pieces and made forfending signs; and they were Ferriers of the Dead.

VI

1

West of Vorgium the hills became long and steep. Forest thinned out until there were only isolated stands of trees, and none wherever heath prevailed over pastureland. The soldiers were rarely out of sight of one or more megaliths, brooding grey amidst emptiness. Winds blew shrill and cold, drove clouds across heaven and their shadows across earth, often cast rainshowers. Yet here too it was the season of rebirth. Grass rippled like green flame, mustard and gorse flaunted gold, flowers were everywhere – tiny daisies, blue borage, violets, hyacinths, cuckoopint, speedwell, primrose, strewn through filigree of wild carrot and prickle of blackberry. Only willows had thus far come to full leaf, but oak and chestnut were beginning, while plum blossoms whitened their own boughs. Bumblebees droned, amber aflight. Blackbirds, starlings, sparrows, doves, gulls filled the sky with wings and calls.

Farmsteads were apt to be far apart, tucked into sheltering dells: a thatch-roofed wattle-and-daub house for people and animals together, perhaps a shed, a pigpen, a vegetable garden, an apple tree or so. Mainly folk in these parts lived by grazing sheep and, to a lesser degree, cattle. They were all Osismii, and Gratillonius would not have been able to speak with them had he not picked up some of their language as a boy. It used many words unique to itself, words he thought must trace back to the Old Folk. Invading Celts, centuries ago, had made themselves the leading families of the tribe and mingled

96

their blood with that of the natives, but more thinly, this far out on the peninsula, than elsewhere in Gallia.

Some words, he thought with an eerie thrill, must stem from another source, from Ys. They resembled none he had heard before, but stirred vague memories in him of names he had met when studying the history of the Punic Wars.

Although folk were friendly, much excited to see legionaries, he didn't stop for talk except one evening when he chanced to camp near a dwelling. There he learned that the neighbourhood had suffered little from raiders, being too poor to draw them, but the western shore was an utter wreck apart from Gesocribate and Ys. The former was tucked well into a narrow bay and Roman-defended. The latter fronted on Ocean, but – The farmer signed himself to his Gods in awe of the power protecting that city. He would be glad to come under its guardianship. Unfortunately, Ys claimed only a few eastward miles of hinterland.

Disturbance crept about within Gratillonius. What forces indeed did such a minikin state command, that it endured while Rome crumbled?

He found himself thinking about that again when his squadron reached the coast and spent a night at Garomagus. He and his father had called there several times, in years as lost as the lives they had found. Small but bustling, the town once embodied those industries, that prosperity, which ringed its great bight: ceramics, metalwork, salt, and garum, the fish sauce Armoricans exported to the farthest ends of the Empire. Now, as sunset smouldered away, Gratillonius stood fingering a shard of a jar, among the burnt-out shells of buildings surrounding a forum where only he and the whimpering wind had motion.

He saw no bones lying about. Survivors who crept back

to town after the final sack must have buried their kindred before abandoning their homes. Stains still darkened a fountain gone dry, where the heathen had held a sacrifice, and rubbish littered pavement. A book sprawled mildewing outside a church, its cover stripped of jewels, its vellum capriciously slashed. Gratillonius bent over to peer at the rain-blurred pages and recognized Greek letters and ink drawings. A Gospel. Christian or not, the dead book saddened him. He carried it into the church and laid it on the altar.

Later the moon rose, a day past the full. Unable at first to sleep, he wandered from camp. Following the stream beside which the town had nestled, he came to the mouth and turned on to a beach. Wavelets on the bay glimmered and lulled, sand scritted underfoot. The air was not very cold. He made out stars, old friends, the Bears, the Dragon, the Lion that heralds the northward-swinging sun. Tonight they seemed remote and alien. Did they really rule over the fates of men? Most people believed so. If they were right, then the star of Ys – Venus? – was still ascendant; and the Mars of Rome was sinking?

Without having pondered the matter, which could have led him to question seriously a tenet of his religion, Gratillonius had always doubted astrology. At most, he supposed, whatever planet a man was born under might influence him; but so would the heritage of blood and circumstance that he had from his parents. Manhood required him to make his own fate.

But if the blind circle of the spheres was not what kept Ys alive: what did? He should have learned far more than he knew before embarking on this mission. The knowledge had, though, not been there for him, in any chronicles he could find or any spoken accounts he could elicit. Ys kept itself wrapped in enigma – how?

For no good reason, he remembered another evening a

few days back, and a great owl he had glimpsed above a glade. Why should that make him shiver? He turned from shore and sought his tent.

2

Out of what had been Garomagus, a road ran almost due west along the coast, twenty miles or a bit less to the Gobaean Promontory. It was merely gravelled, like most secondary Roman routes, but well maintained. The troops started early and marched with redoubled briskness. This night they would be in the fabulous city.

They had covered half the distance when they came to a pair of stones flanking the track. Ten feet tall, those granite pillars were not prehistoric; weather had softened their squared edges, but the characters chiselled into them were still legible. Gratillonius dismounted to read. On the southern column, a gracefully curving alphabet was unknown to him. On the northern he found Latin, surely the same message. His finger traced what his lips murmured: *'In the names of Venus, Jupiter, Neptunus, here I mark the frontier of land that has been of Ys since time immemorial, along this Redonian Way. Hold me and my sister sacred, for we bear the Oath, for ever binding. Raised DCLXXXVIII AVC obedient to orders of the SPQR, year XIII since the Sign came upon Brennilis, who with C. Julius Caesar did make the Oath.'*

'Old,' Gratillonius whispered. 'Four and a third centuries. But the wording – I've seen things like this elsewhere, from nearly that far back – the wording here is – ' a chill went up his spine – 'unusual.'

Eppillus looked around. 'Boundary marker, eh?' he grunted. 'Where are the sentries?'

Grass waved in a salty breeze, down to a cliff's edge on the north, with water agleam beyond it under a clear sky, and southward up to the spine of the peninsula. Afar in that direction, the men could just spy a flock of sheep near some wind-gnarled trees, but no other sign of habitation. Out where sunlight winked on whitecaps, sails showed boldly coloured across the arc of vision. They were too remote for Gratillonius to be certain, but he supposed they belonged to fishing boats. Ys took little from its modicum of thin-soiled hinterland; its communion was with the sea.

'I don't imagine the city feels any need of pickets,' he answered slowly. 'Relations with the Osismii, and with Rome, have been peaceful. Trade must go unhindered, and across a long stretch, too. "Redonian Way." That seems to mean the Ysans think of this as their road to the Redones in eastern Armorica – nowadays to Condate Redonum – though those tribesmen seldom get to these parts.'

'But what about pirates?' the deputy argued. 'Pirates could land and walk on in.'

'They don't. Something keeps them away. I don't know what.'

'The old Roman Gods?' Cynan asked from his place as today's standard bearer. 'Do They still have power . . . in this place?'

'Those are not Roman, those Gods the stones bespeak,' Gratillonius said. 'They're only Latin names. Romans used to suppose any Gods they met were the same as their own, but it was never true. You, my friend, must know better, must know Sulis is not really Minerva or – See, the inscription puts Venus first. A mother Goddess? Maybe. If we could read it, the second stone would tell us something very different from the first, about the Gods of Ys.'

'The demons!' Budic exclaimed. He raised his arms. 'Christ Jesus,' he beseeched, 'watch over us, drive off the powers of darkness.'

'Fall in,' Gratillonius snapped. 'Forward march.'

Mithras, Lord of Light, ride with us, Your soldiers, he thought as he sprang back on to his horse. He could not make it feel like a prayer. Had he wandered so far, into such foreignness, that the God of his fathers no longer heard him?

Angry at his weakness, he tried to thrust the question away. What was there to fear? Most likely less than anywhere else in the Empire, here where robbers dared not come. However lonesome, the landscape was gauntly beautiful. Ys of the marvels awaited him, and would scarcely deny him obedience. His demands would be modest in any case, simply that Ys remain at peace, and help keep the rest of western Armorica at peace, while Maximus campaigned. The leaders of the city could not fail to see how they too would benefit by an Emperor strong and able.

And afterwards – why, that grateful Emperor ought at the very least to bestow senatorial rank on a man who had served him well. Perhaps he would lift the man's entire kin out of the curial class. And the officer would go on to mighty deeds, power, wealth, undying fame.

With an abrupt shock, Gratillonius realized that he did not know what his ambitions were. Hitherto he had been content to live day by day. When he thought about the future, he hoped for eventual promotion to senior centurion, followed by retirement in a home he would acquire somewhere among his Belgic tribesfolk. There he would have a woodworking shop for pleasure, horses, dogs, a cat to sleep on a sunny windowsill. Of course, he would already have married and begotten sons . . . Never before had he imagined the world open to him. Did he truly want it?

A bulk ahead drew his attention. 'Keep on,' he ordered, and turned his horse off the road on to a point of land. What he found was the remains of a fortress on the brink of a precipice. Ditched and triple-walled, it was from before the Romans, and long unused. Grass billowed across ridges and mounds that had been earthworks. Yards below, waves foamed and growled; overhead, a gull cruised mewing.

The sight was like an omen of mortality. Gratillonius drew the sign of Mithras, wheeled his mount, and hastened back to the van of his party.

The end of the headland wasn't far now. He knew this road went to a maritime station the Romans had built, back when they maintained a constant presence; later the Ysans manned it for them. From there, he supposed, the way would turn south till it went down to the bay where the city was. Impatience leapt in him. He wanted to gallop straight across. But that wouldn't be dignified. Besides, grass and brush might well conceal footing dangerous to a horse. His heels prodded the animal into a trot while he reined in his spirit.

At the bend in the route he diverged for a look down a side path. Under granite of the promontory, above rage of water among rocks and reefs, he saw the ruins of the station. Holes knocked in walls – whether by enemy rams or by storm-driven surf – gaped full of darkness. Rain had washed away the soot of the fire that consumed roof and dock; he glimpsed only a few charred timbers from either, tumbled and bleached like driftwood.

'This happened years, maybe decades ago,' he muttered. 'Ys is supposed to be safe. But already then – '

Eppillus trod forward to stand by his leader and see. 'Maybe their Gods are dying too,' he said. Yet the rusty

102

voice and the barrel-shaped figure somehow called Gratillonius back to hopefulness. Here was reality, prosaically Roman. Whatever ghosts haunted this country were no more solid than those cloud shadows which the sea wind sent scudding over it.

'We'll see,' the centurion answered. 'Onward!'

Southbound, he passed a hillock which he suspected covered more wreckage. He scarcely noticed, for tower-tops were coming into view ahead. When he reached the descent, there was Ys.

From this height the road swept to a deep dale, walled on both sides by the land. Thus protected, the northern slopes were fit for more than rough pasture. Orchards and woodlots stood around the red tile and white walls of wealthy homes, the thatch and clay of clustered cottages. Brown plots amidst the greenness showed where gardens would soon be bearing. The southern side of the hollow was less occupied, because it climbed steeply to form another headland. Between those two nesses was the bight which Ys filled. Eastwards the valley ran lengthy, well populated, towards distance-blue hills.

Soldier's training made Gratillonius first survey the terrain. A branch way plunged directly down to a short bridge between this promontory and the wall around Ys. Another road led from the eastern city gate, inland. An arm of it swung north, and then east under the heights, to a grove of oaks, after which it became a mere trail.

On the near side of the shaw, Gratillonius spied three large wooden buildings around a courtyard giving on that road. Beyond the trees, in a low swale, was an amphitheatre, modest in size but clearly Roman save for – something subtle, some difference he could not identify from this far off. There the highway went south, and then east again out of sight. Elsewhere ran several dirt roads, and a gravelled one out on to the southern cape, which held a pharos at the tip. From the far hills, down the middle of the valley, cutting through the grove, gleamed a narrow canal.

His gaze sought Ys. Strange, he thought as he caught his breath – part and parcel of the strangeness everywhere around – that he and his father had traded as close as Garomagus, yet not until now had he glimpsed Ys of the hundred towers.

Thus they bespoke it around Armorica. If the count was not really that high, if this was in fact a rather small city, what matter? Ys soared out of the sea.

Its wall formed a rectangle about a mile long, to which were added semicircular ends of a diameter slightly less. The shore arc snugged close between the two forelands, and there the rampart loomed fifteen feet. Westwards its elevation above water would depend on the tides, which Gratillonius knew to be large. He could only wonder how deep those foundations lay. Red-brown, the material must have been quarried from the cliffs. A band of colour below the parapet, a frieze, relieved the murkiness. Twin turrets lifted battlements over each of the three landward entrances. Along the western arc, if he gauged rightly, a fourth pair stood about a hundred and ten degrees apart, to guard the harbour and its marvellous gate.

He could not discern that basin from here, because too many buildings were in the way – towers indeed, high, narrow, reaching for the sky out of the crowd of lesser structures. Mosaics and patternings formed brilliant fantasies up their sides. Glass, gold, even tiled and patinaed copper caught the early afternoon sunlight and flung it back in a dazzle. A slight haziness, borne in from Ocean, made the sight a dream. He could scarcely believe that human beings dwelt yonder, not elves or Gods.

But the first of the Caesars had walked those streets, the first Augustus had ordered those outer defences erected. Gratillonius had come to reclaim a heritage.

The knowledge thrilled in him. 'Silence!' he cried at the amazed swearing of his men. 'Dress ranks. We'll enter in Roman style.'

The Ysans had paved this section of the way, since gravel would have washed downwards. Hoofs rang on stone. Gratillonius tightened knees against the hairy warmth of the horse. Weight pulled hard on him, hauling him on towards the sea.

Faintly through the wind he heard a trumpet call, and another and another. Watchmen had glimpsed his soldiers. The land portals stood open and he supposed townsfolk would soon be swarming forth – past the smithies and carpenter shops and other worksteads that stood just outside along the eastbound road – unless an official delegation forced itself in front of the crowd.

But the first human motion he spied was at the oak grove. Several people came from the house. For an instant they paused in the courtyard to stare. Then a man took the lead, loping out while the rest scurried after. Clearly they meant to intercept the newcomers.

Gratillonius thought fast. Amidst what scanty information he had been able to gather, much of it doubtless false, was a story that the King of Ys spent the three days and nights around full moon in a sacred wood, and that at all times he must hold himself prepared to fight any challenger for his crown. Last night had ended the period in this month; but he might have lingered for some reason. If not, those might be priests of importance . . . and priestesses? Gratillonius identified women among them. Probably he would do best to meet them as they wished, allay whatever fears they had, ask that they accompany him into town.

A rutted track offered a shortcut between this road and

105

the one that led to the grove. He gestured to his men and turned off, angling downwards.

3

The parties met nearer the shaw than the city. They halted a few feet apart. For a space there was stillness, save for the wind.

The man in front was a Gaul, Gratillonius judged. He was huge, would stand a head above the centurion when they were both on the ground, with a breadth of shoulder and thickness of chest that made him look squat. His paunch simply added to the sense of bear strength. His face was broad, ruddy, veins broken in the flattish nose, a scar zigzagging across the brow ridges that shelved small ice-blue eyes. Hair knotted into a queue, beard abristle to the shaggy breast, were brown, and had not been washed for a long while. His loose-fitting shirt and close-fitting breeches were equally soiled. At his hip he kept a knife, and slung across his back was a sword more than a yard in length. A fine golden chain hung around his neck, but what it bore lay hidden beneath the shirt.

'Romans,' he rumbled in Osismian. 'What the pox brings you mucking around here?'

The centurion replied carefully, as best he was able in the same language: 'Greeting. I hight Gaius Valerius Gratillonius, come in peace and good will as the new prefect of Rome in Ys. Fain would I meet with your leaders.'

Meanwhile he surveyed those behind. Half a dozen were men of varying ages, in neat and clean versions of the same garb, unarmed, their own hair braided but beards closely trimmed. In form they resembled Osismii, except for tending to be more slender and dark, but the visages of four were startingly alike, long, narrow, curve-nosed, high-cheeked. Brothers? No, the gap between a grey head and a downy chin was too great.

Nearest the Gaul stood one who differed. He was ponderous of body and countenance. Black beard and receding hair were flecked with white, though he did not seem old. He wore a crimson robe patterned with gold thread, a mitre of the same stuff, a talisman hanging on his bosom that was in the form of a wheel, cast in precious metal and set with jewels. Rings sparkled on both hands. In his right he bore a staff as high as himself, topped by a silver representation of a boar's head.

The women numbered three. They were in ankle-length gowns with loose sleeves to the wrists, of rich material and subtle hues, ornately belted at the waist. Above hung cloaks whose cowls bedecked their heads. Gratillonius guessed their dishevelled appearance was due to haste, after his sudden advent, rather than to carelessness.

The Gaul's voice yanked him from his inspection: 'What? You'd strut in out of nowhere and fart your orders at *me* – you who can talk no better than a frog? Go back before I step on the lot of you.'

'I think you are drunk,' Gratillonius said truthfully.

'Not too full of wine to piss you out, Roman!' the other bawled.

Gratillonius forced coolness upon himself. 'Who here is civilized?' he asked in Latin.

The man in the red robe stepped forward. 'Sir, we request you to kindly overlook the mood of the King,' he responded in the same tongue, accented but fairly fluent. 'His vigil ended at dawn today, but these his Queens sent word for us to wait. I formally attended him to and from the Wood, you see. Only in this past hour was I bidden to come.'

Gratillonius laughed. 'He was sleeping it off, eh?'

The man shrugged and smiled. 'After so much time alone with three of his wives – ' He grew serious. 'Let us indeed go meet with the rest of the Gallicenae and leading Suffetes. This is an extraordinary event. My name is Soren Cartagi, Speaker for Taranis.'

The Gaul turned on him, grabbed him by his garment and shook him. 'You'd undercut me, plotting in Roman, would you?' he grated. A fist drew back. 'Well, I've not forgotten all of it. I know when a scheme's afoot against me. And I know you think Colconor is stupid, but you've a nasty surprise coming to you, potgut!'

The male attendants showed horror. A woman hurried forth. 'Are you possessed, Colconor?' she demanded. 'Soren's person when he speaks for the God is sacred. Let him go ere Taranis blasts you to a cinder!'

The language she used was neither Latin nor Osismian. Melodious, it seemed essentially Celtic, but full of words and constructions Gratillonius had never encountered before. It must be the language of Ys. By listening hard and straining his wits, he got the drift if not the full meaning.

The Gaul released the Speaker, who stumbled back, and rounded on the woman. She stood defiant – tall, lean, her hatchet features haggard but her eyes like great, lustrous pools of darkness. The cowl, fallen down in her hasty movement, revealed a mane of black hair, loosely gathered under a fillet, through the middle of which ran a white streak. Gratillonius sensed implacable hatred as she went on: 'Five years have we endured you, Colconor, and weary years they were. If now you'd fain bring your doom on yourself, oh, be very welcome.'

Rage reddened him the more. 'Ah, so that's your game, Vindilis, my pet?' His own Ysan was easier for Gratillonius to follow, being heavily Osismianized. ''Twas sweet enough you were this threenight agone, and today. But inwardly – Ah, I should have known. You were ever more man than woman, Vindilis, and hex more than either.'

'My, my lord, you rave,' stammered Soren. 'Be calm, I pray you, for your own sake and everyone's.'

'Calm – after what *you* said to me when yon invaders came in sight?' Colconor's shout was aimed past him, at a younger woman: tall, well-formed in a rangy fashion, her face recalling Minerva in its cold regularity and grey eyes. 'You adder, you sorceress, you – you Forsquilis, trafficker with devils – ' Then she returned him a look that sent a shudder through the centurion.

'Colconor, dear, please, please,' begged the third woman. She was big and plump, with brown eyes and pug nose. Her manner was mild, even timid. Was she less formidable than her companions? 'Be good.'

The Gaul gave her a leer that was half a snarl. 'As you were good, Maldunilis? 'Twas your tricks more than aught else that kept me belated in the Precinct. But meseems you too were conspiring my betrayal – '

He swung on Gratillonius. 'Go, Roman!' he roared. 'I am the King! By the iron rod of Taranis, I'll not take Roman orders! Go or stay; but if you stay, 'twill be on the dungheap where I'll toss your carcass!'

Gratillonius fought for self-control. Despite Colconor's behaviour, he was dimly surprised at his instant, lightning-sharp hatred for the man. 'I have prior orders,' he answered, as steadily as he could. To Soren, in Latin: 'Sir, can't you stay this madman so we can talk in quiet?'

Coiconor understood. 'Madman, be I?' he shrieked. 'Why, *you* were shit out of your harlot mother's arse, where your donkey father begot you ere they gelded him. Back to your swinesty of a Rome!'

It flared in Gratillonius. His vinestaff was tucked at his saddlebow. He snatched it forth, leaned down, and gave

Colconor a cut across the lips. Blood jumped from the wound.

Colconor leapt back and grabbed at his sword. The Ysan men flung themselves around him. Gratillonius heard Soren's resonant voice: 'Nay, not here. It must be in the Wood, the Wood.' He sounded almost happy. The women stood aside. Maldunilis seemed shocked, though not really astonished. Forsquilis breathed what might be an incantation. Vindilis put hands on hips, threw back her head, and laughed aloud.

Eppillus stepped to his centurion's shin, glanced up, and said anxiously, 'Looks like a brawl, sir. We can handle it. Give the word, and we'll make sausage meat of that bastard.'

Gratillonius shook his head. A presentiment was eldritch upon him. 'No,' he replied softly. 'I think this is something I must do myself, or else lose the respect we'll need in Ys.'

Colconor stopped struggling, left the group of men, and spat on the horse. 'Well, will you challenge me?' he said. 'I'll enjoy letting out your white blood.'

'You'd fight me next!' yelled Adminius. He too had been quick in picking up something of the Gallic languages.

Colconor grinned. 'Aye, aye. The lot of you. One at a time, though. Your chieftain first. And afterwards I've a right to rest between bouts.' He stared at the women. 'I'll spend those whiles with you three bitches, and you'll not like it, what I'll make you do.' Turning, he swaggered back towards the grove.

Soren approached. 'We are deeply sorry about this,' he said in Latin. 'Far better that you be received as befits the envoy of Rome.' A smile of sorts passed through his beard. 'Well, later you shall be. I think Taranis wearies at last of this incarnation of His, and – the King of the Wood

110

has powers, if he chooses to exercise them, beyond those of even a Roman prefect.'

'I am to fight Colconor, then?' Gratillonius asked slowly.

Soren nodded. 'In the Wood. To the death. On foot, though you may choose your weapons. There is an arsenal at the Lodge.'

'I'm well supplied already.' Gratillonius felt no fear. He had a task before him which he would carry out, or die; he did not expect to die.

He glanced back at the troubled faces of his men, briefly explained what was happening, and finished: 'Keep discipline, boys. But don't worry. We'll still sleep in Ys tonight. Forward march!'

By now people were spilling out of the city. Three of Soren's attendants stood in line across the road to keep them from coming farther. This combat would be a rite, not a spectacle. The other three ran ahead, passing by Colconor, to make things ready. Evidently all of them were household staff in yonder place. Since their attitude was not servile, that must be an honoured position.

The Speaker walked at Gratillonius's left, the women at his right. Nobody talked.

It was but a few minutes to the site. A slate-flagged courtyard stood open along the road, flanked by three buildings. They were clearly ancient, long and low, of squared timbers and with shingle roofs. The two on the sides were painted black, one a stable, the other a storehouse. The third, at the end, was larger, and blood-red. It had a porch with intricately carven pillars.

In the middle of the court grew a giant oak. From the lowest of its newly leafing branches hung a brazen circular shield and a sledgehammer. Though the shield was much too big and heavy for combat, dents surrounded the boss, which showed a wildly bearded and maned human face.

111

Behind the house, more oaks made a grove about seven hundred feet across and equally deep.

'Behold the Sacred Precinct,' Soren intoned. 'Dismount, stranger, and ring your challenge.' After a moment he added quietly, 'We need not lose time waiting for the marines and hounds. Neither of you will flee, nor let his opponent escape.'

Gratillonius comprehended. He sprang to earth, took hold of the hammer, smote the shield with his full strength. It rang, a bass note which sent echoes flying. Mute now, Eppillus gave him his military shield and took his cloak and crest before marshalling the soldiers in a meadow across the road.

Vindilis laid a hand on Gratillonius's arm. Never had he met so intense a gaze, out of such pallor, as from her. In a voice that shook, she whispered, 'Avenge us, man. Set us free. Oh, rich shall be your reward.'

It came to him, like a chill from the wind that soughed among the oaks, that his coming had been awaited. Yet how could she have known?

The storehouse door crashed open and Colconor strode forth. He had outfitted himself well for a barbarian – conical nose-guarded helmet, scale coat reaching to his knees, calf-length leather boots reinforced with studs. His left hand gripped a small round shield. The longsword shone dully in his right.

'Well, well, you're here 'spite of being a Roman,' he gibed. 'Let's have done fast. I've business with yon traitor wives of mine.'

'My lord, your demeanour is unseemly,' Soren protested. 'It cannot please the God.'

Colconor spat. 'I've given Taranis deaths enough whilst I was King. Think you He'd want a lackey of Rome instead?'

'Kneel.' Soren pointed to a spot below the tree. Gratil-

112

lonius and Colconor obeyed, side by side. An attendant
brought water in a bowl, another a sprig of mistletoe.
Soren used the herb to sign the contestants as he chanted
a prayer in a language Gratillonius did not recognize at
all.

Thereafter: 'Go forth,' said the Speaker for Taranis in
Ysan, 'and may the will of the God be done.'

Colconor led the way between the red house and the
stable, in among the trees. Gratillonius followed, never
looking back. Light rays struck between branches still
largely bare. Shadows welled up in the farther depths of
the grove. Last year's leaves rustled underfoot, smelling
of damp. Moss and fungi grew on fallen boles. A squirrel
darted ruddy, like a comet foretelling war. Gratillonius
heard a pig grunt – wild, sacred to whatever mystery
dwelt in this place?

Near the middle of the shaw was a grassy space, narrow
but clear. Colconor stopped and faced about. 'Here I'll
kill you,' he said in a voice gone flat.

Gratillonius raised his oblong Roman shield. Javelins
would be useless under these conditions, and he bore just
the shortsword in his fist, the dagger at his hip. Fleetingly,
he wished he had had a chance to swap his parade mail
for workaday armour. He smiled bleakly at himself. This
was good equipment despite the damageable ornamenta-
tion. It was with such gear that Rome's legionaries had
conquered much of the world. However, they did it in
disciplined units, each a single, many-legged machine.
With two men alone, the barbarian outfit was as useful,
maybe better.

Mithras, he thought, I stand as a soldier, obeying my
orders. Into Your hands I give my spirit.

Then at once he became entirely seized by the business
before him.

The fighters circled, seeking an opening. It was always

113

an odd feeling to Gratillonius when he looked into the eyes of an enemy. A perverse comradeship –

Colconor lunged. His sword whirred down. Gratillonius moved his shield slightly to intercept. The blow thudded loud, radiated back through handle and arm, pulled the strap hard across his shoulder, but the metal rim of the plywood stopped it. He stabbed. Colconor was skilled too. The point smote into the soft pine of the Gallic shield and stuck for an instant. Colconor twisted it while he slashed at that wrist of Gratillonius. So confined, the long blade was awkward. The centurion had time to block it with his own shield. He freed his weapon and tried for a knee. Colconor recoiled. Blood wet a ripped trouser leg, but from a minor cut.

Colconor bayed. He kept his distance, sword leaping, crashing, seeking. Gratillonius must stay on the defensive, unable to counterattack with his smaller blade. His shield did not catch every blow. Two rang on his helmet, one hit mail, one slid along a greave. They hurt.

Coldly, Gratillonius peered beyond his foeman, found what he sought, began manoeuvring. A frenzied Colconor dogged his step-by-step retreat. Gratillonius got his back against a great trunk. Colconor yelled and hewed, right, left, up, down, metal a-clang among the rising shadows. He bounced about like a wolf slashing at a bull.

Gratillonius spread his feet right-angled and tensed his knees. Abruptly he released the left. He pivoted, and Colconor nearly ran past him. Gratillonius jabbed. Colconor drew back . . . and now it was he who stood pinned against the tree.

Gratillonius gave him no time to work his way out of the trap, but moved in. The longsword dinned on his helmet. A shallow slash opened on his forearm. Then he was close. He feinted at the legs. Colconor lowered his shield to cover. Gratillonius drove the boss of his own

114

straight into his enemy's belly. Scales or no, wind whooped out of Colconor. Gratillonius brought the top edge of the shield aloft, catching Colconor beneath the chin. Bone crunched. Red ran forth. Colconor wailed.

Gratillonius saw a rare opportunity. He drove his sword upward and home. It entered at the cheek and went on. He felt bone give, and next the soft mass of the brain. That was a chancy stroke, but therefore unexpected. Blood gushed from Colconor's mouth and nose. His face became a Gorgon's. He crumpled and flopped. Gratillonius withdrew his sword and reinserted it beside the larynx, to complete the task.

For a while the centurion poised over the corpse. Breath went in and out of him, cool and cooling. He felt sweat chilly on his skin and smelled it, an arrogant odour. His mood was calm, though. He had done what he must – good riddance to bad rubbish – and inspection showed his wounds to be trifling.

He'd not wipe his steel on Colconor's greasy, death-fouled clothes. Squatting, he used earth and old leaves. Meanwhile he considered what might happen. King of the Wood? That doubtless entailed duties, he didn't know what, but seemed to bestow a certain amount of power as well. Thus a prefect who was also the monarch should be able to carry out his mission very handily.

Regarding the slain man, he realized that Ys would expect him, too, to fight future challengers, until at last one of them bested him. He shrugged. Surely he could cope while he finished his work here. Later he surely could leave. At worst, he and his men might have to cut their way out, or send for reinforcements; but he would regret that if it happened. The Ysans were probably decent people, on the whole. He'd try to do well by them.

Today he'd be busy with whatever ceremonies they held. He said a belated noontide prayer, added a word of thanks, and stooped to close the eyes below him and straighten out the body. Colconor had been brave enough to deserve that much.

As he performed the office, Gratillonius noticed anew the chain around the fallen man's neck. Wondering at something so delicate on someone so uncouth, he gave it a tug and drew forth from under padding and mail the object it held – an iron key, longer in the shank and more intricate in the prongs than he had ordinarily seen.

A talisman? Gratillonius felt the unknown touch him, cold as the wind. With reverence he laid the key back on the breast. Rising, he sought the red house.

VII

1

When he strode into sight, his men drew blade and gave him three honest cheers. Soren led the Ysan males in genuflection. The women remained standing. Maldunilis's soft features offered shyness, uncertainty, but from Vindilis and Forsquilis blazed an exultation terrifying in its savagery.

At once events swept Gratillonius along. Soren conducted him into the house. He saw that the columns of its portico represented a man, bearded and majestic, who bore a hammer like that which hung at the Challenge Oak, and attributes such as eagles, wild boars, and stylized thunderbolts. The name Taranis he recalled from former visits to Gallia, as well as the same image. So the Ysans had made Taranis their chief God? Gratillonius suspected matters were not that simple.

Within, the right half of the house was a feasting hall, high-raftered and gloomy, where fire licked out of trenches in a clay floor and smoke stung eyes before escaping from a hole overhead. Pillars upholding the roof formed two rows of idols, some clearly Celtic, others impossible for him to identify. Wainscot panels behind the built-in benches along the walls seemed to depict heroic tales. Banners hung from the crossbeams, sooted and frayed with age. Magnificence so rude must have stayed in use because ancientness made it holy. 'Is this the temple of the God?'

Soren shook his head. 'No, Taranis has a splendid

117

marble fane in the city, and many lesser shrines. This is the House of the King, also known as the Red Lodge. Once he was required to live here always, with each Queen spending a night in turn. But for centuries, now, it has only been during full moon, and he summons those wives or other persons whom he will.' He paused before adding, grimly matter-of fact: 'Of course, wherever he may be, he must come back when a challenger strikes the Shield. The resident staff dispatches a messenger.'

Again a prickling went through Gratillonius's skin. Colconor could have left at dawn today for the comforts and pleasures of town. In that event, the Romans would have entered Ys directly, and might well have settled matters with the city magistrates before even meeting the King, who would most likely have decided to accept what he could not easily or safely change. Instead, though, three of his – wives? – had kept him carousing, and at the same time piqued him, as subtly and cruelly as a bull-fighter, until he stormed forth when he saw the new-comers and, in besotted fury, forced the quarrel that ended in his death.

And just how had he done so? Gratillonius knew himself for a short-tempered man, and the insults he suffered were unforgivable. Yet he was a legionary officer on duty. For the sake of Rome, he should have armoured his pride in dignity and merely returned contempt – not plunged headlong into action of whose consequences he had no idea. What demon had entered him?

A burning log cracked. Flames and sparks leapt high. Shadows moved monstrous in dimly lit corners, and it was as if a rustling went through the blackened banners overhead.

Gratillonius ran tongue over lips. 'You must understand, Priest Soren – '

'No, my lord, I am simply the Speaker.' The interruption was bluff but not discourteous. 'I serve Taranis by leading certain rites and by helping govern the worldly affairs of His temple. Otherwise I am a Councillor of the Suffetes and the director of a Great House – an industry. You, sir, are the ordained one, high priest and, in a sense, Incarnation.'

'You must understand,' Gratillonius persisted, 'that I am a Roman citizen in the service of the state. I am also a votary of the God Mithras. Never ask me to compromise my conscience about either of these things.'

He could not be sure, in the dusk, whether Soren showed a flicker of unease. The man did reply steadily: 'I do not believe we need fear that. If I am not mistaken, Mithraists may and do honour other Gods. For the most part, a King does as he will. Apart from meeting his challenges – and I would not expect any to you for a long while, my lord – apart from that, a King's reign is very much what he himself makes it. Ys is old. Through the hundreds of years it has seen many different kinds of men on its throne, Romans among them. But come, please.'

The second half of the Lodge was divided into smaller rooms. These had been modernized, with glass windows, tile floors, frescoed plaster, hypocaust heating. Furniture was comfortable. It included a remarkable number of chairs, with arms and backs. Gratillonius remarked on that and was told that such seats were common in Ys, and not confined to the rich, either.

There was no space for a full-panoply bath, but a large sunken basin had been filled for him. Servants helped him out of his armour and undergarments. He sank gratefully into hot, scented water. His encounter had strained him more than he realized, and Mithras knew what would come next. He needed a rest.

Emerging, he had his injuries poulticed; just the cut on

his arm received a precautionary bandage. Thereafter he enjoyed a skilled massage, was anointed, was guided to a chamber where new raiment lay. Resembling Soren's but more sumptuously worked, the robe fitted him well, as did the soft shoes. He supposed the house kept several wardrobes in different sizes. His pectoral was a gold sunburst, hung from a massive chain and set with pearls and rubies. However, instead of a staff he would bear a full-sized sledgehammer, whose oaken haft and rounded iron head were dark with antiquity. True to his religious vows, he declined the laurel wreath offered him.

More men bustled around than before, making preparations. Soren had gone to oversee matters in the city, and no Ysan present had much if any Latin. His halting Osismian won Gratillonius a little information from the chief steward, about what was happening and what to expect.

Trumpeters and criers went through the streets. '*Allelu, allelu!*' resounded between walls and up into heaven. There followed words in the ancestral language of Ys, which had been Punic. Few other than sacerdotes and scholars knew it today, but it was sanctified. The message then repeated in the vernacular. '*The King is dead, long live the King! In the names of Belisama, Taranis, Lir, come ye, come ye unto the coronation of your lord!*'

The steward's account continued from the immediate past to the present and immediate future.

From the temples of the Three, Their images rolled forth on wagons never used for aught else, drawn by paired white horses for Belisama, black for Lir, red for Taranis. Folk garlanded themselves and heaped the wains with what greenery and blossoms they could find. Led by drums, horns, harps, they went singing and dancing out of the gates and to the amphitheatre. The clear weather, which gave no cause to unroll the canvas roof, seemed to them a good omen. Some must stay behind, though, making ready for a night's revelry.

The royal feast would be more sedate. Huntsmen tracked down a boar, out of the half-wild swine that ranged the Wood. At risk of life, they captured it in nets and hung it above the body of Colconor. There they cut its throat and bled it, down on to the fallen King. Stewed in a sacred cauldron, its flesh would be the centre of a meal here at the Red Lodge.

Taken aback, Gratillonius asked what would become of the human remnant. Ys, he heard, was like Rome in forbidding burials within city bounds; and the cemetery out on Cape Rach, under the pharos, had long since grown to cover as much land as could be allowed. Dead Ysans were taken to sea on a funeral barge and, weighted, sent down to Lir. But a former King lay in state in the temple of Taranis until he was burned, which was too costly for anyone else. A warship took his ashes out near the island Sena. There they were strewn, given to Belisama (Ishtar, Isis, Ashtoreth, Aphrodite, Venus, Nerthus . . .), the Star of the Sea.

As for his conqueror, following the victory feast, he spent his first night in this house. Thereafter he was free to move to his city palace. If he chose, he could visit his Queens in their separate homes, or call them to him –

'Queens!' burst from Gratillonius. 'Hercules! Who are they? How many?'

'The Nine, my lord, the Gallicenae, high priestesses of Belisama. But, um, the King is not compelled – save when 'tis Her will – Forgive me, great sir, a layman should not talk of these matters. They touch the very life of Ys. The Speaker will soon rejoin you and explain what my lord needs to know.'

Dazedly, Gratillonius received a herald, all in green and silver and with a peacock plume on his head, who

121

announced that the processional was beginning. They must want their new King consecrated immediately, he thought. Well, they believed that somehow he embodied a God, or at least the force of that God, upon earth.

Outside, it was late afternoon, and the air boisterous. Soren waited with several fellow dignitaries of his temple. Nearby stood the legionaries. He had made arrangements for them to march along and have seats, later to be quartered in town: unusual, but then, every King was unique. How many had fought, won, reigned, fought, perished, how many ghosts were in this wind off the sea of Ys? Long hills, stark headlands, glimpsed towers and gleam of waters beyond, seemed remote to Gratillonius, not altogether real; he walked through a dream.

Where Processional Way, which led to the Wood, met Aquilonian Way, which ran out of the city's eastern gate, the Gods received their King. The idols of Taranis and Belisama were handsome work in marble, twice life size, done by Greek sculptors whom the Romans brought in as a gesture of alliance in earlier times, He the stern man, She a woman beautiful and chastely clad. The emblem of Lir was immensely older, a rough granite slab engraved with Celtic spirals. Later Gratillonius would learn that that God was never given human shape. Sometimes folk described Him as having three legs and single eye, in the middle of His head, but they knew that was only a way of bespeaking something strange and terrible.

A jubilant crowd followed the wagons. Gratillonius had a feeling their joy was not pretended. Colconor appeared to have made himself hated – mostly among the first families of Ys, whom he daily encountered, but their anger would have trickled down to many commoners. And yet there had been no thought of overthrow, assassination, anything but enduring that which the Gods had chosen to inflict.

Unless – Again bewilderment laid hand on Gratillonius.

As the servant in the house had said they would, the throng moved eastward, down on to low ground, and neared the amphitheatre. It was Roman-built, a gracefully elliptical bowl of tiered benches within an outer wall of marble whose sheerness was relieved by columned doorways and sculptured friezes. Nevertheless Gratillonius confirmed the impression he had got on the promontory, that it was alien. The proportions were not . . . quite . . . classic. The portals were pointed. The fluting and capitals of the pillars hinted at kelp swaying upwards from the sea bottom. The friezes mingled seals, whales, Northern fish with fabulous monsters unlike centaurs or gryphons, and with curious Gallic symbols. How much mark had Rome ever really made on Ys?

The people swarmed in right and left while the sacred cortege entered by a centrally southern archway, through a vaulted passage and out on to the arena. This was not sanded, to take up blood, but paved. A spina told Gratillonius that chariot races were held. That low wall ran down the middle of the arena, leaving space clear at either end; there rose posts for the hoisting of scorekeeping markers. In the middle, however, this spina broadened into a cornice, a balustraded stone platform. Stairways led up to it, as they did to the boxes in the stands reserved for magnates. That meant, Gratillonius realized, this place did not see beast combats – nor human, he felt sure.

When benches had filled with brightly clad spectators, the Gods made a circuit of the arena before stopping under the cornice on the south side. Gratillonius noticed that Belisama was in the middle. Soren told him to bow to Them as he, accompanied by the Speaker, went up on to the platform. Acolytes followed, bearing ewers, censers, evergreen boughs. Behind them, a rawboned grey-

123

beard carried a bronze casket. It was a position of honour; his robes were blue and silver, and Soren had introduced him as Hannon Baltisi, Lir Captain.

Standing aloft, these celebrants waited until a hush had fallen. The lowering sun still spilled brilliance down into the bowl, though shadows lengthened and chilled. A trumpet rang, high and icy sweet. From the middle northern archway came a band of girls and young women, gorgeously cloaked above white gowns, bearing tall candles in silver holders. 'The vestals, virgin daughters and granddaughters of the Queens, those who do not have vigil today,' Soren murmured to Gratillonius. They moved wavelike to ring and spina while they sang:

> 'Holy Ishtar Belisama,
> Lady of the starry sky,
> Come behold Your sacred drama
> Taught to men by You on high.
> You the Wise One are our teacher.
> Spear-renowned of ancient days,
> Hear the words of Your beseecher.
> Mother, come receive our praise.

> 'Great Taranis, heaven-shaker,
> Lord of sky and inky cloud,
> You the rain- and thunder-maker,
> Wrap not this Your day in shroud.
> Shed Your light on Your procession.
> Bless us with Your golden rays.
> Giver of all good possession,
> Father, come receive our praise.

> 'Lir of Ocean, dawn-begotten,
> Lifter of the salty tide,
> Be Your servants not forgotten
> When in hollow hulls they ride.
> Lord of waves and rocks, bereaving,
> Draw us into safer ways,
> And, our fears of wreck relieving,
> Steersman, come receive our praise.

'Threefold rulers of the city,
Star and Storm and Ocean Deep,
For our praise return us pity
While we wake and while we sleep.
Grant we keep our worship faithful,
Sung aloud in sacred lays.
Turn on us no faces wrathful.
Holy Three, receive our praise.'

And now arrived the Nine. Those whom Gratillonius had met this day were become as strange to him as were the rest, in gowns of blue silk bordered with figures akin to the friezes, white linen wrapped high over their heads and pinned by orichalcum crescents, faces stiff in solemnity. Pace by pace they approached the stairs and ascended one by one. A tall old woman led them . . . they seemed to be going in order of age . . . Soren spoke the name as each paused before Gratillonius, bent her head above folded hands, then entered a rank forming on his left hand and stood like soldiers, war captains of the Goddess, nothing further of humility about them . . . Quinipilis, Fennalis, Lanarvilis, Bodilis, Vindilis, Innilis, Maldunilis, Forsquilis –

Dahilis.

Dahilis rammed through Gratillonius. He would not confuse that name. O Gods, she was so much like Una the neighbour girl whom he loved when he was fifteen and ever since had sought to find again, for Una must needs marry wealth in Aquae Sulis if she would help her father stave off ruin . . . Dahilis reached to the base of Gratillonius's throat. She was slender though full-bosomed, her hue very fair save for the tiniest dusting of freckles over a short, slightly flared nose; her mouth was soft and a little wide, dimples at the corners; her face was heart-shaped, high cheekbones delicately carven, chin small but firm; her dress brought out the changeable blue-

125

green-hazel of big eyes under blonde brows; her movements kept an endearing trace of coltishness, as young as
she was . . . When she looked at him, her look was not
like that of any of the others, proud or rapt or victorious
or wary. A blush crept up from her bosom, her lips parted
and he heard her catch her breath before she moved on.

Invocations sounded forth, first in Punic, next in Ysan.
Gratillonius could not make himself pay close heed.
Reality struck him in the stomach when the Lir Captain
opened his casket and held it out to the Speaker, who
lifted forth a key on a fine golden chain. Gratillonius
knew that key. 'Kneel,' Soren commanded, 'and receive
the Power of the Gate that is the King's.'

Gratillonius obeyed. When the loop went over his head
and the thing hung from his neck it felt heavy, and as if
so cold as to freeze his heart through the pectoral and
robe. That passed over. He forgot it in the next moment,
for out of the casket Soren had brought a crown.

'Receive the sigil of your lordship and the blessing,' the
Speaker said.

'No, I cannot,' Gratillonius whispered.

Soren almost dropped the circlet of golden spikes.
'What?'

'I told you I follow Mithras,' Gratillonius replied in
hasty Latin. 'When they raised me to Soldier of the
Mystery, I was thrice offered a crown and must thrice
refuse it, vowing never to wear any, for the God alone is
Lord.'

'You shall – ' Soren broke off. Glances clashed. He
made a wry mouth. 'Best not risk a disturbance. The Key
is what truly matters. Hannon, keep silence. Gratillonius,
may I briefly hold the crown above your head? Answer,
quick!'

I must not let them order a Roman about, passed
through the centurion. 'Do that and nothing else. Or I'll

fling it from me. My legionaries sit yonder, still armed.'

Soren flushed. 'Very well. But remember Colconor.'

Gratillonius heard a buzz go around the seats at the change in the ceremony, but it died away and everything further was soon completed. Afterwards the maidens led the Queens out; Suffetes came down from their boxes to meet the new King in the arena; the amphitheatre emptied; last, the Gods of Ys went home to Their temples, to abide the future.

2

After sunset the wind loudened and bleakened, driving rainclouds before it low above the land. The first few spatters were flying when the magnates bade their host goodnight and departed with their lantern bearers for the city, a mile hence. Gratillonius left the door and paced the length of the hall.

It had been a polite gathering, but cautious and formal, when neither side knew what to make of the other. He was no desperate adventurer or runaway slave, he was an agent of the Empire, come to serve its purposes; and though he promised those would enhance the welfare of Ys, he could not blame its leading men if they took that incident of the crown as a bad sign. He had to win their trust. Before he could do so he must understand them in some measure, and what his position among them really was. Well, he thought, tomorrow I'll begin, I'll take my earliest few steps into the labyrinth.

He grew aware that the household staff had assembled before the wall that divided the two portions of the lodge. Flickers of firelight and lamplight showed them expectant. What, more procedures? He stopped and waited.

The chief steward touched his brow, salutation to a superior. 'Is my lord ready for bed?' he asked.

'Oh, I . . . I'm not sleepy, but I suppose I may as well – '

'Presently comes the bride of my lord's first night.'

'Uh?' No, he would not reveal perplexity. Had he, with his limited knowledge even of Osismian, misunderstood something? Well, let that happen which the Gods willed. Certain it was that he had slept solitary for months. He felt sudden heat in his loins. Of course, if they went by precedence of age – maybe he could blow out the lights and use his imagination. 'Aye,' he said, as calmly as might be, 'let us do what may beseem this occasion.'

Servants guided him to a well-outfitted chamber, helped him disrobe, brought in a flagon of wine, cups, cakes and cheeses and sweetmeats, several lamps, incense which they set burning, and left. Abed, unable to lie down, Gratillonius sat with arms folded across nightshirted knees. Warmth from the floor, fragrance from the sandal-wood and myrrh, enfolded him. Noise of wind and rain sounded remote beyond the shutters. Much louder was his heartbeat.

Nine wives – He wondered wildly what his duty was towards them. He had married them in a heathen rite and because he had no choice if he was to carry out his mission. When he was done here and could go home, need he legally divorce them? He should ask a Mithraic Father. Yet meanwhile they were human, they could feel pain, and, O Gods, there would likely be children –

Faintly there reached him a hymeneal hymn. It could only be that. His pulse quickened still more. Who had arrived? Wrinkled Quinipilis, bitter Vindilis, handsome Forsquilis, what could happen with any of them? Somehow they had *known* he was on his way hither.

The door opened. 'May all Gods bless this holy union,'

said the steward. Dahilis entered. The steward closed the door behind her.

Dahilis.

She stood as if frightened. One small hand fumbled at the brooch of a rain-wet cloak. She swallowed before she could speak. 'My lord King, is . . . is Dahilis, his Queen . . . is Dahilis welcome?' Her voice was a little thin, but the timbre caused him to remember meadowlarks.

He surged from the bed and went to take both her hands in his. 'Welcome, oh, indeed welcome,' he said hoarsely.

The cloak came off. He took it and tossed it aside. She had changed to a simple gown of grey wool whose belt hugged it against her slimness. Her hair was piled high, held up by a comb. He saw that it was thick and wavy, sun-golden with just a tinge of copper. He clasped her shoulders, looked down, and said in his lame Osismian, which he tried to give an Ysan lilt: 'How wonderful that you, you, should seek me this night.'

She lowered her gaze. 'They, the Sisters, they decided it when – when we called you, my lord, called you to deliver us.'

He did not want to think about that, not now. 'I will strive to show kindness . . . unto all – Fear me never, Dahilis. If ever I blunder into wrongdoing, tell me, only tell me.'

'My lord – ' She received his embrace, she responded, the kiss lasted long, she was not skilled but she was quick to learn, and eager.

'Well, uh, well,' he laughed breathlessly, 'come, let us sit down, refresh ourselves, get acquainted.'

Her glance was astounded. 'Col – ' she began, and checked herself. Colconor, he thought, Colconor would never have troubled to put her at ease. (Supposing that he, Gratillonius, could do it in this first encounter.)

'Already you are being kind,' she whispered.

They took chairs opposite each other at the table. He felt in a remote fashion what a curious arrangement that was. But naturally, she was used to it. He poured wine. When he was about to add water, she made a shy negative gesture, so he refrained too. Her cup trembled as she lifted it. The drink was dry and full-bodied, warming both flesh and spirit. He thought he would readily learn to like taking his wine like this.

'Do you speak Latin?' he inquiried in that language.

'I can try,' she gave him back with difficulty. 'We study it in vestal school. But I've seldom had any practice since.'

He smiled. 'Between the two, we'll get along.' And thus they did. Sometimes it required much repetition or search for a word, but that became part of a game they played, helping them feel more comfortable with each other; and he found himself actually beginning to acquire Ysan.

'I know well-nigh nothing, Dahilis,' he said. 'You understand, don't you, I did not intend to take the Kingship. I stumbled into it.' Her look sharpened, and he hurried on before she could respond. 'I do not even know what questions to ask. So let us talk freely, dear. Will you tell me about yourself?'

She dropped long lashes. 'Naught is there to say. I am too young.'

'Tell me anyhow.'

She lifted her eyes. A bit of mischief danced forth. 'If you will do likewise, good my husband!'

He laughed. 'Agreed. Not that we can say much in an hour, or two. How old are you, Dahilis?'

'Seventeen winters. My father was King Hoel, my mother Tambilis. Queen Bodilis was her daughter too, my older half-sister, by King Wulfgar. But mother died in my fifteenth year and . . . and the Sign came to me.'

And Colconor, then reigning, took her.

'There is, is scarce anything else, my lord,' Dahilis said, 'but I think I shall be glad you are King. Pray won't you speak of your own life?'

When ever was a man loth to parade his exploits before a lovely girl? thought Gratillonius. Nevertheless he kept the tale laconic. Her eyes widened and widened. To her, Rome must be as glamorous as Ys was to him. And he travelled on affairs of Rome . . .

When her clothing fell to the floor, he saw that above the cleft of her breasts was a tiny red crescent, its horns to the left, like a birthmark. She noticed his attention drawn to it from other sights, touched it, and said diffidently: 'This? 'Tis the Sign. Ever when a Gallicena dies, it appears on one of the vestals. That consecrates her a priestess. I know not why Belisama chose me out of all the rest – but oh, this night I thank Her that She did.'

And afterwards she snuggled close to him and murmured drowsily, 'Yea, I do thank Her, truly I do thank Her, that She made me a Queen of yours. Never erenow have I known what glory She may bestow.'

His lips brushed along the summery odour of her hair. 'And I thank Her too,' he said.

VIII

1

'It were well that we talked together, unheard, you and I,' said Quinipilis. 'Would it please you to walk the wall? Then I could also show you somewhat of this your newly-won city.'

Gratillonius looked more closely than hitherto at the eldest of the Gallicenae. With five-and-sixty winters behind her, she still bore herself tall. A once opulent figure had become stout, her hands were gnarled by the ageing that had made her gait rocking and painful, her visage was furrowed and most teeth gone; but underneath abundant white hair, gathered in a Psyche knot, grey eyes gleamed wholly alive, while good bones and arched nose held a ghost of her youthful comeliness. She was simply clad and leaned on a staff whose ferrule was plain iron. Her house was unostentatious, requiring just a pair of domestics, for she used only a part of it. Yet he felt he had never encountered anyone else more truly like a queen.

And her note borne to him at his palace, written by herself in excellent Latin, had less requested his presence than summoned him. He believed he could not well decline. His few days in Ys had overwhelmed him more than they had taught him. He badly needed advice. Still, not knowing what she wanted, he had come in some uneasiness.

'Is that what my lady intended?' he asked.

Quinipilis brayed a laugh. 'Oh, ho! Did you fear me

dragging you from lovely Dahilis to soothe my lust? Me, barren, crippled, my face like forty leagues of bad road?' She patted his arm. Her palm was warm and dry. 'Nay, I gave up that three reigns agone. King Hoel and I were good friends, no more. As I hope you and I shall be, Gratillonius.'

'As you were not with Colconor,' he ventured.

Her mood darkened. 'Never. Oh, he had me, again and again, for well he knew how I abhorred it from him. However, that was less bad than what he made the rest of the Sisterhood suffer. He had the animal cunning to sense it would be dangerous to goad me overmuch. And indeed, at the last –' She shook her head. 'No matter. 'Tis behind us, thanks be unto you. We should take counsel for the morrow, foremost concerning that Sisterhood.'

'I will be grateful, my lady.'

'Then let us begone. A mummy like me does best to use the morning, for she is weary by afternoon.'

'Could we not spare you, stay here and talk Latin?' asked Gratillonius in that language. 'I'm told all educated Ysans know it, more or less, but don't suppose your slaves do.'

'Servants, boy. Temesa and her husband are free, and well rewarded,' Quinipilis replied sharply in her mother tongue. He was already able to follow it fairly well, though his speech stumbled. 'We have no slavery or serfdom in Ys. Too much have we seen of what they have done to Rome.'

'I've heard of Ysans capturing and selling folk.'

'Aye, abroad, among the barbarians. Ys lives mainly by her ships. Most are fishing craft and merchantmen. A few are raiders. But do stop spilling my scanty time and come along. I'd fain point out this and that, and see how you respond. 'Twill tell me things about you. And I want to make you practise Ysan.' She grinned. 'Besides what you've been cooing at Dahilis.'

Gratillonius felt himself redden. He helped her on with her cloak and resumed his own. Otherwise he wore the shirt, decorated jacket, breeches, and low shoes that were everyday male garb in the city. They were of fine material but of colours more subdued and cut more simple than was usual among the well-to-do here. As King he could have carried a sword, but was content with the knife at belt which was all that unauthorized persons were allowed to have on the streets. He did not care to be conspicuous this day. Best might be if he went unrecognized – though that was unlikely, when his companion was one whom everybody must know.

They left the house. Like its neighbours, it was of rectangular outline. Dry-laid sandstone blocks and red tile roof glowed mellow beneath rays of a sun that was as yet not far above the eastern towers. It gave directly on the street, and the flower garden behind it was minute, for even this wealthy district was crowded. Most homes nearby were larger, rising two or three storeys, smoothly stuccoed, figured with inlays or frescos. What those showed might be scenes but were often ideals: spirals, Greek keys, geometric arrangements. The effect was brilliant in the clear, cool air, as if jewels had tumbled out of a great coffer.

Not being a commercial thoroughfare, the street was narrow, nonetheless paved and clean. Ys required the hauling away of rubbish. Upon inquiry Gratillonius had learned that the sewers did not drain into the sea, which would have angered Lir, but into tanks of fuller's earth in chambers excavated below the city. From time to time these were emptied and the muck carted inland, where farmers were glad to have it for their fields.

Most people he saw as he walked were menials, in vivid

liveries, on errands to and from markets and the like. The rich who dwelt hereabouts were already off to their businesses, while their wives were indoors managing the households. He met an occasional artisan carrying tools for some task, and flocks of children too small to attend any of the various schools, and sometimes an elderly person or a leisured youth. Where leaded windows stood open, he glimpsed a few pets – a songbird, a cat, a ferret. Ys lacked room for larger creatures, except draught animals admitted only on to major routes.

To him, folk generally looked happy. Well, he thought, why should they not? The city-state is at peace, safe, less prosperous than formerly but in no dire want, seemingly well governed. True, for years it lay in the shadow of Colconor, but the harm he could do was limited, and now I have plucked him out of the world.

'Yours seems a nation the Gods have favoured,' he said.

'They've sent us our share of grief,' Quinipilis answered, a bit harshly.

'Whence came Ys? I've heard tell it stems from Carthage of old, but little else. 'Tis a puzzle to me how Ys could flourish this long a while and remain obscure abroad.'

'Bodilis can best recount the history. She's the scholar among us. Seek her out.' Quinipilis paused before she added: 'Seek them all out, and soon. Aye, liefest would you lie with Dahilis only: that's graven upon you. And we are seldom jealous of each other, and . . . the yoke of Colconor united us. However, we brook not scorn. If naught else, that would through us dishonour the Goddess.'

'I, I will do my best, my lady. But I've so much to learn, so much to do – '

She smiled at him. 'Verily, if you be the man of duty I

135

suppose.' A chuckle. 'Feel no pity for yourself. They may not be equally well-favoured, but nine wives with incomes of their own should fulfil the daydreams of the friskiest young fellow. Well, eight, though I trust you'll reckon me a helpmate. That had better suffice, you know.'

He sensed an underlying meaning. 'Nay, I do not know.'

She turned grave, almost motherly. 'You are the King; the Father is in you. We are the Queens; the Mother is in us. Never will your manhood fail with any of these your wives. But never will you have your way with any woman else.'

He stopped short. 'What?'

'That is the law of Belisama, Who is present at every act of procreation.' Her voice went steely. 'Colconor tried, and could not, and that is one thing which made a monster of him, though he did find tricks whereby his whores in Old Town might give him pleasures of a low sort.' Again the tone softened. 'I think you will be too proud for that.'

'It . . . it is not a wish for – Nay. A man is more than . . . a penis. But, I have heard that only daughters – '

Compassion spoke. 'Aye. We bear no sons. Ever. This too is the law of Belisama; for we are Hers.' Quinipilis squeezed Gratillonius's hand. 'Surely it is honourable to father Queens.'

Stunned, he accompanied her in silence when she walked on. 'You shall, my dear, you shall,' she said presently. 'Those of us who are of childbearing age will open their wombs for their liberator as they would not for Colconor, no matter how that maddened him. The Goddess gave unto Her first priestess in Ys the secret of an herb which bars conception – '

Mithras lives, he thought. Mithras will not leave me bound for ever by a heathen spell. When my task here is done, He will free me, and I will go home and beget me sons to bear the name.

He squared his shoulders and rallied his spirit. If nothing else, he had Dahilis, he had Dahilis.

Cheer mounted as he passed through more and more of the city, its variousness and plenitude.

The street climbed gently in this eastern end of town, unlike the steep downwardness of its western half. Near the end he could look over roofs to Elven Gardens; arbours, topiaries, early-blooming flowers. Adjoining, the temple of Belisama was like a miniature Athenian Parthenon – he had seen a drawing in a book – although its marble was not painted but left pure. That was somewhat northwards; southwards lifted the dome of his palace.

The street gave on Lir Way, the principal east–west avenue, and suddenly he was in a millrace of traffic, walkers, riders, porters, oxcarts, mulecarts, donkeycarts, a clattering, a chattering, creaking, calling, whistling, singing, laughing, swearing, dickering, hoping – city folk, farmers and herders out of the hinterland, fishermen, merchant sailors, traders, now and then a party of Osismii or Veneti trying not to be yokels, one party of Redones trying to be Romans, bound for the marketplaces or on other business . . . Few actual transactions went on in this vicinity. It was full of blocky apartment buildings, with statues at intervals to lend stateliness, heroes, animals, chimeras, each with a hint of something neither Greek nor Roman.

Lir Way debouched on the pomoerium, the space kept clear under the city wall for defensive purposes. Beyond that paved ring, and High Gate standing open, Aquilonian Way ran out broad past the amphitheatre, bent southwards to climb the heights, turned east again and sought the distant hills. Immediately in front of the pomoerium, two large edifices flanked the avenue, Warriors' House on the left as a barrack for marines, Dragon House on the right as quarters and conference rooms for their officers. Gratillonius gave Quinipilis his arm when they crossed to the wall and went up the staircase on the north side of the gate.

The tower there was generally called the Gaul. Its bulk, battlemented and severe, reminded Gratillonius of the milecastle at Borcovicium and its kind. This, though, was not mortared in their fashion, but of closely fitted, dry-laid granite blocks, their edges rounded off by the weathers of many a lifetime. And so was the entire wall around Ys. He wondered why.

Sentinels recognized Quinipilis, realized who Gratillonius could be, and slanted their pikes, crashing the butts downwards, in salute. She waved back cheerily. They wore studded skirts like his men, but helmets were peaked, shoulderpieces and greaves flared, cuirasses loricated and engraved with spirals, shields oval, swordblades of laurel leaf shape, cloth never red but blue or grey, insignia abstract – a foreignness Gratillonius found faintly disturbing, as he did not that of Scoti or Picti or Saxons, because this was more subtle.

Quinipilis led a southward course, over the arch above the gate, past that twin tower called the Roman, on around the half-circle of this end. 'I've heard your state has had no army since Caesar made it his protectorate,' Gratillonius remarked.

'Nor do we, nor did we ever,' Quinipilis snorted. 'Why should our men squander their best years in drill, or we pay a pack of flea-bitten mercenaries? Nay, what you see is a cadre of professionals, marines, who double as peacekeepers at home. Besides them, every sailor has training for combat afloat or ashore.'

'Suffices that, in times like these?'

'Aye. Not for an empire, but then, we've no wish to

rule over outlanders. Have you Romans not had enough woes with your Gauls and Jews of yore, your Goths and Vandals today?' He was surprised that she knew of such rebellions, and a touch disconcerted. His task was to keep the Ysans loyal to Rome – to Maximus – and to that end, much history was preferably ignored. 'True, our ships afar may at times meet peril, but no oftener than yours. And as for our defences, what need we fear when the Gallicenae command the weather?'

Once more he halted in startlement. 'My lady, can that be? I mean, well, surely you have the love of your Gods, but the Gods do not always answer human prayers.'

Likewise stopping on the walkway, Quinipilis laughed; it made him recall hearing wolves. 'You misheard me, boy. I said we *command* the weather. Oh, we abuse our power not, lest the Three take it from us. We call upon it only in the worst need. But no few reaver fleets were wrecked among the skerries, until the barbarians learned to leave us be. Landward, you can see, is merely a narrow arc of wall to hold, should attack come from that side; and our sea lanes will stay open for supply. Not that we've had many threats on land either. Caesar himself, flush from his crushing of the Veneti, knew better than to dare an outright conquest of Ys.'

Gratillonius stood for a spell, silent in the breeze that blew tangy off Ocean. A merlon lay sun-warmed under his hand. When he had on a previous circuit leaned over and glanced down through the crenel beside, he had seen the frieze that ran around the wall. A mosaic of coloured stones, it showed sacrificial processions, mythical battles, visions out of the deeps that glittered quicksilver to worldedge.

His glance shot to and fro. Bleak and windswept, the headlands enclosed Ys, Point Vanis reaching away on the north, Cape Rach on the south extending more than two

139

miles westward. At the far end of the latter, beyond its clustered necropolis, he saw the pharos tower. Rocks stood rugged out of the waves, reefs lurked just below, surf burst white and green.

The promontories were of the same dark-red granite as the wall. However, he had learned that Ys stood between them on a downward-sloping shelf of sandstone. Its softness was easily quarried – those caves underneath had yielded much building material as they were enlarged – but it was just as easily gnawed by great tides and murderous currents. Indeed Ys had need to stay friends with Lir.

Well, had it not done so? Did wonder not nestle within its rampart? From this elevation, the city was speckled with silver, sunlight off rainwater in multitudinous rooftop catchbasins. He had been told that these drained into bottomless tanks below ground, set in fine sand within clay cisterns. Water passed through the filtering material to central wells, whence people drew it. In this wet climate there was never a lack. Nonetheless, beyond the Gaul and Warriors' House another water storage place rose high, a tower into which the canal discharged through a culvert. There ox-driven Archimedean screws raised the fluid, whereafter pipes delivered it to the homes of the rich and to public troughs, fountains, baths. He had heard that the canal ran from a spring in the hills, sacred to Belisama, its shrine tended by virgin daughters and grand-daughters of the Gallicenae.

He recalled his wandering mind to its surroundings. Turrets at the wall did not match the height of numerous buildings in the middle and lower town. Those soared from levels of stone to upper storeys of wood, flamboy-antly ornamented, taller than the Emperors had ever permitted in Rome. If the climb was wearisome to a lodging on a tenth or fifteenth floor – one dwelt in Ys!

Gulls winged white between those pinnacles; tops sheened many-hued, tile, patinaed copper, painted gilt.

A faint drumming came up to Gratillonius, the blended noise of wheels, feet, hoofs, machines, pulsebeat of the living city.

'Shall we go on?' Quinipilis suggested.

Where the arc straightened out to run almost due west, Cape Rach thrust a mass inwards that had been too large to chisel away. The architects had taken advantage of this; they need not build a causeway as they must on the northern side. Flanked by those towers called the Brothers, Aurochs Gate opened on Taranis Way, which ran northward to intersect Lir Way at the Forum and thence onward to Northbridge Gate and its defending Sisters. Down on the left, the plaza of Goose Fair bustled with countryfolk bringing their products to market. Savouriness drifted in smoke from foodstalls, merchants cried their wares from booths.

'You've a livelier commerce than aught I've seen elsewhere, even in Londinium,' Gratillonius observed.

Quinipilis shrugged. ''Twas better aforetime, when the Roman peace kept traders safe and Roman money was honest. But we still cope.'

'Roman money? You strike not your own?'

'Nay, what sense in that? Formerly Roman currency was taken everywhere. Now, if we made coins for ourselves, they must either be good, and vanish into hoards like your solidi, or else be as worthless as your nummi. Gold, silver, and bronze circulate within the city but seldom leave it. For most dealings we're back to barter.'

Quinipilis drew breath. 'Yet we have wherewithal for bargaining,' she said. 'Our soil is poor, but its sheep yield a wool long, fine, well-nigh as precious as Asiatic silk. We must import most raw materials, but from them we fashion ships and boats, metalwork and jewellery, cloth, pottery, glassware, of a quality that makes them much desired. Our waters are the source of salt, preserved fish, garum, whale oil, tusks, and such-like exports.

'Though scarcely a foreign ship calls here any more, ours still fare widely, if quietly. When our merchantmen do not sail off trading for themselves, they carry freight for others, from Britannia to Hispania. Our adventurous young men travel out among the barbarians to get amber and furs or to be slavers, pirates, mercenaries – never against Rome, dear – and those who live return at last carrying wealth. Aye, Ys endures.'

Gratillonius's glance flew northward. 'On Point Vanis I've seen the wreckage of a station that was Ysan as well as Roman,' he said roughly. 'It was meant to serve ships when your sea gate must be shut. What happened to it?'

The old woman's staff thudded harder on the stone as she walked. ''Twas nigh three score years agone, in the reign of my father Redorix, when I was a girl. Suddenly, there a score of Saxon warcraft were. The Gallicenae had not foreknown. The crews landed, harried widely about, destroyed the maritime post as you saw. Redorix died in battle against them. Our men cast them back at the wall, and they made off. The Gallicenae sought Sena and raised a gale they hoped would avenge us, but they never knew if it did or no.'

She sighed. 'Prefect of Rome, I will not lie to you. Ys was always less than omnipotent; and now, ever more are our ancient powers flickering and fading. Once any high priestess could heal any sickness by laying on of hands; today, seldom. Once her soul could range afar through space and time; today, few of us can have a vision, and for those who do, it may as well be false as true, with Forsquilis alone granted some measure of assurance. Once – ah, but you too have seen your God in retreat, have you not?'

142

She clutched his wrist. 'We wanted you for more than a liberator, Gratillonius. We hoped for a redeemer. May you be he, and not a destroyer we brought upon ourselves.'

His throat felt tight. 'I will do my best,' he said, 'but remember I am pledged to Rome.'

They walked on in silence to the western arc of wall and along it to the Raven Tower. There a sentry forbade promenading civilians to go farther. Behind him, on the stone curve that ran onwards until the sea portal interrupted it, Gratillonius saw bastions upon which stood rain shelters of leather and light timbers. Beneath them, he knew, were ballistae and catapults. He could have demanded access, but he had already been there and Quinipilis was starting down a stairway to the pomoerium. He came after. Let her be the guide throughout.

While the top of the wall was everywhere level, ground dropped sharply beneath the western half of Ys, which was thus overshadowed. Buildings on his right crowded time-worn, mostly bare of decoration; here was Old Town, where industry and poverty intermingled. On his left, the shipyard extended to the harbour. Quinipilis went along its fence until she reached a street which ran beside it in the direction of the water, called the Ropewalk because it doubled as that. This she took. It was not in use today. Looking into the shipyard, Gratillonius spied a single small vessel under construction, albeit there were facilities for several large ones. As the Queen had said, Ys too felt the hard times that afflicted the Empire.

Where a launching ramp went down to the basin, the waterfront began. Its curve paralleled that of the city wall to seaward, a grand sweep two thousand feet in length, set back five hundred feet. Hard against its stone wharf, warehouses belonging to the great traders reared proud.

But their inlaid façades were faded, and for the most part they seemed almost empty of men and goods. A number of hulls rested between the floating piers that reached out from the dock like fingers. None at this end were big, mainly fishermen in for unloading or overhaul. Their crews were off on leave, and only a few workers moved among them.

Nevertheless the harbour was a noble sight. Water sparkled as if dusted with crystal, lapped, gurgled. Gulls rode it like white boats or skimmed above in a snowstorm of wings. Some young boys were joyfully swimming, oblivious to the coldness of the water; it was a skill that sailor folk desired. Behind lifted the sheer cliff of the wall, ruddy-dark but its upper battlements brave with flags and the cloaks of watchmen.

Halfway along the waterfront, Quinipilis stopped. Here was a break in the line of buildings, for here began Lir Way. It started off through a triumphal arch, raised by the Roman engineers who built the wall but not to commemorate any victory in war. This was the sign of the saving of Ys, of the Pact between the city and its Gods. Beyond, the square of Skippers' Market was astir as dealers took seat in their booths.

The priestess, though, gazed outward, to where the western entry stood open. 'That is the masterwork of all,' she said low.

'Aye,' Gratillonius agreed in awe.

Fifty feet wide, the gap in the wall faced upon illimitable reaches. Ocean itself. The doors on either side were beginning to close as the tide flowed higher – enormous oaken doors, iron-bound and sheathed in copper weathered green, silent and easy on their hinges despite the mass. Hemp and leather sealed their edges. On the bottom, when they shut, they would press against a sill carved out of the rock shelf that upbore Ys.

As yet, ample space remained between them for an

incoming merchantman. Few Romans would willingly put to sea this early in the year, but Ysan mariners were more bold. The craft was leaner and handier than most in the Empire. Gilt trim, horse-headed stempost, red- and blue-striped sails were like a defiance of any dangers. Those sails were being furled, since the wind was not straight from the west and the wall had therefore laid calm on the basin. Towboats darted from their piers on spidery oars. Already their coxswains were shouting bids for the job of bringing the ship in. A customs officer and his amanuensis came out of a door and took expectant stance. Oh, there was still life in Ys!

'You have been on the gate?' Quinipilis asked.

'Yestereven,' Gratillonius replied. The memory thrilled in him afresh.

2

That was the final rite confirming him as King. Lir Captain and a delegation of sailors, deckhands as well as officers, called on him at the palace when the tide was nearly full. They took him out on the wall to the northern edge of the portal. There he looked downwards, at the sea, and they showed and told him how the gate worked.

It was as simple as a heartbeat, and as vital. High on either side, aslant, jutted a great stone block. The feline heads into which these two were sculptured had blurred in the centuries, but their strength abided. Through each, a chain passed over a sheave within. One end of the chain was fast to its adjacent door. From the other end depended a giant bronze ball, cased in padded leather, hollow so that it floated.

'Without this, half the city would lie drowned at high

tide,' Hannon declared gravely. 'Given a spring tide and a hard storm behind it, neither would the eastern side escape. Look. The doors are shaped so that they continue the curve of the wall. This helps them resist the force of the waves. They angle inwards from bottom to top. This makes them *want* to close.

'As the water rises, likewise do the floats, giving ever more slack on the chains and thus letting the doors draw ever more near together. When they do shut, water level in the basin is still some three feet below the wharf. The tide outside goes on flowing, of course, until it may crest close under the battlements; but our city rests safe behind its gate.

'You see the floats are sheathed. This is to keep them from damaging themselves and the wall when storms fling them about. From time to time that protection must be renewed, as must the caulking along the edges and bottoms of the doors. This is done at the lowest tides, on the calmest days. At that, 'tis difficult, dangerous work. The divers who do it are both well paid and honoured. For they keep us alive.

'Now when the sea ebbs, the floats drop, pulling out their chains by their weight, hence drawing the doors open again.'

'A marvel!' Gratillonius exclaimed. 'Indeed the eighth wonder.' And even then it perplexed him that this was all but unknown beyond Ys.

'The Romans wrought well,' said Hannon, 'but only by the leave of Lir; and He set conditions upon that.'

'Um-m-m . . . when the doors do stand wide . . . could not an enemy fleet enter? Or what if there is violent weather?'

Hannon beckoned. 'Come.' He led the way down a stone staircase. Meanwhile, with a huge hissing sound, the gate closed. Gratillonius heard surf rumble outside; he saw the basin tranquil beneath him.

The stairs ended at a ledge halfway down the wall. There stood a capstan, from which a cable ran through another cat's head to the inner top of this door. Hannon pointed to corresponding structures on the opposite side. 'At need,' he said, 'we use these to pull the portal shut against the weight of the floats. And we've a further security – which is in your hands, O King. Follow me.'

He was rather brusque with his lord, Gratillonius thought. But that was understandable. He spoke for his God and his guild. Besides, like everyone before him in his present office, he was a retired skipper who had dared seas from here to Africa, here to Thule.

The doors, like the wall which they matched, had such a large radius of curvature that the inner surface they presented to the harbour was not far from being flat. A narrow, railed walkway reached across either, each terminating in a platform at the juncture. There Hannon and his party took Gratillonius.

On the southern door, a mighty beam – it must have been hewn from an entire oak tree – stood upright, pivoted above a lead counterweight. A cable ran from its upper end to a block high above, and back down to an equally solid cleat. Hannon stepped to the southern platform, released the cable, lowered the beam. The counterweighting was so well done that he could swing the mass up or down by himself. The beam crossed over both doors and settled into a massive iron U bolted to the northern one.

'This holds the portal tight against aught that may seek to come through,' Hannon said. 'We've less dread of pirates than of storms. Even in good weather, you've seen, the doors swing slightly to and fro as the floats bob on the waves. In a gale, those floats are mightily stirred.

Descending into the troughs, they'd fain drag the doors wide apart. Did that happen, especially at high tide, the sea would pour in and wreak catastrophe on Ys. But the bar keeps the gate fast.'

Stapled to the northern door beside the U was a chain on which hung a heavy padlock. Solemnly, Hannon passed it through holes in the beam and the iron, tightened it, and put the hasp of the lock through two links. 'Lord,' he said, 'bring forth the Key.'

The Key Colconor bore – and Kings before him and before him, back to the time when Ys and Rome and the sea made their treaty – Wordless, Gratillonius drew it from off his bosom and its chain of gold over his head. Hannon had him close and reopen the lock, release the bar and haul it back upright and secure it.

'That is our final safeguard,' said the old man. 'In times of threat, from war or weather, we shut the gate, lower the beam, and by the lock make sure that no evil chance can somehow fling it loose from its holder and free the doors to the waves. Always, save if he must needs leave Ys, the King bears the Key upon his person. It is his sacred duty to make fast the gate like this when danger nears, and unlock it when the threat is past. Thus went the word of Lir, Taranis, and Belisama.'

Half numbed, Gratillonius donned the emblem again. 'But what if I were elsewhere, leading your men off to battle, perhaps?' he mumbled.

'Then the Key awaits your return in the Temple of Lir, and I or another high person uses it. As for its loss, the Gallicenae keep the only duplicate; where, is known but to them.' Hannon gave him an austere smile. 'You understand this is all ceremonial, a repeated sealing of the Pact, rather than absolutely necessary. If we must, we can change the lock. Fear not. Our Gods do not forsake us.'

Standing beside Quinipilis, Gratillonius recalled those words. Unthinkingly, he murmured them. She gave him a keen look. 'But someday we may forsake the Gods,' she said.

'For which others, do you think?' he asked very quietly.

Her laugh was bitter. 'I've no fear of Christ. Nay, I feel sorry for the minister the Romans have forced on us. Poor little lonely man.'

'I must tell you that I serve Mithras.' In haste: 'He does not forbid me to honour your Gods, if my acts keep within His law and I hold him in my heart to be supreme.'

'Hm. That may bring you trouble, lad.' Quinipilis brooded. 'But I'll not fret about your Bullslayer either. Nay, what plagues me is a fear that we of Ys may become Gods unto ourselves.'

She began walking again, he beside her. The northern half of the dock was given over to large ships, civil or naval – a number lay empty, idle – and to office buildings ornate behind colonnades. At the end of the basin, woman and man turned left, back towards pomoerium and wall. Below an ascending staircase stood the temple of Lir. Older than the Roman work, small but thick-built, it was pillared with rough-hewn grey stones akin to the menhirs found throughout Armorica.

The two climbed up past the Gull Tower and continued the circuit of the city bulwark. Quinipilis breathed hard and leaned heavily on her staff. Gratillonius offered his arm. She smiled and let him help her. 'You should not exhaust yourself for my sake,' he said.

She smiled. 'Be not sorry. At home I can rest as long

as I wish. Ere many years have fled, I'll be resting snug for ever. Let me now enjoy my good-looking young escort.'

'You have seen much, my lady,' he said with care. 'Methinks you've thought much too, and won wisdom thereby. Will you share it with me?'

'Ha! Scarce would I call myself wise, a hard-drinking hag like me. Anyhow, wisdom lies in nobody's gift. We must each forge it for ourselves, alone, as best we can.'

'But you have known the life of Ys for over half a century. Will you not tell me of it? I do want to be good for your people, but I am wretchedly ignorant.'

She regarded him for a time. 'The omens were unclear when we called you hither,' she said slowly. 'But I dare think it likely that we did well.' Her mood lightened. She cackled a laugh. 'Aye, why should the garrulous crone not gossip as we walk?'

While she narrated, the wall grew straight again beneath their feet and brought them to the higher and newer part of the city, where its powerful families dwelt. At Northbridge Gate the landside length began. They went above the portal. Between those turrets called the Sisters, it gave on a short bridge across waters wild among rocks, to the northern cape. There ran Northbridge Way, along which he had come . . . The pair continued east and then south.

They passed Star House, a Grecian-like building set in a garden near the wall, next to the Water Tower where astronomical observations took place. Those were essential. Although the secular calendar of Ys had become Julian, the religious calendar remained lunar. The holiest festivals were set by the moon and the planet Venus, which were Belisama's; the clans of the Suffetes each took name from one of the thirteen lunar months.

'The learned foregather here,' Quinipilis remarked.

'Philosophers, scholars, poets, artists, mystics – 'tis a setting better for their discourse than a tavern. You'll often find Bodilis amidst them. Belike you'd enjoy it too. You carry yourself soldierly, lad, but I suspect you use that pate for more than a helmet rack.' In Ys the idea was current that consciousness resided in the head.

Mainly, in slow sentences broken by pauses when she must wheeze for air, she spoke of her men. The talk went on past the Water Tower, down the staircase at the Gaul, back through the streets to her house. There Gratillonius bade her farewell. His mind awhirl but his heart warm with the feeling that he had made a friend, he sought home to the royal palace and Dahilis.

4

Now these were the Kings whom Quinipilis knew.

Redorix. He was a landholder near Vorgium until a barbarian raid left him widowed and ruined. Unable to mend his fortunes under the laws of Diocletianus, he went to try his luck at Ys, and overcame him who kept the Wood. The reign of Redorix lasted nine years and was fondly remembered, for he was personable and conscientious. On one of his Queens he begot a girl who received the name Gladwy – the name her mother had borne as a maiden, which was the custom for first-borns of a high priestess. A great horseman, Redorix sought to organize a cavalry troop among the Ysans, but this was not very successful and disbanded after his death. That happened when Saxon rovers appeared. There had been no forewarning, either through agents abroad or visions sent the Gallicenae. Folk wondered if this meant the Gods were failing, or if They were angry because too many Ysans had abandoned strict ancestral ways in favour of pleasure and luxury. The Saxons laid waste the maritime station and neighbouring homesteads. Redorix led his raiders against them and perished in the charge. They assailed the city but could not take it. Archers, slingers, catapults, and boiling kettles wrought havoc on them from the wall. At length they gave up and departed before navy ships out on patrol at sea should return. The Gallicenae raised a storm to hound them, but never knew if it had destroyed the galleys or not. Already Roman commerce was slumping so badly that no effort occurred to rebuild the station.

Calloch. Whenever a King died otherwise than in combat at the Wood, Ys must find a successor as soon as might be. The King was expected to lead his men in war, where his death was not the evil portent that demise from sickness or accident would be. He must always be a foreigner, lest grudges fester and feuds flame in Ys. In Condate Redonum a delegation bought an Osmisian slave, a gladiator. Calloch was happy about this; he would live better, and probably longer, than as a fighter in the arena. For six years he defended himself ably. Else he was not outstanding, and had the sense to stay in the background, letting the Suffetes govern unhindered by him. He begot a number of children, of whom two, by Ochtalis, would become the high priestesses Fennalis and Morvanalis.

Wulfgar. This was a Saxon adventurer, outlawed among his folk for a manslaying that, he claimed, was righteous. Most Ysans believed him, for despite his heritage Wulfgar proved another good King, forcefully taking leadership but considerate of the magnates and mild to the lowly. His greatest service was the enlargement of the navy, which had dwindled under the Roman peace. An enormous strength kept him nineteen years alive. In his reign an aged Queen died, and the Sign appeared above the breasts of young Gladwy. For her religious name she chose Quinipilis. She and Wulfgar enjoyed each other, and of their three daughters, one would become Karilis. He also begot Quistilis-to-be by Donalis, Lanarvilis-to-be by Fennalis, and Tambilis-to-be by Vallilis, as well as numerous girls to whom the Sign never came. These also served as vestals for the required term. Free on their eighteenth birthdays, some married, some renewed their vows and became minor priestesses, some went into curious byways of life: for a strangeness always lay over the Sisterhood. Meanwhile Wulfgar cut down challengers until word got about and none came for a long time. Then at last a second Queen died, and the Sign marked a daughter of his own. She took the name Tambilis. Horrified, he would have refused, but when they were alone in the bridal chamber, the power of the Goddess descended. Unable to help himself, he made Tambilis his, and she became the mother of Bodilis. It was afterwards thought that Wulfgar lost the will to live, as easily as he fell to the man who next arrived.

Gaetulius. This was a Mauretanian auxiliary stationed at Vorgium, who deserted when he saw no future worth having in a military career. While the Gallicenae missed Wulfgar, they did not hold his death against his killer. Such was the will of the Gods; and the slaying of the old King, the crowning of the new enacted the rebirth of the year and of all beloved dead. Gaetulius, though, proved to be a gaunt, ascetic man with a certain streak of cruelty and a temper apt to flare in violence – perhaps because he found himself hemmed in whenever he tried to accomplish something noteworthy and could never make his way through or around the opposition. On Quistilis he fathered Maldunilis-to-be, on Donalis he fathered Innilis-to-be, besides unchosen girls by different Queens. Quinipilis could never bring herself to like him. She discovered

153

she was with child so soon after Wulfgar's death that she was not sure but what it was his. Features and nature revealed it to be of Gaetulius, and the infant grew to womanhood and became Vindilis. The reign of Gaetulius lasted for eleven years.

Lugaid. This was a Scotian from Mumu. He said he was of royal blood, driven out by a feud, but nobody ever learned much about him, for he was a brooding, solitary man. Against the Law of Belisama, Quinipilis regarded him as Wulfgar's avenger. Else he meant little to her. He was not a bad King, and when the mood struck him he sang and played the harp most wonderfully, but otherwise he attracted small love; and it was whispered that, alone, he carried out eldritch rites. By Karilis he fathered Forsquilis-to-be. The mother died in childbed and the girl was fostered by grandmother Quinipilis. The reign of Lugaid was for only four years.

Hoel. When a boy in the tribe of the Namnetes, this person had been sold into slavery for taxes. He ran away and drifted venturesomely about for a long while before coming to Ys and, almost on impulse, taking the Kingship. Handsome and cheerful, he quickly won hearts. He was intelligent, too, but content to stay first among equals, suggesting and persuading rather than invoking the full powers that were his in law. A great sportsman, reveller, and lover, he was likewise strong in battle. (While its wall and its high priestesses protected the city of Ys, its commerce more and more required warlike help.) Hoel took charge of convoys at need. He also led punitive expeditions which taught Scoti and Saxons a lesson they did not forget until after his death. Indeed, under him Ys prospered as it had not done for generations. Trade picked up southwards, especially, with his native Namnetes and on down the gulf as far as Hispania. The wealth and the Southern influences that this brought were not an unmixed blessing – said the old and the moody: for they loosened morals and undermined patriotism. Yet Hoel was deeply mourned when he fell, not least by his wives and their plentiful daughters.

Colconor. This was an Osismian farm hand who fled (after having ravished the wife of another, or so the rumour went) and joined the Bacaudae. There he flourished brutally for several years before he decided to become King of Ys; surely, with his strength, he could hold that position until none dared go up against him. Soon he was hated, less for having struck down good King Hoel than for his coarse and overbearing ways. He was just shrewd enough to avoid provocation immediately unbearable. There did come to be an unusual number of challengers, as had happened in the past when Ys fell under a wicked man, but for five years he prevailed over all. None of the Gallicenae bore him a child, though he had them often and savagely – except for Maldunilis, and hers did not come to term, an ill omen. In his reign Tambilis died and the sign came upon youthful Estar, offspring of Tambilis and Hoel. Estar took the name Dahilis. Colconor had special delight in using her. But whatever he did, he found her spirit too sunny to break, as he found that of her fellow Queens too hard or, in the case of Maldunilis, too loose and lazy. This deepened his rage, as it did his loneliness. In Old Town he had his cronies and toadies, among them harlots who could amuse him despite his impotence outside the circle of the high priestesses. On these people he squandered much of the royal treasury. Perhaps it was not perfect justice that blame fell upon him for the decline in trade and the renewed rise of piracy and banditry since Hoel's time. These things were happening everywhere else, and in general the affairs of Ys went on independently of him.

155

But rightly was Colconor blamed for causing the death of Tambilis, through abuse and heartbreak. Whispers of knife or poison went through Ys. This, though, would have been sacrilege, which might well cause the Gods to end the Pact and Lir to send His waves through a shattered gate. Slowly the Nine groped their way to an answer. If Suffetes could in secrecy persuade men to come strike the Shield, then it would be lawful for Queens to cast a spell drawing hither one whose chances were better and causing him to do battle. The omens they took were ambiguous but did not forbid. And so they gathered on Sena, the holy of holies, and there they cursed Colconor.

Gratillonius.

5

About sunset, clouds blew out of the west across heaven. It was already dark when Soren Cartagi raised a bronze knocker and brought it back down on the door of Lanarvilis.

The homes of the Gallicenae were not together, nor were they far apart, in the neighbourhood of Elven Gardens and the temple of Belisama. Outwardly plain, they were inwardly Roman, from the time when they were built. Yet that time lay almost four hundred years in the past. Each of the nine dwellings had descended from Queen to successor Queen, each of whom had left her traces that never quite went away. Here the knocker, worn smooth by lifetimes of hands, was in the form of a serpent that bit its own tail . . .

The door opened. The steward saw who stood at the threshold and brought hand to brow. While Soren was in civil garb, few ever failed to recognize that broad hook-nosed visage and heavy frame. 'Our lady awaits you, my lord,' the steward reported, and stepped aside. Soren entered. His two lantern-bearers followed. The steward guided the party through the atrium and rooms beyond to a certain inner door, which he swung wide. When Soren had passed through, he closed it and led the escort off. Nobody would venture to question what went on in private between the Speaker for Taranis and a high priestess of Belisama.

Windowpanes in this chamber were full of darkness, but lamps gave ample soft light. It fell on blue carpeting, crimson drapes, fine furniture inlaid with walrus ivory and upholstered in leather. Flagon and cups on a table were cut crystal; a plate for cheeses and spiced mussels was millefiori glass. Lanarvilis took what pleasures she wanted, so they be permissible. What she wanted the most was not.

She rose from a settee and went to meet Soren: a tall blonde woman, small-bosomed and thick-haunched, her nose too wide and her blue eyes too small, but not ill-looking when she took trouble about her appearance. Today she had had her tiring maid do her hair up in an intricacy of knots and braids, topped by a jewelled comb. Ointments and powders gave fresh colouring to a face whose bearer neared her fortieth year. Gold shimmered under her throat, above a gown cut low; those folds of rich brown fabric were kind to a woman who had fivefold been a mother. She took both his hands in hers. 'Welcome and blessing,' she said.

'Elissa!' he blurted, half dazed. 'You're beautiful tonight. What witchcraft made you a maiden again?'

Her smile mingled enjoyment and sadness. 'I was Elissa once,' she murmured; 'but that was long ago. I am Lanarvilis now. Elissa is my daughter by Lugaid, finished with her vestalhood, soon to wed and make me a grandmother.'

'For an instant I forgot,' he said harshly. 'Only an instant. It shall not happen more.'

'Oh, Soren, dear, forgive me,' she begged, contrite. ''Twas myself I felt I should remind. I did wish to receive you well – in celebration – but mayhap 'twas a mistake.' She released her hold on him. 'Come, be seated, take refreshment.'

They placed themselves on the settee, separated a foot or two. She poured. The wine gurgled and glowed. It was a choice Aquitanian, whose fragrance met them before they tasted.

He looked from her, across the room to a mural of Diana the Huntress. 'I've been stewing ever since I got your reply to my message,' he said. 'Why could you not see me earlier?'

'I'm sorry.' This regret was calm, with an undertone of resolve. 'Three Sisters were needed for a certain emprise, and Vindilis asked that I be among them. What is your desire?'

'I decided 'twould be wise to talk beforehand about this Council the King summons. You and I have worked well together over the years.'

'We have that.' She regarded him. 'But what is in your mind?'

'Let us prepare ourselves against surprises.'

'Why, there should be none. For us, at any rate. This Gra – Gra-lo – Gra-til-lonius has met the leaders of Ys severally, well-nigh since he won the crown – since he took the Key. We've all accepted his purpose. The assembly should but ratify our agreement.'

Soren scowled. 'He's been less than candid. *Why* has Rome sent a prefect, after letting generations go by? Gratillonius speaks vaguely of troubles anticipated and

158

the desirability of keeping Armorica out of them. Methinks he knows more than that, and does in truth plan a surprise later.'

Now when Lanarvilis smiled it was not womanly but an aspect remote from humanness, the look of Knowledge. 'Aye,' she said evenly. ''Tis that which concerned Forsquilis, Vindilis, and myself this day.'

He started. 'Forsquilis! Did she learn – ?'

Lanarvilis nodded. 'We believe so. Politically, I deem it very plausible.'

He set his glass down most carefully, lest he smash it. 'Will you tell me?'

She did.

At the end, he drooped his lids, stroked his beard, sipped his wine, and said in measured tones: 'I'd guessed, of course, though I could not be positive. I daresay Gratillonius withholds the news in hopes of first making his grip the firmer. Think you, like me, that 'twill be a shrewd stroke, telling him in Council that we know already? Thus taken aback, he may be the easier to deal with. For sure 'tis, we've no figurehead King here.'

'He does not wish us ill.'

'Nay, but he has his own aims – or Rome's, whatever Emperor's those may come to be. They may not prove the best for Ys.' Soren barked a laugh. 'If naught else, let us ride the current to our advantage. We may perchance wring substantial concessions out of the Imperium.'

Woman again, Lanarvilis laughed too and touched his hand. 'Ever were you the calculating one, Soren.'

'I seek the welfare of my city, my House, my sons, and myself,' he replied. 'What else is there to strive for?'

Her gaze darkened. Unspoken was the truth that they would have wedded, had not the Sign come upon her a single month before the end of her vestalhood.

'Oppose this King when you feel you must,' she said.

'But lay no plots to confound him. I tell you, he is not evil. Else would the Gods have allowed our summoning of him?'

He stared at her through a silence before he breathed, 'Then you did indeed, you Nine.'

'Certes.' Her tone stayed level. 'Did you never suspect?'

'Oh, aye, aye,' he stammered. 'And yet . . . was deed like that done any time before in Ys?'

'Nay, and best 'tis that it not be noised abroad. Mere rumour will die away. The new King knows – Quinipilis told him, on purpose – albeit she doubts he can yet believe it. You do.'

'I must.' Soren passed hand over eyes. 'That morning – ' he whispered. 'What did you do to entrap Colconor? He was strong, and you meant to weaken him as much as might be, but – ' He beat fist in palm. 'A-a-ah, I've heard of his wallowings in the Fishtail brothels – '

The calm went out of Lanarvilis. Tears trickled, blurring the malachite so carefully painted around her eyes. 'Soren, dear, *I* was not there. I knew, I helped plan it, aye, but . . . but never could I do such a thing to you.'

Bitterness lashed: 'Why not? What difference? We're not the boy and girl who babbled endearments under a midsummer moon. Your satisfactions have been plain to see on you. I daresay you await more of them from Gratillonius.'

She drew herself straight and retorted, 'You've taken your own pleasures, Soren Cartagi, and well I know 'tis not been with your wife alone. Should I embalm my spirit? Lugaid was no bad man, and Hoel was grand.' Anger collapsed. She struggled not to weep. 'But oh, how often with them would I pretend to myself 'twas you. And I tried with Colconor, but as nasty as he was . . .'twould

160

have been wrong to have even the memory of you present
. . . whenever he took me, I would go away anywhere
else.'

'Oh, Elissa,' he croaked. They reached.

She drew back before they had quite met. 'Nay. Nay.
We are what we've become. 'Twould be desecration.'

He slumped. 'True.' After a while he stirred. 'Best I
depart.'

She had rallied. 'Not yet, Soren. We *are* what we are,
Speaker for Taranis and high priestess of Belisama, in Ys.
I said we should not conspire against the new King. But
let us think how best we may cope with him.'

IX

1

Unwontedly solemn, Dahilis asked, 'Beloved, have you an hour to spare for me this morning?'

Gratillonius clasped her to him. How wonderfully slender and lithe she was. His free hand cupped a breast, roved down across the curves of hip and belly, rested briefly on golden fleece, returned to chuck her under the chin. 'What, immediately again?' he laughed. 'I'll need that hour to recover my strength, as spendthrift of it as you've made me.'

'I mean talk, the two of us alone.' He heard what a need was hers, and read it in the lapis lazuli of her gaze. 'Oh, I understand you are engaged, you've been around among people like a whirlwind since first you arrived, but if you have any time free – It concerns us both, and the whole city.'

He kissed her. 'Of course, of course,' he did his best to say in Ysan. 'It was never my wish to leave you behind. If you too would discuss affairs of state, why, every magnate and officer should be as delightful.'

At his movement, an object stirred between his shoulderblades – the Key that he must always wear but had put at his back, out of the way. Somehow, shifting it on to his chest again felt like closing a door. He pushed the thought off, banned it from Dahilis and himself.

They left the bed to which they had impulsively returned after breaking their fast, and sought the bath. Dahilis became playful once more, giggling as she soaped him and her and rinsed them clean, diving about in the warm water like a seal. They towelled each other as well but did not call anyone to help them dress. He would summon his barber later, he decided. He slipped on a robe, cloak, and sandals. She took an equally simple white gown belted at the waist, slippers on her feet, a fillet on her head. The yellow tresses she had merely combed and let hang free. Many young women of the best families often used plebeian styles these days, rather than the traditional elaborate coiffures. Ready to leave, she seemed to him a maiden, almost a child.

Hand in hand they wandered down a hallway on which opened the doors of luxurious chambers, across the mosaic of charioteers which floored the atrium, past servants who touched the brow, and out into the morning. Uniquely in Ys, the palace had a walled garden around it, not large but so intricate in its hedges, bowers, topiaries, flowerbeds, paths that one could walk long about and never feel cramped. The building and the outbuildings behind it were likewise of modest dimensions, but ample for their uses and pleasing to behold. The northern and southern sides of the palace formed ideal rectangles, their plaster flaunting vigorous images of wild beasts in a forest. Sculptures of a boar and a bear flanked a staircase leading to the portico and the main door, whose bronze bore reliefs of human figures. The upper storey was set back above a roof of green copper, and itself carried a dome, on top of which the gilt figure of an eagle spread wings.

It was a glorious day, springtime in bloom, each breath like a draught of cool wine. Dew still glittered on leaves and moss, newly born blossoms, crushed shell that scrunched softly underfoot. Birds were everywhere, red-breast, warbler, finch, linnet, wren, singing in a chaos of joy. High overhead, white as the cloudlets they passed, winged a flight of storks, homeward bound.

Dahilis walked mute, her trouble again upon her, until she and Gratillonius reached the wall. Vines growing over its sandstone did not hinder the warmth of sun that it had begun to give back. He spread his cloak over the dampness on a stone bench and they sat down. He laid a hand across the fist she had made in her lap. 'Tell me,' he said.

She stared before her, unseeing, and spoke with difficulty: 'My lord, my darling, I can no longer abide here. Grant me that . . . that I may go to my own house.'

'What?' he exclaimed, dismayed. 'I thought you happy.'

'Oh, I was. Gladsome beyond measure. But – it is not right . . . that I have the King all to myself. Five days it has been. Six nights.'

He clenched his teeth before saying, 'Well, true, I suppose we should – '

'We must! You are the King. And they, they are my Sisters in the Mystery. They too are of Belisama. Oh, do not anger Her! I would fear for you yet more than I already do.'

'I will certainly give them proper respect,' he forced out.

She turned her face to him. He saw tears on her lashes. 'Do more than that,' she begged. 'Cherish them. For my sake at first, if naught else will serve. Later for their own. They are my Sisters. They bore with my childhood flightiness, they were gentle and patient when I grew too restless to study what I ought, the older were like my mother unto me and the younger like loving elder sisters in the flesh. When my father Hoel fell, they upbore me in my grief. When my mother died, they did more, for the Sign was upon me that same night, and – And they consoled me, gave me back my heart, after Colconor, until they had schooled me in how to endure him. And at last it was they, they, they who had the bravery and the

164

skill to bring you. I was their acolyte. Yet me only have you honoured – It is not right!'

She fell into his arms and sobbed on his breast. He stroked her, crooned wordlessly, at length murmured, 'Aye. Indeed. It shall be as you wish. And you speak truly, I've been unwise in this. I can but plead that I've been too taxed with my business among men to think, otherwise, of aught than you, Dahilis.'

She gulped her way to self-mastery and sat straight. He kissed the salt off her cheeks and lips. His mouth slipped on down to the angle between jaw and ear; he kissed the softness of her skin there, too, and drank odours of her warmth and her hair. 'Th-thank you,' she whispered. 'You are ever kind.'

'Nay, now, what else could I be, towards you? And I've agreed you are right. Can you explain to . . . the rest . . . that no insult was intended?'

She nodded. 'I'll go about today doing that, since tomorrow comes my Vigil.'

'What's this?' he inquired.

'You did not know?' she replied, amazed. 'Why, I took it for given that my learned lord – Well, then, Sena is the sacred isle. Always must at least one of the Gallicenae be there. Save at a few certain times, Council meetings or the Crowning and Wedding, when all of us are needed here. Oh, and in war, for safety's sake, though I scarcely believe even the fiercest pirate would dare – We go out for a day and a night by turns, on a special ferry. The crew are navy men whose officers decide they've earned this honour for a month.'

He forbore to ask what the high priestesses did yonder. That might be a knowledge forbidden him. Instead, he regarded her in some slight bemusement before saying, 'You've depths I did not suspect, my sweet.'

The bright head shook. 'Nay, nay. I'm a shallow little person, really.'

'You're unjust to yourself.'

'I am truthful. The deaths of four aged Queens did not touch me, I was only sorry and missed them for a time. Not until my father was slain did I understand what sorrow is.'

'He surely adored you.'

A smile quivered. 'He spoiled me, he did. You are much like Hoel as I remember him, Gra – Gratillonius.' Her Latin weak, she occasionally had trouble keeping the syllables of his name in place. He found it easiest to chop along in Ysan when with her, telling himself he needed the practice.

'Even afterwards,' she continued, 'when I'd stopped mourning him aloud, I'd no real thoughtfulness in me. I expected to serve out my vestal term, and then after I turned eighteen belike marry a pleasant young man, the sort who was in my daydreams.' Her smile writhed away. 'But mother died, and the Sign came, and – ' She stared beyond him. Her fists doubled anew.

'That must have been horror,' he said.

Bit by bit, she eased. 'At first. But my Sisters took me in charge, Bodilis foremost. She's my true sister, you know – half-sister – also daughter of Tambilis, though her father was Wulfgar. But the rest comforted me too, and taught me. Colconor was seldom there for long. When he was finished he'd dismiss me, or fall asleep and snore if it was night. Then I could go home next morning. And when he used me – however hurtfully or, or shamefully – I could leave him. I sent my spirit back through time, or forward, to when things had been better or when someday they would be good once more. Forsquilis taught me how. And most days he let me alone, I could live my own life.'

'Tell me,' he said, trying to help her back to gladness, 'how did you pick the name Dahilis? I know your mother called you Estar. How do any of you Gallicenae choose your names when . . . you have been chosen?'

'They come from places. They bring the blessing of whatever spirit is tutelary. My name means "of Dahei". Dahei is a spring in the eastern hills where the nymph Ahes indwells. I picked that because it is cool and bubbly, hidden among trees. When I was a girl and my mother or Bodilis took me along on a trip to those parts – 'tis beautiful countryside – while she meditated I would seek the spring and give Ahes a garland and ask her for happy dreams at night.'

She sighed, but no longer in misery. 'Could we go together sometime, Gratillonius? I'd like to show you.'

'Of course, when I can find leisure. There's too much on hand now. Hm. You need not feel overly hurried about passing my message on. Your Vigil on Sena shall be postponed. I should have told you, but you make me forgetful of everything outside. And it was preoccupying, making those arrangements – when I was ignorant of all the ins and outs – for a full Council. It meets tomorrow.' He grinned. 'That requires your presence.'

'As a matter of form,' she said humbly. 'I can offer nothing.'

'Your presence, I repeat. We'll need the loveliness.'

'Oh, my own only!' They embraced. 'I did not know,' she breathed in his ear. 'I thought, yea, the new King will carry a better day for us on his shoulders, he cannot help but do that. I did not look for joy such as you've given. Last night after you were asleep, I prayed to Belisama Mother. I prayed you be spared for many, many years – and whatever happens, I might die before you. Was that terribly selfish of me? I'll come back in the sea and wait for you. Always will I wait for you.'

167

'Now, now, I have many a battle in me yet,' he boasted. She strained against him. Arousal stirred. 'M-m, I've a meeting with some Suffetes at noon, but that's hours hence. Shall we?'

She crowed in glee. 'And you thought you'd need more time!'

'With any woman but you I would.' Briefly, he wondered. Quinipilis had bespoken the power of the Goddess . . .

As she skipped along beside his more dignified pace, she said laughing, 'Could we wait long enough for you to be shaved? Later you might grow a beard. 'Tis the style in Ys.'

He rubbed his chin. 'I might. These past days my whiskers have been sprouting at a furious rate.'

'Well, but do put the razor to them this time. When I call on my Sisters and explain, best would be that I not flaunt marks on my face. Not but what they won't know from my gait, dear stallion!'

2

The Forum of Ys had never been a marketplace. It merely received that familiar name from the Roman engineers who reconstructed it as they did much else while the wall against the sea was going up. At the middle of the city, where Lir Way and Taranis Way crossed, it was a plaza surrounded by public buildings. These were likewise on the Roman model, marble-sheathed, colonnaded, stately, albeit of no great size. The temple of Taranis, the baths, the theatre, and the library were still in use. The basilica was also, less often, despite having seen no Imperial official permanently in residence for the past two hundred years. The temple of Mars had echoed empty almost as long, until Emperor Constantinus I required Ys to take in a Christian minister. Then it became a church.

Budic went looking around the square. Mosaics of dolphins and sea horses ringed a triple-basined fountain at the centre. No water splashed; on festival nights, pump-driven oil did, set alight to leap and cascade in fire. At noon today, not many folk were about. They stared curiously at the young soldier. He was out of uniform, but height, pale-blond hair, tunic falling down to bare knees – a garment his Coritanic mother had sewn for him – identified him as a foreigner. Though sunlight descended mild, his calves felt the breeze as a cold caress. His sandals slapped the pavement too loudly.

Because the former temple faced south, the Christians had cut a new entrance in its western side. Mounting the stairs to the portico, he found that door open and passed through. Before him was a stretch of bare floor, the vestibule, ended by a wall – which its peeling plaster revealed to be wooden – that subdivided the great chamber where the pagan rites had taken place. A door in it was also open, giving Budic a glimpse of the sanctuary. It was nearly as devoid of furnishings. The altar block stood in the middle beneath a canopy replacing the cupola of a proper church; the cross upon it was neither gilt nor of especially fine workmanship. At the far end were a table and a couple of seats.

An aged man was languidly sweeping in there, hunched over his besom. Budic halted at the divider. 'I b-beg your pardon, sir,' he ventured.

The other stopped, blinked, and shuffled forward. 'What would ye?' he asked. His Latin had a heavy Redonic accent. 'Be ye a believer?'

'I am, sir, though only a catechumen.'

169

'Well, ye're young yet. Can I help ye, brother in Christ? I be Prudentius the deacon.'

Budic declared his name and origin. Too bashful to seek higher, he asked, 'C-could I see a priest?'

'Priest?' The old man blinked. 'Haven't got any priest. What for? How big d'ye think our congregation be? I only get the name of deacon because I'm baptized and have time to help out with the chores. All the rest of the believers are busy making their livings.'

'Oh. Then the bishop? If I may?'

'Haven't got a bishop either, not here in this nest of heathens. Eucherius is the chorepiscopus. I'll go ask if he can see ye just now. Wait.' The man went off. Budic shifted from foot to foot, gnawed his thumbnail, stared into the sacred room he must not enter before he himself had received baptism. That wouldn't likely be for years and years –

The oldster reappeared. 'Come,' he said, and led the way through a door in the original transverse, marble wall on the left. Having followed a corridor past an unused space, they reached another door. The deacon signalled the soldier to go in.

Beyond was poverty huddled in what had been opulence. The chamber where the pastor made his home, once the temple treasury, was too big for him. However, decent if modest furniture occupied a part, and a threadbare carpet warded off some of the chill. Windows were glazed. At the north end, where a smokehole had been knocked through the ceiling, was a kitchen, crude but sufficient for cooking. Soot from it had obliterated ancient decorations above and had greyed murals. Several books rested on a table, together with writing materials: pens, inkwell, thin slabs of wood, a piece of vellum off which earlier notations were scraped.

Budic halted and made awkward salute. Two people

sat on tall stools at the table. That must be why the
deacon had questioned whether the chorepiscopus would
receive a new visitor. One person was a short, frail-
looking man, grey, Italianate of features, stoop-
shouldered in a robe much darned and patched. He
blinked nearsightedly and smiled uncertainly. 'Welcome,'
he said in Latin.

'Father – ' Budic's voice entangled itself.

'I stand in for the bishop, your proper father in Christ.
But let me call you "son" if you wish. My name is
Eucherius. Where are you from?'

'I am . . . I am a legionary . . . of those who follow
Gratillonius, he who is your King. My name is Budic.'

The pastor winced and signed himself, as many Christians had taken to doing. The woman across from him
turned and asked in a husky, excited tone: 'A man of
Gratillonius? Do you have a message from him?' Her
Latin was excellent.

'No, honourable lady,' faltered Budic, unsure how to
address her. 'I came on my own account. Father, having
leave today, I inquired my way here. We were long on
the march. We got no time for anything but hasty private
prayers. I've much on my soul, to confess and repent.'

'Why, of course I'll hear you.' Eucherius smiled. 'You
come like the flowers of the very Paschal season. But you
have no more need to hurry. Join us. I imagine you too,
Lady Bodilis, would like to know this young man better.
Eh?'

'I would that,' said the woman.

'Budic,' said Eucherius, 'pay respect – not religious,
but civil – to Queen Bodilis of Ys.'

Queen! A woman of the infamous Nine? Yet . . . a
woman of the centurion's? Dazedly, Budic saluted her.

She was a handsome woman, at least: tall, well-formed,
singularly graceful in her movements. Dark-brown, wavy

171

hair lay braided around features blunt-nosed, wide in the cheekbones, full in the mouth. Her eyes were large and blue under arching brows. The gown she wore was of rich material, soft green in colour, sleeves worked with gold thread, its leather belt chased in undulant patterns. A silver pendant in the form of an owl hung on her bosom.

'You can take a goblet from yonder shelf.' Eucherius pointed. 'Come share this mead that my lady was so generous as to bring for the warming of these creaky bones. Don't be surprised. She and I have been friends since first I came here, and that was ten years ago, was it not, Bodilis?'

A fit of coughing seized him. She frowned in concern, reached over to clasp his hand. Budic fetched a wooden vessel for himself and diffidently took a third stool, one of the ordinary low sort from which he would have to look up at the others. Bodilis gestured at the flagon. Well, a queen – whether or not she was a heathen priestess – wouldn't pour for a common soldier, would she? Budic mustered courage and filled his cup.

Bodilis smiled at him. This close, he saw fine lines crinkle at the corners of eyes and lips. 'We share no faith, the pastor and I,' she explained, 'but we share love of books, art, the wonders of earth and sea and heaven.'

'Queen Bodilis has been more than a companion in my isolation,' Eucherius wheezed when he was able. 'She saw to it that I got proper furnishings and enough to eat. The pagan Kings had done nothing about that, and – and there are no more than a score of Christians in Ys. Otherwise this church serves what transient Gauls and sailors are believers. My predecessors dwelt in wretchedness. I trust that speeded their salvation, but – but – Hers is a noble soul, my son. Pray that she someday see the light, or that God will reveal it to her after she dies.'

Sardonicism tinged Bodilis's smile. 'Beware,' she said. 'Do you not skirt heresy?'

'The Lord forgive me. I must remember – ' Eucherius gave Budic his full attention. 'When I can, I travel to Audiarna – Roman-held town, the closest, on the west bank of a river that otherwise marks the frontier – You'd not know the geography, would you? . . . There I make my own confessions, and obtain the consecrated bread and wine. But I cannot travel often. My health – '

He straightened as best he could, with an apologetic look. 'Now it's you who must forgive, my son,' he finished. 'I didn't mean to appear unmanly and chattery, before a soldier at that. It's only, oh, to see a *Roman* again – Are there Christians among your fellows?'

Budic nodded. Eucherius beamed.

'Drink, lad, and let us talk,' Bodilis counselled. 'We've each a bundle of news to exchange, I'm sure.'

Budic sipped. The mead was dry, delicately flavoured with blackberry. 'I'm just a rustic from eastern Britannia,' he demurred. 'This journey has been my first. Well, my vexillation was on the Wall last year, but that was fighting, and garrison duty in between. Nobody told us anything.'

'The Wall last year! Where Magnus Maximus rolled back a barbarian midnight.' Her tone sank. 'Although – What do you know about him? What sort of man is he?'

'I *am* only a roadpounder – a common legionary, honourable lady,' Budic faltered. 'I know nothing about great matters. It is enough to follow my centurion.'

'But you heard talk,' she said fiercely. 'You are not deaf.'

'Well, camp and barracks are always full of rumours.' Budic attempted evasion. 'The lady is very well informed about Rome.'

Bodilis laughed. 'I try. Like a snail reaching horns out of the shell into which it has drawn itself. Word does come in. I'm here today to share with Eucherius a letter lately arrived from Ausonius. He too hears talk.'

'Let us get acquainted,' the chorepiscopus urged.

His story soon emerged, as glad as he was of fresh company. He was a Neapolitan who, after attaining the priesthood, had been sent to the school of rhetoric which Ausonius then maintained in Burdigala, for he showed promise. Exposure to ancient philosophers and to the attitudes of his teacher bred in him a doubt that man since Adam is innately depraved – especially new-born children. When he expressed such ideas on his return home, he was quickly charged with heresy, and had no influential clergyman to argue on his behalf. Though he recanted, his bishop afterwards trusted him with no more than the work of a lowly copyist.

Then it chanced that that bishop received a letter from his colleague and correspondent in Gesocribate. Among other things, the writer lamented that the ministry at Ys had fallen vacant some time ago and there seemed to be no man both competent and willing to take it over. Thus the Church had lost even this tenuous contact with the city – the comings and goings of its traders were altogether unmonitored – and there was no guessing what the powers of darkness wrought around the Gobaean Promontory.

The Italian bishop wrote back proposing Eucherius, and this was agreed to. The feeling among Eucherius's superiors was that in the midst of such obstinate pagans any errors into which he might again stray would make small difference, while he ought to administer the sacraments sufficiently well to whatever few Christians came by. Also, serving in yonder post would be an additional penance, good for his own soul.

Hence he was elevated to chorepiscopus – 'country bishop', as slang put it – with authority to govern a church, teach, lead services, give Communion and last rites, but not to baptize or consecrate the Bread and Wine.

Reaching the city, he learned the language, but remained lonesome, not so much scorned as ignored, until Bodilis's desire for knowledge brought him and her together. She tried to get him membership in the Symposium, the gathering of thinkers at Star House, but the vote failed. For his part, he put her in touch with Ausonius, and those two exchanged letters even though the poet had since joined the Imperial court and attained to a consulship.

Eucherius's own correpondence was perfunctory, confined to his ecclesiastical masters. Beguiling his empty hours was the labour of a treatise on the history and customs of Ys. These had come to fascinate him as greatly as they appalled him; and – who knew? – one day the information might help a stronger man guide this poor benighted people back from the abyss.

Tears stung Budic's eyes. 'Father,' he blurted, 'you are a soldier too, a legionary of Christ!'

Eucherius sighed. 'No, hardly.' He shaped a wan smile. 'At best, a camp follower, stumblefooted and starveling, always homesick.'

'I hear it is lovely at Neapolis,' Bodilis said low to Budic. 'Hills behind and a bay before, utterly blue; the old Grecian city nestled between; and that Italian light and air about which we can only dream here in our grey North.'

'We must forsake this world and seek our true home, which is Heaven,' Eucherius reproached. Another spell of coughing racked him, more cruel than the first. He put a cloth to his mouth. When he laid it down, the phlegm on it was streaked red.

Eppillus having given them leave, Cynan and Adminius set off to see a little of Ys and sample its pleasures. For guide they had Herun, a young deckhand in the navy. They had made his acquaintance at Warriors' House, where the legionaries were quartered together with men of the professional armed service. Those of the latter who were not on duty or standby generally stayed at home, but for the present the Romans had no place else to sleep than the barrack.

While at liberty one wore civil garb, and no steel save a knife whose blade length could not exceed four inches. Adminius thoughtfully tucked a cosh under the tunic he hung on his wiry frame. Cynan was gaudier in the clothes of his native Demetae, fur-trimmed coat, cross-gartered breeches, saffron cloak flapping in the gusty air; from his left shoulder a small harp hung in its carrying case. Herun was attired in Ysan male wise, linen shirt, embroidered jacket open to display a pendant on his breast, snug trousers. The predominant Celtic strain in him showed on big body and freckled face; the beard trimmed close to his jaws and the hair drawn into a horsetail down his neck were coppery.

'Methought we'd go around by Aurochs Gate and Goose Fair, thence wend north for the Fishtail,' he said, slowly and carefully so as to be understood. 'Thus will you pass some things worthy of a look ere we settle down to carouse.'

'That sounds well.' Adminius turned to Cynan and translated into Latin. Meanwhile the three dodged through the traffic on Lir Way and took a street quiet and narrow which wound among the abodes of the wealthy.

'You've seized on to a mickle of our language in the short span you've had,' observed Herun.

Adminius grinned his snaggle-toothed grin. 'A cockroach scuttling about the docksides of Londinium 'ad better be quick, if 'e'd not get stepped on,' he replied.

'Mean you that yours was a hard life?'

'Well, my father's a ferryman on the River Tamesis. Early on, the count of 'is brats began to outnumber the count of 'is earnings. From the time I could walk, I scrabbled for whatever I wanted, over and above my mother's boiled cabbage. That was a lawless as well as a poor quarter, but on the same account, chances would come now and then. To snatch them, I 'ad ter be able ter understand men from around 'alf the world, it seemed. So I got a sharp ear and tongue.'

Herun frowned, labouring to follow. As yet, Adminius perforce spoke haltingly, with a thick and unique accent, using many words that might be common elsewhere in Armorica but were strangers here. It helped that the mariner had encountered some of them on his travels. Patrolling widely around the peninsula, sailing convoy in periods of special danger, Ysan warcraft often put in to rest or resupply. They usually chose small harbours where there were no Imperial officials to encumber transactions.

'At length you enlisted?' Herun guessed.

Adminius nodded. 'I'd made enemies in Londinium. Besides, the legionary's life is no bad one, 'speci'lly when you're good at scrounging and at slipping through cracks in the rules.'

'What are you gabbling about?' demanded Cynan.

Adminius returned to his kind of Latin: 'Aow, nothing but my biography. Don't fret. You'll soon be slinging the lingo too.'

Cynan's dark features stayed fixed in a scowl. 'Maybe

then those warlocks won't strip my purse – when I've learned how to counter their spells.'

'Now, now, don't sulk. It was an honest game. The dice just weren't friendly ter yer. I took my share.' Adminius jingled his own pouch. Like Rome's, the Ysan armed services were paid in coin as well as in kind. Most of what he had were sesterces, of depleted worth but preferable to bagsful of nummi. They would serve for such minor dealings as an evening on the town. 'And I'm not the chap that won't stand a chum a treat.'

Cynan bridled. 'I ask no alms.'

Adminius ran fingers through his sandy hair. 'Mighty near a 'opeless case, ain't you? Why'd you come along if not for a bit o' fun? Consider it a loan. Let the next bout be yours.' He slapped the other on the back. 'Barracks too dull for yer, eh? Well, you'll feel cheerier after you've 'ad a drink and a wench.'

The street passed a walled enclosure, within which rose a domed habitation. Four sentries stood at a grillwork gate: on either side, an Ysan marine and a Roman legionary. Herun saluted in his fashion, Adminius waved at his friends, as they passed by. 'Is this the royal palace?' Cynan asked.

'Got ter be. You know we don't assign anybody ter anywhere else, so far. You and I'll be drawing this duty soon.'

'I understand how the centurion – the prefect – wants men of his on guard. But why not more? And why have natives at all?'

'Eppillus was explaining that ter me. Gratillonius ain't just the prefect now, 'e's the flinking King. It'd be an insult if 'e didn't let 'em watch over their King. And *we* wouldn't like it if 'e didn't let us 'elp.'

Cynan pondered. 'That feels true in me,' he agreed after a space. 'He's a wise one, no?' Resentment flickered afresh. 'At least when my turn comes I won't be cooped up indoors.'

'Easy, lad, easy. Are you really that eager ter start in again on drill and digging latrines? Never fear. Give 'im time ter get the lay of the land, and 'e'll find plenty for us ter do, 'e will.'

Terrain began dropping fast. Except for the residential towers, buildings grew less lavish and more old. Ever higher did the rampart rear in view and, under a declining sun, fill the ways with shadow. The last sellers, buyers, brokers, and hawkers were leaving Goose Fair. Its stones boomed beneath hoofs and wheels; echoes rolled hollowly. The Brothers at Aurochs Gate were outlined black athwart heaven.

Herun turned right, through streets that became mere lanes, half-roofed by overhanging upper storeys between which they twisted. Cobblestones lay lumpy underfoot. More people were about than in New Town – sailors, workmen, housewives, fishwives, children in skimpy tunics, individuals less easily recognizable. Their garments might be flamboyant, rough, or sleazy, but were always cheap. They themselves bore marks of toil and sometimes of past sickness. Yet there was no sign of hunger or alley-cat poverty as in Londinium, nor did the quarter smell sourly of refuse and unwashed bodies. Sea air blew through all Ys, tinged with salt and kelp, chill where walls blocked off sunlight. Gulls cruised white overhead.

The three men halted before a small, rudely cubical structure of rammed earth on a patch of ground defined by four unshaped boundary stones. Between wooden roof and door was inset a solar emblem of polished granite. Despite repairs and replacements which had been made as need arose, the wear of centuries was plain to see. Herun genuflected in reverence.

'What's this?' Cynan asked; his Ysan was sufficient for that.

'The Shrine of Melqart,' Herun said. 'Thus did the founders of the city name Taranis when first they came hither, long and long ago. Later He got temples more grand, and now this is only open on solstice days, with but a single man to make sacrifice. Elsewhere in Old Town, and not unlike it, is the Shrine of Ishtar – Belisama – which opens at the equinoxes. We honour our Gods in Ys.'

He conducted his followers onward. Adminius paraphrased his explanation for Cynan. The Demetan traced a sign in the air. 'Well might they honour their Gods,' he said low, 'they who live on the sufferance of Ocean . . . But you're a Christian, you don't understand.'

'I ain't that good a Christian,' Adminius confessed.

Farther on was another reserved space, this for a megalith man-high, lichen-spotted, darkling. 'Menhir Place,' Herun said, again bending his knee. 'The pillar was here before the city. Out in Armorica have I seen works of the Old Folk that Celts have chiselled their glyphs into, and lately Christians likewise. But our forefathers, and we, ventured not to trouble this that was raised to a God unknown.'

Adminius shivered a bit. As if continuing his earlier sentence, he muttered, 'I know when somewhere is 'aunted . . . Wish I'd brought my cloak. It's got futtering cold.'

Beyond the harbour end of Lir Way and the respectable buildings there, the Fishtail began. It was quite a small slum, less mean than any counterpart in the Empire. Nevertheless dwellers went ragged, slinking or truculently swaggering. Beggars wailed, decrepit whores gestured weary invitations, children shrieked mockery, narrow stares out of hard faces followed the strangers. ''Tis less grim than you might think,' Herun said, 'and the inn we're bound for is easy on the purse.'

It occupied what had once been a fine home. Plaster was mostly gone from bricks, few good tiles remained among cheap newer ones, mere bits were left of relief sculptures beside the entrance. Within, the former atrium, now the taproom, showed fragments of mosaic in its clay floor. The soot and grease of centuries hid nearly all fresco colour, but a stain going halfway up the walls was unmistakable.

'Wotever 'appened 'ere?' Adminius wondered.

'Ancient damage done by the sea, I think, before the rampart was raised,' Herun said. He gestured at a table. Four men sat benched there, drinking. They were weather-beaten, knobby-handed, coarsely clad. 'Greeting,' Herun called to them, and they grunted a response. He and his comrades took the opposite end, ten or twelve feet from them. 'Fishers,' he whispered. 'Decent in their way, but given to overweeningness. Best we leave them be.'

Candles added what they could to light that seeped in through thin-scraped membranes stretched across windows. The air was acrid with smoke, heavy with odours from tallow and an adjoining kitchen. A man who must be the landlord sent a boy pattering over to ask what the newcomers wanted. 'The mead is not bad,' Herun recommended. 'Beware the wine.' He gave their order, and paid when the goblets arrived. 'Be this round on my reckoning. Hail and haleness.'

A woman emerged from an inner room and made hip-swaying approach. She was comely enough, aside from greasy hair and shabby gown. 'Why, Herun, dear,' she warbled through a broad smile, 'welcome. Where have you been all this time? Who are your friends?'

'Mayhap you've heard the Romans are back amongst

us,' the mariner replied. 'They came with the new King. Here are two of them, Adminius and Cynan.'

She widened her eyes. 'Romans! Ooh, how *wonderful*!' She sat down opposite them, next to Herun. 'Be you welcome too, you sightly fellows. If 'tis a romp you'd have, you've sought the right place. I am Keban.'

'Where are the others?' Herun asked. 'This is seldom a busy hour for you.'

'True.' She cast a surly glance at the fishermen. 'They *say* the catch was poor and they've naught to spend on more than a stoup or two. Well, as for the girls, Rael is under the moon; says she feels too badly to do *any*thing. Silis got pregnant and has not yet recovered from having that taken care of. So I'm by myself.' Suggestively: 'I long for company.'

'You shall have some,' Herun laughed. 'But first let's give you the drink you expect.' He signalled the potboy.

Adminius told Cynan more or less what he had heard. The youth's nostrils flared. He gripped his cup till knuckles stood white above the wood, drew shaky breath, and said deep in his throat: 'By the Hooded Three, but I've got a need on that march we made! What would they say if I laid her down right on the floor?'

'They'd say you were a fool, wearing out yer knees when a straw tick goes with the rental. 'Old it in a bit, lad. You'll enjoy it the more.'

The door opened and banged shut again. A man strode in with a sailor's rolling gait. His garb was rough too, and bore a slight smell of fish. Medium tall, he was broad and powerful; his shoulders, chest, and arms might have fitted a bear, his hands were like capstans which had each raised five anchors. Rugged features and green eyes stood within hair and beard whose blackness declared him still fairly young, however much wind and sun and spindrift had turned his skin to leather.

The fishers rose, reseated themselves, and made gestures of invitation. He smiled and waved but steered for the Roman end of the table. "Oo's that?' Adminius asked.

'I know him a little,' Herun murmured. 'His name is Maeloch.'

'Why do they defer to 'im? I thought you said their sort make way for no one.'

'He is a Ferrier. A Ferrier of the Dead. No bad wight, no bully, but have a care of his pride.'

'Mead!' the man roared in a voice to carry through gales. He reached the table, looked down at Herun, and touched his breast. The navy man did likewise. It was the formal Ysan salutation between equals. 'Well met,' Maeloch rumbled genially. 'Who be these strangers?'

'You'd not heard?' Herun replied.

'Nay, I've been at sea this sennight past. Great run of mackerel off Merrow Shoals, if ye can ride out the weather. Now I've a raging thirst and a rampant stand.'

'Your wife – '

'Ah, Betha nears her time again. Another mouth to feed; but still, I'd not risk harming the sprat by pounding on her.' Maeloch went to rumple Keban's hair. She purred and rubbed her cheek against his thigh. He planked himself down beside her. The mead came for the two of them. 'Hail and haleness, all!'

Goblets lifted, except for Cynan's. He glowered, and angrily asked Adminius for translation.

Meanwhile Maeloch's right hand fondled Keban, his left wielded his drink, and he drew from Herun an account of what had happened. It did not quite seem to please him. 'A new King, aye, that's long overdue,' he growled. 'Colconor was offal. Were it not that no Ysan may, I'd've challenged him myself – well, nay, I suppose not; that would've meant forsaking my Betha.' He nodded stiffly at the legionaries. 'But if this King is a swab for Rome – Well, we can hear ye out, ye twain, after I've done my first tupping.'

'I want her now,' Cynan exclaimed. 'Adminius, you said you'd help. Make her price good while I – ' He scrambled to his feet, swung past the table end, and tugged at Keban's gown. 'Where do we go?'

Surprised, she could only titter. Maeloch tensed. 'Hoy, what's this? Let her be!'

'The soldier's want seems more urgent than yours,' Herun said hastily. 'They were many days on their way hither, these guests. Come, drain your cup and let me buy you another.'

'What, me betread wet decks . . . after a Roman?' Maeloch heaved his bulk up like a spyhopping whale. He stepped over the bench. His right hand closed on Cynan's tunic and cloak, under the throat, and hauled the Briton around. His left fist drew back. 'Belay that and begone!'

Cynan whitened. He hissed. His knife came forth. 'Let me go, you filthy fishmonger!'

Herun and Adminius exchanged glances. They leapt, Ysan to Ysan, Roman to Roman. From behind, each threw a lock on the arms of his man. Neither could have held it long, but their voices prevailed: 'Stop, easy, easy, are you mad, would you bring the watch down on us, let's talk, let's be civilized – ' When they felt thews slacken a little, they released their grasps. The antagonists backed a few steps apart and stood with heads thrust out between shoulders, breath harsh in mouths.

Herun: 'Maeloch, hold. He's scarcely more than a boy. Believe me, I know these wights, they've not come to oppress or levy on us. Fain would they be our friends. In the names of the Three, peace!'

Adminius: 'Get yer 'ead out o' yer arse, Cynan! If the centurion heard you'd started a brawl over a 'ore, this early in the game, 'e'd 'ave yer flogged till beetles could dance on yer ribs. Sit down. We'll call for a new round, and maybe toss a coin to see 'oo goes first.'

Everybody eased – also the fishers at the far end, who had sprung clear and made ready for general turmoil. A much relieved landlord offered a free serving. This brought men together. In the beginning they laughed too loudly and slapped each others' backs too heartily, but soon they felt fellowship. Maeloch and Cynan could do no less than swap a rueful handclasp in the Ysan manner. Between Herun and Adminius, the full story of the legionaries came forth, from the war at the Wall and onward. It fascinated the fishers, and required more mead for soothing of gullets. If most purses were lean, Herun and Adminius stood ready to buy. The tale reminded Maeloch of a song about a boatman who had lured a shipful of marauding Saxons on to a reef. He sang it for his Roman mates. Not to be outdone, Cynan unlimbered his harp and offered a ballad from his homeland. He did it well. The company shouted for more.

Keban sat by herself, waiting. One hand cradled her cheek, the fingernails of the other drummed the table.

4

Soon after Imbolc, Niall maqq Echach, King over Mide, left Temir accompanied by his body servants, warriors, learned men, and eldest son Breccan. He did not follow the Queen and their children to that one of their halls which she sought. Instead, he made progress around his realm – sunwise, as he must under gess – and was more than a month about it. This was not very commonly done after the first time, when a King was newly consecrated; but

Niall said he had been so much away at war that he should get to know his folk better and right any wrongs they were suffering.

Indeed he listened, and not only to the powerful men who gave him lodging. Although he never gainsaid the judge in any district, which was not within his right, he heard disputes brought to those worthies, and sometimes offered advice in private before settlement was decreed. His gifts were generous to the poor as well as lavish to the mighty. He was grave or boisterous as occasion demanded, thus making friends among men; and after a night or three, many a young woman came to feel a warmth for him which glowed from her into her father, brothers, or husband.

Some people murmured that he was being shrewd. Although the weather was fair for this time of year and there was no reason to expect lean months, sooner or later they came. The blame for it was less likely to fall on the King if he was well-beloved. Restless Niall might not be at home then to defend himself against charges of evildoing that had angered the Gods. Moreover, his repulse last summer, while not inglorious, called for explaining if he would have warriors follow him willingly on his next adventure.

That he planned one was beyond doubt. Already at Temir he had been in secret talk with men of several different kinds. While his train made its slow way through the countryside, messengers often came speeding with word he did not reveal. Thereafter he was apt to ride off, gazing afar, with none but his guards along and they forbidden to speak to him.

Gossip buzzed. It swelled to a tide when Niall entered Qóiqet nUlat without asking leave of any lord therein, sought Mag Slecht, and made blood sacrifice to Cromb Cróche and the twelve lesser idols. Although he wended back peacefully enough, word of this caused swords to be whetted.

And so in due course he reached the sea, rode down to Clón Tarui, and took lodging at the public hostel there. Day after day he abode, still meeting quietly with men who came and went, but still keeping his own counsel. Since the River Ruirthech that emptied into the bay just south of this place marked the border of the Lagini, the idea arose that Niall had in mind to enforce the Bóru tribute. It had gone unpaid for many years. True, his following here was too small to overcome a whole Fifth of Ériu; but was he making a threat, or was he sending forth scouts and spies to gather knowledge for a campaign in summer? When hints or questions reached him, Niall simply smiled.

The day came at last when he and Breccan had gone hunting, and returned towards eventide. They had started a red deer in the woods northward and chased it down in a breakneck halloo: Breccan's sling had knocked half a dozen squirrels from their trees; everyone was weary and happy. Through cleared lands they now rode, broad and gently rolling acres of pasture and field, bestowed on the hostelkeeper so that that person might give free guesting to travellers. The small round houses of tenants huddled here and there, wattle-and-daub beneath cones of thatch through which smoke seeped into the wind. It had been a day for rainsqualls and continued blustery, although a low sun struck rays like brass through the wrack that scurried overhead. Horses and hounds plodded in the mire of the road. But when the bay gleamed in sight, and the great oblong of the hostel, whinnies and bellings arose, hoofs and feet pounded, the huntsmen forgot how wet and cold they were and lifted a shout of their own.

Suddenly Niall stiffened on the horseblanket. Out of the brume upon the eastern sea, a pair of sails had appeared, above a lean hull – a currach, bearing down on Clón Tarui. 'It's reckless early in the year they've been abroad,' said a guard.

'It . . . is . . . not, I am thinking,' Niall answered slowly. '*Hai!*' He struck heels against his mount. The beast plucked up strength and broke into gallop. Breccan's alone could keep pace; the warriors fell behind. Niall did not heed. Nor did he stop until on the shore.

By then the currach was near. It was large, two-masted, the leather of it holding a dozen men. Sails rattled down on their yards, oars bit water, and the craft drove up on to the strand. One man leapt forth first. Niall sprang from horseback. They ran to each other and embraced.

'Ah, welcome, welcome, darling!' the King cried. 'It's grand you are looking – and all the lads home alive, too! How went the quest?'

The newcomer stepped back. He was bony, sinewy, auburn hair and beard slightly grizzled around a face that weather had seamed and bedarkened. Despite that and his drenched garb, he bore himself with an easy arrogance. 'Bucketing over the sea and trudging over the land,' he laughed. 'Yet well worth the trouble. What you thought might come to pass has done so indeed, indeed. The Roman soldiers have hailed Maximus their lord, and he has left for Gallia with the most of them.'

'Ha-a-ah!' Niall roared.

'Slow, dear master, slow. It does not seem they will be stripping their defences bare for this – not soon – and I'll be giving you some news about the Saxons, also.'

Niall smote fist in palm. 'Nonetheless – !'

The skipper arrived to pay his respects. Niall greeted him well and spoke of venison at the feast tonight. Meanwhile the thin man's glance fell on Breccan, who stood aquiver. 'And might this be your son, my lord?' he asked. 'It's long since I saw him last, and he a babe in arms.'

'It is he,' Niall replied. 'Breccan, my dear, you will not be remembering, but here is Uail maqq Carbri, a trusty man who has gone on many a mission for me – though never, maybe, one that needed as much boldness and wiliness as this.'

'Och, it was not that hard, so don't you be daunting the lad about such things,' Uail said, cockily rather than modestly. 'I know my way about over there, and the speech – a bit of the Latin, too. It was mostly to wander as a harmless pedlar, watching, listening, sometimes getting a soul drunk or furious till his tongue ran free. There was no big secret.'

Niall's look blazed across the waters like the last stormy sun-rays. 'Maximus withdrawn,' he breathed. 'We'd likely not be wise to strike Alba this year, at his heels – not yet – but southwards, Roman will be at war with Roman – ' Again he bellowed. 'Ha-a-ah!'

Breccan could hold himself in no longer. And he saw his chance. He seized Niall's hand. 'Father,' he cried, 'I am going along, am I not? You promised! I shall help you get your revenge!'

Niall swept the slender form to his breast. 'You shall that!'

He let go, stood for a heartbeat or two, frowned, then shrugged. 'It seems Medb will have it so,' he muttered. Straightening, he turned to Uail and the sailors. 'Come,' he said, 'make your boat fast and let's be off to the hostel. The keeper is the widow Morigel, and a fine table she sets. Afterwards . . . I will be querying you about everything you have learned.'

Breccan danced and whooped.

X

1

The chamber in the basilica where the Council of Suffetes met could have held many more than it did this day. It was ornamented only by its stone panelling, but that was superb, mica-sparked granite, veined marble, mottled serpentine, intricate onyx. Large windows admitted ample greenish light. Under the barrel-vaulted ceiling, sound carried extraordinarily well. On either side of a central passage, padded benches in tiers looked down to the farther end. There stood a dais whereon rested a throne. Behind it, the wall curved to form a bay. Against that wall were statues of the Triad, ten feet tall, Taranis on the right, Belisama in the middle, Lir represented on the left by a mosaic slab out of which stared a kraken.

When everyone else was seated, Gratillonius entered, magnificently robed, bearing the Hammer, the Key in view on his breast, but his head encircled by a fillet rather than the royal crown. His legionaries followed in full armour. The crash of hobnails resounded along the passage. At the dais they deployed right and left and came to attention behind it, in front of the towering Gods. Gratillonius mounted the platform and took stance before the throne. Silence thundered down upon the gathering. He raised the Hammer and intoned as he had been taught: 'In the name of Taranis, peace. May His protection be on us.'

The Nine sat together in blue gowns and white headdresses at the left end of the foremost benches. Vindilis rose, spread out her arms with palms downward, and responded: 'In the name of Belisama, peace. May Her blessing be on us.'

By this Gratillonius knew that today she would lead the Gallicenae, speaking for them except when some other had reason to enter the discussion. He wondered why they had elected her instead of, say, wise old Quinipilis. In Vindilis's hatchet features he read an intensity that might prove troublesome. But the Queens moved in their own ways, which it was not for anyone else to question.

Vindilis reseated herself. At the right end of the interrupted arc, Hannon Baltisi stood up. The grey beard flowed from his furrowed countenance over a robe worked to suggest a heavy sea, white manes on green waves. He was not a priest, for the God Whose worldly affairs he guided had none, unless one reckoned every skipper of Ys. But his it was to say, as Captain, 'In the name of Lir, peace. May His wrath not be on us,' and bring the butt of a trident booming down on the floor before he too sat.

Gratillonius handed the Hammer to Eppillus, whom he had designated his Attendant, and stood for several pulsebeats looking the assemblage over. Besides the high priestesses, it numbered thirty-three, all male and all drawn from the thirteen Suffete clans. (He had learned that those corresponded somewhat to the Roman senatorial rank, save that nobody could buy or wheedle or even earn his way into them. Entry was strictly by birth, marriage in the case of a woman, or adoption in the case of a child.) Soren Cartagi was conspicuous among them in the red robe and mitre of his role as Speaker for Taranis. Like Hannon, he represented the corporation of his temple, though he had no ritual part in the proceedings today. He could also, if he chose, argue on behalf of the Great House of Timbermen which was his.

Three men belonged ex officio to the Council – Adruval Tyri, Sea Lord, head of the navy and marines; Cothortin Rosmertai, Lord of Works, who oversaw the day-by-day administration of city business; Iram Eliuni, Lord of Gold, whose treasury function had become almost nominal. The Sea Lord wore ordinary Ysan clothes of good material, his colleagues had decked themselves in togas.

A few more togas were visible among the rest. The majority had selected robes, or else shirt and trousers. Not every garment was sumptuous, for Suffete status did not necessarily mean wealth. The delegates from guilds had themselves been fisher, sailor, wagoner, artisan, labourer, or the like. Even some heads of Great Houses had been poor in their youths. However, most had not, for these firms generally stayed in the same families through many generations.

Thirty-three men. Gratillonius's gaze searched across them. No two were alike; and yet – The aristocrats of Ys had consciously set barriers to inbreeding. None could marry within his or her clan. Brides from outside were usually made welcome. A couple might adopt a promising youngster from among the commons or the Osismii, in hopes of invigorating the bloodline. Nonetheless, again and again he met the 'Suffete face', narrow, high-cheeked, aquiline, a memory in flesh and bone of lost Phoenicia.

Well. Best to start. He remained standing but assumed an easy posture. 'Greeting,' he said in Ysan. 'First will I thank you for your forbearance. This honourable Council meets four times annually, I hear, around equinox and solstice. Thus you've but lately completed a session, and have affairs of your own awaiting your attention. Although the King possesses the right to order a special assembly when he sees fit, I have striven to make clear that mine today is for the welfare and safety of Ys, and not capriciously in future will I call you back. Rather will I hold frequent private conference about our shared concerns as these arise; and ever will you find me heedful of you.'

He smiled. 'I trust we can finish within a few hours. You know why we are here. 'Twould expedite matters if we, or at least I, used Latin. Else must I slowly mangle my way through your language, which does it no credit. My hope is that soon I shall be in better command of it. Meanwhile, has anybody aught in disfavour of Latin?'

Hannon lifted a hand. Gratillonius recognized him. 'Myself, no,' he said in an Armorican seaman's form of that tongue. 'There must be some who've not wielded it since school days, but if they may talk Ysan, well enough. My lord King, when you've trouble understanding something, I suggest you ask for translation. Likewise for whoever don't follow you very readily.'

'We need a single interpreter,' Soren pointed out, 'or we will be babbling into each other's mouths.'

'I propose Queen Bodilis,' came from Vindilis. 'She's both learned and quick-witted. Are you willing, Sister?'

'That I am,' replied Bodilis in scholar's Latin.

Gratillonius regarded her. An attractive woman, he thought, seems to be in her mid-thirties, best years of a woman's life, my father always told me. The knowledge that he would bed her stirred him – unexpectedly, when Dahilis sat right beside her. Bodilis returned his glance with calm, candour, and a slight smile.

He cleared his throat. 'Thank you,' he said. 'Let me begin by explaining my purposes. I've already done that as best I was able, to several among you. But for the rest, it could be that what you heard at second or third remove has suffered in transmission. Afterwards we can discuss everything, and I hope at the end you'll formally ratify my programme, and then take a share in it.'

Increasingly, he felt sure of himself. This did not seem too different from addressing the soldiers of his century on the day of a mission. He wondered for an instant if, somehow, the fact of cooperation with Bodilis had heartened him. However brave a front he presented, when he first entered this chamber the strangeness of all that was around him had been daunting.

'I realize you've had well-nigh every sort of man for King in Ys,' he went on. 'As for myself, you know I am a legionary: Gaius Valerius Gratillonius, centurion, hitherto serving in Britannia. There, last year I helped kick the Scoti and Picti back from the Wall. I've heard what pests the Scoti are to you also. I'm a Briton, Belgic, of curial family; and I've visited Armorica in the past.

'Now you should be quite clear about this, that I did not come here with any intention of making myself your King. It happened. Frankly, I'm still not sure just how it happened. But we've got the fact of it before us, solid as your headlands. And . . . it may be through the favour of the Gods. Not many people seem to have liked Colconor.' That drew a few chuckles. 'I don't know if I can be another Hoel, but I mean to try.'

He took up earnestness as he would have taken up his shield: 'My task was, and is, to be the prefect of Rome in Ys. You haven't seen my like since time out of mind. Nevertheless, the treaty – the Oath – remains in force. Ys is a foederate of Rome. It has duties towards Rome, which it may be called upon to fulfil. And Rome has duties towards Ys, which I am also here to see fulfilled. To that end, it may prove valuable that I've won the powers of your King.

'Not that I intend to abuse them, nor throw my weight around as prefect. My assignment is simple. There is reason to fear trouble in the Empire. Gallia in particular may well be in upheaval. I cannot imagine you'd want Ys drawn into that. As far as possible, your city has always kept aloof. My task is to lead you in staying at peace. No more, no less. For that, we cannot sit passive. If Roman Armorica – western Armorica, at least – if it becomes embroiled, Ys can hardly stay out. And Rome, which I serve, will take yet another wound, a wound that could prove hard to staunch.

'What Ys must do is lend its aid to the cause of peace, of order. Legates and governors elsewhere may wish to take sides in the fight. We need to keep them home. A word here, a bribe there, a show of naval strength yonder – that should suffice. What exactly shall we do? I plan to work that out in concert with the leaders of Ys, and then get it done.

'That's all. Later we'll consider together what else we can undertake, in the better day that I believe lies ahead. But first we must weather the storm that's brewing. I want your agreement to this, followed by your best efforts – under me, the prefect of Rome and now your King – to carry out the mission. For the welfare of Rome and of Ys!

'Thank you.'

He folded his arms and waited. After a hush, Soren said, 'My lady Bodilis, could you put that in Ysan for the benefit of any who may not have caught every word?'

'I can paraphrase,' replied the Queen. 'Meanwhile let each of us be thinking of what this portends.'

She stood and spoke. Gratillonius admired her handling of the matter; she seemed to express things more clearly and compactly than he had himself.

When she finished, a buzzing went along the benches, until Sea Lord Adruval declared bluntly, 'We can't navigate in a fog. And foggy you've been, O King, when we talked before. What is this menace we're supposed to prepare against?'

'I have not said, because I am not party to secrets of

state, nor am I a prophet to read the future,' Gratillonius answered. 'What my commander gave me to understand was that great events will soon happen, and they may get violent. I pray it be less bad than the Magnentian War, and the outcome better. But we must wait for word, and hold ourselves ready to act on it.'

Vindilis did not signal request to be recognized. Silence fell immediately upon all others when the spokeswoman of the Gallicenae announced in a steely tone: 'I can tell you more than that. Gratillonius's superior, who dispatched him to us, is Magnus Clemens Maximus, Duke of the Britains. The legions in that diocese have hailed him Augustus. They have crossed over to Gallia and are warring for the purple. Gratillonius,' – her eyes burned at him – 'you are not stupid. I suppose he never told you outright, but you must have understood; and you are Maximus's man.'

The Suffetes gasped. Thundersmitten, the King of Ys cried, 'How can you know?'

'By the same means we knew of your coming.' Vindilis gestured towards the woman on her left. 'Forsquilis went in a Sending.'

'What's this? Priestess, we've only your naked word.'

Soren's ruddy visage darkened. 'Do you call the Gallicenae liars?' he shouted. A growl as of shingle under surf lifted around him.

Quinipilis rose, leaned on her staff, raised her free hand for attention. 'Be not hasty,' she said in Ysan. 'Gratillonius is new among us. He means well. And he *is* King and prefect. Give him a chance to learn.'

The centurion wet his lips. 'I'm certainly willing to listen,' he said. 'Do explain.'

'That were best done in private,' Vindilis answered, 'between Forsquilis and yourself.'

'Well – that is, if the lady agrees – ' Gratillonius's look

went to the Pallas Athene face of the seeress. No expression relieved the coldness of its lines when she nodded. But Dahilis, even in this moment, flashed him an impish grin and jerked a thumb upwards.

'Aye, this is no place to reveal a mystery,' said Bodilis in Ysan. 'The Power reaches beyond speech. Let us go on with the business of our assembly. At eventide Forsquilis can show the King what she chooses.'

A mollified Soren agreed: 'Very well. Shall we stipulate that the Empire is again at civil war? Since Maximus could not arrange to rally Armorica behind him as he has the Britannic legions, it is to his advantage that Armorica stay neutral while he campaigns east and south of it. Gratillonius's orders are to assure this. He may be right about it being best for Ys too, provided we do not provoke resentment in the Imperium, should Maximus fail. Let us discuss it, and then go on to ways and means.'

Gratillonius stood soldierly and helpless while debate began.

2

He could not guess what awaited him at the house of Forsquilis. They walked there in silence, unaccompanied, after the meeting dissolved. Dusk lay blue upon the world; the earliest stars trembled forth. From this high part of the city he could see over the battlemented bowl of night which it had become, to a mercury glimmer in the harbour basin and the vast sheening of Ocean beyond. Right and left gloomed the headlands; out on Cape Rach, fire burned atop the pharos, red, unrestful as a seeking eye. Air was cool, slightly sweetened by a lilac in a stone basin at her doorstep, and wholly quiet.

Lamplight spilled yellow across the paving as a manservant bowed the two inside. 'Dinner is ready, my lady and lord,' he said. Savoury odours confirmed it.

Forsquilis glanced at Gratillonius. He saw that her eyes were grey, like those of the Minerva – the Athene whom she so much resembled. No, he thought confusedly, that Goddess wears a helmet and carries a spear and shield. But what Gorgon's head may this woman bring forth, to turn men into stone?

Her Latin was fluent: 'I sent a messenger during the day, directing a repast be prepared. Does this please the King?'

He attempted a jest. 'Can't you read the answer in my mind?'

Her solemnity reproved him. 'No, unless by strong magic, which might not work; and without dire need, it would be no decent thing to do.'

Flushing, he gave his cloak to the servant, as she did hers, and they went directly to the triclinium. Atrium and corridor showed bucolic scenes that he suspected she had never bothered to have altered, nor had those who lived here before her, for they looked old. The dining room likewise was antique; but perhaps she found jarring whatever pattern was on the floor, since reed mats covered it. The furnishings were table and chairs, Ysans never having reclined at their meals. On a richly decorated cloth stood costly ware. He wondered if this was on his account and ordinarily Forsquilis ate austerely. Her slenderness suggested it.

He wondered, as well, just why she reverted to her mother tongue while they settled opposite each other: 'Difficult has today been for you. Shall we now take our ease and refresh ourselves?'

'You are . . . considerate,' he responded, deciding to stay with Latin. Why burden himself needlessly in a taut situation? 'I'll try. Though it has for certain been difficult. Pardon me if I can't put matters aside at once.'

It was not that the Council had, in the end, denied him support. It was that that had been considered, and finally given, almost as if he, the prefect, were a mere courier – at most, an ambassador: as if Ys were not subordinate to Rome but deciding independently that its interest lay in emerging to some degree from the secrecy it had kept around itself.

For the first time, he saw Forsquilis's lips curve upwards. 'Think you 'twas my fault? Well, in a way. But would you not have done the same if you could, for Rome?'

A servant in livery of black and gold brought bowls and towels for the washing of hands. Another poured unwatered wine, a third set forth appetizers, boiled shrimp, pickled eggplant, raw fish, sauce of garum and minced onion. They ate well in Ys who could afford it, not gluttonously but well.

Gratillonius lifted his beaker. Relief swept through him. 'Right! And there's no real conflict between us. I admit being, m-m, surprised. It's hard to believe you'd know what Maximus is doing before I myself have heard. I held back the information about his intentions because, frankly, I wanted the upper hand, if anything untoward happened. But you'd have got it as soon as I received whatever word he sends. He will be good for the Empire, and that means he'll be good for Ys.'

'We trust so, we of the Sisterhood. We called on the Three to give us the right king, and you are the one They brought.'

Gratillonius felt a shiver. He was of Rome, a soldier, a civilized and educated man. Maximus had ordered him here for excellent, logical reasons. He must not believe it had really been the work of alien Gods, and witches, and

– He might have dismissed the idea if Forsquilis had raved at him or made mystical passes or done anything but sit there, more and more fair to behold, talking quite evenly – No, not that either. In her tone, in her eyes, there went ghosting something else. He could imagine that she lived on the fringe of the Otherworld.

He snatched after ordinariness. 'Well, let's see if we can slack off as you propose. You've heard about me, but I know nothing about you. Tell me.'

Her look dwelt long and seriously upon him. 'Dahilis spoke true,' she murmured at last. 'You are a kindly man. You may well prove a second Hoel.' And then it was as if a shudder of her own went beneath the controlled exterior. 'Although the omens were obscure,' she whispered. 'But we live in such an age of breakup –'

He *would* not peer into those dim and lawless depths, not yet, not yet. He took a fragrant gulp and a pungent bite. They brought him back to the understandable earth. 'You were wife to Hoel?' he asked.

She nodded. 'The Sign came upon me when Quistilis died, a year before he did. I was fourteen. He was gentle. But I was bearing his child when he fell. What Colconor did, that caused me to lose it.'

A red lump on the floor or in the bed or the privy, that might have stirred for a minute, Gratillonius thought. Freezingly: She tells it in such calm, as if it happened to somebody else long ago. Her soul was withdrawn. Will it ever return?

'May I ask how old you are?' he said.

'Twenty winters.'

Dahilis was not much younger . . . 'You are wise beyond your years, Forsquilis.'

'I had nowhere else to go but into the arcane,' she told him quietly.

– She showed him a little after the meal, during which

they had discussed safe matters. (Not that that was dull; each had endlessness to talk about.) A curtained chamber, dark save for a lamp made out of a cat's skull, held within its weaving shadows a shelf of scrolls and codices, a female figurine in clay that she said was from ancestral Tyre, inscribed bones, herbs dried and bundled, flints that perhaps had been shaped by the Old Folk as some said or perhaps were thunderstones as others said . . . 'These things are not needful in themselves, Gratillonius.' Her eyes glistened huge in the murk. 'They are but teachers and helps. As I wait entranced, my spirit fares forth. It is a power that once belonged to every Queen. But in this age when the very Gods are troubled and faltering, it has only come to me. Do you remember an owl, of the great sort called eagle owl, at midnight above a glade in Armorica – ?'

– In the bedroom she said gravely, 'Let us hallow ourselves, Belisama be with us.' When she unwound her headdress, he saw that her hair was golden-brown. When she let her gown fall, he saw that she was shapely.

The Bull arose. Fleetingly he remembered Dahilis. But this would be her wish.

All at once Forsquilis laughed aloud and pointed. 'Oh, but the Goddess has been generous!'

Ugliness stabbed: how could she tell? She had known just Hoel and Colconor, had she not? Maybe, during the reign of the beast King, maybe her Sending had prowled into homes more happy?

No. He would not think further. He could not. The Bull was in him, the Bull was he.

Astonishment followed. With Dahilis he had gone slowly at first, soothing her fears, finding his way towards what pleased her. He had looked for this Athene to be likewise, if she did not simply lie there and accept. But

201

she was hastily up against him, her hands seeking and urging. When he laid her down and entered her she yowled. In the morning he recalled the changeableness and unknown depths of the sea. His back was clawed red.

XI

1

A light rain turned the world cool and horizonless on the afternoon when Gratillonius came to call on Bodilis. She admitted him herself. 'Welcome, lord King.' Her tone and her smile made him believe she meant it.

Entering, he threw back the cowl of his cloak and undid the brooch. Beneath, he wore everyday Ysan garb lately tailored for him. Raindrops sparkled in the auburn curls of the beard he was growing. It still itched sometimes, but he had decided he should show his people every sign he could of his oneness with them. 'I am sorry – ' he began.

'O-oh, mother! Is *he* the King?' An eight-year-old girl darted from a doorway, tawny locks flying about an elven countenance.

'Now, Semuramat, bow like a proper lady,' Bodilis said. Although warmth pulsed in her voice, the child obeyed at once, whereafter she stood staring out of enormous eyes.

'Greeting,' the man said in Ysan. 'I am . . . in truth your new stepfather. For this is your mother, is she not? What is your name?'

'S-s-semuramat,' the girl whispered. 'My lord.'

He saw her tremble. The Queens had kept their daughters away from Colconor as much as possible, which became nearly all the time; but there would have been an aura of hatred and terror. 'Be not afraid, Semuramat,' Gratillonius urged. 'I expect we shall be happy together. Hm. Do you like horses?' She nodded twice and thrice.

'Well, suppose you come for a ride on my saddlebow as soon as I have a free hour, and we'll get to know each other. Afterwards we may perchance look into finding you a pony.'

Bodilis laughed. 'Don't overwhelm the poor creature!'

'I'd fain be the friend of this household,' he replied earnestly. 'As I was about to say, I'm sorry to have let seven days go by since the Council, ere sending word I would visit you now if you desired. You may have heard how I've been at work, getting to know the city's defences above all. Three of those days I wasn't even in town, but riding around the hinterland on inspection. At night I'd fall asleep as if into a well.' Alone. Not that purely male companionship and concerns were unwelcome, however much he missed Dahilis.

'Go back to your work, dear,' Bodilis directed. When Semuramat had pattered off, she explained to Gratillonius, who was hanging his cloak on a peg: 'My servants are presently out to fetch what's needful for a worthy supper. I've ever made my daughters help in the house. Princesses should have skills too.'

'And discipline, of a loving sort,' he approved.

She regarded him for some while before murmuring, 'So you understand that also. Few are the men who'd show your regard for a woman's feelings. Oh, mine were never hurt; well did I see why you must stay absent. Yet it gladdens me what you have revealed of yourself.'

The compliment made Gratillonius flush. He had been returning her look with pleasure. She was simply clad, in a grey-blue gown with silver stars embroidered on the neckline and sleeves. A belt of crimson mesh snugged the cloth around fullness of bosom, hip, and thigh. He admired the strong bones in her face, and her eyes were like those of Dahilis, her half-sister. There seemed to be no tensing, no qualms in her. She took his hand as naturally as if they had been man and wife for years. 'Come,' she said, 'let us talk.'

They passed from the entryroom to the atrium. He saw that, while its floor was antique Roman, the frescos were not. Their colours bright and fresh, they depicted a vividness of dolphins in waves, sea birds skimming overhead. The style was not quite representational; elongated lines and curves hinted at more than this world knew. Seeing him notice, she said with a touch of diffidence, 'Mayhap I should not have covered up the old art. I did first copy it on to vellum, that future generations may have a record. But it was tedious stuff. Whoever inherits this house from me can get rid of mine if she dislikes it.'

'What?' he exclaimed. 'You painted it yourself?'

'I dabble at things. But come onwards. 'Twould be most honorific to receive you in this chamber, but 'twill be more – real – if we seek to my scriptorium.' Bodilis laughed. 'Besides, Semuramat is not allowed there, not till she grows older and more careful. She's a darling, but she'd pester the life out of us.'

'I gather you've other daughters.'

Bodilis nodded. 'Two. They are both wild to meet you, of course. But Talavair is standing vigil at the Nymphaeum, and Kerna is at her studies in the temple. She'll be home for supper.'

'The girls are . . . Hoel's?'

'All three. The Sign came upon me in Lugaid's reign, but he fell almost immediately afterwards. Talavair will finish her vestal term this year. She has a young man picked out for herself. A year hence, I may well be a grandmother!'

'What of – Kerna, is that her name?'

'Oh, she's just fifteen, and studious. She intends to renew her vows at age eighteen and become a minor priestess. Not that that debars marriage. However, most men are reluctant to take a wife whose duties will often have her away from home. Former vestals who enter the priestesshood most commonly do so after having been widowed.'

They had left the atrium and gone down a hallway beyond. The layout of this house was similar though not identical to that of Dahilis's or Forsquilis's, and unlike the usual Roman. Bodilis opened a door and led Gratillonius through. He found a room nearly as spacious; later she would explain that she had had the wall removed between two former bedchambers. Lamps of a shape as graceful as her gait brightened the dullness that today seeped through windowpanes. One burned on a table, beneath a legged small pot that it kept warm. The oil was olive, nearly odourless. Flagons of wine and water stood beside it, glass goblets and earthenware cups, a plateful of titbits. Shelves around the walls held scrolls, codices, the portrait bust of a woman solemn and beautiful, ivory and bone miniatures of fleet animals. A much larger table filled the far end of the room. Writing materials littered it, open books, brushes and paints, botanical specimens, shells, rocks, a flute, a cat asleep in the middle of everything.

'Pray be seated,' Bodilis said. 'Would you thin your wine according to your taste?'

'What's in the pot?'

'An herbal infusion. I seldom drink wine save at supper, and then little.' Bodilis smiled. 'I fear you'll find me drab company.'

'Contrariwise, I think.' They took chairs. 'I'm no heavy drinker myself, most times. May I try a cup of your brew?'

The tisane was fragrant and sweet-acrid, good on a chilly day like this. 'I heard aright; you are a scholar,' he remarked.

'Well, I enjoy learning things. Also out in the open – I love to ramble about the countryside or go forth in a boat

– but nearsightedness does somewhat hinder me there.'

'You seem at work on something literary.'

'Translating the *Agamemnon* into Ysan. A pity that scarce any of us today read Greek, but better my poor words than no Aeschylus at all.'

'How did you learn?'

'I taught myself, from a textbook and lexicon I had sent me. Eucherius, the Christian minister, gave me more instruction, and corrected my pronunciation. They still use Greek where he hails from in Italia.' She grew quietly ardent. 'Oh, Gratillonius, you have so much to tell too! What the folk of Britannia are like, their tales and songs and – For me 'tis twice wonderful that you are come.'

He dropped his glance downwards, into his cup, as if to seek an omen in its murkiness. 'I think you will be mainly the teacher,' he murmured. 'The Ysan language – '

'Already you handle it rather well. I might be able to help with vocabulary. We make much use of synonyms, for example.'

'And the history, the lore, everything below the surface. That is why I – I wanted to visit you first.'

'Ask me what you will,' she sighed, 'but remember I lack the wisdom of Quinipilis, the forcefulness of Vindilis, the witchcraft of Forsquilis, the charm of – Well, I'll try my best.'

He heard pain in her voice, raised his eyes, and saw lines at the corners of her mouth, as if she struggled not to show what she felt. It came to him: I'm a blundering ass. She thinks I don't see anything in her but her mind. I never meant that. Jupiter thunder me, no! But if I instantly say she's lovely, she may suppose I'm only snorting after yet another new female body.

He groped his way forward. 'Ah, let's talk a while like ordinary human beings. I want to know you, Bodilis. Tell me of your life.'

She shrugged. 'Naught to tell. 'Tis been well-nigh eventless.'

He guessed that, of the Nine, she had had the most resources, the broadest reaches of escape for her spirit, during Colconor. He did not care to think about it. Instead – He tugged his chin. The whiskers were still too short, but he oughtn't scratch his face. Slowly, he said, 'You remarked on your middle daughter's wish to remain with the temple after she's free to leave. Was that yours too, when you were a girl?'

The glance she gave him was startled. Then, inch by inch, she leaned back, smiled on him, finally found words. 'Aye. The Sign did come upon me when I was the age that is Kerna's now; but ever had I been a child moody and solitary.'

'Was that because of . . . the circumstances of your birth?'

Again she regarded him closely for a spell. 'Gratillonius,' she breathed at length, 'you are a remarkable man. You truly are.'

'Nay,' he tried to laugh, ''tis but that a military officer must needs gain some skill in guessing about people.' He sobered. 'Would you liefer not talk of this? I shan't press you.'

She reached to stroke his hand. 'Why should I hang back? Dahilis must have told you things, and . . . and if the Gods are willing, we will be together, you and the Sisterhood, for many years.' Her look drifted off and came to harbour at the bust. 'You know my father Wulfgar begot me on his daughter Tambilis. It was the will of Belisama, no sin among the Gallicenae, but I am told he fell to brooding, and within a year lay dead at the hands of Gaetulius. Certain it is that this left a shadow on my mother, who did not regain gladness until Hoel came. By him she had Dahilis-to-be, you recall. But hers had been a sombre house for me to grow up in. I fled into my books and my walks and – all you see around you. My wish was to become a minor priestess, for life.'

'Instead you became a Queen,' he said low.

She coloured. 'Hoel made me, too, happy. Not that his was any great intellect. He confessed I could bewilder him. But he was gutsy and kind and well knew how to make a girl purr. And his friends, his visitors, how they could talk of marvellous things and mighty deeds! He loved to invite foreigners to the palace; they blew in like winds off the sea. Later I began to frequent Star House –'

She broke off, snapped after air, finished bleakly: 'Under Colconor, the Symposium kept my soul alive.'

'Oh, my dear!' he said in pity.

She shook herself, confronted him, and retorted, 'I ask for no balm, Gaius Valerius Gratillonius. My life has been better than most on this earth, despite everything.' Her tone softened. 'And now you are King.'

Silence fell. He drained his cup and filled a goblet with wine, undiluted. Once more she looked away from him. Blood went in and out of the cheek he saw, like drumbeats. He knew what she was thinking of, and surely she knew that he did.

He cleared his throat. 'Well. I see. Um-m . . . whose is yonder bust?'

'Why, Brennilis.' Her relief was plain to hear. 'Brennilis of the Vision, Brennilis of the Veil. 'Tis uncertain whether the portrait was done in her time or is imaginative, but I like to believe this is indeed how she appeared.'

'Who was she?'

'You know not?'

'I am an ignoramus, remember.'

'Well, then,' she said cheerfully, 'what better way to

209

pass the hours ere we dine than for me to relate a little of
the history of Ys?'

2

The oldest records were fragmentary, but tradition held
that the site was discovered by Himilco when he came
exploring up from Carthage some eight and a half centuries agone. Returning, he recommended that a colony be
founded there. What Carthage required was a way station
and naval base for its trade with the far North. Britannic
tin, Gallic furs, German amber, honey, hides, tallow,
timber, walrus and narwhal ivory, together with the
Southern goods which paid for them, needed protection
as well as transport.

No mere outpost could long be maintained at such a
remove. Hence it must be a town, capable of feeding and
defending itself. Since few of the then prosperous Phoen-
icians were willing to leave home, they recruited widely
about the Mediterranean lands. Prominent among those
who immigrated in the early decades were Babylonians
fleeing the Persians who conquered and destroyed their
city, and Egyptians resentful of Persian rule.

Legend said that when Himilco was first investigating
the region, men of his were slain in their camp every
night. At last he tracked down the monster that was doing
this thing, and the sailors put an end to it. The creature
had laired in a passage grave. The Old Folk whose bones
lay there, grateful to be at peace again, promised that
settlement here should flourish as long as the dwellers
were likewise at peace with the Gods; but if ever there
was a falling out, the sea would reclaim its own.

Perhaps because of this, the city was consecrated to

Ishtar, for She was powerful over all the elements and was the Star of the Sea. Soon afterwards the mixed colonists identified Her with Isis and established an order of priestesses to serve Her.

Otherwise the community was subject to Carthage, though at its distance this was nominal, amounting to little more than a governor from the motherland. As it grew and enlarged its own trade, wealthy men began to chafe under even so light a yoke.

More or less at the same time as the founding of the city, the Celts had arrived, overrunning the aboriginal population and intermingling with it to produce the Gauls. The aristocrats of the new tribes were generally descended from the invaders. It was natural for the city to make alliance with neighbour natives against further newcomers. Wars and raids had harmed those nearby folk enough that they were willing to accept Punic leadership.

By now the name 'Beth-Ishtar' or 'Beth-Isis' had become shortened to 'Ys'.

The city was often endangered, more than once besieged. Yet, supplying itself by sea, it outwaited the enemy Celts, who never were very good at sitting still. Water was the worst problem, a fact that may have enhanced the sacredness of its sources in the minds of the people – although the Gauls venerated springs and streams too. The constant need for fighters and workers, in a commonalty still small, bred repugnance for the practice of sacrificing children to Baal Melqart, and eventually its discontinuance. However, prophecy and tradition agreed that from time to time some great blood offering must be made the Gods.

Gradually warfare eased off. While rivalry with the seagoing Veneti remained strong and occasionally flared into battle, Ys developed ties to the Osismii, as that mingled breed of Old Folk and Celts called themselves.

Intermarriage became frequent, deities were identified with each other, rites and institutions conjoined, the very language of the city Gallicized.

In Ys the Triad became paramount among Gods. Ishtar-Isis most often bore the name Belisama, which meant 'the Brightest One'. Melqart assumed the name and attributes of the Celtic sky God Taranis. Lir, Whose cult was more ancient than colony or tribe, took unto Himself the awe and dread of the sea.

These evolutions were not barbarizations. They went hand in glove with political changes. Increasingly occupied against Rome, Mother Carthage gave Ys ever less consideration. Finally the magnates expelled the governor and established a Council of Suffetes on the Phoenician model. For the head of state, they took from various Gauls the idea of the King of the Wood – who was ordinarily no more than a figurehead, and whose death in battle replaced the former sacrifice of children.

The Sisterhood of the Nine grew from both Punic and Celtic roots. It was recruited from among the daughters and granddaughters of Queens, albeit most of the latter were born to ordinary men. Such a girl took holy orders at age seven and served as a vestal until age eighteen. She generally lived at home, but went to temple school and, when old enough, spent days and nights on end in religious duties within the city or at the Nymphaeum. At the close of her term, she was free to do whatever she liked – unless first the Sign had appeared on her and she had been wedded to the King and enrolled in the Gallicenae. After the third generation a given line of female descent was released from all obligation, for then the blood of Incarnate Taranis was thinned down to mere humanness.

If she chose, upon completion of her vestalhood a princess could renew her vows, or at any later time, and become a minor priestess. The temple would also accept other volunteers who qualified, train them, advance them according to what abilities they showed; but of course no such outsider would ever become a Queen.

Ys looked upon vestalhood as a divine privilege. It had its worldly benefits as well. Besides an excellent education, a maiden received a generous stipend. On going into civil life she got additional gold and goods, as a dowry for herself or investment capital if she did not elect marriage. The temple could well afford that, for much of the wealth of the state flowed into it from holdings, offerings, and bequests.

Ysan commerce waxed. The city commanded only meagre natural resources, other than what it wrested from the waters, but skilled workers turned imported raw materials into wares that, exported, won high prices. Merchantmen on charter and adventurers among the barbarians brought in wealth of their own. When Rome finally sowed salt where Carthage had been, it made no large difference to Ys . . . although some folk wept.

For a hundred or more years afterwards, the city prospered. It had no imperial ambitions; it was content with its modest hinterland and outlying island of Sena. Nor did it need more than a small, efficient navy, chiefly for convoy and rescue duty – when its Gallicenae could raise a storm at will. Its ship went trading and freighting throughout the North; likewise throve its manufactures, brokerages, entrepots; and its poets, artists, dreamers, magicians.

Yet the sea at whose bosom it lay was ever rising . . .

The Veneti had always been troublesome. When Julius Caesar came conquering, Ys gave him substantial help against them. When he had crushed and decimated those foes, he visited the city in person.

What happened then would be hidden from the future.

Brennilis of the Gallicenae had had a vision while in a prophetic trance, and somehow she prevailed upon the tough and sceptical Roman. He actually appointed a soldier to slay the King of the Wood and succeed in that office – a young favourite of his, thus a sacrifice on the part of them both. Other things which were done required eternal silence: for Belisama had revealed that a new age was come to Ys. Archivists of the city believed that this was why Caesar made no mention of it in his writings.

The upshot was that Ys became a foederate of Rome, paid a reasonable tribute, accepted a prefect and his staff, enjoyed the benefits of the Roman peace and otherwise continued its wonted life.

To be sure, as Armorica was Romanized, there were effects upon this city too. On the whole they were benign. Indeed, Rome saved Ys from destruction. The Vision of Brennilis warned that sea level would mount and mount until waves rolled over everything here, were measures not taken. As defensible as it was between its headlands, this site ought not to be abandoned; but already people were moving to higher ground.

From the time of her revelation, onwards through her long life, Brennilis was the effective ruler of Ys. In her old age she won for her people the help of Augustus Caesar. To her he sent his best engineers, that they erect a wall against the waters. They did much else while they were there, but the wall and the gate were their real accomplishment, for which the city gave them a triumph.

That labour did not go easily. Besides the sea to contend with, they had the folk. The Romans thought it ridiculous that the wall be built as high as Brennilis demanded; they did not live to see tides eventually surge where she had foretold. Nor could they understand why they must not use enduring concrete. They insisted on it, and not until storms had repeatedly wrecked their work and snatched lives from among them did they yield. True, they then wrought honestly, in dry-laid blocks of stone so well shaped and fitted that a knife could not slip between. But they never understood why.

Brennilis and her Sisters did. In her Vision, Lir had told her that Ys must remain hostage to Him, lest it forsake its Gods in the eldritch days to come. He would only allow a wall that He could, at need, break down, for the drowning of a city gone faithless.

The gate was no defiance of this; Ys required one if it would receive ships as of yore. Sealed in copper, oak endured for many a decade. Sometimes the doors must be replaced – machinery and multitudinous workers doing it in a few hours of the lowest tide and deadest calm, followed by three days and nights of festival – but the necessity came seldom, and Ys abided.

Yet also, as lifetimes passed, it drew ever more behind the Veil of Brennilis. This too had been part of her apocalypse, that the Gods of Ys were haughty and aloof, that They would not demean Themselves to plead for worshippers against a new God Who was to come, but would, rather, hold Their city apart unto Themselves. For all its splendour and prosperity, Ys grew obscure. Chronicles which described it gradually crumbled away without fresh copies having been made, burned in accidental fires, were misplaced, were stolen and never recovered, were scraped clean so that the vellum might be reused for a Gospel. Curiously few Roman writers ever referred to it; and of those who did, their works had a similar way of becoming lost.

A part of this may simply have been due to regained autonomy, as Roman commerce and government began to fall apart. Longer and longer grew the periods during which the Emperors saw no reason to send a prefect; at last, none came. Payment of the tribute was more and more often delayed by bad communications; at last, Septimius Severus remitted it altogether, in thanks for help the city had given him against his rival Albinus. That was the final intervention of any consequence that Ys had made. Thereafter it looked to its own.

But it was not totally isolated. The storms that racked the Empire inevitably troubled Ys as well. Trade shrank, Scotic and Saxon raiders harried the waters and the coasts, inland barbarians pressed westwards, evangelists of Christ led men away from the Gods of their fathers. Among the Gallicenae arose a feeling that they had come to the end of still another age. What would the new one bring? None could foreknow. Like a creature of the sea, Ys drew into its shell and waited.

3

By candlelight in the bedroom. Bodilis showed no mark of being past her youth, save for maturity itself. Smiling, she went to Gratillonius. 'How can I best make you welcome?' asked her husky voice.

She responded to him, in movement of loins and hands, in soft outcries; but always there was something about her that cared more for him than for herself; and before they slept, she murmured in his ear, 'I pray the Goddess that I be not too old for bearing of your child.'

XII

1

Suddenly fog blew out of the west. Then wind died while cloud thickened. *Osprey* rolled to the swell, the eyes painted on her bows as blindfolded as eyes in the skulls of the men aboard her. Barely did sight reach from stem to stern, and the masthead swayed hidden. It was as if that formless grey also swallowed sound. There was nothing to hear but slap of waves on strakes, slosh in a well where the live part of the catch swam uneasily about, creak of timbers and lines and of the sweeps where crew toiled – and dim and hollow, at unknown distances and in unsure directions, those boomings which betokened surf over the rocks around Sena.

Maeloch drew his hooded leather jacket tighter. Leaving the prow of his fishing smack he went aft, past the four starboard oarsmen. Sheeted fast, the lugsail slatted to the rocking. Despite chill, air was too dank for breath to show. As Maeloch neared, the helmsman slowly changed from a phantom to a mortal like himself, beard as wet as the sail, leathery face stiffened by weariness.

'How fare ye?' Maeloch asked. 'Need ye a relief?'

Usun, his mate, shrugged. 'Not so much as the deckhands. Might be one o' them and me should spell each other.'

'Nay. While we keep sea room, their task is but to maintain steerage way. Should we find ourselves drifting on to a skerry or into a snag, aye, they'd better row their guts out. But worse will we need an alert steersman. My thought was ye might want to change with me and go stand lookout for'ard.'

Usun sagged a little over the tiller. 'If ye, who captain us through this passage on those nights, if ye be lost – '

'Who'd not be, as long as we've wallowed in this swill?' Maeloch snapped. 'Would Lir fain destroy us, why couldn't He ha' sent an honest gale?'

'Ha' ye gone mad?' Usun exclaimed, shocked. 'Best we join in vowing Him a sacrifice if He spare us.'

'He got His usual cock ere we set forth.'

'I – I've promised Epona – '

'As ye wish.' Maeloch's rough countenance jutted on high. 'Myself, I'll deal with the Gods like my fathers before me, straightforwardly or not at all.'

Usun drew back. Ever were the Ferriers of the Dead an arrogant lot, not only because they enjoyed exemption from tax and civic labour but because – the source of their privileges – they met the unknown, on behalf of Ys. But Usun, who was himself along on such crossings, had not thought the captain's pride would go this far.

Maeloch filled his lungs and shouted: 'D'Ye hear me, out there? Ahoy! Here I stand. Drown me if Ye will. But remember, my eldest living son is a stripling. 'Twill be years till he can help bring Ye your wayfarers. Think well, O Gods!'

The fog drank down his cry. Louder snarled the surf, and now there was in it a hiss of waves as they rushed across naked rock. Two crewmen missed a beat. The vessel yawed. Usun put the steering oar hard over. His own lips moved, but silently.

Something passed alongside. A splash resounded. Maeloch trod to the rail and peered downwards. Foam swirled on darkling water. Amidst it swam a seal. Twice and thrice it smote with its rear flippers. The front pair kept it

218

near the hull. It raised its head. Great eyes, full of night, sought towards Maeloch's.

For heartbeats, the skipper stood moveless. Finally Usun saw a shiver pass through him too. He turned about and said, well-nigh too quietly for hearing: 'Stand by to give what helm I call for.'

But striding off, Maeloch trumpeted: 'Pull oars! Full stroke! We're going home!' The seal glided beneath and beside him.

When he reached the bows, the creature swam on ahead, until he could barely see it through the swirling grey. Once it glanced back at him and made a leap. Thereafter it started off on the larboard quarter.

'Right helm!' Maeloch roared. 'Stroke, stroke, stroke! Give it your backs, ye scoundrels, if e'er ye'd carouse ashore again!'

Dread was upon the men, they knew not what this portended, nor knew what to do save obey. To and fro they swayed on their benches. Their breath loudened. Sweeps groaned at the tholes, throbbed in the waves. 'Steady as she goes,' Maeloch ordered. The seal swam on.

Surf crashed to starboard. On the edge of sight, a reef grinned. Yet *Osprey* had clearance enough. 'Might that be the She-Wolf?' Maeloch muttered. 'If 'tis, we've tricky navigation before us.' The seal veered. 'Left helm! . . . Steady as she goes.'

Stroke, stroke, stroke. The waters bawled, seethed, sank away and sighed.

– The sun must have been low when the mainland hove in view, shadowy at first, later real, solid, the southside cliffs of Cape Rach. Men dared utter a ragged cheer. With their last strength they brought the battered and tarry boat into her home cove and laid her to at Ghost Quay. Oars clattered inboard. Feet thudded on close-packed stone as sailors climbed on to the dock, caught mooring lines, and made fast to iron rings set in boulders. The hull rolled, rubbing against rope bumpers hung on a log secured to the wharf.

At the stempost Maeloch slowly lifted his hand, waved, let the arm drop again and watched the seal depart.

Usun sought him. A while they stood in silence. Fog seemed thicker still, or was it only that night drew near? They could make out a pair of companion smacks at the quay, rowboats drawn on to a strand which had become cobble-hemmed and tiny at high tide, nets across poles. A track wound up the steeps, to join roads towards the pharos and Ys. A second trail went under the scarp. At its end, a deeper dimness showed where those few rammed-earth cottages were that bore the name Scot's Landing. A hush had fallen. Cold gnawed in through garments and flesh.

'Ye men'll sleep aboard,' Maeloch said at length. 'We've our catch to prepare for market in the morning, ye know.' Only he and Usun among them dwelt here, where some were boatowners like him and all were haughty – however poor – and a little strange, concerned less with affairs of the Fisher Brotherhood and the city than with things that were their own. 'But I'll dispatch boys to tell your kin ye came back safe.'

'How did we?' one sailor whispered.

'I know not.'

'You . . . a Ferrier of the Dead . . . know not?'

'What I do those nights is a mystery to me too,' Maeloch answered starkly. 'Ye've heard what folk tell, that Gallicenae who've died may return in the shape o' seals, abiding till those they loved ha' fared out to Sena. No dream has told me if this be so or not. But when yon swimmer appeared, I had a feeling we should follow her.

'Goodnight.'

He left the craft and trudged towards his home. There

his wife Betha kept vigil, among their living children and the babe that was great within her. For his sake she was invoking Belisama, Our Lady of the Sea – and, silently or by secret tokens, beings about whom the fisher women never told their men.

2

The day was bright when Innilis came to the house of Vindilis; but within lay dimness and quiet. 'Welcome,' said the older Queen, with a smile such as was rarely seen on her gaunt countenance. She took both hands of Innilis in her own. To the servant who had admitted the visitor: 'We twain have matters of discretion before us. Let none disturb.'

The servant bowed. 'Never, my lady.' This was not the first time he had been so commanded. As half-sisters, both daughters of Gaetulius, unlike though they were in aspect, this pair might be expected to cherish one another. In any event, it was not for him to question what the Nine did, or even wonder.

Vindilis led the way. Innilis must hurry to match her strides. They passed through the atrium. Like Bodilis, Vindilis had had the walls of hers painted over; but these now bore only spirals and Greek keys, black on white.

Beyond was what she called her counsel chamber. Light fell greenish through leaded panes to reveal mostly bareness: a table, a few chairs, a broad and backless couch upholstered in red. A niche held a statuette of Belisama. On a shelf below it were a lamp and an offering of evergreen. Refreshments waited on the table.

Innilis bowed to the shrine and signed herself. After a moment, Vindilis did likewise. The image had nothing about it of serenity. Rather, it showed the Goddess spear in hand, dress and unbound hair flying, astride a night wind like a stream or a snake – Her persona as the Wild Huntress, leading through the air the spirits of women who died in childbed.

Vindilis turned to Innilis, laid hands on her shoulders, kissed her on the lips. 'How went it?' she asked, more softly than was her wont.

'Oh – I – ' Innilis looked away. Her fingers, fragile as reeds, twisted together. 'He was not unkind. Not knowingly.' In haste: 'I'm sorry to arrive this late. Three people begged my help at the same time.'

'You could not well refuse, if you had no duties more urgent,' said Vindilis. 'Nor would you ever. Be seated. Here, let me pour you some wine. 'Tis that sweet Narbonensian you like.' As she bent to pick up the flagon, light sheened on the silver streak in her hair and the raven coils around it. 'What were their needs, those people? Illness?'

'For two.' Innilis settled herself. 'One is a man I've seen erenow. His dropsy was coming back. I gave him foxglove; that helps. But, poor soul, he has scant strength any more to earn his living. I think soon the temple must consider him and his family deserving of aid.'

'You may be too tender-hearted, as often erstwhile.' Vindilis sat down opposite her guest. 'Go on. You need talk for easing of your mind. Let me be your physician and prescribe it.'

Innilis shook her head, drank unsteadily, and replied: 'The second was the worst. A girl with a raging fever, none knew why, least of all myself. I could but give her tisane of willow bark, for cooling of her poor little body, and invoke the Mother.'

'If any of us can heal any longer by the Power of the Touch, 'tis you, Innilis. You She still heeds. As well She might.'

222

The younger priestess reddened. 'I am not worthy. Yet I pray that She will . . . The third was an old man on his deathbed. He wanted a blessing.'

'*Your* blessing.'

'Oh, but 'tis only a rite of comfort.'

'That is just why 'tis best coming from the one of us whom everybody loves.'

'I . . . I spent a while more at his bedside. That is what really delayed me. I had my harp along, and gave him some songs he liked. If only my voice were better.' Innilis's was high and thin.

Vindilis regarded her for a spell that lengthened, her own chin cupped between hands. After fourteen years of consecration, Innilis hardly seemed changed from the thirteen-year-old girl on whom the sign had appeared in the reign of Hoel – not even by the daughter she had borne him. Short, slight, ivory-skinned, lips always parted beneath a tip-tilted nose, eyes large and blue, she let her hair flow freely, a light-brown cascade down her back, like a commoner maiden, save when occasion demanded she dress it. Her gown today was glowing saffron, but jewellery lay nowhere on her.

Vindilis, clad in silver-accented black with a Gorgon's-head pendant, lifted goblet. 'Drink again, darling. I know 'twill not be easy for you to tell me about yesterday.'

Innilis's lashes fluttered wildly. Red and white pursued each other above the fine bones. 'There is, is naught to tell,' she stammered. 'I said he . . . was courteous, told me he re-re-regretted he'd not been able sooner to . . . pay me his respects, and – ' Her words trailed off.

'What further?' Vindilis asked sharply.

Innilis spread her hands, a gesture of helplessness. 'What could there be? What know I to talk about with a man? We both tried, but long silences kept falling, until supper came as a release. Then he suggested – What

223

better had we to do? I told you he meant well.'

Vindilis sighed, considered, abruptly set her vessel down hard and inquired, 'Should I tell you first about my time?'

Innilis nodded, mute, staring down at the tabletop.

Vindilis leaned back, crossed her legs, frowned into space, crooked a finger as if summoning memory to report in full. Her tone was impersonal:

'Well, he arrived at the hour agreed, mid-afternoon. That was earlier than with you, but we knew we had much to discuss. He'd taken the trouble to ask about me beforehand, and actually said he was sorry I'd dismissed Runa for the day; said he looked forward to meeting another daughter of Hoel, who must have been a good father. And he said he'd got a feeling that Quinipilis paid me less heed when I was a child than she did her older girl – since Karilis-to-be was by Wulfgar, whom she liked, and I by Gaetulius whom she did not care for – and Gratillonius wondered if this was why I was reckless and rebellious in my school days. But when he saw his prying was offensive to me, he stopped, and after that our discourse became intelligent.

'He started by asking what we priestesses, both high and minor, *do*, other than conduct our rites and the affairs of our temple corporation. Naught boorish in that question; he begged pardon for his ignorance and said he hoped to remedy it. So I talked of counselling the troubled, healing the sick, teaching the young, taking part in the public business day by day as well as when the council meets – everything, save that he sheered somewhat away from our spells, the thought of those making him uneasy. Ha, this may be a whip wherewith to chastise stout drayhorse Gratillonius, if he gets over-frisky!

'But now he was merely appealing for my help. Nay, wrong word. In soldierly wise, he put it to me that he and

224

I, all the Nine and their lesser Sisters, should work with him for the safety and well-being of Ys. That talk went on for hours. When at length we took a repast, neither of us noticed what we ate or drank. Yea, methinks I could come to like Gratillonius, as much as lies in me to like any man.'

Silence entered and pressed inwards. Finally Innilis breathed, 'Also after he – he spent the night?'

Vindilis laughed, with neither mirth nor bitterness. 'We went to bed, of course. I'd told him the Goddess would be angered were not the sacred marriage consummated, except with a Queen like my mother who's so old the moon no longer rules over her. He was taken aback, but then smiled a bit and said, "I carry out my orders." When he began to feel of me, I asked that he mount at once. He did. He took a time about it, as busy as he'd been with others, but wrought no harm, and was satisfied with the single doing. At least, he lay straight down to sleep. In the morning I told him men do not arouse me; Hoel tried often and failed, Colconor was disgusting. Gratillonius might do best to leave me in peace. Could we not be partners, aye, and friends? Dahilis, or anyone, would be welcome to all such honours due me. He laughed and kissed my hand. We parted amicably.'

Vindilis's brow darkened. 'Although,' she said in a harshened voice, 'I must needs conceal what I felt, knowing that the same evening he would seek you.'

Innilis lifted her gaze. 'Oh, but I told you he was kindly.' Her speech wavered.

'Once and no more, as with me?' pounced Vindilis.

'Nay – but – '

Vindilis sucked air in between her teeth. 'Ah, well might I have foreseen. 'Tis my fault, I should have taken more of his goatishness on myself . . . for you. Though you are too beautiful – '

225

'I, I never besought him. He might have stopped, but I never thought to ask. And he was so eager, and between times he looked at me so mildly, stroked me and murmured. I – it seemed not to matter that it had hurt.'

Vindilis reared in her seat. 'Badly?' she grated.

Innilis made fending motions. 'Nay, nay. Be not angry. Please. 'Twas but that he is big and I was, well, dry at first . . . and later, when I was not, I remembered how Hoel sometimes gave me some pleasure, and I thought mayhap Gratillonius – '

Vindilis rose, came around behind Innilis, stood smoothing the long brown tresses and crooning, 'Poor sweetheart, poor little sister-wife.' In Hoel they had shared a father for the child that each bore. 'You were very brave. Now rest, be at peace, be happy. 'Tis over and done with. Presently we'll find a way to take the burden off you too. He may well have been inflamed because you reminded him somewhat of Dahilis. And surely she will be our ally, whether she know it or not.'

Vindilis bent over to pass lips across Innilis's cheek. Her fingers plucked at the silken cord and amber button which closed the neck of Innilis's gown. The younger woman turned her head. Mouths met and lingered. In Colconor they had shared misery which brought them together.

Afterwards on the couch, Innilis said through tears, 'This *must* be right. The Mother *must* smile on us.'

'She has not cursed us, throughout these years, has She?' Vindilis replied drowsily. They had been over this ground before.

'Nay. She has kindled love in us.' Innilis clenched a fist. 'But oh, if only we need not keep it secret!'

Wind whooped above glittery waters, made sails dance, drove white pennons across a vast blue field. It stung tears from the eyes of Gratillonius when he squinted into it. Between that and the glare, he could just make out a low, dark streak in the west: Sena, where again today Dahilis stood her lonely watch.

'Uh, you were saying, sir?'

Eppillus's rusty voice recalled Gratillonius to himself. He grinned, half abashed. 'Pardon. My mind wandered.'

'Well, the centurion has a peck o' things to think about. And they don't sit still neither, do they? Wriggle around like worms, I'll bet.'

'The more reason to use this chance. Come.' The two men resumed their walk atop the wall. Passing the Gull Tower, where a sentry saluted, they went above the harbour basin towards the gate. 'The seaward defence is holding a practice. I wanted you to watch, and tell me what you think.'

On the bastions, rain shelters had been dismantled and removed. The war engines crouched amidst the men who served them, spaced at intervals, three bolt-shooting catapults to each great stone-throwing ballista. Gratillonius and his deputy stopped at the first they encountered, which was of the former sort. Light by comparison, it did not require the recoil-absorbing wall reinforcement of the latter kind, and was much easier and faster handled. 'Heed us not,' the King told the team officer. 'Get on with your business.'

'Aye, my lord,' said the Ysan. 'We're about to start. 'Twill go quicker for the following rounds, but skeins get slack in damp weather – as my lord knows, being a soldier.'

He called for winding. The men at the lever arms threw their weight into the work, twisting two vertical strands which, with the frame, flanked the trough. Meanwhile others were bringing ammunition and stacking it. 'Hold,' the officer ordered. The winders withdrew their levers from the sockets. Pawls clicked into notches. For a moment the wind alone gave tongue.

With a small hammer, the officer tapped the right skein. It sang, a deep bass note. Into the sinew and horsehair of which it was braided had been woven something resonant. Head cocked, the officer listened until the sound died away, before he struck the mate and heard it out. 'Hm,' he said, 'not quite balanced yet. Give this'n a half turn more and we'll try again.'

Equal tension was necessary so that the missile, when loosed, would not rub against the groove, and when free would fly straight. Eppillus whistled to behold such a method of gauging. Gratillonius smiled wryly. He would never command Ysan artillery. His ear was too poor; at home, his fellow centurions had requested him to refrain from singing in their presence.

Satisfied, the chief had the casting arms inserted in the skeins. The strong bowstring linking their opposite ends was to propel a slide which in turn pushed a long, iron-headed bolt down the groove. The machine had already been laid for elevation and direction. Now a windlass creaked, drawing the string back against the resistance of the skeins, until the slide engaged a locking mechanism at the base of the slotted beam. The chief undid skein pawls. 'Would my lord like to send the first shot?' he asked. 'Methinks 'twould bring us luck.'

Gratillonius nodded, stepped forward, pulled the trigger that released the engagement. The catapult whirred and thumped. The bolt sprang forth, nearly too fast to see.

Other engines had likewise begun to shoot. Their targets were several rafts anchored at varying distances. Boats rested nearby on their oars, bearing scorekeepers, eventually to haul rafts and spent missiles back. But the exercise would go on all day while tide ebbed and flowed. Afar, a naval galley stood by to warn off any merchantmen that might appear.

Eppillus's small eyes bulged with fascination. These designs and procedures had countless differences from the Roman. Gratillonius must nudge him twice to get his attention: 'Move that paunch of yours, you. We want to inspect every emplacement on this arc.'

They did, walking to the gate and back to the tower, where they descended. Thrum, shouts, horn signals rang in their ears till well after they had passed the temple of Lir. 'I don't think we need look the south side over,' Gratillonius decided. 'They're quite satisfactory, wouldn't you say?'

'I would. Oh, a funny style they've got, but I've seen Romans shoot worse. Naming no units, by your leave, sir. I'd say between their engines and their warships, they're plenty secure to seaward.'

Gratillonius frowned. 'That's a thing I want to talk over with you. We may have very little on hand in the way of navy, from time to time. Remember, our mission is to make sure not only of Ys, but this whole end of Armorica. That may call for a show of force at certain places. I'll send discreet letters to their officials as soon as I know what the situation is in the east, but those may not be enough. Meanwhile, what's keeping me busy is preparing for contingencies here.' His chuckle was rueful. 'Ysans can be as stubborn and slippery as any Imperials.'

Eppillus rubbed his bald spot. 'Hm, well, I'm no

seaman, o' course, but I'd still hate to row up at that artillery. And I suppose the city infantry would be on the wall too. Plus every civil mariner in town, eh? Not that a sailor who's never been on a parade ground would be worth too much if a real army hit him.'

They walked on by the ancient sanctum of Ishtar and through the mean streets of the Fishtail. Gratillonius had said he wanted to go by an obscure route, where he would less likely be recognized and detained by petitioners, gawkers, or Suffetes. Eppillus was the guide through this quarter. His familiarity with it amused Gratillonius – although doubtless the old roadpounder spent more tavern time gabbing about his past life than in gambling or wenching.

'That's the main business before us today. I've been dismayed at how little I've got to see of my own men. But with everything else besieging me – How are they doing?'

'Haven't your honour guards been smart, sir?'

'They have. And when I've asked them the same question, they say, "Fine, sir." What would you expect them to tell me under those circumstances? I'm counting on your honesty.'

Eppillus stroked the broken bridge of his nose. 'Well, we've had our problems, but they're mostly behind us and I needn't pester the centurion with 'em. Sitting around in barracks wasn't good for the boys. The centurion will understand. Now that we're busy again, not just drill but patrols and field exercises, why, they're shaping up fast. Give me another ten, twelve days and I'll have them back in crack condition.'

'Splendid!' Gratillonius felt it would do no harm if he slapped the burly shoulder beside him. 'We'll proceed to the royal palace and talk at length. I've things to tell you. Between us we can work out the right ways to use our troops. When we're done, I'll see to it that you go back to Dragon House with a bellyful of the best food and wine Ys has to offer. Which is plenty good, believe me.' For the sake of Roman prestige, Gratillonius had insisted that his deputy be lodged among the marine and naval officers.

'I know. Thank you, sir.' Eppillus gusted a sigh. 'Though I got to admit those fine things are kind of wasted on me. I'll settle for a stoup o' Dobunnic red, a roast o' pork, a heap o' cabbage, and a slice o' bread – fresh from the oven, if my wife was baking that day.'

'When you return home and retire to your bit of a farm, eh?'

'Mithras willing. I'll stick with the centurion till he leaves here. When will that be, sir?'

'Mithras knows. In two or three years, let us hope. The trick will be to stay alive till then.'

– At the palace, a stranger waited.

A Roman. A military courier. He bore the first communication Gratillonius had received, other than rumours out of the hinterland. It was a letter directly from Maximus.

4

When Forsquilis heard what the King wanted to speak of, she raised a palm. 'Nay, not here. Come with me to the secretorium.'

In her chamber where flamelight flickered through the eye sockets of a cat's skull, shadows made the small female image from Tyre seem to stir, herbs sharpened the air with their memories of wildwood, she sat down facing him. Her hands rested quietly on her lap, her visage bore the calm and pallor of Pallas, but the grey gaze was darkened in this dusk and stars of red fire-glow moved within it. 'Now say,' she commanded.

In his mind Gratillonius clung tight to the handfast world outside. 'Maximus reached Gallia on the day you declared. His legions have swept all resistance before them. Not that there was much. His opposition had little more to set against them than poorly trained auxiliaries. Some legionary units did arrive, hastily called from the eastern frontier or out of Hispania, in time to give battle – but of those, whole cohorts went over to the eagles of Maximus. He writes that he was in danger of outrunning his supply train, and this was among the reasons he had no chance to dictate a message earlier. Flavius Gratianus, co-Emperor, was in Lutetia Parisiorum. Maximus marched on that city. When he got there, the garrison rebelled and forswore Gratianus. Maximus entered without hindrance. Gratianus had fled. Maximus is – was – making ready to pursue, defeat him decisively, lay grip on the whole of Gallia and Hispania.'

'What will he have you do?' she asked low and tonelessly.

'Oh, I'm to send back a report by his courier, continue in my mission, keep him informed. We'll soon have a new and better Augustus, Forsquilis.'

'And what will you have me do?'

'I think you know already.' Gratillonius must moisten his lips. His armpits were wet enough. 'Ys looks well prepared. Aye, not only to defend herself but to carry out the task Rome has given her. Yet . . .'tis unforeseeable what may happen. The Empire is in turmoil. Its legions guarding Britannia and the East are stripped to the bone. Beyond the frontiers prowl wolves.'

'You said we can stand off attack. Not that I think any barbarians would be so mad as to try.'

'But Rome, Rome –'

'Ah.' Forsquilis sat quite still. Misshapen glooms danced in silence. At last: 'You ask that the owl fly forth again.'

'Aye.'

'And, if need be, the Nine take a hand, seek to order the tides of time.'

He mustered courage. 'You did it with me.'

'That was for Ys,' she answered sternly.

'If Rome falls, can Ys long endure?' he pleaded. 'Bethink you how alone she will stand, while darkness deepens and the sea rises higher.'

She was mute another while.

'This is a strange thing you seek,' she then said, like one who talks in her sleep. 'But these are strange years. I must think. Later I must meet with my Sisters. I will call you here when we have decided.' Her eyes came back to him and focused. 'Go.'

He left. Not until he was outdoors did he let himself tremble.

5

The temple of Taranis was a majestic edifice on the west-northwest edge of the Forum – Roman-built on the colonnaded Roman model, save that it enclosed an open courtyard, its temenos. Only the south wing of the building was given over to worship. The rest held offices, treasury, a hall with sumptuous kitchen nearby for the sacred banquets of the seasons, and a conference room for the Speaker.

There Soren Cartagi privately received Queen Lanarvilis. On the wall behind his chair of state, under an inlaid Sun Wheel, hung weapons of war, surrounding a gold-trimmed Hammer. On the wall to his right a mosaic depicted the God victorious over Tiamat of the Chaos; windows, above a writing table, occupied the left side; bookcases flanked the entrance which he faced. For Lanarvilis, a throne of equal dignity had been brought. However, this day he and she wore plain silk with simple embroidery.

His fist lay knotted on the chair arm, his mouth was stiff, he must wrench the words out: 'Thank you for coming, my lady. Believe me, I've no wish to ask about . . . what concerns you yourself. But for the good of Ys – after you have spent time alone with our King – can you tell me aught new?'

Faintly, she flushed, although she held her own voice level. 'Those before me spoke truth. He is a well-intentioned and able man.'

'For Rome.'

'The cause of Rome is the cause of civilization: which means that 'tis equally Ys's.'

Soren shook his head. 'Always have you thought more highly of Rome than it deserves, my dear. You dream of a greatness, a grandeur of soul as well as domain, that has long since died, if ever it truly lived. I've dealt with the Empire; I know.'

'Soren,' she said quietly, 'let not your resentment speak for you. Whatever you think – and I myself am not so dewy as to believe in any human perfection – still, the fact is that Gratillonius has our welfare at heart, is moving strongly to assure it, and seeks our advice, inquires about our wishes. He spent hours talking with me, and listening, too, as if I were a man.'

'What was the drift of this?'

'Well, he . . . he'd heard you and I often confer and work together on behalf of our temples. Thus much of his querying concerned you. You've been polite but aloof, he

234

said. And he needs your active help, the more so when the Lord of Works is in opposition to him.'

'Indeed?' Despite everything that roiled in his breast, Soren's interest awoke. 'How is this?'

'Gratillonius wants fortifications on the headlands. Immediately.'

'Hm.' Soren tugged his beard. 'Little can be done that fast.'

'Well, he spoke just of mantraps, with here and there a dry-laid piece of wall to protect archers and slingers. He fears an assault from the sea while our navy is off supporting our envoys to the Roman governors.' Lanarvilis laid finger to chin. 'Nay, "fear" is wrong. He wants precautions taken. They will require a work levy.'

'Ah. Does he understand what that means?'

'He does. I had him describe it to me.'

Soren hesitated. 'I intend no offence, dear, but in your desire to think well of him, you may have credited him with a better grasp of matters than he has. Would you tell me what he said?'

'Why – ' She paused, shrugged, and recited: 'Taxes to Ys may be paid in money, in kind, or in labour. The labour is limited to public works, to a short maximum period in any year, and to times when it will inflict no undue hardship. Since most construction was completed long ago and needs little maintenance, no such levy has been imposed on the poor for generations.'

Soren smiled grimly. 'I can see why Cothortin Rosmertai digs in his heels. 'Twould upset his administrative routine. Does Gratillonius realize that?'

'Certes. And he's not such a fool as to ride down a Lord of Works whose future friendship will be worth having. He asked me if I could lend my good offices – and prevail upon you – to persuade Cothortin. I agreed. I'll speak to my Sisters also.' Warmth: 'Glad will they be to have this additional token that the Gods meant well by us when They answered our call.'

Soren winced. 'You admire him, then. And not only because he is Roman.'

Again she flushed, but lifted her head and replied proudly: 'Aye. Had the Sign come upon my daughter' – by Lugaid – 'while Colconor reigned, I would have made her kneel, and with this hand slashed her throat, lest he get her. Yestereven Gratillonius cleansed me of him. As he is cleansing all Ys.'

Soren scowled. 'He may yet scrub too hard, he with his foreign God. 'Twould not be the first time the Three withdrew Their favour from a man.'

Pain crossed Lanarvilis's face. She rose and reached towards him. 'Oh, Soren! Close that wound in you. Speak no ill omen. Bethink your sons and the city that shall be theirs.'

He hunched his shoulders. 'So be it,' he growled. 'I'll help. For Ys. And for you who wish it.'

6

'Ah-h-h,' Maldunilis breathed. 'That was good. You wield a mighty sword.' She giggled. 'How soon will you sheathe it anew?'

Gratillonius lifted himself to an elbow and looked down at her. Afternoon sunlight came through the windows to glow across an expanse of sprawled flesh. They had gone to bed shortly after he arrived, for there seemed nothing else to do. Innilis had at least, shyly, proposed a game of draughts . . . Maldunilis was tall and plump, with brown eyes and reddish-brown hair now lank from sweat. Although her father had been Gaetulius, the heavy features recalled grandfather Wulfgar. Yet she was by no means ugly, and had shown her new husband a certain lazy sensuality which made the Bull roar loud within him.

'Give me a while,' he laughed.

She raised herself too. The copious breasts slithered around as she reached for a bowl of sweetmeats on a stand beside the bed. Their fragrance blended into the closeness of the room. No matter that she kept the largest domestic staff of the Nine, always a measure of slovenliness prevailed in this house.

She offered him a confection. 'Thank you, nay,' he said. 'I've small tooth for such.' She fluffed up pillows to lean against and munched it.

'Aye, maybe best you keep your appetite,' she answered. 'The cooks are preparing a feast.' Archly: ''Twill take hours. How shall we spend them?'

Well, he thought, since I've set aside the time till sunrise, why not dawdle about? Gods know I need a rest, a little freedom from responsibility. She's a simpleton, but amiable and a pretty good lay. Unlike some.

The tiny crescent on her bosom seemed abruptly to burn. How had the Sign come to Maldunilis, of all Gallicenae daughters? he wondered. The ways of Mithras could be mysterious, but the ways of Belisama – of the Three Who brooded over Ys – were those of the wind, lightning, the sea deeps, falling stars, death in the night.

He sat straight in the rumpled bedding, crossed arms over knees, and suggested, 'Shall we get to know each other better? Tell me of yourself.'

She yawned, scratched, fumbled after a second sweetmeat. 'Why, naught's to tell. I was never a, a scholar like Bodilis or a seeress like Forsquilis or a politician like Lanarvilis or – I am only me. I do what I am supposed to, and harm nobody.' She smirked. 'Command me, my lord.'

'Oh, surely something,' he protested, while observing that she did not even ask for his story.

She put a hand on his thigh and slid it along an insinuating path. 'I can tell you that I love to futter. Hoel enjoyed me.'

He could not forbear to bark, 'Colconor?'

'Aye. He wasn't very heedful, but nor was he as bad as they said. Once he saw I liked having him on me, and I'd willingly do *whatever* he wanted – as I would for you, O King – he did no worse than spank me sometimes, and that only made this big bottom of mine tingle. He'd have treated me better yet had I given him a child. And I did open my womb, I left off the Herb, but the babe dropped out of me early.' Maldunilis nuzzled Gratillonius. 'I'm sure you can give me one that lives.'

He froze.

'What's the matter, my lord?' She sounded plaintive.

His breath came hard and harsh. 'That day – in the House of the King, ere I arrived – '

She nodded. 'Vindilis and Forsquilis and I were keeping him there. Waiting for you.'

'But – but for them it was a necessity – like Brutus striking down Caesar because he hoped to save the Republic. You – '

She smiled. 'Why not enjoy? That was why my Sisters picked me for the third. Colconor would know I wasn't feigning. Instead it doubled the pleasure to know I helped prepare the way for you, his conqueror.'

The most horrible thing, he thought in a distant part of himself, the ghastliest thing was her innocence.

It thundered in his head. He rolled around and sprang to the floor. Tiles felt cold beneath his feet. Somehow he could chatter, 'Pardon me, this is not courteous. Of a sudden I've remembered pressing affairs of state. I must begone.'

Her face screwed up. 'But my feast!' she wailed.

'Eat it in health. Invite somebody else. Do what you will. I must away.' He scrambled into his clothes.

She blubbered a bit. However, she made no effort to keep him, just sat in bed watching while her hand travelled absently between bowl and mouth.

He strode out into the street. A clean wind blew off the sea. He would go to his palace, he decided, take a hot bath, don fresh raiment. Only there in Ys was it permissible to keep horses. He would have one saddled and gallop off across the hinterland, alone.

His Queens – Nobody remained but Fennalis, and she was the mother of Lanarvilis. Flat-out against the Law of Mithras, to lie with both daughter and mother. He would explain that to Fennalis sometime soon as kindly as he was able. They said she was a friendly sort, usually cheerful, bustling about upon charitable works. Besides, with seven living children by Wulfgar, Lugaid, Gaetulius, and Hoel, she might well be past the rule of the moon. Dismiss Fennalis. He had carried out his duty by the lot of them.

It didn't matter which had known beforehand of that whore-hearted conspiracy to entrap a man. Dahilis had not. She had merely appealed to her Gods for deliverance.

Ignoring persons who hailed him, Gratillonius stalked through Ys. He would ride the roads above the sea until his horse could go no more. Then he would return, bathe anew, dress well, and seek the house of Dahilis.

With her he would abide as long as the Gods allowed. Let people say whatever they chose. Was he not the prefect of Rome?

XIII

The word had gone forth around Mide: again this year would the King at Temir carry a spear abroad. Let ships and currachs gather at the mouth of Boand's River. Let those noble landowners who owed him warlike service make ready themselves and their men, to meet well-provisioned once seed was in the ground and cattle on their way to upland pastures. Let any other man who was free to do so and wished for adventure, glory, and plunder come too. Niall maqq Echach would await them and lead them – this time not to Alba, where fighting and loot had been splendid but where the Wall of Rome still stood – this time south to golden Gallia!

First there must be the rites of Beltene, welcoming in the summer and striving to make it fruitful. Throughout Ériu, folk would rise before dawn to gather the dew for its powers of cure. Women washed their faces in it to make themselves fair, men their hands to make themselves skilful. Women then drew the magical first water from the well and left flowers behind; men set up a bush before the house, and prepared to defend it against whoever might steal it and the luck it carried; youngsters plucked healing herbs, together with blossoms for shrines, horse bridles, every place that might please the Goddess. Later in the day came exchange of gifts, balls bearing the signs of sun and moon, followed by hurling-games played with these, which could well lead to brawls and bloodshed. Youths and maidens went in procession around the countryside, singing, acting out Her coming, celebrating Her gifts of life and light. Families made no marriage pacts, because that would have been as ill-fated as it was to be born this day. However, many couples plighted troth of their own for the year to come or renewed it, and made love upon the earth.

Food was cold, for all household fires had been put out the evening before. At sunset the dwellers in each neighbourhood left their revels and solemnly gathered on the highest ground nearby. While bards or poets sang and druids watched for portents, a chosen man kindled new flame with flint and steel, to make twinned bonfires. Into these folk cast their festival bushes and whatever they had that seemed unlucky, so that fortune might consume misfortune. Farmers drove their cattle between the blazes, for protection against murrains. Those who thereafter went home carried along some of the needfire to relight their hearths. The hardier stayed on till sunrise, for doings that left them weary and a little dazed the next day.

In these observances, every king of a tuath and his queen took a leading part. The King and Queen on Temir must do so on behalf of the whole land. Niall had foreknown he would have no time to himself on the day and night of Beltene; and immediately afterwards would come the whirlwind of busking for his expedition. Yet he had felt the need of some calm counsel.

Therefore he had walked out upon the eve preceding the holy dawn. He went in company with his druid Nemain maqq Aedo and with Laidchenn maqq Barchedo, who had become chief among his poets.

As busy as he had been, this was late in the day. Weather had brought rainshowers, though free of the cold east wind or frost that would have boded ill for the coming season. Now clouds drifted low and leaden beneath an overcast that quite hid the sun and laid an early twilight in the valley. Breezes plucked fitfully at grass and leaves. Odours of growth had given way to dankness. Homebound rooks cawed afar, otherwise silence abided the night.

Niall took the northward road, between the Rath of Gráinne and the Sloping Trenches, thence downhill. Well-kept, it was not unduly muddy or rutted; but at this hour it stretched empty, nothing bordered it save meadow and coppices, no firelight gleamed from houses in view. The sole brightness, and it wan, came off the spearheads of Niall's four guards, who encompassed the three great ones at a respectful distance, and off a golden torc around the neck of the King. Although he was still magnificently clad, after receiving guests who arrived during the day, dusk was fading all colours.

'Best we not linger outside overly long,' counselled Nemain. 'The síd will soon be opening and letting their dwellers loose.' The eve of Beltene was second only to that of Samain as a time when unhuman beings went abroad through the dark.

Niall tossed his bright head. 'We can turn our cloaks inside out and bewilder them,' he said.

'So do people suppose,' Laidchenn answered; 'yet I could tell you many a story, my dear, about those who put overmuch faith in that trick. Even washing in one's own piss is often not shield enough. For Those Beyond may have deeper ends than leading us astray or altogether out of the world.'

'Well, what I have to say is quickly said,' Niall snapped.

'Then say it,' murmured the druid.

The King's mood gentled. He stared before him, down into the gloom towards which he walked. Trouble freighted his tone: 'This I could not utter in the hearing of others, lest they think I was afraid and so, themselves, falter. But to you two, my hearts, I can speak without misunderstanding. And what I have to ask of you is whether you can read any warning signs, in this night before us when sorcery reigns, or whether you can cast any guardian spells – for my warfare after I am off upon it.'

'Have you cause for dread?'

'I have not. Would I of my free will take men who trust me on a venture I deemed unwise?'

'Nevertheless you are uneasy,' said Laidchenn.

'It is about my son, my son Breccan. He burns to prove himself. A while ago, in a gladsome moment, he lured me into a promise that he could come along on this voyage.'

'Surely you, of all men, will not begrudge your boy his chance to win fame.'

'But he is so young – '

'No younger than yourself, when you returned from Torna's house to claim your birthright.'

'I was stronger than he is. Och, he will grow to be a goodly fighter if he lives. But at present he has still his mother's slimness.' Niall's voice wavered, seemed to speak of itself, as if he could not stop it. 'And, O Ethniu, your face – '

'You loved her.'

'As Diarmait loved Gráinne. I do yet, though she be fourteen years in her grave. Breccan is all that remains of her.' Niall's hand slashed swordlike through the air. 'Enough!' he barked. 'This grows unmanly. I, your King, am calling on you two for your counsel and help.'

'Is that right for Breccan's own honour?'

'Hold!' said the druid. 'Our lord simply asks, Laidchenn – asks what may be done to stave off needless woe. Had King Conaire been better advised, he would not have broken the gessa upon him and thereby come to perish in Dá Derga's hostel. Let us take snares from the path of the young stag; wolves he can battle himself.'

His staff thumped the ground as they trudged on mute. Ahead of them an oakenshaw enclosed the road. Its outer trees stood limned against heaven, branches reaching like the arms of gnarled giants, while between them gaped darkness. Wings ghosted overhead and vanished among those shadows. Somewhere a belated cuckoo called.

Laidchenn started. 'That cry! An evil sign at just this time.'

'It is not evil for us,' Niall replied, 'for it came from the right, which means luck.'

'Before we can take thought and cast the yew chips for divining,' said Nemain, 'we must know more of what you intend. You have not given out much.'

'Lest word somehow reach the Romans and warn them,' Niall explained.

The druid nodded his white head. 'That is clear. However, with us two you can feel safe, darling, else why have you sought us? Now tell us where in Gallia you mean to raid.'

'From the supplying you have ordered,' observed the poet shrewdly, 'I doubt you plan on the north coasts.'

'You are right,' Niall answered. 'They have been well picked over. Besides, I seek no clash with Saxons, like two flocks of carrion crows quarrelling over some bones.'

'Have a care,' warned Laidchenn. 'Those are birds of the Mórrigu that you bespeak.'

Niall laughed, which shocked his friend afresh, before he asked, 'Sure, and may not a man jape a little within his own family?'

The druid nodded, though his demeanour had turned solemn. Niall's claim to lordship rested on more than his having often fed the flocks of the Triple Goddess of war. Many men believed that the hag with whom he had lain as a youth had not only been the Sovereignty of Mide, but Herself.

'Well,' said the King, 'it's of more than Saxons I am thinking. Foremost, there is Ys.'

They went under the oaks. It was not quite so dark there as it looked from outside, but murky enough, the sky a blue-grey glimmer behind barricading leaves, boles and boughs heavy in shadow. 'Ys!' exclaimed Nemain. The name cracked through stillness. 'Heart of mine, you are not thinking of attacking Ys, are you, now?'

'I am not,' Niall declared. 'That would be madness. That wall and those guardian witches – Indeed I have no wish to fall on Armorica at all, at all. Ys is a Roman ally. War among the Romans should cause it to reach a protecting hand over its whole end of the peninsula. We will steer wide of Ys. And this is one thing I am hoping you can help me do, keep the favour of Manandan while we are that far out at sea.'

'Where do you mean to go?' Laidchenn asked.

'Around and southwards, to the mouth of the Liger and up that river. There lie rich farmlands, towns, a city. With strife drawing men away, they should be thinly defended – worse off than Alba, where last year's fighting will have left the Romans wary and prepared.' Despite that which gnawed in his breast, exultation made Niall laugh. 'Oh, fine shall our harvest be!'

The trees thinned out. Not much more light straggled through, when dusk had been deepening. Sufficient remained for the men to glimpse an eagle owl depart from the shaw: sufficient to flicker across great wings and glisten on great eyes before the bird disappeared from sight, southbound.

Nemain halted and stood staring at it. Uneasily, his companions drew close to him. 'What is the matter, wise one?' breathed Niall at last.

The druid bent his thin shoulders. 'I do not know. I felt something uncanny there. Come, best we turn about at once and get into shelter before full night has fallen. It will be very dark.'

– Obedient to his gess, Niall rose at the dawn. Fireless, the hall was dolmen-black. Straw rustled dryly under his feet. He groped at a bolt and pushed the shutters from a window. The sky had cleared; the first silver flashed through drifting mists and back off dew; though chill, the air already smelled green. He took a long draught of it.

Suddenly he stiffened. From a beech tree nearby he heard the melodious cry of a cuckoo – too early, too early in the morning, and a harbinger of death if heard from within a house at Beltene.

Yesterday the cuckoo had promised better. Well, signs were often unsure. Niall turned from the window. Nemain would be taking omens and Laidchenn making a powerful song, for the sake of Breccan. The King must remain undaunted.

XIV

1

From the harbour and the markets, through the Forum and over the high ground where the wealthy dwelt – from the philosophers at Star House to the marines in Warriors' House – from Scot's Landing under the cliffs to the noisy workshops outside High Gate – from mansions on the heights above the canal to the hamlets of the valley floor – the whisper flew around Ys and its hinterland. Something tremendous was afoot. This morning the state barge bringing a Queen back from her Vigil on Sena had not, first, taken another out to replace her. All the Nine were gathered together in the temple of Belisama.

In various ways, a few men knew that this was at the behest of the King. None but he knew why.

When Gratillonius left the palace he went alone. A King here could do that if he chose, could walk about or ride abroad, be a man among men. It was the Emperors who sat in a shell of splendour, god-kings with humanity under their feet, those who were not merely gloves on the hands of ruthless real men. Through Maximus, when his victory was complete, Rome would gain back her soldier-Emperors of old.

In a plain, hooded cloak, Gratillonius followed the streets as they wound down to Lir Way and upwards on the other side. Traffic had begun to bustle along the thoroughfare. Some persons recognized him and touched fingers to brow; when he noticed, he acknowledged with a nod and passed on. Two or three approached, clearly hoping to ask favours. His dismissing gesture sent them off. The King might be on sacred business.

It was not the practice for him to hear petitioners or give alms, anyhow. Such things were handled by the Suffetes, Great Houses, guilds, temples. Occasional rulers in the past had distributed largesse or heard complaints . . . occasionally. Thus far, Gratillonius had not, if only for lack of time. Besides, it was not what a centurion did. Lately, at odd moments, he had wondered if he should institute a regular court – twice a month, perhaps – open to whoever had found no better recourse. But he would be unwise to rush into that, without more knowledge of the city and its customs than he yet possessed. Magnates might resent what they felt as an intrusion on their ancient functions. His mission required that he keep them cooperative, and already there was friction aplenty.

Such children as had tagged after him at a distance gave up when he, seeking calmness, entered Elven Gardens. A wall with guarded portals kept the general public out of these exquisitely contoured and cultivated grounds. He found himself alone. If any else were present, the intricacy of paths, hedges, bowers kept them well off, despite this preserve being less than a hundred yards across.

Stillness underlay birdsong. Flowerbeds were hallways, hedges walls, trees roofs; each petal and leaf seemed in its perfect place, as though sculptured. Nowhere were trails, staircases, arched bridges wider than for two people to walk abreast, and nowhere could he see more than a few paces before their curves went out of his view. Yet he had no sense of crowding. Sunlight and shadow made secret depths. A statue of a nymph or faun, or a fountain where stone dolphins played, or the chiming of a streamlet would leap out at him. The forenoon coolness was full of fragrances.

At the farther end he came forth before the staircase to

the temple. It climbed steeply, unrailed, from surrounding flagstones. There he had an overlook across much of the city, its towers agleam between shouldering headlands which had turned emerald and gold, the sea beyond whose daughter Ys was, sails like wings beneath the burning Wheel of Taranis. It was not the first time since his arrival here that beauty had taken him by the throat, and he a hardened roadpounder.

He mounted to the building. It resembled the Parthenon of Athens, in smaller size, though a close glance showed aliennesses – columns more slender, with capitals suggestive of kelp and surf; a frieze of women, seals, cats, doves, blossoms, sheaves, in a style that flowed like water or wind; the marble left bare, weathered to the hue of pale amber.

Bronze doors stood open. Gratillonius entered into a foyer radiant with mosaics of the Mother's gifts to earth. Attendants waited, minor priestesses – who were mostly in their later years – and young vestals. Among the latter he noticed one he had not seen before. Therefore she could be no child of any of his wives. Her mother must be dead; judging by her apparent age, her father had been Hoel. She was of plain appearance and seemed a little dull-witted. He gave her no further thought.

The women greeted him ceremoniously. He replied as he had been taught to and let a maiden take his cloak. Beneath, in deference to this place, he wore a scarlet robe trimmed with ermine, the Wheel embroidered in gold upon the breast. Above it, out in view, hung the Key. That last was as much emblem as he really needed.

A senior led him through a corridor around that great chamber where the threefold image of the Goddess oversaw services. At the rear was a room for meetings. It was amply impressive. In sombre stonework, the four walls showed Her leading Taranis back from the dead to His reconciliation with Lir; present at the act of generation, while dandelion seeds blew and bees flew past the bed; triune as girl child, woman, and crone; in the van of the Wild Hunt. Windows above illuminated the high white headdresses of the Gallicenae. Blue-robed, they sat benched in a half-circle before the dais on to which Gratillonius stepped. His guide closed the door and departed.

Gratillonius looked down into the faces of his wives. Briefly, he was daunted. What strangeness was it that had fallen over them? Wry old Quinipilis; lean, intense Vindilis; Forsquilis, half Athene and half she-cat; sensuous, indolent Maldunilis; shy Innilis; stout, kindly, grey Fennalis; her daughter Lanarvilis, earnest and in some hidden way sorrowful; Bodilis, beneath whose warmth and learning he thought he had sensed steel; darling Dahilis –

No, *she* had nothing but love in her gaze. And as for the rest, he must not let his feelings about them, especially about certain of them, unduly influence him. In their own view they had acted righteously, after intolerable provocation. Seemingly they knew things and wielded powers that were beyond him – that was why he was calling on them – but he should not stand in awe of them, either. He had knowledge and abilities of his own.

Muscle by muscle, Gratillonius relaxed. He smiled. 'Greeting,' he said. By now his Ysan was adequate, and daily improving. 'My thanks for heeding my summons. I think you understand 'tis for the good of the people. I, a man and a foreigner, am still ignorant of much. If we ought to begin with a prayer or a sacrifice, tell me.'

Fennalis stirred on her seat. 'We cannot,' she snapped, 'with you in this house, you who follow a God Who does not hear women.'

Startled, Gratillonius grabbed after a handhold within himself. What possessed this generally cheerful little

250

person? Offence at his never having slept with her? She had seemed to accept his awkward explanation that it was against his religion – ruefully, he suspected, but no more than that, for she was in fact past childbearing age. Usually bustling about on her charitable works, carelessly dressed, she was the last of the Nine whom he would have expected to show intolerance. Her snub-nosed features had stiffened.

'I . . . I revere Belisama, of course,' he tried to respond, 'and all the Gods of Ys.'

'They sent him to us!' Dahilis cried. Appalled at her own brashness, she covered her mouth; but her eyes still shone defiant.

Quinipilis laughed. 'Shall we save the squabbles for long winter evenings when there's naught else to do?' she said. 'This council has business more interesting. At the same time, nay, Gratillonius, we need no rite. Such may come later. Today we are but met to reach a decision.'

'It is a very grave decision, however,' Lanarvilis replied. 'Questions of statecraft . . . We should have other men on hand, the Speaker for Taranis, Lir Captain, the Sea Lord – '

'I will certainly be in conference with them,' Gratillonius promised. 'I'll have them out to the Wood when, shortly, I stand my full-moon Watch there. But first I must have the willingness of the Gallicenae.'

Vindilis scowled. 'That turns on the willingness of the Gods. Who dares try to read Their minds?'

'Aye,' said Bodilis softly. 'And even without hubris, what may stem from a terrible deed? Agamemnon did not truly sacrifice Iphigenia for a fair wind – the Gods wafted her away to safety – but Clytemnestra knew this not, and so murder led to murder until the curse on the house of Atreus was fulfilled.'

'Hold on,' Quinipilis admonished. ''Tis no delicate

251

balancing of ifs and maybes we have before us, 'tis a practical question not unlike the last such that we Nine faced. Meseems we came rather well out of that one.'

Bodilis smiled a little. 'I agree. My inclination is to do what the King asks. Without Rome, what is Ys? I only urge that we think first.'

Maldunilis looked bewildered. 'What is this? Nobody has told me,' she complained.

'You didn't trouble to listen,' Dahilis said in scorn.

'I – I think – no, wait – ' After Innilis had tried several times, her Sisters realized that she hoped to utter a word, and indulged her. 'That's . . . not fair to Maldunilis. Did anybody ever seek her out and ask what she thought? I've no real understanding of it myself. I don't. Gratillonius wants us to raise a tempest . . . against some barbarians who aren't our enemies . . . Well, why?' She sank back in confusion. Vindilis gave her hand a reassuring clasp.

The man saw that matters were getting away from him. He cleared his throat. 'It may be best to lay everything out in plain sight, no matter how much you already know,' he said. 'Forsquilis, will you explain what you have discovered?'

The seeress nodded. All eyes turned her way. Though she remained seated, it was as if she had stood up, tall and prophetic.

'You remember Gratillonius asked me to make a Sending, widely about,' she told them. 'The Empire is at war with itself. Our fleet is off to keep western Armorica at peace. But might barbarians, then, take the chance to strike at Ys? Or might a Roman faction? We needed forewarning.

'With your consent, I agreed. My spirit flew forth over land and sea, to look and listen. What it found, I have reported to him but not erenow to every one of you. Hark ye.'

The centurion was still unsure what truth lay in her. He believed her sincere; but lunatics as well as charlatans infested the world. Nevertheless he had got his glimpses of the unexplainable; and his duty was to use every possible weapon for Rome. After sleepless nights, he had decided to try this.

If Forsquilis could really send her ghost abroad and understand what it heard, no matter in what language, then it might well be that the Gallicenae had those other powers they claimed.

She was so calm about it! 'There are no plans against Ys. The Armorican Romans mean to stay quiet. Some resent our show of naval strength, regardless of its being made as a polite hint rather than a threat. More of them, though, find it a godsend, the very excuse they longed for to avoid the risk of taking sides; and they have prevailed on the rest. Barbarians are astir along the denuded eastern frontiers, but that is remote from us.

'It is in Hivernia that I found fresh grief being prepared for the West. A chieftain – a king, a great king, the master behind last year's attack on Britannia – means to take advantage of civil war in the Empire and launch an onslaught up the mouth of the Liger – very soon.'

She ceased. Stillness descended while each priestess withdrew into herself.

Then: 'Oh, wonderful!' Maldunilis piped. 'The River Liger, 'tis well south of us, is't not? Won't the Scoti sail far around Ys?'

Forsquilis nodded. 'They've abundant respect for us.'

''Tis a piratical raid, you told me, not an invasion,' Lanarvilis said. 'Is it then any concern of ours?'

''Twill be a massive raid.'

Gratillonius regained the word: 'That's my fear. Portus Namnetum lies not far upstream, a vital harbour for this entire region. Because of the war, 'twill be poorly defended. If the barbarians take and sack it, as well they may, not only will shipping around Gallia Lugdunensis suffer. The whole Liger valley will lie open to later attacks.' His forefinger tried to draw a map in the air. 'Can you not see Armorica, Ys, cut off, and Rome suddenly bleeding from a huge gash of a wound? I ask you to defend the well-being of your children and grandchildren.'

'Or that of Maximus?' Fennalis challenged. 'You'd have us wreak harm on folk who wish us none.'

'But who intend doing hideous damage elsewhere to those who never harmed *them*,' Bodilis retorted.

Quinipilis nodded. 'We need to kill them where we can as we need to kill foxes in a chickencoop, though the chickencoop happen to be our neighbours'.'

Bodilis laughed. 'You might have found a metaphor more dignified, dear. But I agree. I cannot believe the Gods of Ys would forbid a strategy of defending civilization itself.'

'Under our King!' Dahilis shouted.

'The Nine alone cannot – ' Lanarvilis began, and broke off. 'Well, you said you would consult with Soren, Hannon, the leading Suffetes ere anything is decided.'

'I am aware I must have their support,' Gratillonius answered. 'But I cannot speak meaningfully with them unless first I have yours.'

Forsquilis shivered. 'My Sending has felt cold winds blowing out of the future,' she mumbled. Aloud: 'The Gods have granted Ys a proven leader. Let him lead.'

'We should . . . give him his chance . . . this time,' Vindilis said slowly. A dark fire burned in her. Innilis clung to her hand.

Fennalis made a slight shrug. ''Twould be foolish of me to cross my whole Sisterhood. Very well. You may be right.'

'Pray somebody tell me what 'tis we're to do!' Maldunilis begged.

Gratillonius gave her, and all of them, his reply.

2

An eerie thing happened as Niall maqq Echach was leaving Ériu.

His warriors were gathered where Boand's River met the sea. Tents, which had settled over the hills like a flight of wild geese, were now struck. Grass would soon heal campsites, for the season was well on; it had taken a while after Beltene to finish work and then trek here. Wagons and chariots stood ready to rumble home. Banners lifted above bright spearheads where men surrounded their tuathal kings. The currachs that would bear most of them were still beached, but several ships lay anchored in the shallows. Everyone waited for the Temir King to board his.

Racket and brawling were silenced, clangour was hushed. Rain misted. The cool smells of it came from earth, growth, cattle, smoke out of wide-strewn shielings, the waters that beckoned ahead.

Niall strode forth. The greyness around could not subdue the saffron in his tunic, the woad in his kilt, the gold at his throat, the steel on his spear, least of all the locks that streamed from brow to shoulders. His left fist gripped a shield painted the colour of fresh blood. Behind him came his son Breccan and his guardsmen, hardly less brilliant. Beside him on the right walked his chief poet Laidchenn maqq Barchedo, on the left his chief druid Nemain maqq Aedo.

His ship lay before him. She was a galley of the Saxon

255

kind, clinker-built, open save for small decks fore and aft, seats and thole-pins for rowers along the bulwarks. Oars lay ready across the benches. Down the middle stretched mast, yardarm, and sail, bundled together on two low racks, not to be raised unless a following wind should arise. The stempost lifted proudly, carven and gilt, a Roman skull nailed on top. Black the hull was, rocking and tugging at its stone anchor, eager to be off to war. Cargo filled the bilge, supplies and battle gear laid down on planks.

Niall had come near enough to hear eddies rustle and chuckle, when the thing came to pass. Out of the grey rain flew a raven. It was the largest any man there had ever seen, its wings like twin midnights. Arrow-straight it glided, to land on the upper rim of Niall's shield and look into his face.

Heavily though that weight struck, the shield never wavered. Not for one step did the King falter. The point of the beak was an inch from the bridge of his nose and could in two pecks take out his eyes; but their blue looked straight into the jet behind that beak, the while he said low, 'Hail and honour, if this be She Whom I think.'

A gasp and a moan blew through the host. Breccan yelled and stumbled back before he mastered his terror. The guardsmen milled in confusion till their captain spoke a command and got them back at their lord's heels. Laidchenn raised the chiming rod that proclaimed him a poet, inviolable, before he went on along beside Niall. The knuckles were white where Nemain clutched his staff.

Niall stopped at the water's edge. 'I promise You many slain,' he said, 'but this You know I have given and will give. Is there anything else that You are requiring?' The bird did not stir nor blink. 'Is it that You have a word for me, darling? I listen. Ever have I listened, and when at last You call me, I will not be slow to come.'

The grisly, beak moved, touched him lightly on the forehead. Wings spread. The raven went aloft. Thrice it circled low above Breccan maqq Nélli. Then it flapped back up into unseen heaven.

Men were casting themselves to the ground, making signs against evil, vowing sacrifices. Niall and his company stood firm. He did shift the spear to the crook of his right arm, and laid that hand upon the shoulder of his son.

After a time Nemain said softly, 'This is a wonder and an omen. I am thinking that that was the Mórrigu Herself.'

'As Medb, She has . . . favoured me,' Niall answered. 'I remember tales of how She has thus appeared to armies before a battle.'

Breccan clenched his fists. 'What happened to them afterwards?' he cried. His voice broke in a squeak. At that, a blush drove the pallor from his face, like rage overwhelming fear.

'Why, some won the day and some fell,' Laidchenn told him, 'but always it was a battle from which fateful issue welled.'

Niall regarded Breccan. 'Her message was for you too,' he said.

'Choosing him for undying fame,' Laidchenn offered.

'Choosing him, at least,' Nemain muttered into his beard.

Niall shook himself. 'Enough of this. Quickly, now, before the lads give way to terror. Sing some heart back into them, poet!'

Laidchenn rang his chimes, took forth his harp, smote the strings. Men roused from their bewilderment when they saw and heard, for he commanded unseen dominions of his own, whence words came forth to blast, blight, or bless. The trained throat spoke from end to end of the hundreds:

'Well may it be that this means
Mighty ones at work,
Willing we all gain honour.
I invoke victory!'

Niall raised his spear on high. His call rolled out: 'The
Mórrigu is with us! Rejoice!'

The kings who were gathered saw their King run into
the water. It sheeted white about his knees. One-handed,
he grabbed the ship's rail and swung himself aboard.
There he immediately seized a red cock which lay trussed
in the prows. With his sword he cut those bonds, so that
the bird fluttered and cawed wildly in his grasp. 'Manandan maqq Leri, you will be granting us the passage of
Your sea, that we may bring You glory!' He put the
victim against the stempost. A sweep of his blade
beheaded it. The death struggle laved the Roman skull
with blood. 'Onward!' he roared to his men.

A cheer lifted, ragged at first, but ever louder and
deeper. Weapons flashed free. Standard bearers whipped
their poles to and fro until banners were flying as if in a
gale. Breccan shuddered in exaltation. Laidchenn and
Nemain kissed him on the cheeks, then stood waving
farewell as he embarked and the guards followed. Ready-
making went swiftly. The anchor came up, the oars bit,
the King's galley stood out to sea.

That was the signal for the rest to start. They swarmed.
The fleet was on its way.

Even in this weather, that was a grand sight. The ships
were not many, and aside from Niall's had no more crew
than needful. They were meant mainly to carry home loot
and captives. But the currachs were everywhere, lean and
low, coursing like hounds around horses. Some of those
leather hulls could hold only four or so warriors, but in
others were better than a dozen. As they got away from
land and met real waves, they no longer simply spider-

walked; they danced, they skimmed, they soared. Chants of oarsmen went back and forth across unrestfulness, surf-sounds.

Those not at this work were busy getting things ship-shape. By the time they were done, the salt was in their nostrils to whip their blood alive. They agreed that the raven had been a marvellous vision, a holy vision, fore-telling slaughtered foes, plundered lands, and return to fame. Breccan was so rapt in dreams of it that Uail maqq Carbri, skippering the royal ship, relieved him of duty just to keep him out from underfoot.

Dim on the right, Ériu would be Niall's guide for the first few days. At eventide, whenever possible, his folk would camp ashore. Given their numbers, they need not fear attack by the Lagini, since it would be clear that they were peacefully passing by. However, wind, fog, seas, or rocks might sometimes force them to lie out overnight. After crossing the channel where it was narrowest, they would use Alba the same way – more or less; there was no sense in anything but a straight dash across the Sabrina firth, and safe campgrounds would be hard to find in Roman country.

At the southwestern tip of Dumnonia the men must either hope for a spell of fair weather or settle in and wait for it. Ahead of them would be days and nights on the open sea, as they steered clear of Armorica and its Ysan she-druids, then turned east for the Liger mouth. True it was that they could be rowing that whole while, watch and watch, or sailing if Manandan was kind. But they must see sky well enough to hold a course. Otherwise – 'We might blunder our way to Tír innan Oac,' Niall had laughed. 'Likeliest, though, we'd only gladden the gulls and sharks, and they have not any great name for the returning of hospitality.'

The plan was quite sound, he went on to say. Armorican fishermen regularly worked farther out than he proposed to go. Jutish traders and pirates regularly made trips as long, also beyond sight of land, between their homes and Alba. And had not his Milesian ancestors sailed the whole way up from Iberia?

The voyage met no worse trouble than kept men on their mettle – until the first night beyond Dumnonia, in the very Ocean.

Heaven was clear, the moon full, so that vessels need not keep dangerously close together to stay in sight of each other. This was twice good, because they had got the wind for which rowers longed and were under sail. It crooned low and not too cold, when you ran before it; waves whooshed and gently rumbled, gleams and silvery traces swirling over the obsidian of them; ships rocked, surged, talked to themselves in creak of timbers and tackle. Niall, who stood a lookout himself, had finished his turn and was about to go join the crew who slept nested together down the length of the hull. Muffled in a cloak, he took a moment of ease on the foredeck. Starboard, larboard, aft, his fleet came along like leaping dolphins. The eye sockets of the trophy skull gaped towards Rome.

Something caught his gaze. He turned his head upwards. Broad wings slipped by. An eagle owl . . . at sea?

It swung away and vanished eastwards. Niall said nothing to the other man, who had not seen. That night the King slept ill.

3

In the morning Eppillus took the legionaries out on Redonian Way to the far side of Point Vanis. The whole thirty-two were present. Gratillonius had relieved the honour guard of duty, observing that he would not be at the palace for a while. After his required stay at the Wood, he would be busy in and around Ys, and lodging in Dragon House so he could readily confer with officers of the armed forces.

The Romans tramped smartly off. It was a clear, calm day. Sunlight glared on their metal. A few fleece-ball clouds drifted overhead as lazily as bees droned about wildflower blossoms. On the promontory the grass was thick and intensely green, studded with shrubs and boulders. Under Northbridge, the sea churned and roared among rocks between the headland and the wall of Ys; but everywhere else it reached in sapphire brilliance, its calm broken only where it went white over reefs. Far and far away, a streak of darkness marked Sena. The pharos at the end of Cape Rach, beyond sky-striving Ys, seemed in its loneliness to be calling to the isle of the Nine.

Where Redonian Way bent east, Eppillus barked: 'Halt! Fall out.' He turned to face the men. 'You've been wondering what this is for. Well, I didn't know myself till yesterday when the centurion told me. We're going to do a little drill, boys, a little war game. That's how come I ordered you each to bring a baton. Save your real swords. You might be needing 'em.'

'Eh?' said Adminius. 'D'you mean we're expecting an attack? Why, just last night, down in a 'ore'ouse, I was talking with a chap back from Condate Redonum, and 'e was telling 'ow it's all serene. Maximus is way off south by now, driving the opposition before 'im.'

Eppillus squirted a jet between his front teeth, to spatter on a breast-high wall of dry-laid stone about ten feet long. A couple more were nearby. Already they looked as ancient as a beehive-shaped rock shelter for shepherds in the distance. 'This wasn't built against no Roman troops,' the deputy said. 'What use in that? It's to protect archers and slingers from enemy coming up out o' the water. One thing you'll do today, my fine fellows, you'll learn and learn well where the lilies are.' – as Romans called mantraps of the kind that Ysan labourers had here dug for them. 'Wouldn't want a stake up your arse, would you?'

'Saxons!' Budic exclaimed.

Cynan shook his head. 'No such rovers anywhere near,' he replied. 'The fishers know. I was talking myself – with Maeloch; you remember Maeloch, Adminius – he and I've got to be pretty good friends – '

'As broody as you both are, I can see that,' the man from Londinium said with a gap-toothed grin. 'Wot d'you do, sit around arguing whether Lir or Nodens is 'arder ter please?'

'Silence!' Eppillus rasped. He planted his legs well apart, put hands on broad hips, and glowered at the troops. 'Now listen close, you braying jackasses. I don't want to have to say this twice. Ask your stupid questions today. Later on, each one costs an hour's pack drill. Got me?

'Well, then. Maybe once in a while one or two o' you's come up for air out o' his beer and noticed how the centurion's got work started on land defences. The city could stand off any barbarians that might land, sure; but he don't aim to *let* them land and go around scorching the countryside. That'd make a hungry winter for us, wouldn't

262

it? Did any such thought ever stir in your dim little minds?'

Having captured their full attention, he relaxed his stance and lowered his tone. 'Ah, the centurion's a deep one, he is. But I didn't understand how deep, myself, till yesterday, when he called me in. Brace yourselves, boys. This is uncanny.

'Somehow, he didn't say how, he knows there's a big fleet o' Scoti at sea. It's bound for the Liger mouth, to loot and lay waste that whole fine country. The garrisons there are stripped because o' the war. Gratillonius don't figure he can allow this, not at the back o' Maximus Augustus.' He drew breath, hunched forward, dropped his voice close to a whisper. 'Well, somehow, and believe me, I didn't ask how – somehow he knows a great storm's going to come out o' this clear blue sky, and blow the Scoti on to the rocks around Ys and drown them!'

Rocking back on his heels, thumbs hooked in belt, he let the men mumble their amazement, clutch their lucky charms, speak their hasty prayers. When he judged the moment right, he grinned and said:

'Easy, now. You've got nothing to be scared of, less'n you're a Scotian. After last year on the Wall, I don't suppose any o' us in the Second Augusta bear those headhunting devil-cats much love. Our job is to make sure o' them. You see, all their boats may not be wrecked. Some crews may make it ashore. If we let them go, we'll have a dangerous nuisance on our hands, or worse, for months to come. If we don't – if we cut 'em down as they straggle up from the water – why, not only will we be saving ourselves future trouble, we'll be doing Mother Rome a whopping big favour. Every Scotian we nail is one that won't ever go raiding again.'

Cynan cleared his throat. 'Question.' Eppillus nodded. Cynan turned and pointed over Ys, towards Cape Rach.

'I mentioned I've become friendly with a fisher captain. I've visited him and his family in that tiny village down under the southern cliffs. They don't call it Scot's Landing for nothing, deputy. It's the only good place to put in hereabouts, aside from Ys itself, and pirates have used it in the past.'

'That was long ago, wasn't it?' Adminius protested.

'What matters,' Cynan snapped, 'is that Scoti still use it now and then. Not for hostilities, no. But small traders from Hivernia drop in to do business without paying Ysan duties. Or Scotic fishers blown off course come to refill their water casks.'

'I know,' Budic interposed. 'They are from the south of Hivernia. Many are Christian. Father Eucherius was telling me about them.'

Cynan sneered. 'Is it impossible for a Christian to be a pirate? Besides, surely, if he's not a fool, the chief of this Scotic fleet that Gratillonius . . . foresees – surely he's provided himself with information about these waters and pilots who know them, even if he doesn't intend anything against Ys.'

Adminius rubbed his chin. 'M-m, you've a point there, chum.'

Cynan's sombre stare challenged Eppillus. 'This is my question,' he said. 'Why are we being assigned here? Why not down at Scot's Landing?'

A smile relieved the heaviness of the deputy's features. 'Ho, a damn good question, soldier. I'm going to tell the centurion you asked it. He's said he needs leaders from among us. You might make vinestaff someday.'

Cynan did not return the smile, simply folded his arms and waited.

'Well,' Eppillus explained, 'the centurion knows what you do, and more. He's made ready. The fishers are a tough lot, nobody you'd care to meet in a brawl. Ysan marines will be on hand too, to help them hold Cape Rach. The centurion himself will stand by in town, at the head of a striking force which'll go wherever it's needed the most. But that leaves this place.'

He pointed. What had once been a path, worn away by neglect and weather to a poor excuse for a trail, dropped down between brambles, over the edge of land and out of sight. 'That goes to the ruins o' the Roman maritime station,' he said. 'Possible place for boats to put in. Maybe not likely, but possible. The centurion wants to cover all bets. He's decided to place a few men here, few but good. That's us, and you'd better measure up. We'll have Ysan sharpshooters with us, and we can send for reinforcements if we need them – like I told you, he'll be standing in reserve – though I hope we won't.'

'With luck,' said Adminius, 'we won't get any custom.'

Eppillus laughed. 'Oh, I'd like some, not too big for us to handle by ourselves, but enough to look good when the centurion writes his report. Bonuses, promotions, and such, you know. I expect Maximus will be generous to them as deserve it. New-made Emperors always have been, I hear.' He rubbed his hands. 'Maybe extra acres for my bit of a farm when I retire?'

Straightening: 'All right! If there are no more questions, let's get cracking.'

4

No barge of state took the Gallicenae out to Sena. That would have been too dangerous – after dark, when few sailors dared come near the rocks around the island, and on a mission as dread as was theirs. None would do to navigate but Ferriers of the Dead.

Just past the full, the moon stood low above the cliffs. It threw a shuddery bridge over waters otherwise dark as heaven, closer to hand flecked by foam-gleams that were like fugitive stars. Quiet though air and sea were, whiteness snapped its teeth across the reefs strewn everywhere about. The stillness seemed to deepen the chill that always followed sunset, out away from land.

A pair of boats could carry eight women with sufficient rude dignity. Oars creaked, not loudly, almost the sole human sound. The smack *Osprey* went first. Two of her passengers sat silent in the bows near the lookout, two in the stern, where Captain Maeloch had the helm. He knew this passage so well that in fair weather he would merely need warning of something unexpected, a driftwood log or a piece of wreck.

Dahilis had settled closest to him, legs curled beneath her on a cushion, at the larboard rail. She could not have been altogether lost in meditations, for from time to time she glanced up to where his beard jutted athwart the Bears. For his part, he stole some looks at her. Very fair she was with her cowl thrown back, hair aglow in the dimness. Above her reached those stars called the Maiden. Finally their glances chanced to meet, and turned aside in confusion, and she smiled at herself while he scowled at himself.

Low and flat, the island drew nigh in sight. A small stone building with a squat tower made blackness behind a dock where a lantern glimmered red. The lookout finally did call soft words as he gestured, and Maeloch gave orders and put his helm accordingly. The boat thudded against rope bumpers. The lookout sprang off with a line which he made fast to a bollard. Maeloch tossed him another line for the stern and lifted and secured the steering oar. Flame-light showed that it was old Quinipilis who had had today's Vigil and now stood waiting.

Dahilis rose. Maeloch offered his arm. 'Let me help you, my Queen,' he said softly.

'Thank you,' she answered, which many of the wellborn would not have troubled to do.

He guided her over the deck, jumped to the wharf, and gave her support as she followed. No matter the unknown deed in which she was about to take part, impishness broke forth and she whispered, 'That was needless. I'm no cripple. But I enjoyed it. I hope you did.'

'My Queen – ' For one of the few times in his life, he was taken aback. Hastily: 'Um, 'tis not for me to do aught but obey here. However, best will be if ye ha' done ere moonset. The tide will've got tricky – nasty rips. But we'll abide your pleasure.'

'I think not 'twill take very long, that which we go to,' she replied, serious again. 'Remember, you and every fisherman, sail not out tomorrow, nor till the King gives you leave.'

'We'd no thought of that,' he said, 'after being told how all ye Nine will come back with us tonight.'

Quinipilis beckoned. Dahilis went to join her Sisters. Slowly, in single file, they walked off. Harsh grass, grey under the moon, wet kelp, pools where strange small creatures scuttled, were the other signs of life upon Sena. But three seals followed along the shore till the trail went inland, then lay afloat as if awaiting the high priestesses' return.

At the Stones Quinipilis set her lantern down and lifted her arms. She led the women in their prayer to the Three and in the sacraments of salt and blood. They kindled no wood this time, for their doings were apart from the element Earth. Rather, they sacrificed Fire to Air by raising the lantern hood and blowing on the flame till it burned furiously, then to Water by quenching the candle in a bowlful of brine. Hands joined, they danced solemnly around the menhirs while they chanted:

'Wind of the West, awaken! The wolf is again a-prowl.
The ravening reaver of sheepfolds has lifted his head to howl,
And the watchmen shudder in summer to hear those wintry sounds.
Wind of the West, awaken! Unleash now on him your hounds.

'Calling on Lir, we loose you to harry our enemy
That dared to depart from the heathlands and hunt upon His sea,
And His waves shall answer your whistle, and come to course the beast
Wildly through brakes of spindrift, relentlessly to the East.

'Calling on Lord Taranis, the Guard of the city wall,
We order up horror and havoc, lest what is worse befall,
And we lend your hand His hammer where storm-flung squadrons go
On to the waiting skerries, that heavy may be the blow.

'Calling on Belisama, Our Lady of Life and Death,
Whose kisses put warmth in the newborn and stop the old man's breath,
And Whose stars betoken Her peace in the dawn and the sunset skies,
Doom will we deal to sea wolves. O Wind of the West, arise!'

XV

1

On his second and third nights at sea, Niall again glimpsed the owl. It came out of the eastern darkness, swung silently above the Roman skull, turned back and vanished in empty distances. Other men saw it too, and muttered of it to comrades who had not. Before fear could spread through his fleet, the King commandeered a currach and had himself rowed to the nearer vessels. 'It is nothing to frighten us at all, at all,' he declared to them. 'No natural bird, surely; but it's done us no harm, has it, now? Maybe a poor wandering ghost, such as we've charms against. Maybe a scout for the witches of Ys, but if so, it's telling them we mean no harm to their country. You'd not be letting a single fowl scare you, would you, my darlings?'

The bold beauty of him, as he stood spear in hand and seven-coloured cloak about his wide shoulders, breathed courage into everyone. What further thoughts he had, he kept to himself.

It had been easy to get about thus on the water, for the airs had turned crank, foul when any whatsoever blew, and craft crawled forward on oars. Everywhere stretched Ocean, barely rocking beneath a cloudless sky, and sunblaze blistered fair skins. Niall could only guess where he was. However, he said, one more day must certainly put them well south of the peninsula, after which they could seek land. There they would get their bearings and, hugging the shore, proceed to the Liger mouth.

But on the night before this change of course – the

269

third night, some hours after the owl had passed by – clouds began piling up in the west. Like black mountains they were, and ever more tall they grew, while stronger and stronger became the wind that skirled from them. By dawn it was a full storm.

No man saw that sunrise. There was naught but a faint lightening of what had been utter murk. Heaven was hidden. Wrack flew beneath like the smoke of burning houses. Monstrous were the waves, towering over hulls as they rushed and rumbled by, their backs white with foam, the hollows of them shading from green on top to abyssal black in the troughs. Their crests blew away in blinding froth. Wind filled the world. It struck fangs of cold into the bones of men, it lashed them with bitter scud, it grabbed their garments and sought to drag them leeward to their drowning. Often a burst of rain and great hailstones flew down upon it and streaked across the fury round about.

Niall's folk could do naught save hold their galley head on to the seas. Those who were not at the oars were bailing – buckets, cups, helmets, boots, whatever might keep the water a-slosh no higher than their ankles. The ship pitched, bow down till the stempost flailed amidst spume, bow up and a flood of tears from the eye sockets of the skull. Timbers groaned in anguish. Otherwise the warriors were helpless, driven before the tempest towards wherever it would have them.

Niall went back and forth, balancing himself against the surging as a lynx would. Labour was gess for him, the King; his part was harder, to keep heart in his followers. 'Good lads, brave lads, it's fine you are doing. Sure and Manandan is proud of you. And what a tale you'll have to tell by your hearthfires!'

But once when he was aft, he let himself falter. Nobody was in earshot, in this tumult, besides Uail maqq Carbri

270

at the helm, and he a close friend and indomitable. His back to the blast, Niall peered right and left. He made out a few currachs, riding better than the galley but no more able to hold a course. The rest of the fleet was lost to sight in grey chaos, scattered, perhaps much of it already broken and the crews sunk. His shoulders slumped. 'I wonder if we should give Manandan a man, that He soften his anger at us,' he croaked.

Uail, the old mariner, shook his head. 'We should not,' he answered through the racket, 'for I am thinking this is no work of His, but of Lir, His father. And Lir is the truly terrible – no handsome charioteer but a Force that will not be swerved by anything in human gift.'

Niall shuddered. 'Who raised Him?'

Uail shrugged, squinted into the storm, devoted himself to his tiller.

Niall started forward again, bench to bench. His son Breccan was among those bailing. Without the brawn to row, bare-legged under a kilt, the prince kept on somehow when grown men had crumpled up, worn out and numbed by the cold. He looked aloft at the King. His golden hair was plastered to his cheeks, as sodden as the shirt that clung to his lanky frame, and his eyes seemed enormous, dark-shadowed by weariness, in the face that was his mother's. The rhythm of his pail checked. He flashed a grin and a thumb-sign of defiance at his father, before he bent back to his task and sent another load of water over the side.

'Medb with us!' Niall shouted. 'I did well to bring you!' After that he was cheerful –

– until the first white spurtings and bestial growls told how the fleet had drifted in among reefs.

Uail bawled orders which the roars of Niall passed onwards against the wind. Regardless of the danger of getting swamped, the danger of tossing about was worse.

Oars churned. Many a wave dropped away from a blade, hissing in mockery, and the stroke smote air. Yet the ship did get turned around. She could not fight her way west, but she could wallow along under some measure of control, claw off the rocks that surrounded her, seek to keep alive.

Save when rainsqualls whooped by, the skies had paled somewhat and Niall could see farther than erstwhile, through a weird brass-yellow light. The gale had slackened just a bit too, so that there was less spindrift to whip his eyes. Yet whistling and bellowing and deep sucking noises filled his ears, while the seas ran even heavier. He witnessed currach after currach dashed against a skerry and its ribs smashed to splinters. Men would tumble out of the wreckage, flop for a ghastly moment, and go under, unless the surf rolled their bodies on to a ridge. Flotsam from a second galley, sundered, her crew and cargo spilled, went swinging past. At the edge of vision he spied a low-lying duskiness which he knew from mariners' accounts was the island Sena.

More craft were getting through than lost. Let them understand the King was too, and rally after they had passed these shoals! Niall fetched men from the bailers, Breccan among them, and had them step and secure the mast. That was long and perilous toil. Once the pole fell, caught a man's arm against the rail, made mush and shards of it. He swooned from the pain. Coolly, Breccan cut a strip of clothing and bound the hurt lest he bleed to death. Meanwhile his fellows got the mast in place. Raising sail would have been madness, but the King's banner fluttered aloft, colour streamed in the spray, a hoarse cheer lifted through the hull.

Though the sun remained withdrawn, Niall reckoned the time as late afternoon.

Standing lookout in the bows, he was the first to make

272

out the shadow ahead. It grew as the storm-clouds had done, rising, solidifying, until ruddy cliffs and the turmoil at their feet were unmistakable. The mainland.

Chill struck Niall in the breast. Then wrath leapt on high. He raised a fist. 'I see. It is you yonder who have done this to us,' he said between clenched teeth. 'Why, why, why?

'Well, you shall mourn for it.'

Wind continued to slacken, clouds to thin, the range of eyesight to stretch. The seas were still enormous, impossible to go against, but at least men could work partly across them, could pick the general direction in which a vessel was to be forced landward. Niall saw what he supposed were all the survivors of his fleet, or most of them – less than half the grand host which had sailed from Ériu, battered, awash, the strength wrung out of their crews, but alive, alive.

He saw which way they were setting. If only he could yell across the waters! His flag was a forlorn signal which few would likely fathom.

He could merely do what seemed best, or least bad. Niall moved aft. Amidships, he squatted, tapped Breccan on the shoulder, and said to the dear face: 'Lay off that. Tell everybody to stop, take a rest, try to get warm. I think soon we'll be fighting.'

'Oh, father!' It was a joy to see the joy that flamed in the youth. Breccan caught Niall's hand between both his. Niall rumpled the wet hair and went on to Uail astern.

'You've a plan, master,' said the steersman.

Niall nodded. 'I wish I had a better one. It seems the witches of Ys have been working for our destruction. How likely would it else be that we were blown straight on to this deadly ground? Medb, come help us get revenge.'

He swept a finger around. 'Look,' he said. 'We cannot

beat back west. Seamanship would have us bear as much north as we may, try to round Armorica and win the Alban Channel. With her weight and draught, this ship is able. But wind and waves are opposed, and overwhelming to the currachs . . . Have we any more galleys left us? I see just the poor currachs, riding on top of the sea and thereby debarred from making more than a little way across it . . . One by one, they are bound for yonder headland.' .

'For Scot's Landing beneath it.'

'I know. Remember how much I inquired before we left home.'

'Since they are forced on to a lee shore, those with men aboard who know it pick the only safe spot. The rest follow.'

'It is not safe,' Niall said grimly. 'I think Ysan fighters are waiting there to slay them as they debark.'

'That could well be.' Uail regarded his King. 'You've a plan, master,' he repeated.

'I do that. *We* can work north. Never would I willingly forsake men who've trusted me. Have you not told me of another landing beyond the city?'

'I have. It is on the far side of Point Vanis, as they call that part. The Romans had a station there, but Saxons destroyed it and nobody has used it since.'

'We will. If the Ysans plotted this, as I do believe, then they expect that whoever came through the reefs alive will seek haven at Scot's Landing. There they'll stand prepared. Now our lads, however wearied, should give a good account of themselves. But I doubt they can force a passage to the heights and refuge in the hinterland. The Ysan aim must be to kill most and drive the rest back to the hungry waters. We, though – here we've a shipful of the finest warriors in Ériu. We'll dock at the old station, hurry overland around the city, strike the Ysans from behind, scatter them and join our comrades. After that, the enemy should sit earthed behind his defences till the weather clears and we can fare homeward.'

'Homeward? . . . Well, it took Lir Himself to make Niall maqq Echach retreat. We'll bring back our honour, if nothing else.' Uail hesitated, even while he strained at the oar. 'But what if the other approach is guarded also?'

Niall's head lifted haughty as his banner. 'Why, we'll cut our way through.'

'Row, you scuts!' Uail cried. 'Stroke, stroke, stroke!'

Four currachs, which happened to be far enough north, managed to follow. Doubtless the foe was watching and would guess the intent; but given his need to man the southern harbourage, could he stem *this* tide? The hope of rescue, vengeance, and glory swelled higher in Niall than ever did lust for a woman.

Passing the headland, where the pharos stood like a sinister phallus, he was almost unaware of the white fury of water churning between it and the city wall. This was his first sight of Ys. He caught his breath.

The rampart shot up sheer, a cliff itself, topped by crags that were turrets. The very smoothness of that height, the marshalling of battlements above, even the frieze of playful, colourful shapes aloft in the granite, made it more awesome than the ruggednesses which abutted on it. The gate was shut – barred and locked, Niall had heard – and the floats that opened it at low tide dashed back and forth, up and down, on waves that ramped and foamed. When one of those padded balls struck stone or metal-sheathed wood, a drum-boom rolled huge and hollow through the wind, with an iron rattle from the chains.

Behind the wall rose towers like frozen cataracts, rainbow-hued; and on the slopes beyond were terraces, gardens, gracious dwellings; and suddenly, briefly, Niall thought he saw why the Romans in Alba had given him such stubborn resistance.

He had his men to save. The galley drove onwards.

2

Another cloudburst struck, fiercer and longer than any before. Rain slanted down in sheaves of spears; hail skittered off stones and made hoar the grass it had flattened; wind shrilled till a soldier's head rang in his casque. At last, as quickly as it had come, it went. The gale was dropping too. Through a brief rift in heaven, a sunbeam smote out of the west, from low above the waves, and shattered dazzlingly on them.

Eppillus trudged to the path and a little way through its mud and cascades, for a look below. When he saw, he stopped and whistled softly. Somehow, during the squall, a ship of the Saxon kind and four boats had made fast at the ruins of the wharf. They were vomiting warriors.

'Son of a bitch,' he muttered to himself. 'More than we bargained for.' Slipping and swearing, he climbed back up and trotted across to where his legionaries stood ranked. Native archers and slingers stared over their defensive walls, read his visage, and readied their weapons.

'If we wanted a fight, Mithras has been mighty generous,' he rasped. 'We can't hold the path against as many as are coming. Scoti are like goats anyway. Most o' them 'ud scramble around and take us from the rear. Budic, boy, hit leather.' He jerked a thumb at a horse tethered nearby. 'Go tell the centurion we got a hundred or worse bandits on our hands here and could use whatever reinforcements he can spare us.'

276

The Coritanian snapped a salute, leapt to the saddle, and was off. To the rest, Eppillus continued: 'What we'll do is deploy in a half circle beyond the barriers. I drilled you in the manoeuvre; now let me stir those pea soup memories o' yours. It breaks the line, but just the same, man for man you're better than any two unarmoured barbarians. Besides, the idea is to let the lilies and the sharpshooters take some o' them first. I expect they'll get together after that and go hooting away inland. Whoever they've happened to point themselves at, stand firm. Everybody else watch me. When I swing my sword over my head, like this, you run to me, around any enemy. We'll take tight formation while he's busy with those first few of us and hit him wherever he looks ripest for it. Got me? All right, to your posts. Hang in there for Mother Rome, not to speak o' your flea-bitten necks.'

He stumped to his place at the middle, directly opposite the trailhead. Though the wind was falling off, its chill bit through metal, wool, and flesh. Drenched, grass moved sluggishly under its flow. A second sunbeam pierced the tattered, flying gloom and lit wildfire over the wetness. He remembered such weather from his boyhood in Dobunnia – but there the countryside was tamed, neatly kept, graced with trees along the roads and in the paddocks where cattle grazed red, farmsteads such as the one which waited for him – not bleak and open above a city where sorceries laired; and the storms came in honest wise, of themselves. Eppillus swore, spat, planted his flat feet firmer on the ground, and loosened blade in sheath.

The Scoti appeared. Leading them was a very tall man. His shield was blood-coloured. The sea had not dimmed the brightness of his steel, garish clothes, beard, or the locks that streamed yellow from under a helmet. His billowing cloak half concealed a younker who bounded on his right. Behind him spilled his followers. Their weapons whirled, their yells resounded, thinned but sharpened by the wind.

Before drawing his own sword, Eppillus dropped hand to a pouch at his wrist and squeezed it. The shape of the thunderstone within was comforting. 'Sweat us out some luck, will you?' he said. 'Mithras, Lord o' Battles, into Your keeping I give my soul. Come on, stone, I know you can do your job.'

As he observed, his heart bounded for joy till he thought it must be making the hair on his chest quiver. The foe had forgotten even such schoolboy discipline as their sort had shown in Britannia. They swarmed forward any old way, howling at the wide-spaced Romans.

Bows twanged. Slings snapped. Barbarians lurched, stared and scrabbled at arrows in them, fell to earth and lay writhing while blood pumped forth. Skulls shattered in a gush of brains where lead smote. Beneath other men turf collapsed, pits opened, their screams rose faintly from the stakes at the bottom whereon they were skewered. Why, this alone may panic them, Eppillus thought.

No. Their leader shouted. His sword flared aloft, a beacon. The wild men heard, and saw, and rallied to him. He has the magic, Eppillus thought. I've seen it before. The centurion has some, but this fellow got all there was to get.

The stripling loped ahead, probing for traps with a spear. In a loosely gathered pack, the Scoti came after. They were too fast for missiles to inflict many more casualties. Reaching the wall on their right, they overran it and butchered its Ysans in passing. The tall man stayed in their van. His sword flickered back and forth like lightning. Drops of blood dashed off it into the wind. He turned left and made for the centre of the defence.

He's aiming straight at *me*, Eppillus realized. He knows what he's doing. It's like last year over again.

The deputy waved his blade on high. From the corners of his eyes he saw his men leave their posts and converge on him. Good soldiers, good grumbly roadpounders. But here came the Scoti.

Roman javelins flew. They stopped too few of those bastards.

Still ahead of his warriors, the tall man reached Eppillus. His blade whirred. The deputy's shield caught the blow. Its violence tore through hand and arm and shoulder to rattle his teeth. He shoved the boss forward. The Scotic buckler intercepted that. Eppillus brought the top rim of his shield upward, trying for the jaw. The tall man swayed easily aside. His sword swung underneath.

Eppillus felt the impact as something remote, not quite real. Abruptly his left knee gave way. He shifted weight to the right foot and stabbed. His point went into red-painted wood. The barbarian cut him across the forearm. His hand lost its grasp, he let go of his sword. His shield overbalanced him on the crippled left leg. As he fell, another blow took him in the neck.

Battle thundered over him. Armour or no, he felt ribs break. It didn't hurt, nor was the blood that ran out of his wounds anything but warm. He was afar, a boy, lying at ease in a meadow where honeybees buzzed. Dimly he heard shouts, clash of iron, thud and grunt and saw-edged shriek. He tried to think what it meant, and could not, and gave himself up to sleep in the great summer.

Those of the Scoti who put their currachs alongside Ghost Quay and sprang on to it made a mistake. Ysan marines stood there, full-armoured, shield by shield in the Roman manner. From that fortress the laurel-leaf blades darted out. Archers and slingers on the path above sent a steady hail. Soon the close-packed stones were buried under corpses and entrails, while the water beneath foamed red.

Others among the incomers sought east of the wharf. They could beach their leather boats under the trail that led to Scot's Landing, though time was lacking to secure these and most soon drifted away. Meanwhile the crews must climb a steep and rocky slope to the path – where poised the sailors of Ys. That became a desperate battle.

Holding the high ground, the shellbacks finally prevailed. Such of the barbarians as survived withdrew to the water's edge, panting and snarling. A lull fell over the combat.

The wind was likewise dying down. Waves still ran gigantic, casting whiteness yards aloft where they burst on reefs and cliffs, but their ferocity was spending itself. The storm had done its work; now nature would fain rest.

Maeloch wiped his axe on the shirt of a dead foe-man. Rising, he leaned on the weapon, drew long breaths, stared outward.

'What be ye thinking about so hard, skipper?' asked Usun at his side.

'I wondered what'll become of the enemy fallen,' Maeloch answered.

Usun was surprised. 'Why, I suppose the funeral

barge'll take them out and sink them, save as with anybody else but a King.'

'Aye. But after that, what? Will they knock on our doors call us to ferry *their* spirits off – and to where?'

Usun shivered, he who had lately filled edged metal with furiousness. 'Gods, I hope not! They'd find scant welcome on Sena. Can we cast a spell to keep them down, d'ye suppose?'

'Not ye nor me, mate. Let's ask our wives to try. 'Tis the women that stand closest to death, like they do to life.'

4

Dahilis had never altered the house she inherited from her mother. To her its softly tinted pastoral frescos had once been signs of love and peace, afterwards of refuge, lately of joy. She did fill vases with flowers in season; and in her bedroom she had replaced an ivory image of maternal Belisama with a wooden one. It was crude, but it had been carved for her when she was a child by an adoring manservant.

In dimness scented by roses, she knelt before the niche, raised her hands, and begged:

'All-holiest, ward him. If he must go to the fight, ride before him, Wild Huntress. Keep him safe, Protectress. And if he is hurt – he is so brave, you know – make him whole again, Healer. For the sake of Your people. Who else is more wise and good? Oh, let him live many, many years. When time comes for the Sacrifice, may it be me who goes instead of him. Please.'

Her voice dropped to a whisper. 'But not ere – well, you know.'

The last few days, while Gratillonius was too busy to visit her, she had been sick in the mornings; and for more than a month, she had had no courses. She could hardly wait to tell him.

5

The King's reserves were standing by at Warriors' House, with horses bridled and saddled just outside High Gate. Thus when Budic delivered his news they were on their way immediately.

Galloping up the road on to Point Vanis, they saw the Scoti swarming down. What was left of the legionaries, about two dozen, followed closely but no longer pressed the attack. Maybe if Eppillus had been in command – but he wasn't. The knowledge rammed into Gratillonius. Indeed an overwhelming force had landed here. It must have been more skilfully led than barbarians usually were, too. Plain to see was that, in spite of their losses, the Scoti had outflanked the Romans before those could dress ranks, killed several, and held the remainder off by rearguard action. Since they were not bound east towards safety but south towards Cape Rach, their intention must be to aid their fellows at Scot's Landing. If they took the Ysans there in the back, they might well clear that whole area and evacuate every raider who was alive.

'By the Bull,' said Gratillonius, 'it shall not be. Ghost of Eppillus, hear me.' He cast reins over his horse's nose, a signal to the well-trained beast that it must not stray, and jumped to the ground. In their strange bright armour, his marines did likewise. They assumed formation and quick-marched to intercept the Scoti.

There was no mistaking the enemy chief, a tall, golden-

282

haired man, like some pagan God of war. I'm going after him first, Gratillonius decided. Once we've taken him out, the rest will be dung to our pitchforks.

Now it was the Scoti who were outnumbered – and unarmoured, fatigued, many among them already wounded. As the marines advanced, the legionaries did too, from behind. The chief shouted and beckoned. His followers rallied around, formed a primitive shield-wall, started chanting their death-songs. They would not perish easily.

Gratillonius at its centre, the Ysan line made contact. Everything became delirium, as always, except that the marines and the legionaries worked in coordinated units. Gratillonius could see his target man over the heads of others, but in the chaos that man had got elsewhere and was hewing away at Romans. 'Ha-a-a! Ha-a-a!' Clang and bang, tramp and stamp, thrust and parry, Gratillonius pushed inwards.

A last, violent gust of wind went over the headland. A raven flew upon it.

Gratillonius was never sure afterwards what had happened. He remembered a woman, titanic and hideous, lame, swarthy, sooty, a cast in her left eye, who wielded a sickle that mowed men like wheat. But that could not be right, could it? Surely the truth was just that somehow the Scoti battled their way through the onslaught, heaped casualties in windrows, won back to the trailhead and thence to the sea. Gratillonius had taken a blow on the head which, helmet or no, left him slightly stunned for a while. He must have suffered an illusion. That others had had the same was not uncommon in combat.

In the end, after they had done what they could for their own injured and cut the throats of whatever foes lay crippled, he and his troop stood at the brink, looking down. They saw the galley beating along the point on oars. The coracles trailed after. 'That remnant is not in simple retreat,' Gratillonius deemed. 'They still aim to give reinforcement below Cape Rach. Well, we'll see about that.'

He almost regretted the killing. If Rome had civilized Hivernia, long ago when that was possible, what soldiers for her its sons would be!

6

Hulls rolled, pitched, yawed, shuddered. Spray sheeted over the bows. Yet close in to land the seas were no longer too heavy to row against, with the currachs in the galley's pathbreaking wake. The reefs farther out took most of their rage. It would have been mortally perilous to venture there. Niall had another reason as well for staying near the cliffs. 'The shortest way is the swiftest,' he explained to Breccan. 'The sooner we reach our people at the harbour, the fewer of them will die.'

The boy hugged cloak around shoulders. Legs braced and hands clutching rail, they were standing together on the foredeck. Bailing was not immediately needful – a boon, when the crew were dwindled and so exhausted that turns taken on the benches were brief indeed. 'Can we truly help them?' Breccan wondered.

'We can, if the Mórrigu be with us still.' Awe tinged Niall's voice. He had seen the Mother of the Slain at work on the battlefield. 'This game is not played out, darling. I think that not all the players are human.' His gaze brooded over the waves. 'What we'll do is engage the enemy yonder while those of our men ashore who've lost their boats – the which they'll have had no chance to make fast – come aboard. Thereafter we'll stand out, escorting what currachs are left. With more men, this ship can get about readily again. The currachs may want towlines from us to escape the maze of rocks we must thread; or if any get wrecked, we can try to rescue the crews.'

'Will not the Ysans pursue? I've heard tell of their war fleet, and they know these waters as we do not.'

'Those ships are elsewhere, my heart. Otherwise they would have attacked us before ever we could make any landings. For the masters of Ys knew we were coming. It can have been none but their she-druids that caused us to be blown here.' Niall's fist smote the rail. 'May each be raped by a demon, and may the whelps he gets on them tear them apart in the birthing.'

Breccan looked troubled. 'Father, always you told me to honour a worthy foe. And they've been bonny fighters here. They have.'

'They set on us with their magical tricks when we meant them no hurt whatsoever.' Niall sighed. 'Ah, but Ys is fair and wonderful. Let us escape, and I'll forgive the folk if not their rulers.' A smile crossed his lips. 'Why, someday I'd like to come back, in peace. Behold. Let your eyes revel.'

They had rounded the point and were about to pass the city at a distance of several hundred yards. High and high the walls gleamed, and the towers beyond; it was as if the voyagers had truly crossed Ocean and come to Tír innan Oac. The very rowers stared and marvelled as they toiled.

Breccan shaded his brow from the spray. 'Father, something is different. See, there on top. The little sheds are gone, and – what *are* those things?'

'You've the eyesight of youth,' Niall said. 'Let me try – Cromb Cróche!' ripped from him. 'Those are killing machines! Helm over, Uail! Get us away!'

The air had gone quiet and cold. Waves ran noisily, but

not so much as to smother the deep drone and thud which sounded from either side of the sea gate. Boulders the size of half a man came flying, tumbling, arching over with a horrible deliberation. Six-foot shafts, their iron heads murderously barbed, flew straight between them.

A splash erupted alongside. The galley rolled on her beam ends. Aft, Niall saw a direct hit on a currach. And it was no longer there, merely bits of it afloat, and two men who threshed about for a small span until they went under.

'Row!' Niall bellowed. 'Pull out of range before they target us!'

Two bolts smote the larboard planks. Their points protruded into the hull. Their shafts dragged, waggled, got in the way of oars. Another pierced a currach, which filled and drifted useless. Men of the third boat drew close and tried to save those who clung to the wreckage. A ballista stone sank it.

'We cannot help,' Niall groaned. 'We'd only die ourselves.' Nor did any chance remain of giving aid at Scot's Landing. The galley must now get so far from Ys that her crew would have all they could do to keep her off the skerries. By the time she could labour around to the south shore, that battle would be over.

'Manandan, I offer You a bull, white with red ears and mighty horns, for every lad of mine who comes home,' Niall cried. Surely some could win back to such vessels as had not floated away, and thereupon ride it out, maintain sea room, finally steer for Ériu. Oh, let it be so!

Niall drew sword and shook it at the city. A sunset ray broke through clouds to glimmer along the iron, and to make brilliant the armour of the Ysan artillerymen. Tears mingled with salt water beneath the eyes of the King.

'Father, don't weep,' Breccan said. 'We did well – '

A bolt took him in the stomach, cast him down into the

286

bilge, and pinned him there. His blood spurted forth. For a moment he struggled, flailing arms and legs, like an impaled beetle. He choked off a scream. Then he mastered himself and forced a smile.

Niall reached him, knelt, and tried to pull the bolt free. It was driven in too hard for even his strength. Useless, anyway. Breccan was sped. 'Father,' he gasped, 'was I worthy?'

'You were that, you were, you were.' Niall hugged him and, again and again, kissed the face that was like Ethniu's.

Soon Breccan lay quiet, save that the ship made limbs and head flop. His blood and shit sloshed about in the bilgewater.

Niall rose. He clambered back on to the foredeck. Three splashes in the waves, followed by no more, showed that he had drawn beyond reach.

He raised the sword he had dropped when Breccan was hit. He lifted it by the blade, in both hands, letting the edge cut his right palm till red flowed down the steel. None was in his countenance, which was as white as the eyeballs of his dead boy. Looking towards the beautiful city he said, low and evenly:

'Ys, I curse you. May the sea that you call yourself the queen of rob your King of what he loves the most, and may what he loves afterwards turn on him and rend him. May your sea then take yourself back to it, under the wrath of your Gods. And may I, O strange and terrible Gods, may I be he who brings this doom upon you. For my revenge I will pay whatever the price may be. It is spoken.'

Trailed by the last of its currachs, the ship went in among the rocks. Three boats got away from Cape Rach to join them, but one was presently ripped open and the men drowned. Darkness fell. The survivors found anchorage of a sort. In the morning they started home.

XVI

1

Ys jubilated. That evening the Fire Fountain was kindled in the Forum. Its jets and cascades of flame would make luminous the next six nights, for which the Nine had promised fine weather – part of the celebrations, both solemn and sportive, that would give thanks for victory.

In certain houses happiness was absent. Among them were those which had lost a man in battle. Some other people had their different misgivings.

At sunrise Gratillonius left the palace. He did not seek the gate for its ceremonious unlocking; the waves were still running too high. Instead he went alone, in a hooded cloak, unrecognized by such few persons as were abroad this early, to the Forum. Oil to the fountain was turned off just as he came on to the plaza; a little smoke lent acridity to remnant mists.

Mounting the west stairs of the former temple of Mars, he heard the voice of Eucherius the Christian pastor quaver out of a bronze door left ajar. He frowned and halted. Evidently the daily Mass was not over yet. He recognized the blessing that followed Communion, having caught snatches of Christian liturgy throughout his life. A coughing spell interrupted it. Well, then, they'd soon be done in there. It would be bad manners to enter just now. Gratillonius composed himself.

Half a dozen worshippers came out. The catechumens, who did not number very many more, had already heard the part of the service that was permitted them and gone off. These, the baptized, were four women and two men, of humble station and getting along in years. They didn't notice him. When they had passed by, he went into the vestibule. At the inner door he looked beyond, into the sanctuary, where Eucherius and old deacon Prudentius were occupied. Softly, he hailed.

'Oh – the King!' The small grey man was astonished. They had been introduced, but as hastily as Gratillonius felt was halfway polite. He had had too much pressing business. Eucherius left Prudentius to put away the portable tabernacle of the Host, which in Ys was little more than a wooden box in the usual turret shape. The chorepiscopus trotted forward to take his visitor by the forearm. 'Dare I hope – ?' His shy smile faded out. 'No, I fear not. Not yet. Were you waiting outside? You would have been warmer in this room. It's open to everybody.'

'I don't belong,' Gratillonius answered. 'But I thought I should give you a sign that I respect your faith.'

The pastor sighed. 'You wish I would respect yours. Well, I do. From everything I have heard, it is an upright creed. I am sorry – I should not be, but I am – that I may not concede you more than this.'

'I've come on a matter touching yours.'

'I can guess what. You are indeed a virtuous man. Let us go talk.' Eucherius led the way through the corridor around the sanctuary to his quarters. There he offered bread, cheese, and water; he had nothing better. Gratillonius partook sparingly.

'Eight of my soldiers died yesterday,' he said. 'Seven were Christian. Their legion and funeral society are away off in Britannia. It behoves me as their commander to see that they get the kind of burial they wanted. When I inquired, I learned that no Christians are ever laid in Ysan soil.'

Eucherius expressed sympathy before he nodded.

'True. Any burials near the city have long been forbidden, since men decided the necropolis should spread over no more valuable land. Not that the faithful could well rest there. And pagan sea funerals – ' He grimaced, as if in actual pain. 'Ah, poor souls! Father, forgive them, for they know not what they do. They mean well, too, but – but even Queen Bodilis, who has been so benevolent to me – My son, you have at least seen the outer world. How can you partake in these gruesome rites?'

'It's not forbidden me as a Mithraist. The Lord Ahura-Mazda created many beings less than Him but greater than men. Besides, I don't agree the Ysan practices are bad. They sacrifice no humans, like the Germans.' Gratillonius drew aside from the combat in the Wood. 'Nor do they sanction those obscene things that get done in the name of Cybele.' Irritation roughened his tone. 'Enough of that. Graves are allowed inland. Some farmers and shepherds, who'd rather keep their dead close by, bury them on their own property. Why doesn't your church maintain a plot?'

'None has been granted us. We have nothing but this building. I doubt anybody would sell us an ell of ground to consecrate, supposing I could raise the money. They would be superstitiously afraid of offending their Gods.'

'I see. What do you do, then?'

'There is a churchyard outside Audiarna, the Roman town at the southeast border. It's not too far, about a day's journey by wagon. I have an arrangement with a carter, and with my fellow minister yonder.' Another fit of coughing racked the thin frame. Concerned, Gratillonius noticed how bloody was the sputum. Eucherius gave him a sad smile and murmured, 'Forgive me. I should not detain you, who must have much else to do. Send one of your soldiers who is a brother in Christ, and between us he and I will take care of everything.'

'Thank you.' Gratillonius rose, hesitated, and added, 'If you have any needs in future, ask. I don't think you'll find me unwilling to help.'

'Save where it comes to propagating the Faith?' replied Eucherius gently. 'Regardless, yours is a noble spirit. Do you mind if I pray to my God that He watch over you and someday enlighten you? As for – charitable works or the like – oh, Bodilis may have some ideas.' His eyes burned fever-brilliant in the gloom. 'Give her my love.'

2

Soren Cartagi sent an urgent message to the royal palace. The King should promptly meet with the Nine, as well as with Lir Captain and the Speaker for Taranis. 'No surprise,' Gratillonius snapped. He set the hour of noon and dispatched the courier to inform everybody named. At the time, he escorted Dahilis to the basilica. Twenty-two legionaries followed them. Some limped, some displayed bandages. Eight more lay dead, and two were an honour guard on the last journey of their seven Christian comrades.

The King wore a robe of splendour; the Key hung out in sight on his breast. He had better cut a potent figure. When he had mounted the dais before the eidolons of the Triad and, having formally opened the session and heard the invocations, gave the Hammer over to his Attendant, he was much too aware that that man was not Eppillus. Recovering himself, he nodded gravely at the eleven faces that looked up into his.

'Well met, I trust,' he said. 'Though belike 'tis matters of import you would bring forth, let us strive to move them expeditiously. We all have many urgent duties, both secular and religious. The Gallicenae should resume their cycle of Vigils, while those in the city attend not only to the Gods, but to the hurt and the bereaved among our folk. My lords, your Great Houses and those who serve them have many calls on your attention in the wake of recent events. As for myself, I must see to public business that has gone neglected, as well as re-establishing communication with our navy and with Roman officials throughout Armorica.'

Hannon Baltisi stirred his rawboned length on the bench. 'Well may you do that last, O King,' he growled, 'as heavily as we've paid out for the benefit of Rome. Can you get us any reimbursal of the debt?'

Gratillonius had expected this. Lir Captain was devout to the point of fanaticism. In his days as a shipmaster, he said, he had often encountered the Dread of Lir. He had also seen, spreading through the Empire, a Christianity from which he awaited nothing but evil. 'Methought we'd talked this out beforehand,' Gratillonius replied mildly. 'Ys dare not let barbarians lay waste the civilization which nurtures her also. We had the means to prevent it, and did, at remarkably small cost for the harvest we reaped.'

'Nonetheless, cost! And never have I agreed that our action was necessary. While Ys remains true to Him, Lir will guard her. Why should we make enemies among tribes with which we could very profitably trade?'

'We may do that, now that we have chastened them. I know their kind; they respect naught but strength.' Gratillonius drew breath. 'If we are to discuss policy, we should have summoned the whole Council of Suffetes.'

'Nay,' rumbled Soren. 'That's for later; and in honesty I must say I think you, lord King, are more nearly right. But you are wrong in other ways. You have forgotten the primal charge laid upon the King of Ys.'

Gratillonius nodded. 'He is the high priest and in a

sense the Incarnation of Taranis. Aye. But you know that *this* King is also your prefect.'

'And he is no Colconor!' Dahilis cried. Glances turned to her. She reddened, touched her lips, then squared shoulders and gave back a defiant stare.

Gratillonius smiled. 'Thank you, my dear,' he said. 'Let me remind this honourable assembly, 'twas understood when first I mounted your throne that I'd have much on my hands, things too long ignored that must be set aright, new things for which there is an aching need. 'Twas with your consent that I devoted myself to them. What's happened since shows that you were wise to go along with me.'

'That's past,' Soren declared. 'The time has come when you should in earnest assume your sacral duties.'

'Gladly will I, insofar as Mithras allows.'

Teeth flashed in Soren's beard. His burly form hunched forward. 'Then why do you refuse to lead the thanksgiving sacrifice today?'

'I explained that to the priest who asked me yester-even.' That had been one of those Suffete men who, otherwise occupied with their own everyday affairs, were initiated into certain mysteries and therefore authorized to conduct the rites of Taranis. The Speaker was among them, but tradition decreed that once he had taken that office he no longer acted as a flamen.

'He should have approached me earlier,' Gratillonius reproved. 'Then I would not have committed myself to be elsewhere at the time set. 'Tis a holy commitment which I cannot break, just as it appears the hour for your ceremony is now unchangeable. Well, my presence is not absolutely required. Choose a priest to take my place. As for me, surely the God will think Himself best served by a man who has first honoured the claims of manhood.'

'And what, pray, mean you by that?'

Here comes the crisis, Gratillonius thought. Beneath his robe he tautened himself like a soldier before battle. He kept his voice calm: 'You may have noticed that Quintus Junius Eppillus, my deputy, is not here. He fell in defending Ys. As do I, he worshipped Mithras. This day he shall have the burial he deserves.'

Soren scowled. 'The necropolis was closed lifetimes ago.'

'He should not lie there in any case, nor be cast to the eels. Such is not the way of Mithras. I'll leave him on Point Vanis, looking towards the Britannia to which he longed home, but forever guarding this land.'

A gasp went among the Gallicenae, save for Dahilis, who had already been told, and Bodilis, who was clearly perturbed. 'Nay!' shrilled Vindilis. 'Forbidden!'

'It is not,' Gratillonius retorted. 'That's grazing commons. A headstone will do no harm. Rather, 'twill recall his bravery on behalf of Ys.'

Hannon bit off word after word: 'It seems my lord King is misinformed. The necropolis was not closed merely because 'twas encroaching on land needed by the living. 'Twas draining down into the sea. Why think you we haul away our sewage from pits, 'stead of letting cloacas open in the bay? Corruption of His waters is a mockery of Lir. Men at sea must beg His pardon ere they relieve themselves. Let Ocean have clean ashes of a fallen King; let His fish otherwise have clean, undecayed flesh.'

'One grave high on a foreland will not – '

'The precedent!' Lanarvilis interrupted.

Quinipilis raised her staff and suggested, 'Could you not lay your friend to rest inland, Gratillonius? I'm sure almost any landowner would allow, aye, believe 'twas lucky and pay honours ever afterwards to the dead man.'

That was the sticking point, precisely because it was reasonable. Gratillonius had picked the gravesite on impulse, out of sentiment, a wish to give good old Eppillus some small compensation for the farm he would never return to. Only later, when he explained to Dahilis why the priest had left with such a scandalized expression, did she remind him of the prohibition. He had quite forgotten it until then.

Now he could not compromise. His authority had been challenged at its foundation; if he failed to maintain it, he would soon fail as the prefect of Rome.

'I fear that would be to break a vow I made before my God,' he stated. 'Moreover, with due respect, 'twould be wrong if Eppillus – the memory of Eppillus – became a yokel godling. His soul has earned more. Nay, he shall lie in earth which his blood has hallowed. It will not be a precedent. I will proclaim that this memorial is unique, revering every man who ever gave his life for Ys.'

He folded his arms just beneath the Key. 'This is my will,' he told them most quietly. 'Bethink you, my ladies and lords.' He made no least gesture at the motionless iron rank of his men.

Not much further was said. Hannon himself had no more desire for a confrontation than did Gratillonius. One by one, the gathering mumbled assent.

Still, success was exhilarating, giddying. Gratillonius wanted to make them happy too, make them again his well-wishers. He raised his palms. 'Let me give you the glad tidings,' he said. 'Queen Dahilis is with child.'

A murmur, not really surprised, went among the women. Bodilis and Quinipilis, at her sides, embraced her.

Goodwill rushed over Gratillonius. Let bygones be bygones. If Colconor had been wronged, the swine wasn't worth avenging. Certainly that incident should no longer encumber the King in his politics and his daily relationships.

'Hear more, O Sisters of hers,' Gratillonius continued.
''Tis true I've perforce postponed many of my tasks; but
as her time approaches and she is hampered, why, we
shall all get to know each other better.'

Vindilis flushed as if struck. Fennalis sneered. Quinipilis frowned and shook her head slightly. Bodilis bit her
lip. Lanarvilis and Forsquilis stiffened. Maldunilis and
Innilis seemed to accept, and Dahilis was radiant – she
had felt so guilty about having him to herself when he was
with any woman whatsoever – but he realized in some
dismay that somehow he had said the wrong thing, and it
could not very well be unsaid.

3

Sunset cast scarlet and gold over the half of heaven that
reached above Ocean. Water glimmered and glowed
beneath the cliffs. Sounds of surf came muted. A breeze
ruffled the grass on Point Vanis. It came from the north,
cooling the day's warmth, bearing a smell of salt and
maybe, maybe, of fields in Britannia.

Six legionaries bore the freshly made coffin of Eppillus
to the grave that had been dug and lowered it down. Then
they saluted, wheeled, and marched back to the city in
formation. As Christians, they could give no more honours to their officer. Four stayed behind: Gratillonius,
Maclavius, and Verica, the Mithraists in their vexillation,
together with Cynan, who had offered his help. Funerals
were not forbidden to noninitiates; after all, wives, daughters, mothers, young sons, companions had farewells to
make.

Not before had the believers held a service. That might
have been disruptive, on the march and during the settling

in and the preparations for war. They had contented themselves with private prayers. This evening they stood together in the presence of eternity.

The three rankers took the spades they had carried and filled the hole. At first clods fell on wood with a sound like footfalls; afterwards the noise was muffled, until the low mound had been patted down to await wildflowers. A headstone would come later. Gratillonius had not yet decided what the epitaph should be. Name, position, unit, of course – and, perhaps, the old Roman 'STTL . . . *Sit tibi terra levis* – May the earth lie light upon you.'

Meanwhile he spoke the sacred words. Holding the grade of Persian within the faith, he could do that, though best would have been if Eppillus could have had his valediction from a Father. ' – Since this man our comrade has fared from among us – '

The soul was surely bound for Paradise. How long its trek would be, no mortal could tell. Eppillus had talked of feasting with Mithras; the God must set a grand table! But seven gates stood on the road to the stars, each guarded by an angel who would only let the soul pass when it had undergone a further purification. To the Moon it would leave its vitality, to Mercurius its voracity, to Venus its carnality, to the Sun its intellectuality, to Mars its militancy, to Jupiter its pride, to Saturnus the last of its selfhood; thus would it attain the eighth heaven and the Light, to be forever One with Ahura-Mazda. Gratillonius found the thought of Eppillus trudging on that pilgrimage peculiarly lonely.

But farewell, farewell.

Colours died in the sky. It shaded from silvery in the west to royal blue in the east. The earliest stars trembled forth.

'Let us go back,' said Gratillonius.

Cynan plucked at his sleeve. 'Sir,' he murmured, 'may I have a word with you, apart?'

Surprised, the centurion looked into the sombre young visage a heartbeat or two before he nodded. They went off to the trailhead above the cliff, up which the enemy had stormed. Peace breathed around them.

'What do you want, Cynan?' Gratillonius asked.

The Demetan stared outward. His hands wrestled each other. 'Sir,' he forced from himself, 'would it be . . . possible . . . for me . . . to join in your rites . . . hereafter?'

'What? But you're a Christian.'

'It means nothing to me,' Cynan said hurriedly. 'The centurion knows that. Else why would I be here? I offered to my tribal Gods, they seemed more real, but – I always wondered, and then the other day – ' His tongue faltered.

'What happened?' Gratillonius prompted.

'You know!' Cynan exclaimed. 'That ghastly giantess who entered the battle.'

A prickling went through Gratillonius's skin. 'What? Did you too have that, that delusion?'

'Not me alone. I've talked with others.'

'Well,' said Gratillonius carefully, 'I suppose the Scoti may by some kind of magic have called in some kind of creature to help them at the last. Little good did it do them.'

Cynan clenched his fists and twisted about to face his leader. 'Sir, that isn't it! I'm not afraid of Halfworld beings. But I saw . . . I saw an old, animal horror, and it lives inside me, inside everybody, and . . . and nothing can keep it from us but a God Who is not mad. Will you teach me about yours?'

Gratillonius forgot military discipline and hugged him.

Stepping back, his wits restored, the centurion said, 'You'll certainly be welcome to worship with us if you'll accept the discipline. But just as a postulant, a Raven. If you do well, I have the power to raise you to an Occult. No more. Initiation into the true Mystery needs a Father.'

'Someday I'll find one,' Cynan replied ardently.

It burst upon Gratillonius like sunlight through clouds: Why not?

Votaries of Mithras were scattered through the Empire, their congregations isolated, often persecuted. There must be some in the cities and barracks of Armorica, not to speak of Britannia and the rest of Gallia. In Ys they could find tolerance, the Brotherhood free and open. Not that they could settle here as a general thing, but they could come for prayer, elevation, heartening upon earth, strength for the wayfaring afterwards. Moreover, most being soldiers, such ties with them would help him draw together a defensive webwork for the whole province.

He could not found or lead a Mithraeum. That required a Father. But he could cherish the dream and work for its attainment.

4

With the round of the Vigils broken, Bodilis volunteered to be the first who started afresh. The order of rotation was not important. What mattered was to have a Sister on Sena – always, apart from special circumstances – in communion with Our Lady of the Sea and the souls whom She had taken unto Herself.

Bodilis thought she might be the best of the Nine to go forth after the gale, simply because of having both strength of body and an orientation towards natural philosophy: for she did not expect that the cycle could in fact be immediately resumed. She proved right.

Though morning seas rolled as gentle as rocks and riptides allowed, the barge of state that bore her could not make land. The wharf was gone, except for a few splintered bollards. It would have been dangerous for a vessel of any size to approach. Instead, a jollyboat carried the high priestess to shore. Its oarsmen waited while she walked to the building and, afterwards, around the entire island.

That took a pair of hours, during which the sailors kept reverent silence. From time to time they glimpsed her, in a cloak of the blue that was Belisama's colour, moving over rocks and treeless flats. Before them was the sight of the building and the damage it had suffered. It was a small, squared-off structure of dry-laid granite from which a tower jutted, on the east end of Sena. Billows dashing over the low ground had displaced several blocks at the bottom, visibly though not enough to cause collapse. On the frontal western side, window glass was shattered, shutters torn off, the oaken door a-sag on its hinges.

The calm of this day became a chilling reminder of what had passed. Waves lapped, chuckled, glittered green, azure, white, streaked with dark tangles of kelp. A few seals cruised to and fro, close in to shore; it was as if their gazes too followed Bodilis. Gulls, guillemots, puffins, cormorants winged beneath cloudlessness. Through the air went a current of summer's oncoming warmth.

She returned and had the men bring her back to the barge. There she nimbly climbed the rope ladder to the deck and sought the captain. 'We go home at once,' she told him. 'The place is unfit. It needs restoration.'

The officer was bemused, a little shocked. 'How, my lady?'

Bodilis smiled. 'Be at ease. This is not the first time over the centuries that that has happened. The worst was in the era of Brennilis, when Ocean destroyed everything.

It was among the warnings by the Gods against making the wall around Ys otherwise than according to Their will. These repairs ought take no more than some days. Furnishings and holy objects shall be replaced as well, likewise stocks of food and water – aye, in particular the cistern must be emptied, cleansed of salt, supplied with fresh sand and charcoal. The Stones abide as always. However, the hearthsite there would benefit from attention.'

The captain tugged his beard. 'But what of the House itself, my lady? Restoring yon blocks will be hard labour, impossible for women to do, if the Queen will pardon my saying so.' A thought struck him. 'Could the King's soldiers lend their skills? The Romans are the greatest engineers in the world.'

'Nay. Even Brennilis's Romans were only permitted to draw up plans and give advice. Among men, none but husbands or sons of former vestals may ever betread this island above high-water mark, and then only when the necessity is beyond doubt and after they've been blessed in certain ancient rites. At that, once they are done, all we Nine must come out and reconsecrate everything. Gratillonius is a good man, but he would never be able to understand – ' Bodilis broke off. 'Come, unship the sweeps, let us begone.'

XVII

1

After the victory celebrations, Ys settled back down into the ways of peace. Those did not mean idleness. Besides workaday tasks and repair of storm damage, there were preparations for the great midsummer festival. However, folk no longer tensed themselves against the morrow. The Scoti were broken, the Saxons would surely heed that lesson, the Romans of Armorica stayed quiescent, and – word trickled from the palace, to which couriers brought letters – Maximus was campaigning, successfully, in the South. A person dared again take a certain amount of ease.

Even Gratillonius did. Most of the time he kept busy. He must confer with the individual Suffetes, try to win their confidence, wrangle over ends and means, defence, outside relations, how to refill city coffers that Colconor had emptied, what reforms were desirable in a civil service ossified with age, countless petty details. Without compromising the status of King or prefect, he also tried to make the acquaintance of ordinary people, their needs and wants, strengths and failings.

Still, he could now take some recreation, set up a woodworking shop for himself, go riding, hunting, sailing. He could devote more attention than erstwhile to Dahilis. (As yet, aware that he had blunderingly given umbrage to his other wives, but unsure how to make amends, he met them only publicly, when at all. Dahilis too kept silence about the matter. He knew, and knew that she knew, that to some extent they were selfishly grasping what time remained to them before her fruitfulness was so far along that they had better sleep apart.) He and his soldiers, Mithraist and Christian, could properly observe that Sunday whose holiness they shared.

He could instruct Cynan in the Faith.

He received the Demetan in a room of the palace meant for private talks. On the upper floor, it was small and plain save for frescos of pastoral scenes, narrow-windowed, sparsely furnished. The first day when Cynan came happened to be rainy, which cast a dimness as if this were indeed a crypt of the Mystery. A servant showed the visitor in, closing the door after him. Cynan snapped a salute. In Roman tunic and sandals, painstakingly barbered and scrubbed, he could not altogether hide surprise at sight of his chief.

'Greeting,' said Gratillonius from his chair. 'At ease. What's the matter?'

'The centurion is . . . very kind,' replied the newcomer huskily.

Gratillonius studied the darkly handsome face, the muscular body, the hillman beneath the civilized shell, before he murmured, 'At ease, I said. Outside this room we are legionary and officer. But here – the first thing for you to learn is that in Mithras are no worldly ranks. No high or low, rich or poor, free or slave.' He smiled. 'So what's bothering you?'

Trembling, Cynan blurted: 'You aren't like before, sir! I didn't really see it till now, but you aren't.'

Gratillonius considered. He wore Ysan shirt, jacket, and breeches, as he usually did except when overseeing his troops. Though close-cropped, auburn moustache and beard had reached their full growth. As yet his hair was too short to draw into a horsetail, but it fell beneath his earlobes and was confined by a fillet. Aye, he found himself thinking in Ysan, the lad may well wonder what sorcery beyond the sea gate has flowed its tide over me.

'I have to be King oftener than prefect, remember,' he said in his plainest Latin. 'Remember also, Mithras doesn't care about your outside. Only your inside, your spirit, counts. Do sit down.' When his guest had obeyed, he himself poured wine for them both. 'Let's talk.'

He couldn't lighten the mood. Cynan wasn't that sort; and, of course, this wasn't that kind of occasion. Gratillonius could, though, seek to penetrate the bashfulness – and the fierce pridefulness – that stood between them. 'Before we start,' he went on, 'we should know each other better. I picked you to come along, back in Isca, because I'd seen you fight like a demon beyond the Wall. But why did you volunteer?'

Cynan stiffened. 'It was an adventure, sir.'

'Can you look me in the eye and smile when you say that? Listen, son, if you're afraid to be honest, Mithras will not make you welcome. And if I punished you for your honesty, He would disown me.'

Blood pulsed up into the young countenance. A fist clenched. 'Very well, sir!' the Demetan cried. 'I wanted to travel and fight, not do drill at headquarters. But I did not want to travel with Maximus and fight Romans. My home village was near the coast. I came back from hunting in the glens and found the Scoti had been there. What they hadn't plundered, they'd burnt. They killed the men, my father, my older brother. They gang-raped my mother. They bore off my young brother and two sisters for slaves. I swore I'd live for revenge. I lied about my age and my Gods, to join the army. I gloried when we cut down the vermin in the North, and again here – oh, sir, you were Vengeance itself! Then that troll-thing on the battlefield – and afterwards, when you gave Eppillus his honour – *That's* why I've come to your God!' He covered his face and wept, long, coughing sobs: no Roman now, a Celt.

Gratillonius let him have it out, and comforted and calmed him, and could finally begin:

'I'm not the best by a long shot to explain the Faith. A lot I don't understand myself. I only rate as Persian, the fourth grade. But maybe it's good for you to hear about it first in simple soldier lingo.

'Persian . . . The Faith came from Persia, Rome's old enemy, but a worthy foe. Often a man learns more from an enemy than a friend. And, of course, it wasn't always war; and others than Persians were believers; and as the ideas moved into the Empire, Greek thinking, and later on Roman, worked them over.

'Before and above all, for ever, the One from Which Everything comes – ' He checked himself. The concept of Time – Aeon, Chronos, Saturnus, the Source, the Fountainhead – was for the higher ranks, those allowed into the sanctuary. You didn't pray to the Ultimate anyway.

'Above all Gods,' Gratillonius said, 'is Ahura-Mazda. He's also called Ormazd, Jupiter, Zeus, many names. Those don't mean much; He Is, the High, the Ever-Good.' He found himself slipping into the words of the Lion from whom he had received instruction. Well, they were doubtless better than any he could put together. 'Below all Gods is Ahriman, Evil, Chaos, maker of hell and devils and misery. The story of the world is the story of the war between Ahura-Mazda and Ahriman. So is the story of your soul, lad. They war for it the same as they do for the whole of Creation. But you don't have to stand by helpless. You can be a soldier yourself.

'Then your Commander is Unconquered Mithras.

'He is the God of light, truth, justice, virtue. Because these come into being, suffer, and die – like mortals, or like the sun that rises and sets and rises again – you'll see

Mithras shown with two torchbearers, the Dadophori. One torch is upright and burning, the other is turned down and going out.

'Our Lord Mithras was born from rock, which some say was a cosmic egg. It was on the banks of a river, underneath a sacred tree. Only shepherds witnessed this, and came to adore Him and bring offerings. But Mithras was naked and hungry in the cold winds. From the fig tree He plucked fruit and from its leaves He made Himself garments. Then His strength came to Him.'

Gratillonius paused before saying slowly: 'This happened before there was life on earth. I don't understand that myself. But why should a man be able to understand the Eternal?

'The first battle of Mithras was against the Sun. He overcame His noble foe, and received the crown of glory from Him. Thereafter He raised up the Sun again, and They swore friendship.

'His second battle was against the Bull, the first of living creatures that Ahura-Mazda made. He seized It by the horns and rode It, no matter how much He was hurt, till It was worn out and He could drag It to his cave. It escaped, and the Sun sent the Raven as a messenger, bidding Mithras kill the Bull. Against His will, He did this. He and His dog tracked It back to the cave where It had returned, and He took It by the nostrils with one hand while with the other hand He plunged His knife into Its throat.

'Then from Its body sprang life upon earth, from Its blood the wine of the Mystery. Ahriman sent his evil creatures to destroy this life, but in vain. A great flood covered the world. One man, out of the humans alive in those days – one man foresaw it in a vision, and built an ark that saved his family and some of every kind of being. Afterwards Ahriman set the world afire, but this too it survived, thanks to the labours of the Lord Mithras.

'Now His work on earth was done. With the Sun and His other companions, He celebrated a last supper before He ascended to Heaven. Ocean tried to drown Him on His way, in vain. He is among the immortals.

'But He's still our Commander in the war against evil, that shall end on the Final Day when Ahriman is destroyed, and the righteous are resurrected, and peace reigns eternal.'

For a while was silence. Unaccustomed to speaking at such length, Gratillonius had gone hoarse. He didn't think it would be impious to take a long drink of wine, not much watered.

'I have heard a little of this before,' Cynan said low. 'But you make it . . . real.'

'If so, I'm glad,' Gratillonius answered, 'though it's no credit to me. Thank the Spirit. You think about this. Ask questions. I'll have more to tell, the next few times we meet. After that, if you still feel you want to join – and mind you, if you don't, I won't hold that against you, because every man has to find his own way – if you still do, I'll initiate you as best I can.'

2

Dahilis wished to visit the Nymphaeum and seek a special blessing upon her unborn child. To her delight, Gratillonius said he would come along. The distance was less than ten miles, so no servants or provisions were needed, other than a basket of food for a light midday meal. He did take three of his legionaries, explaining that, while there was nothing to fear, they maintained the royal dignity. Dahilis laughed and clapped her hands in glee. She had long hoped to know the Romans better, her husband's trusty men. These were Maclavius, Verica, and Cynan.

On horseback, the five of them went out of High Gate. Beyond the smithies, tanneries, and other clangourous or malodorous industries forbidden within town, they turned off paved Aquilonian Way on to a path running due east along the middle of the valley, beside the canal. This cut through the southern edge of the Wood of the King. Though the day was glorious and the leafage all green and gold, Dahilis shivered in the shadows of the oaks and reached to take Gratillonius's hand. She recovered her merriment as soon as they were again in the open.

'Isn't it beautiful?' she exclaimed. 'Aren't the Three good and kind, that They made this for us?' She gestured around. Beneath a vault of light where a few clouds wandered and many wings beat, the valley sides lifted intensely verdant. Pastures were starred with wildflowers. Orchards stood rich near farmhouses thatched, earth-walled, but snug and neatly whitewashed. Groves and gardens framed mansions – red-tiled, tawny-plastered, glass agleam – on the heights. Dwellings of lesser size and luxury but in the same pattern, wide-strewn over the slopes, radiated a sense of well-being. A breeze lulled warm, bearing odours of blossom, growth, soil. Canal water glittered and chuckled above its bed of fitted stones, between its narrow banks where moss made softness; frogs leapt, dragonflies hovered lightning-blue. High and high overhead, a lark carolled.

Gratillonius smiled on her. 'No doubt,' he answered, 'but it suffers by comparison with you.' Indeed she was lovely. Her head was bare and she had not piled her hair in the elaborate coiffure of a noblewoman but let it flow free, like a maiden's or a commoner bride's, past the pert features and down her back, as yellow as the loosestrife nodding in the grass. A gown of silver-worked samite was belted close around a slenderness which the life within had, thus far, not changed. Skirts hiked up for riding astride, her legs might have been turned on the lathe of a master craftsman who was also a Praxiteles, save that they seemed about to start dancing. How tiny were her sandals!

'Oh, my,' she laughed, 'you're becoming quite the courtier, darling. Beware lest you lose your proper Roman bluntness.'

The path climbed leisurely, leaving homes behind and passing through rail-fenced meadows where cattle grazed. Ysan territory held scant ploughland; the city got its grain from the Osismii. An occasional boy or girl dashed to gape at and hail these remarkable passers-by, the big man in his fine tunic and breeches, the three in flashing metal, the fair lady. Dogs clamoured. Dahilis waved and warbled greetings.

They stopped in a shady place to eat and rest. Dahilis served forth the bread, butter, pickled fish, hard-boiled eggs, wine. Cynan shook his head, walked off, stood gazing into the distance. 'Isn't he well?' the Queen asked, concerned.

'He practises certain austerities before a religious rite,' Gratillonius replied.

'Oh.' She shied from the subject. Verica and Maclavius were nothing loth to entertain her. Seeing that she winced at mention of war, they talked instead about their Britannic homelands. Her eyes grew still more huge. 'I do hope we can go there someday, Gratillonius, beloved, you and I – to *your* country.' The centurion refrained from saying how unlikely that was, or how risky and wretched.

The unguarded frontier was not far when path and canal bent north and wound steeply upwards. The waterway became natural, a string of small, chiming falls and

309

whirly pools. Forest grew thick, casting sun-flecked dusk-iness, and the air turned cool. When at last he came forth and saw the Nymphaeum, which he had done just once before and then briefly, Gratillonius was almost startled.

This was no mere pergola. The grounds occupied a couple of acres, the nearly flat bottom of a hollow under the hilltops, open to the south. North, east, and west the terrain rose somewhat higher, slopes and crests covered with wildwood. On the east side the holy spring welled from a heap of boulders whereon stood a statue of the Mother in Her serenity, shaded by a giant linden. All the waters flowed together to make a broad, clear pond, whence issued the stream that fed the canal. Swans floated upon it. Around it, and in a swathe leading to the building on the west side, a lawn reached silk-smooth, aglow in the afternoon light; peacocks walked there. The grass was bordered by flowerbeds, hedgerows, bowers, laid out with a sweet simplicity. The Nymphaeum itself was of wood, as befitted these surroundings, but on colonnaded classical lines, painted white. Modest in size, it was nonetheless large-windowed, airy, exquisite. A pair of cats, sacred to the Goddess, lay curled in the portico, while Her doves cooed above.

Here, said belief, the female spirits of nature came, to bathe on moonlit nights and flit frolicsome among the trees by day. Here too would stag-horned Cernunnos often come, drawn by their beauty, to this one place in the world where the forest God was not terrible; it was said that breezes at dawn and sunset were His lovesick sighs. No few wedding parties sought the Nymphaeum, and mothers-to-be like Dahilis, and folk weary of spirit, beseeching benison. Gratillonius's band dismounted, secured their horses, and approached in a reverence that was joyous.

Priestesses other than Queens, and descendants of

Gallicenae serving their vestalhoods, occupied the house by turns. Seven, robed in plain blue and white, they came out while the newcomers went up the stairs. The girls among them gasped and squeaked as they recognized the King. The aged leader bade him a welcome grave but not awed. When Dahilis spoke her desire, the old one smiled and laid a gnarled hand on her shoulder. 'Verily shall you have a blessing, child – at once, or as soon as you have rested from your journey if you need that.' The leader looked at Gratillonius. ''Tis a solemnity not for men. Could you absent yourselves an hour or two? You may like to accompany your steeds to the guardhouse; that's a pleasant stroll in this weather, and the warders would be glad of a chat. Afterwards you shall sup with us and spend the night. Aye, you may stay as long as you wish.'

'I thank my lady,' said Gratillonius. This was exactly what he had counted on. 'Duty demands return to Ys tomorrow, but until then we gratefully accept the hospitality of the Goddess.'

'Guide them, Sasai,' directed the leader, took Dahilis's elbow, and led the Queen inside.

A girl of sixteen or seventeen advanced awkwardly and, mute, proceeded down the stairs. Gratillonius recalled her; she had been at the temple of Belisama when he came to ask a storm of the Nine. She was tall, heavy-hipped, thick-ankled. Her head was small, with stringy brown hair, thin lips, underslung chin, and too long a nose. When he drew alongside her, she reddened and cast her glance downward.

His men led the horses behind him on a woodland trail that began at the rear of the Nymphaeum. Quietness brooded. He wanted to be friendly. 'Sasai, is that your name?' he asked the maiden.

'Aye, lord,' she mumbled, always watching the ground.

'Who is your mother?'

'Morvanalis. She is dead.'

Gratillonius swore at himself. Of course. He had met all the children of his wives. With an effort, he remembered who Morvanalis had been, the full sister of Fennalis, both born to Calloch and Ochtalis. As for the girl, judging by her age – 'Your father was Hoel?'

'Aye, lord.'

Silence stretched. He searched for words. Finally: 'Are you happy, Sasai?'

'Aye, lord,' said the monotone.

'I mean, well, do you think you will continue in service of the Goddess after you turn eighteen?'

'I don't know, lord.'

Gratillonius sighed and gave up. The poor creature must be dull-witted as well as homely and ungainly. He doubted she could catch a husband or shift for herself. So let her take the vows of a minor priestess; Belisama would shelter her.

The walk was short to the guardhouse and its stable. A dozen marines were barracked there, in case of danger – not that misfortune had ever stricken these hallowed precincts or the wildest of men dared to violate their peace. The warders were indeed pleased to have company and broke out the mead. Gratillonius had already met some and convinced them that the new King could be a comradely sort. Romans and Ysans sat yarning longer than he had expected, until he must hurry back.

Dahilis sped down the lawn to hurl herself into his arms, never mind stateliness. 'Oh, beloved, it was so wonderful, and the omens – the omens – She'll be like none ever before her – *your* daughter!' She stood on tiptoe and crammed her lips against his.

– Supper with the women was simple but savoury. Once grace had been said, talk became animated. Soon Verica and Maclavius were at their ease too. Cynan, fasting, had gone straight to the guestroom he would share with them.

At sundown the other three soldiers left the triclinium and went forth. The superior had given them permission to pray to Mithras, if they did it off the grounds. They found a glade where the last rays streamed level between boles. On the way back, despite piety, Gratillonius felt cheerful enough to be jocular: 'Don't oversleep, boys.'

Again Dahilis waited outside for him. 'Shall we take a walk ere we retire?' she proposed. He was willing. Hand in hand they sauntered about through the dusk, under the early stars. No nymphs appeared, but she was amply sufficient.

In their own chamber she slipped off sandals and belt, pulled gown and undergarments over her head, let everything fall and reached towards him. A single lampflame cast glow on cheekbones, eyes, the dear vessel that was her belly. Elsewhere shadows caressed her. She smiled. 'Why stand you there like that?' she breathed. 'See you not how I want you?'

'Is it . . . seemly . . . here?'

'You marvellous fool!' she trilled. 'Where is it more right to make love?'

When they did, he felt as though Belisama were truly present.

3

Gratillonius had told his dreams to wake him at dawn, and they obeyed. Windowpanes were grey; the room brimmed with murk, chill, and silence. He could barely see Dahilis beside him. On the pillow, in its flood of tresses, her face looked like a child's. How long were

313

those lashes. Babywise, she was curled up under the blanket. He rose as easily as he was able, but the leather webbing under the mattress creaked aloud.

Her eyes fluttered open. He stooped to kiss her. 'Hush,' he whispered. 'I go to my sunrise prayers, and maybe afterwards a jaunt in the woods. Sleep on.' He had not told her his real intent, because he knew it hurt her to be reminded that his faith debarred her. If he did now, she would be too excited to rest, and that might not be so good for the unborn. She smiled and closed her eyes again.

He had clean garb in a bag, which he donned, but when he was shod and combed he took something additional and threw it over his arm. Soft-footed, he left the room and groped his way to a rear door. None of the priestesses or vestals was awake; their services were at noontide, full-moon midnight, and the heliacal rising of Venus. His men awaited him outside. They also wore white tunics, together with military cloaks against the cold. Wordless, they gave him the Roman salute and formed single file, Cynan last. Stars glimmered yet in the western heavens, but the east was lightening. Mists drifted over pond and turf. Dew laved sandalled feet. Only the clear ringing and clucking of water had voice.

The day before, scanning the heights, he had decided to go northeast. The trail was barely a trace, gloom loured between the trees, men rustled through underbrush and stumbled on roots, but the rivulet they followed sang and glistened for a guide. It took a while to find the sort of place for which Gratillonius had hoped, but then it was perfect, as if Mithras Himself had chosen it. The hillside broadened to form another hollow, like the one where the Nymphaeum stood save for being tiny. Issuing from a spring a little farther up, the stream ran bright, here a whole three feet wide and better than ankle-deep. Beech, hazel, thorn crowded around, night still in the depths among them but crowns silvery under the dawn. They did not grow too close for free movement. Instead, masses of convolvulus twined stems and lifted white chalices. Dew was brilliant on those leaves.

'We are come,' said Gratillonius. 'Let us prepare ourselves.'

Following an invocation he gave, he was first to strip and wash himself in the purifying water. Maclavius and Verica went in next, then stood on either side of Cynan while the postulant did likewise. These three resumed their tunics, heedless of being wet and cold, but Gratillonius had donned a robe and Phrygian cap.

'Kneel,' he said, laid hands on the head of the recruit, and asked for divine favour.

Radiance burst forth. The sun cleared the eastern treetops. Gratillonius, Maclavius, and Verica said the morning orison; Cynan stayed aside.

The Mithraist legionaries had brought flint, steel, tinder, dry wood, and an object which Gratillonius had had a smith make for him. As they, whose rank in the Mystery was Soldier, started and blew on the blaze, Gratillonius the Persian led Cynan through memorized responses. They rang firm into the quiet.

The bed of the fire was soon hot. Maclavius took the branding iron by its wooden handle and held it in the coals. 'Kneel,' ordered Gratillonius again, 'and receive the Sign.' Cynan obeyed. Gratillonius accepted the iron from Maclavius. Cynan watched unflinchingly. Verica came from behind to brace him by the shoulders. Gratillonius strode from the fire with the iron red in his right hand. His left brushed back a lock that had fallen over Cynan's brow. For an instant, looking down into those eyes, he recalled how he had slashed this face on shipboard. The weal was long gone. The brand of the Sun would never go, quite, though in time it would fade to as pale a mark as was on him and the other two men. Speaking the Word of Fire, he put the iron to the forehead. Breath hissed between Cynan's teeth, the sole token the Demetan gave. A roasting smell marred the air. Gratillonius withdrew the iron, gave it to Maclavius, and bent to help Cynan rise. 'Come,' he said. Together they went back to stand in the stream. Gratillonius scooped a handful of water and let it run over the angry red sigil. 'Be welcome, Raven, to the Fellowship,' he said. He embraced the new brother and kissed him on both cheeks. They returned to earth, wading through the convolvulus. 'It is done,' Gratillonius said.

A cry ripped across his awareness. Swinging about, the men saw Dahilis under the trees. Her hair was dishevelled, her gown mud-stained. Tears coursed down her countenance.

'What are you doing?' Gratillonius roared in his shock, and heard Cynan snarl: 'A woman, at this holy hour?'

'I couldn't sleep, I followed your tracks in the dew and went on upstream, I thought we – O-oh,' she wailed, 'oh, I'm sorry, I'm sorry, but 'tis dreadful what you've done. I dared not speak till now – ' She lifted arms and gaze heavenwards. 'Belisama Mother, forgive them. They knew not what they did.'

As ever in crisis, Gratillonius's mind leapt to action. He confronted the men. 'She has not profaned the ceremony,' he said in Latin with all the authority he could muster. 'This is no Mithraeum, just a site that was suitable, open to anyone, and she did not interrupt. Mithras is satisfied. You be too.' Inwardly, he could only hope he was truthful. He himself had not been instructed in the deepest lore of the Faith.

When he saw them glowering but calm, he went to stand before Dahilis. His arms longed to hold her close

316

and dismiss her despair. Instead he must fold them and say levelly: 'We have done no harm, no sacrilege. We held an initiation. That requires flowing water, and there is none in Ys.' A sardonic part of him remembered that city Mithraeums commonly drew it from a tank. But of course there was no Mithraeum in Ys.

'Don't you . . . don't you *see*?' she stammered. 'This stream – from Ahes – it flows to join Her most sacred water – and, and you, your male God – '

He decided that it would not be unwise to close his fingers gently on her forearms, look straight into the lapis lazuli eyes, and say, quite sincerely: 'My dear, in the end all Gods go back to the One; and as for me, I am the high priest and avatar of Taranis, Her lover. If I have done wrong, on my head be it; but I deny that I have. Ask your Sisters. Meanwhile, fear not.'

She gulped, shuddered, straightened. He wished he could console her. Abruptly her smile kindled, however tremulous. 'Why, I am, am with you always, Grallon – Gratillonius, beloved,' she said. 'Cynan, I'm sorry if I . . . disturbed you . . . at a wonderful moment . . . and belike naught was profaned. And, and here is the spring of Ahes, *my* nymph, my patroness. Surely she'll listen when I ask her to intercede with Belisama – Shall we be friends again, we five?'

The King thought in a leap of joy: With so high a heart, she may well fulfil the omen she spoke of, she may well bear us a daughter who'll be remembered when Brennilis herself is forgotten.

Dahilis looked about. 'Why, see the convolvulus,' she exclaimed as vivaciously as might be. 'Is't not fair? Could you wait a little, kind sirs, while I gather some?' She became busy doing so. Her chatter went on: ''Tis medicinal, but we grow it not in the city or nearby, for 'tis apt to overrun gardens. My Sister Innilis has told me her sup-

317

ply's run short, for ever does she go about as a healer among the poor in Ys. Belisama's Cup, they call this flower. Know you why? The story is that once, long, long ago, a wagon was hopelessly mired. She came by in the guise of a mortal and told the carter She would help him free it. He laughed and asked what payment She wanted. 'I give My gifts for love,' She answered, 'but now I thirst. Would you give me some of your wine?' Said he, 'Well, I'd not grudge a woman that, but alas, I've no cup with me.' She plucked a convolvulus flower, he filled it, She drank, and thereupon the wheels rolled on to firm ground. Aye, the Goddess can be tender.'

And terrible, Gratillonius thought. Dahilis loaded her arms. The dew on leaves and blossoms was cool, almost cold, like moonlight.

4

Innilis needed pretty things around her. The house that she inherited she had had painted rosy pink on the outside; within, the walls became pale blue trimmed with gold, where they did not carry paintings of blooms and birds. Delicate objects filled the rooms, statuettes, crystal, silver, as well as gauzy hangings. Most she had not bought, for she lived quietly and spent much of her stipend on alms and charitable works; she had received it from people who rejoiced to behold her joy. Two servants, man and wife, sufficed her. They were apt to go about their work he smiling, she singing.

Ocean sheened as if polished beneath a late sun when Vindilis arrived. Innilis let her in. They two could merely exchange salutation and looks while the woman attendant stood by. 'Welcome, oh, welcome,' Innilis whispered. She drew breath and turned to the servitor. 'Evar, the Queen and I have m-m-much to discuss. We'll sup – after dark, I suppose. I know not when, I'll tell you at the time, it need only be a light collation. Come.' She hastened from the atrium. Vindilis strode at her side.

In the conference room, they closed the door and curtained the windows. Thereafter the kiss went on and on. ''Tis been so long,' Innilis half sobbed, her cheek upon Vindilis's small bosom.

'Aye,' Vindilis replied into the fragrant brown hair. Nobody else in Ys had heard her croon. 'But this time is ours. We've done our duty, now we may have our reward.'

Innilis stepped back, keeping hands linked with hands, stared up into the gaunt visage before her, and said sadly, 'Not yet may I take much ease, dear darling. Those men worst hurt in the battle – many wounds have become inflamed – men lie tossing on their beds, sometimes raving, while their wives and children know naught to do save pray.'

'And call on you,' Vindilis added. ''Tis ever thus. You, the Sister of mercy.'

Innilis shook her head. 'Nay, you know better. Bodilis, Fennalis, Lanarvilis – '

'They do what they can, but the grace of the Goddess is in your touch.'

Innilis flushed. 'You've had your work too.'

'In truth.' Vindilis's tone hardened. 'Our King would fain turn everything topsy-turvy. Along with much else, he wants changes in management of the public treasury, starting with inventory of every coffer, religious and civil alike. I must agree 'tis not necessarily a bad thing. I'd no idea how slipshod record-keeping had become in the Temple. Yet the Nine shall retain control of its finances. Quinipilis and I are overseeing the work. Her strength flags early in the day, so most of it falls on me.' She laughed. 'That's why my note said we should meet here. At my house, some female prothonotary is like to burst in at any moment with a question.'

Innilis's smile lighted the chamber. 'Well, you *are* here,' she sighed, and swayed close again.

They undressed each other with many endearments and little jests. There was a broad couch. They sank on to it. Hands, lips, tongues went seeking, caressing. Time passed unheeded.

The door opened. Dahilis came through. She carried a basket full of Belisama's Cup. 'Innilis, dear,' she called happily. 'Evar told me you – ' She dropped the basket and choked off a scream.

Vindilis bounded to her feet. 'Shut the door!' she hissed.

Numbly, Dahilis did. Her glance went from the lean, crouched form with fingers crooked like talons, to Innilis huddled back on the couch, an arm across her breasts, a hand over her loins, mouth parted, eyes widened till the blue was ringed in white.

Vindilis stalked forward. 'You meddlesome witling.' Her fury was like the iceberg that flays a ship. 'How dared you? How dared you?'

Dahilis retreated. 'I didn't know.'

'Vindilis, darling, she couldn't have,' Innilis quavered. 'I should have told Evar . . . not to let anybody in, not even a Sister . . . I forgot. I was so glad y-you were coming . . . I forgot. 'Tis my fault, mine alone!' She cast herself down on a pillow and wept.

Vindilis halted. 'Well, I might have noticed and seen to it, but I didn't,' she said. 'Whatever the blame, we'll share it, as we've shared our hearts.'

Dahilis squared shoulders. 'Belike this was . . . the will of the Goddess,' she said. 'Certes 'twas never mine.'

320

'I'll yield you that.' Vindilis picked up her cloak and covered her nakedness. Grimly: 'What we must decide is how to cope with the matter.'

Dahilis went to the couch, knelt beside it, threw arms around Innilis. 'Cry not, little Sister, cry no longer,' she begged. 'I love you. I love you best of all my Sisters. Never will I betray you, nay, not to my lord himself.'

Vindilis let her continue murmuring, soothing, stroking hair and brow, while she reclad herself fully. When at length Innilis was quiet, save for gulps and hiccoughs and nose-blowing, Vindilis fetched a nightgown from the bedroom. Dahilis helped Innilis draw it on. Its fluffiness made her seem a child. She sat up near the head of the couch, the other two sat on the foot, and they looked back and forth through dimming light.

'I thank you for your loyalty, Dahilis,' said Vindilis.

'Well, you were kind to me in the past,' responded Dahilis.

'Less kind than I might have been. I see that now. But 'tis not my nature.' Vindilis paused. 'Nor is it my nature to care for men.'

Dahilis cast a troubled regard at Innilis, who faltered, 'I, I know not what my nature is. Hoel and Gratillonius – but they never taught me!'

Dahilis bit her lip. 'That may be my doing. I've been . . . greedy . . . about him. I fear that's offended the Goddess.'

Vindilis bridled. 'Think you *this* has?' she challenged. 'Nay, we twain gave each other the strength to endure Colconor. Thus we could carry out our duties, and not go mad. Love is the gift of Belisama. Should we spurn it, for a man who cares naught?'

'You wrong him,' Dahilis protested. She clenched her fists. 'Aye, there I think is your sin, that you turn your

321

back on the King the Three sent to deliver us. Innilis . . . you, at least . . . oh, do!'

'I can try,' came the whisper. 'If he will. But never can I forsake Vindilis.'

'That may perhaps be – Who am I to say? Who are we?'

Slowly, Dahilis unclenched her hands. She stroked them over her belly, once, and calm flowed after them. Rising, she looked straight at the two and said:

'I promised I'd keep faith with you, and I will. But we must find what is right. Let us think where we may seek. Tell me when you feel ready. Until then, farewell, my Sisters.'

She walked out. The hem of her skirt scattered the spilled flowers.

XVIII

1

A short way north of Warriors' House where fighting men on duty had barracks, the Water Tower raised its great bulk higher than the adjacent battlements of Ys. A conduit under city wall and pomoerium led the flow of the canal there; ox-turned machinery pumped it to chambers near the top, whence pipelines redescended beneath pavement and carried it off to certain temples, important homes, fountains, and baths. The pipes were ceramic, because people here had a notion that lead was slow poison. Otherwise, and mainly, they depended on catch-basins and storage tanks with sand filters; rainfall kept those well enough filled.

The roof of the Water Tower held an observatory. Many Ysans did not trust in astrology, but many others did. In any case, stars and planets were vital to timekeeping, navigation, religious rites. Moreover, there was an ancient tradition of gathering knowledge for its own sake. This work required a building hard by to contain instruments, library, scriptoria, auditorium. The Romans who remodelled Ys gave it a new Star House, in an Athenian style modified for the Northern climate. It came to be the meeting place of philosophers, scholars, poets, artists, visitors, who had interesting things to tell, citizens whom the Symposium voted into membership.

A King could not be denied. Few had availed themselves of the privilege – more than once or twice, at any

323

rate. Gratillonius wanted to, but had not hitherto found time. Now he could go.

A supper would be followed by free conversation, which might well outlast the night; but first the afternoon was for formal discussion. Word that the King would attend had brought well-nigh everyone who belonged. Decently clad though never sumptuously, most wearing togas, they reclined like the ancients on couches arranged in a circle, a couple of dozen men and Queen Bodilis. Between each pair, a small table bore dilute wine, raisins, nuts, cheese, which barefoot youths – noiselessly, always listening – kept replenished, not for the gratification of stomachs but to maintain clear heads while the drink lubricated tongues. The room was austere unless one considered the beauty of its marble and onyx or the extraordinarily clear, almost colour-free window glass.

Today the president of the symposium was Iram Eliuni, otherwise Lord of Gold. A short, bald-headed, fussy man, he was not without humour as he said, 'Fain would I begin by lodging a complaint against our distinguished guest, Gratillonius the King. For generations my office was a sinecure, and I have had leisure to cultivate learning. Of late, he insists the treasury *do* something.'

He cleared his throat and proceeded: 'However, that is not the topic chosen for this gathering. 'Twas agreed by the committee that faith – that which men believe is the nature of God and Spirit, the meaning and destiny of Creation – that this is the highest and deepest question to which our souls can aspire. Moreover, if men be sane and righteous, belief will determine how they think, how they behave. In sooth, if you know not the faith of a man – or a woman, of course, my Lady Bodilis – then you understand that person not at all. Is this stipulated? Aye. Accordingly, we shall in mutual respectfulness investigate each other's religions. Gratillonius?'

Forewarned, the Roman could answer readily: 'You wish me to explain mine? Well, to be frank, I doubt I can say much which this group knows not already. Mithraism was widespread when Ys was close-knitted to the Empire. You must have descriptions. I'll be glad to talk about whatever you want to hear, as long as 'tis allowable for me, but I really think 'twill suffice to assure you afresh that I can and do honour the Gods of Ys . . . barring minor matters of ritual which count for naught . . . and if I've overstepped my bounds, 'tis been for lack of information, not of good will.' He looked around the circle, face by face. Bodilis, in a grey gown, wore perhaps the gravest expression. 'Let me make a request,' said Gratillonius. 'Let me ask you first about your religion. I pray you, enlighten me.'

'Where'd we begin?' asked a hoarse voice. Several men smiled. The inquirer was among the four regular members who belonged to no Suffete family – an artisan, but in his free time an experimenter who studied the behaviour of material objects.

'Perhaps by starting with history, which you recall we've talked about, Gratillonius,' suggested Bodilis.

'We have,' the centurion replied. 'Sirs and my lady, I've knocked about in the world. I know how often the Romans of old were mistaken when they reckoned a foreign God to be the same as Jupiter or Neptunus or Whoever. Thus far I've not been able to make entire sense of your Ysan pantheon. No disrespect; I simply haven't.'

'For example?'

'Oh . . . some of your Gods appear to come from the South or from Asia, but some are Gallic. And yet not Gallic. Taranis Himself – here in Ys He has taken the primacy from Lugh and the hammer from Sucellus, neither of Them having any cult among you as far as I

325

know – ' Gratillonius ventured a smile of his own. 'Help me understand what I have become!'

Esmunin Sironai said, almost inaudibly out of his thin chest: 'I trust you realize that we, at least we who are educated, do not take ancestral myths for literal truth, as if we were Christians. They are symbols. As different languages, or different words in one language, may denote the same thing – albeit with subtle variations of aspect – so, too, may different Gods represent the same Being. They change with time as languages do, They develop, according to the evolving needs of Their worshippers. The very heavens change through the aeons; nevertheless, the reality of Heaven endures.' He was the chief astrologer, once tall, now frail, white-bearded, nearly blind. Under his direction his students, who loved him, continued his researches: for he was not satisfied with Ptolemaeus's depiction of the universe.

'Mayhap 'twould help if the chronicle of the Gods were set briefly forth,' propounded Taenus Himilco. 'Parts you will have heard, Gratillonius, but not the whole, nor in orderly wise.'

A murmur of assent went around the circle. 'Do you do this,' Iram Eliuni decided. 'You are best qualified among us.' Of aristocratic appearance and bearing, with a seat on the Council of Suffetes, Taenus was also a landholder near the Wood of the King. He knew not only what city dwellers thought, but what countryfolk did.

At Gratillonius's urging, he commenced:

'In the Beginning, Tiamat, the Serpent of Chaos, threatened to destroy Creation. Taranis slew Her. But She was the mother of Lir, Who therefore waylaid Taranis and killed Him. Heaven and earth were plunged into darkness, until Belisama descended into the underworld. At a fearful price, She ransomed Taranis and brought Him back; and She made peace between Him and Lir. A condition of this peace was that Taranis must die over and over, until the End of All Things, though He would ever be reborn. This mystery we enact in Ys. Formerly 'twas by yearly human sacrifice. Today 'tis in the person of the King. He dies in battle, he is resurrected in the victor, who fathers new life upon the Gallicenae, the chosen of the Goddess.

'In a sense, therefore, every daughter of King and Queens is divinely engendered. Only nine at a time are actual avatars. The rest live common human lives. Likewise do persons born of congress between other divinities and mortals. We have families claiming descent from, say, Teutatis, Esus, Cernunnos – mine – or from female deities by mortal lovers, Epona, Banba . . . 'Tis mere ancestry, unattested save by legend. More meaningful, mayhap, though vague as sea-fog, is a tale that in the Ferriers of the Dead flows blood of cold Lir . . .'

Silence fell. Gratillonius nerved himself to break it: 'The Ferriers. I've heard of them. But nobody wants to speak of it. What does happen to the dead?'

'That no one knows. The stories are many, many. Ghosts haunting their homesteads, barrow-wights, the Wild Hunt – dim Hades or utter oblivion – Here in the city and along the coast, we bury our dead at sea, as you know. Their bodies. The Ferriers have the task of bringing the souls out to Sena, for which terrifying reason they are exempt from tax or civic labour. Yonder, 'tis thought, Belisama judges those souls, though some say Lir shares in it. Many say that certain are reborn – that dead Gallicenae, especially, may become seals, which linger until they can accompany their own beloved into the Beyond – But we do not pretend to know.'

'As you Mithraists do,' Bodilis said coolly.

Gratillonius flushed. 'I know not what will become of me,' he snapped. 'A man can but strive to earn salvation.'

327

'A *man*. Is it denied to any who are not washed in the blood of the Bull? That would admit only the wealthy to Heaven.'

'Nay!' exclaimed Gratillonius, doubly stung that she should be the one who gibed. 'The Taurobolium – that ugly business where the worshipper stands in a pit and the blood bathes him – that's for Cybele. The Great Mother, they call her.'

'You were sanctified by the blood of a King. Why should others not be sanctified by the blood of the Bull?'

'As you will. 'Tis not required among them either. The rites are open to women.' Gratillonius stopped himself from admitting how closely the Temples of Mithras and Cybele had often cooperated. He had never liked that cult, where men driven hysterical had been known to castrate themselves. Let women follow Christ, Who was good enough for his mother. 'When we slay a beast to Mithras, we do it with dignity, as He did.'

'I pray you, I pray you!' Iram cried. 'This is a comparison of views, an exchange of cognizances. Debates, if debates are desired, must be arranged separately.'

Gratillonius suppressed his temper. 'Well, about human destiny,' he said, 'many of my fellowship believe 'tis controlled by the planets, but I confess to doubts about that. Could the learned Esmunin enlighten us?'

'I am not in the least sure of the horoscopes I cast,' replied the old man, 'although I do my best as duty demands. If there is fate, then methinks 'tis on a grander scale, the forces of it all but incomprehensible to us. The apparition of comets, enigmatic eclipses, precession of the equinoxes – '

It became fascinating.

Gratillonius would happily have stayed as late as the last philosopher, but soon after the meal Bodilis plucked his toga and said low, 'Come away with me. We've things to talk about.'

Despite lingering resentment, he knew she would not request this idly, and made his excuses. No armed guard was necessary hereabouts; a lantern bearer sufficed, a boy who did not know Latin.

'I'm sorry I angered you,' Bodilis said in that language. 'But given the opportunity, I thought I must.'

Astonished, Gratillonius glanced at her. Stars threw more light on her face than did the glow bobbing ahead. He studied its strong moulding as if for the first time until, confusedly, his gaze roved off, past the towers to the vast glimmer of Ocean. The night was cool. Footfalls rang.

'You see,' she said presently, 'you do not understand free women. If you're to reign as we both hope, you need to. I gave you a taste of what you've been giving us.'

'What do you mean?' he protested. 'My mother, my sisters – no slaves they. Nor most of those I've known.'

'But not equals either,' she retorted. 'We Gallicenae are. Never forget that.'

'What have I done wrong?'

She sighed, then smiled and took his arm. 'Not your fault, really. Everywhere else, unless perhaps among some of the barbarians, women are underlings. The Romans honoured their matrons, but gave them no voice in affairs. The Greeks shut theirs away in houses; no wonder that became a nation of boy-lovers, as dull as they made their poor women! Your cult won't admit them.

329

The Christians will – but subservient, looked at askance as vessels of temptation, denied any possibility of ever administering the sacraments. How could you know?'

The Great Mother – no, She was a screeching Asiatic. Tonight, around him, Gratillonius felt that majesty of Belisama, to Whom belonged moon and stars.

He swallowed. 'Did I insult you Nine? I didn't mean to. Dahilis said nothing.'

'She wouldn't. She's too loving. Nevertheless I suspect she has urged you pay more heed to her Sisters.'

'Well – she has – but – '

'Ah, I speak of pride, of what is due, not of lust, though the flesh does have its just demands. Think back, for example. When you announced Dahilis was pregnant, and this would release you in due course to service the rest of us – Do you like being patronized?'

'No! But – but – '

She laughed softly and held his arm the tighter. 'Dear Gratillonius. You've never been a man more than now when you flounder helpless. Do you imagine I'd have bothered trying to teach Colconor? Why, Hoel himself could not understand. He might have – he was not stupid – but he would not make the effort, he would not patiently listen. In you there is hope.'

'I will . . . listen, as long as seems reasonable . . . and try to do what's right,' he said carefully, 'but I will not humble my manhood.'

'Nobody asks that of you. It's simply that we will not humble our womanhood.'

They went on in silence until they reached her home. There Gratillonius tipped the boy and dismissed him. Inside, servants had gone to bed, as short as the nights were now growing, but had left a pair of lamps burning in the atrium. Light fell amber upon Bodilis. She whirled

330

about and seized him. 'Come,' she said huskily, 'don't wait, the hours are wearing away.'

She had been good before. This time she was magnificent.

3

Rain came misting out of the sea, to hide the towers of Ys and make its streets twilit ravines. Dahilis and Innilis felt it on their faces, like the kisses of a thousand ghosts. They drew their cowled cloaks as tight as they were able while walking. Despite the apprehension in them, they were glad to reach the house of Quinipilis.

The high priestess let them in herself. She had thrown a shawl over a gown often patched; wool stockings and straw slippers were on her rheumatic feet. Carelessly combed, her hair made a white lion's mane. 'Welcome!' she hailed. 'Stand not there getting wetter, come inside where 'tis halfway warm. I've mulled wine on the brazier, or I can brew up some tisane if you'd liefer.' She waved them through and rocked after them. 'Pardon my appearance. Your note asked for a private talk, so I gave the staff this day free. Ordinarily I do not meet folk until I've got my jowls neatly tied up against my ears.'

'We, we meant not to cause you trouble,' whispered Innilis.

'Nonsense, child. You've given me unassailable cause to stay away from the temple and slop about here. Toss your cloaks anywhere.' Quinipilis led the way to a room off the atrium. Like the rest of her establishment, it was somewhat garishly decorated. The furniture was battered but serviceable. 'Be seated. At ease, as our good centurion would say. We've the whole day if we want, not so? –

and a kettle of soup cooking. Made it myself. My cook's no slattern, but she *will* put in too few leeks.'

They sat down and, for a space, sipped mutely from their beakers. Across the rim of hers, Quinipilis squinted at the guests. When she deemed the moment ripe, she said: 'The trouble is yours, plain to see, and a bitter grief in you. Tell me whatever you wish.'

Twice Innilis tried to answer, and could not. She shrank back in her chair, clutched her cup, and fought against tears.

Dahilis squeezed her hand before taking the word, low but almost steadily, looking straight into the eyes of Quinipilis: ''Twas my thought that we seek your counsel, you, the oldest and wisest of us. We wanted Vindilis along, but she refused – sought to keep us from going – If you find her more aloof and haughty than ever, that will be the reason.'

'Age in itself brings no wisdom, dear. But I have seen a thing or two in the past. Say on.'

'This is a thing that could destroy. Yet I d-dare not call it wrong. I found out by sheer chance, unless 'twas the will of the Goddess . . . Innilis and Vindilis are lovers.'

Quinipilis bared what was left of her teeth in a sound-less laugh. 'Ho, is that all? I've known for years.' Innilis gasped. The wine splashed from her cup and stained her lap. Quinipilis ignored that, smiled at her, and said kindly, 'Fear not. I'm sure none else has suspected. Me, I'm curious about people. Their bodies speak more honestly than their tongues. I've learned a bit of the language.'

'But what shall we do?' Dahilis pleaded.

Quinipilis shrugged. 'Need we do aught? This cannot have been the first time in the centuries. Nine women to one man may be sacred, but 'tis not natural. Yet Ys has done rather well throughout its history. 'Tis only that its folk have inherited, from their Carthaginian forebears, an abhorrence. I believe Belisama understands.'

She gazed afar. Her voice dropped. 'Poor Innilis. And poor Vindilis. I was never the mother I should have been to her, my Runa, Vindilis-to-be. There was Lyria, you remember, my daughter by Wulfgar whom I'd been so fond of. Aye, 'tis fair to say I loved Wulfgar; and you cannot remember, being too young, what a bright, beautiful child Lyria was. Then Gaetulius slew Wulfgar, and on me begot Runa. Oh, I never hated the little one; she could not help having the father she had. I did my duty by Runa. But to Wulfgar's daughter Lyria I gave my love. And then in the reign of Lugaid the Sign came upon Lyria, and she took the name Karilis, and she died in giving birth, and to this grandchild who is now Forsquilis I passed on the love I had borne for her mother . . .'

She shook herself. 'Enough. 'Twas long ago; and who can command her heart? Do your duty as a Queen. Whoever else may be in your life, provided 'tis not adulterously another man, that person is your own.'

'But I hate keeping a secret like this from Gratillonius,' Dahilis mourned. 'It touches him so deeply, though he know it or not. And, and he is the King we prayed for. We owe him our loyalty.'

'What loyalty has he shown us?' demanded Quinipilis.

'Why, why, he has been – kind and sage and strong – ' Dahilis's cheeks burned. 'Aye, certain things he's neglected, but that's my fault as much as his, and Bodilis told me she's spoken to him and he paid close heed – '

'That is well,' said Quinipilis. 'Mistake me not. I like him very much. I fear lest he lose the favour of the Three. Mayhap this . . . between you and Vindilis, dear Innilis – mayhap 'tis Their punishment of him, even though it began ere he arrived. If They do no worse, we should give thanks for mercy.'

'That's my terror too,' Innilis forced forth. 'That the

333

Gods are affronted as They were by . . . the earlier King. When Dahilis discovered us – could that be Their sign, Their warning?'

Quinipilis came to attention like an old hound that has caught wolf-scent in the wind. 'Eh? What's this? Meseems you've more on your minds than you've yet told.'

'We do,' Dahilis answered. Struggling for every word, she related how Gratillonius had held his Mithraic rite in a stream hallowed to Belisama, and afterwards been unrepentant. 'He swore 'twas no harm; and he *is* so strong and clever that, that I made myself believe him – but then this next thing happened, and I cannot sleep for fright – Counsel us what to do!'

'Hm. Hm.' Quinipilis tugged her chin. 'This is bad, I think. He's already defied Lir, d'you see, by burying that soldier of his on Point Vanis. And I scarce imagine Taranis is pleased that Gratillonius has dawdled about getting Him daughters on the rest of the Nine. The Gods are patient, but – '

She rose and paced, hands clasped behind her back, though an occasional wince showed that each step cost her pain. The younger women sat dumb, their stares following her to and fro. Finally she halted, loomed above them – her tall form against the window seemed to darken the room – and said:

'He is worth saving. The best hope, I swear, Ys has had in my long lifetime, or longer than that. Wulfgar and Hoel were good men too, but they lacked the skills of war and governance that seem to be Gratillonius's, nor, in their day, did such storm-driven tides beat on our gate as are now rising. If he refuses to expiate his sins, we Nine must do it for him. Is that not ever the lot of woman?

'How? I cannot tell. In matters like this, I'm a simpleton: too much earth in me, too little fire, air, or seawater. Let me ask of Forsquilis. Young though she be, that

334

grandchild of mine is deep into strange things. Well do we know.'

Dahilis and Innilis shivered.

''Twill take time, doubtless,' Quinipilis went on. 'Meanwhile, we'll do what we can to make amends and fend off divine anger. First, I'd say, Gratillonius *must* rightfully honour and make fruitful those of the Gallicenae who are able. If he'll not take the first step towards that, they – we – shall have to.'

Dahilis bowed her head. 'I've tried,' she mumbled. 'And, and Bodilis says she did reproach him, and afterwards he and she – How glad I was. He keeps telling me, though, he keeps telling me he'll . . . see to the matter . . . when I've grown heavier. What else can I do?'

Quinipilis rasped a chuckle. 'What, need the Crone instruct the Wench? Your blood knows the answer.' She sighed. 'You've been too proud, all you lasses. You've concealed your hurt. Have you thought that that might have overawed him? Belike he's unaware of this, he tells himself he only want Dahilis, with whom he's in love. But underneath – he knows you have powers – and . . . every man dreads failing with a woman. Which he never will with any of you; but does he truly realize that?'

She laid a knotted hand on the head of Innilis. 'Seek him out,' she urged. 'Set fear aside. Open yourself to joy. Ah, I remember.'

'I w-w-will do my best.' The words came high and thin.

Quinipilis stood a while looking down at Innilis. It was as if that look went past clothes and the skin beneath, to flesh which had been torn and knitted poorly, to frail ribs and narrow hips. Whatever of the restorative Touch that had once belonged to every Queen lingered in Innilis, it sufficed not for the healing of herself.

Finally the old woman said low: 'I was forgetting. The birth of your child by Hoel nearly killed you; and Audris

335

is sickly and not quite right in the wits. Aye, a strong reason for you to seek where you did.' Stooping, though the motion wrenched a groan from her, she hugged the other. 'Take what time you need, girl. Nerve yourself. Let others go before you. Dahilis will be your ally. And there is the Herb. If the Gods did not smite the Nine for bearing Colconor no child, why, surely they'll condone you safeguarding your health, mayhap your very life. But when you feel ready, go to him. Never be afraid of loving him.'

XIX

1

Festivals surrounded Midsummer. In part they were religious. On the Eve, bonfires blazed around the countryside after dark, while folk danced, sang, coupled in the fields, cast spells, asked welfare for kith and kine, house and harvest – across Armorica, across Europe. In Ys, day after day processions went chanting to rites at every fane of the Three. Most were parades as well, where the Great Houses, the Brotherhoods, the Guilds turned out in their best, where the marines marched smartly and, this year, the King's legionaries outdid them. There were traditional ceremonies: the weavers presented Belisama with a brocaded robe, the horsebreeders gave Taranis a new team for His wagon, the mariners sailed forth and cut the throat of a captured seal that Lir might have the blood – the single seal that Ysans were allowed to kill throughout the year. There were other offerings to other Gods, deeds ancient, secret, and dark.

Midsummer was likewise a season of secular celebration. It was a lucky time to get married in. It was a time for family reunions, grandiose feasts, youthful flings that elders winked at. The short, light nights were full of song, flutes, drums, dancing feet, laughter. Green boughs hung above every door. People forgave wrongs, paid debts, gave largesse to the needy. Few slept much.

Yet Midsummer was also worldly, political. The day after solstice was among the four in the year when the Council Suffetes always met.

Often this had been scarcely more than an observance, soon completed. Behind its strong wall and, belief went, the subtle Veil of Brennilis, Ys had been free of many things that aggrieved the earth. But nothing is for ever.

On the dais of the basilica chamber, Gratillonius raised the Hammer and said: 'In the name of Taranis, peace. May His protection be upon us.'

Lanarvilis rose to say: 'In the name of Belisama, peace. May Her blessing be upon us.' So the Nine have chosen her for their principal speaker at this session, Gratillonius thought. Why? Because she's a good friend of Soren Cartagi, who generally opposes my policies?

Hannon Baltisi stood. 'In the name of Lir, peace. May His wrath not be upon us.' The trident butt crashed on the floor.

Gratillonius gave Adminius the Hammer to hold. A while he stood watching the faces before him – long, narrow Suffete faces for the most part, but not altogether, certainly not on stout Soren or craggy Hannon or, except for traces, any of the Gallicenae. They returned his reconnaissance. Stillness deepened. Best get started, he thought.

'Let me begin by thanking you for your patience and support in these past difficult months,' he said. Flashing a grin: 'Today we can talk Ysan.' A few lips flickered upwards, not many. 'We've weathered a mighty storm. The seas still run high, but I know we can reach safe harbour if we continue pulling together.' Don't remind them how they quibbled and bickered and sometimes came near rebellion. They never quite went over the brink. That's what counts.

'We broke the Scoti. They'll not come again soon, if ever! We kept ourselves from embroilment in the Roman civil war, and kept Armorica out of it too, by our direct influence on our near neighbours and theirs on people farther east. For this, Magnus Maximus is grateful. I have letters from him, which some of you have read and all are welcome to. Having served under him, I can tell you that he rewards service; and he is not far now from winning his Imperium.

'But we have work yet undone, we in Ys. I think the Gods have laid a destiny upon us. We have become the outer guard of civilization itself. We must not fail in our duty.'

Hannon barely signalled for recognition before he stood up, greybearded patriarch, and snapped: 'Aye, we know what you want, you. To keep our whole strength marshalled, however the cost may bleed us. For what? For Rome. King, 'twas I who showed you the mystery of the Key, and loth I am to clash with you – for you are at least an honest man – but why should Ys serve Rome, Christian Rome who'd forbid us to worship our Gods – and yours, Grallon, yours?'

Adruval Tyri, Sea Lord, heaved his burly form erect. As head of the navy, and a former marine, he could say: 'Hannon, with due respect, what you speak is walrus puckey. A grandmother of mine was Scotic, my mother was half Frankish, I've travelled about both trading and fighting. I *know* the barbarians. What d'you want? That we haul in our warships, keep none in commission save the usual coast guard, and thereby avoid offending the Saxons? I tell you, if you buy the wolf off with a lamb, next twilight he'll be back wanting the ewe. The Gods have given us a King who understands this.' He ran fingers through thinning red hair. 'Heed him, for Their sake!'

Hannon glowered and growled, 'What do you wish in truth, lord?'

They returned to their benches. Gratillonius cleared his throat. 'This,' he said. 'We've a Heaven-sent opportunity.

339

Armorica has been spared war, thanks largely to Ys. 'Twill accept our leadership, eagerly, at least until such time as the Imperial issue is decided. I'd have us work with the Roman authorities throughout the peninsula. We can help them rebuild signal towers and establish a line of beacon fires ready for ignition. We can keep our fleet on standby for them, who have almost none – for, if the Scoti are no longer a menace, the Saxons remain, and are worse. In exchange, the Romans can defend our landward frontiers.'

Soren stirred. 'What need have we of that?' rumbled the Speaker for Taranis. 'What on land endangers Ys?'

'The threat to Rome, if naught else,' Gratillonius replied: 'which is the threat to civilization, I tell you. Sirs and ladies, Ys cannot feed herself. Trade is her life. Let Rome fall, and this your city will starve.'

Lanarvilis rose. Grace had never imbued her long body or heavy haunches; but the blonde hair lifted on high like a helmet as she said quietly: 'I would not gainsay the King – not at once, on a single point of issue – but mothers must needs look further ahead than fathers. So I ask this assembly, although we may indeed find some cooperation expedient – ultimately, does Ys the free want to rejoin that Rome which has become a slave state? Had we not better keep our distance and trust in our Gods? Bethink you.'

She sat down. Gratillonius swallowed hard. The worst was, he couldn't deny to himself that her question was quite reasonable. If it had not happened that his own Mother was Rome – Clearly, his rampart for her would be years a-building. Well, a mason necessarily went brick by brick. Today he might lay two or three. He cleared his throat for a response.

2

In ancient times the King had stayed always at the Sacred Wood, whither the high priestesses sought by turns, and whatever men he invited. Gradually it came to be that he visited the city to preside over various ceremonies; and these visits lengthened. When Julius Caesar's man won the crown and refused to sit yawning in the primitive House, he merely confirmed and completed what had been the case for several reigns before his. Thereafter the Kings moved freely about and inhabited a proper palace in Ys.

Yet while Taranis thus allowed His law to be lightened, it could not be abolished. The King must return to meet every challenger, slay or be slain. Moreover, save in war or essential travel or when a major ritual coincided, he must spend the three days and nights around each full moon out in the Wood. His presence there being the sole requirement, most sovereigns had taken a wife or two along, and sent for friends, and passed the time in recreations which ranged from decorous to debauched.

Dahilis felt horror of the place. Beneath those shadowing oaks Colconor had killed her father and might have killed Gratillonius, whose blood would also someday nourish their roots. After she confessed this, just before his initial Watch, he had kissed her and gone off to sleep alone.

The duty was otherwise not irksome. Free of distractions, he studied material from the archives, practised the language, conferred at length with magnates he summoned, pondered the tasks before him, and maintained his regular exercises to keep fit. About the underlying finality he was unconcerned. He awaited no rival soon. Such advents were, in fact, generally years apart. Any fighters who did come, he felt confident he could handle. Eventually his strength and speed must begin failing; but he did not mean to be here that long, although at the present stage of things he saw no sense in planning his departure.

The morning of this third moon dawned already hot. Clouds banked murky in the east and rose higher hour by hour, while a forerunner haze dulled the dwindling western blue; but no breeze relieved the wet air or freshened its musky odours. Soren and the priests who officially escorted Gratillonius sweated beneath their robes so that they stank. They were as grateful as dignity permitted when he offered them beer at the House. He, who had tramped and fought in armour, suffered less, but was glad to strip down to a tunic after they were gone.

Servants had carried along pens, ink, parchment. That last was costly stuff for the letters he meant to write to various Imperial officers of the region, but papyrus was not to be had, as disrupted as trade routes were on both land and sea, while wood was simply too plebeian. Well, he thought, this material should be impressive, emphasizing the capabilities latent in Ys and, by the bye, offsetting his awkward style and vagrant spelling. Only afterwards was it to occur to him that Bodilis could have corrected those.

The hall was the most nearly cool place to be. He ordered a table and chair brought in and settled himself down to work. It went slower and harder than he had expected. After a while his jaw and back ached from tension. He wasn't sure why. Maybe a ramble in the grove would help. He set off. That was about noon.

At once he was alone. Utterly alone. Around him the trees brooded, huge boles, twist-thewed branches, claw

342

twigs. Their leaves made a gloom through which a weird brass-yellow light struck here and there, out of a sky gone sooty and steadily darkening further. Silence weighed down the world, fallen leaves too sodden to rustle underfoot, brush stiff as though straining after any sound, never a bird call or squirrel chatter or grunt from a wild boar whose blood was to wash the corpse of a King, nothing astir save himself; but fungi glimmered like eyes. Even the canal, when he reached it, seemed to flow listless, tepid, forbidden to quench his thirst.

Gratillonius scowled. What was the matter with him? He was no superstitious barbarian, he was a Roman . . . But Romans disliked wilderness. It was beyond their law. In its depths you might meet Pan, and the dread of Him come upon you so that you ran screaming, blind, a mindless animal, while His laughter bayed at your heels . . . A Presence was here. He felt It as heavily as he felt the slugging of his heart. It might be of Ahriman. Best he return.

As he did, he heard the first muttering of thunder.

He breathed easier after he got back to the Sacred Precinct, its courtyard flagged and swept, open to heaven and on to Processional Way, with a view beyond of the heights, garden-garnished homes, pastureland above the cliffs of Point Vanis where Eppillus kept his long watch. Yet he was still beset by portents he could not read. As he stood there, clouds covered the last western clarity, grey yonder, blue-black where they mounted out of the east. Summer's verdancies were discoloured, bruised. Dominant in the courtyard reared and sprawled the Challenge Oak, shield hanging from it dully agleam with brass that the hammer had smitten over and over. Between its outbuildings loomed the House, crimson hue somehow bringing forth the brutal mass of timbers, grotesqueness of images that formed its colonnade. When

343

Gratillonius looked away towards Ys, the city at its distance appeared tiny, fragile, a fantasy blown in glass.

Suddenly as a meteor flash, he became aware of the three on the road. How had he overlooked them? They were almost here. He forced steadiness upon himself. A wind sprang up, soughing in the treetops and tossing them about. The hammer swung on its chain, hit the shield, belled in a mumble. Lightning flickered afar. Thunder rolled more loud.

The three halted before their King. Under their cowls he saw Forsquilis, Vindilis, Maldunilis. He could not quell a shudder.

'Greeting, lord,' said Forsquilis. 'We have come to attend you during your sentinel stay.'

He sought to moisten his lips, but his tongue had gone dry too. 'I thank you . . . However, I did not ask for . . . your company.'

Vindilis's look smouldered in the bony face. 'You hardly would,' she replied. Did a whiplash of spite go through her tone? 'Not of us three out of the Nine.'

Forsquilis lifted a hand. 'Peace.' Calm, resolution were upon her Athene countenance. The grey eyes took hold of Gratillonius's and would not let go. 'Aye,' she said, 'just we three, who held Colconor here until his doom could find him. That was needful evil. The hour has come to set it right.'

Maldunilis sidled close to tug Gratillonius's sleeve. 'We'll be sweet to you, yea, very sweet,' she said, and giggled.

Lightning flared anew, brighter; thunder boomed; the shield rang. Gratillonius felt a surge of anger as heartening as the wind. 'Now look you,' he snapped, 'I accept your intention as good, and mayhap I have been neglectful, but we'll settle all this in rational wise, later.'

'We will not,' Forsquilis answered. While her tone was

344

level, she had let go of her cloak, and it flapped at her shoulders like great wings. 'This is something that must be, lest the time-stream flow still worse awry. I have made a Sending. It did not reach the Gods, that is not in my power, but it did come near enough to hear Them whisper. Follow me.' She strode towards the House. Numbly, Gratillonius obeyed. Vindilis and Maldunilis flanked him.

Beyond the doorway, the hall gaped cavernous. The staff had lit fires in the trenches against the approaching storm, but their light only bred shadows which seemed to make move the carven pillars and wainscots, the tattered banners from battles long forgotten. Smoke stung nostrils and blurred vision. The crackling of wood was merely an undertone to the halloo of wind outside.

'Go,' Forsquilis ordered the assembled manservants. 'Be off to town, fast, ere the downpour catches you. Come not back till the moon has waned.'

Gratillonius confirmed with a stiff nod. What else could he do?

'We'll see to you,' Maldunilis tittered in his ear. 'Oh, we will.' His flesh crawled at her touch.

When they were alone with him, the three shed their cloaks. Underneath, they were royally dressed. As one, they confronted him. 'Lord King,' said Forsquilis gravely, 'in us – you and your Queens – the Gods are on earth. We are seed and soil, weather and water, the cycle of the year and the tides, of the stars and the centuries. We engender, we give birth, we nurture, we protect, we dream, we die, we are reborn in our children at the springtime and we die again in the harvest at autumn. If ever in this we fail, Ys perishes; for we are Ys.

'Therefore let that which was done here in hatred be now done in love. Let the wombs that were shut be opened. Let the dead quicken. Taranis, come unto Belisama.'

Lightning burst. Its flare through doorway and smoke-hole made wan the fires. Thunder wheeled after, down and down heaven. Hailstones rattled before the wind, whitened the ground, clamoured on the shield. In a mighty rushing, the rain arrived.

It was as if Gratillonius stood aside and watched another man go into the arms of Forsquilis. Then there was no Gratillonius, no woman, there was only that which happened, which was everything that there was.

– Lamplight glowed throughout the bedchamber, but its Roman accoutrements seemed unreal, infinitely remote; and the light was not soft in the eyes of Forsquilis, it turned them yellow, like a hawk's. Her visage had become Medusa's, gold-brown locks spread snakish over the pillow, she wrapped long arms and legs about him and cried out as her hips met his plunging.

– 'I did wrong to bid you go away,' Vindilis breathed in the dark. 'Give me another daughter, a new babe to cherish.'

'But you told me you liked not – '

'I should have told you what I do like. Hoel could not understand, but Bodilis and Dahilis say that you listen.'

'I do. For I want you – you, not just a body lying still – '

'Let us try, let us see. Give me your hand to guide – '

– The sleepy noontide sun cast richness over Maldunilis where she lay. 'We're going to drain you dry, you know,' she laughed, and somehow that was not impious, for the Gods have humour too and it is not always ironic or cruel; love and death have their ridiculous moments, that the spirit may be refreshed. With Forsquilis and Vindilis playful on either side, Gratillonius saw that Maldunilis honestly desired him and was quite ready to adore him. His ardour torrented.

– The Bull was in him, he was the Bull, rampant among his cows, although in glimpses of self-awareness he knew it was a bull seal he had been thinking of, out on a rookery reef near Sena.

– The last night ended as dawn paled the sinking moon. All four were so weary and sore they could barely drag themselves to their feet. Nonetheless Gratillonius and Vindilis, aye, Vindilis went forth to stand in dew and wildflowers across the road. 'Now do you believe?' she asked quietly.

'I seek to,' he answered.

Across her dark head, lifted against the sky, the white streak gleamed like a warrior's plume. 'We have been Gods. Belike 'twill never happen again. Flesh would burn to ashes. Nay, we shall return to what we were, perhaps a little wiser, a little stronger, but always mortal. Yet we have been Gods.'

The sun rose, bearing the glory of Unconquered Mithras. Gratillonius gasped.

He was silent when Speaker and priests led him and his Queens back to Ys. Dahilis met him at the palace, kissed him, said in tender mirth that he had earned a good long rest. She took him to a room curtained and cool, and left him by himself.

A sunbeam struck through. Gratillonius went to that window, opened it, leaned out, holding his palms and his branded brow up to the light. 'Nay, I do *not* understand!' he cried. 'What came upon me? What was it?' He heard, surprised, that he had called in Ysan. He fled to Latin. '*Tene, Mithra, etiam miles, fidos nostris votis nos!*'

XX

1

Adminius was the new deputy to Gratillonius. Few would have thought the lean, snaggle-toothed scrounger and japester a wise choice, but he quickly vindicated the centurion's judgement, laid his authority firm upon his remaining twenty-three fellows, kept them in sharp form, maintained cooperation with the Ysan regulars and popularity among the Ysan folk.

The municipal theatre at the Forum operated, on grants from the Great Houses, during the four months around Midsummer, when daylight could provide illumination after working hours. For the most part it offered classical drama, music, readings; dance, gymnastics, and sports were for the amphitheatre outside of town. Not until a month after solstice did the soldiers have leisure to go. Gratillonius kept them too busy strengthening defences and executing joint manoeuvres with the marines.

Finally, though, Adminius announced a party. 'We'll march down in formation, 'spite of being civil dressed, impress everybody proper, and take in the show. Don't be afraid. It's the *Twin Menaechmi*, lots of fun – dirty jokes in there too, if you're quick enough on the uptake. I sneaked inter a performance once when I was a brat in Londinium. Afterwards we'll 'ave a banquet at the Green Whale. Some of you already know 'ow good a table Zeugit sets. The city's paying, by way of a bonus for our services in the late unpleasantness. And then you're free to go waste yer substance in riotous living – but I want

348

you back in barracks and fit for duty at sunrise, d'you 'ear?'

It was therefore a shock when a spokesman for the patrons announced that the theatre was proud to present the *Agamemnon* of Aeschylus in a new Ysan-language translation by the most gracious Queen Bodilis.

'Wot the Sathanas!' Seated on the right of his contingent, Adminius turned to his neighbour opposite, a portly and patrician Suffete. 'Excuse me, sir,' he said in the vernacular, 'aren't they doing Plautus this eventide?'

'Nay, that is tomorrow.' The man smiled superciliously. 'I daresay our way of counting days straightforward, rather than backwards from ides and nones, is confusing to Romans.'

'Oh, bloody Christ.' Adminius addressed his men in Latin: 'Sorry, boys. I got the date wrong. Wot we'll be seeing is . . . m-m, I think it's an old Greek tragedy.'

Scowls and growls went among them. Cynan, beside the deputy, started to rise. 'Well, let's go,' he said. 'I'm in no mood for – '

Adminius grabbed his arm. 'We stay. This is a civilized country, and we owe it ter Rome and the legion ter make a good impression on the natives. You'll take in some culture, s'welp me 'Ercules, if I've got ter 'old yer noses and pour it down yer flinking gullets.'

A disapproving buzz went along the close-packed benches. Sullenly, the men resigned themselves. At least they would be able to follow the lines, more or less; none of them knew Greek.

The theatre was of the Roman kind, a semicircular bowl before a stage, roofless although with arrangements for spreading a canvas top in wet weather. However, differences were many, most of them more subtle than its comparatively small size. The upper gallery was point-arched, supported on columns slim, unfluted, their capitals in the form of breaking waves. A box aloft there was empty, reserved for the Gods. Female roles would be taken by women, not prostitutes but honoured artists. In a well below the stage sat an orchestra with horns, flutes, syrinxes, sistrums, cymbals, drums, harps, lyres. It played for a while, a heavy, moody music; then, as the cloth-of-gold curtain was rolled down, it fell silent, until a lone trumpet call resounded.

Scenery portrayed the front of a cyclopean palace, altars before it. A backdrop showed night, slowly brightening to day as layers of gauze were withdrawn. An actor stood peering outwards. He bore spear, shield, archaic armour; the great helmet descended to make his mask. After a space motionless at his sentry post, he sighed and began: 'O Gods, relieve me of this weary watch, this year-long waiting like a guardian hound with no more rest than elbows 'gainst the roof above the hall of the Atreides! Too well I've learned to know the midnight stars – '

Cynan's eyes widened. 'Mithras!' he whispered. 'That's the way it *is*.'

'Shh,' Adminius cautioned. But when the beacon fire blazed afar to proclaim the King's return, he himself let out a cheer.

Thereafter the soldiers spoke never a word; but often they drew breath or smote knees with fists.

When finally Clytemnestra had scorned the chorus and starkly told Aegisthus that they twain would rule; and another trumpet call died away; and the audience applauded and went out into the sunset street – Adminius said, 'Wow!'

'Those women, those poor brave women.' Budic was not ashamed to shed a few tears.

'What happened next?' Cynan wanted to know. 'That Orestes they spoke of, he must have done something. Are there more plays?'

'I've heard Greek plays go in threes,' Verica answered. 'Maybe Queen Bodilis has translated the rest. Or maybe she will.'

'Well, anyhow, she did a damn good job on this one,' Maclavius declared. 'Especially seeing she's a woman. Only a man who'd been a soldier could've written it.'

'He understood more than soldiering, I can tell you,' said Budic with the loftiness of youth.

'That was a lucky mistake you made, deputy,' remarked Guentius, and general agreement murmured from the rest.

Adminius laughed. 'Fine, fine! We might as well appreciate wot's around us. I've a notion we'll be 'ere quite a spell.'

2

Summer advanced in triumphal procession. Colts, calves, lambs, kids grew long in the legs and full in the haunches. Apples, plums, cherries burgeoned in orchards. Freshly cut grass filled hayfields with fragrance. Bees droned about heather, clover, gorse, replacing the tribute men had exacted from them earlier. Carts laden with produce trundled out of Osismiic lands, to return full of wares from workshops and the sea. Poppies and cornflowers bejewelled roadsides. Children grew scratched on the hands and purple about the lips, gathering wild blackberries. Young storks, geese, ducks flopped overhead, in training for the trek south. On clear nights the Swan, the Eagle, and the Lyre stood high.

While he still had much to do, most of it of his own making, Gratillonius began discovering time for himself. More and more Ysans, great, humble, and ordinary, were coming to accept him as a man when he was not being the

351

sacral King. He could poke around town, ask people about their work, listen to legends related by granny or gaffer, put a child on his knee and tell it a story while dinner was cooking in some house where he was a guest. He could whistle up his crew and take the royal yacht, a trim and swift little galley, off for a day on the water. With a few bodyguards he could go a-horseback, hunting or simply exploring, well past the frontier. He could sit up late over wine, talking with scholars, philosophers, men of affairs, visiting skippers, everybody who had something worth listening to; and Bodilis was not the sole woman among them. He could participate in sports, watch contests and shows, hear music and readings, wander into books, lie on his back in the open and look at the clouds and find images in them until he drowsed off. He could practise his handicraft.

That last was especially precious to him, because so long denied. As a boy on his father's villa, he had been forever making things. As a soldier, he became the one in the cohort to see when some job of repair was tough or some tricky apparatus needed devising. However, this was limited, since the engineers and other specialists had their pride. Mostly Gratillonius had whittled, cut leather, that sort of thing. Now he had his own workshop, a shed by the stable behind the palace. (None but the King was allowed to keep horses inside the city.) He filled it with hand tools, lathe, whatever he ordered. Although no joiner – he hoped eventually to teach himself that fine art – he fashioned furniture, household oddments, items for garden and travel, serviceable and not bad-looking. From the royal hands, they made welcome gifts.

He had been thus busied all day, a while after the inland Celts had celebrated their feast of Lug. Evening closed in. Smilng, pleasantly at ease, he put things in their places and left the shop. Outside, the sun was down and

352

dusk settling in. Swallows darted after mosquitoes, shadows against violet. Most flowers had finished blooming, but trees and hedges made the air sweet, while rose mallow stood pale against walls. Before him, he thought, lay supper with Dahilis, just the two of them, and whatever might follow. He divided half his nights among the other five Gallicenae who expected it, Bodilis, Forsquilis, Vindilis, Maldunilis, Lanarvilis, when they were not having their courses or he was not elsewhere. It was never tense with them any more, and sometimes it was very good, and they seemed content to let him be with Dahilis otherwise, at least until such time as it would endanger her child. The fullness upon her made her, if anything, more dear to him than ever, if that was possible.

Entering by a back door, he smiled at a servant who saluted and went down a hall lit by wax candles in bronze sconces, to the bedroom and its adjacent bathing basin. There he would cleanse himself and change into fresh clothes, not formal but colourful, cheerful, matching her spirit.

He entered and halted. She was there, dressed for the street. Beside her was Innilis, clad in a gown of sheer silk richly bordered with floral patterns. A star in gemmed silver gathered it low above her breasts, so that the Sign of the Goddess was plain to see. The women stood hand in hand. Lamplight darkened the window but gleamed off the rich brown hair of Innilis, delicate features, teeth white between lips always slightly parted.

'Uh, greeting,' Gratillonius said, taken aback.

Dahilis came to him. 'Darling, I go home this eventide,' she told him. 'Today did my Sister here seek me and give me the joyful news that she feels ready to be your true Queen.'

Gratillonius stared across her shoulder at Innilis. 'What a surprise!' he blurted, and noticed he was embracing

Dahilis. 'I had no wish, well, no wish to force aught on anyone.'

'I know.' Innilis clasped fingers together. 'You were kind to wait while I . . . while I sought the Goddess within myself.'

''Twas not easy for her,' Dahilis murmured against Gratillonius's collarbone. 'Help her. I'll call again tomorrow. But we Nine, we've agreed Innilis should have time, days, in your company. Be good to my little Sister. Oh, but I know you will.'

Strange, passed through Gratillonius, strange that Dahilis thinks of Innilis as her little sister, when Innilis is – what? – a decade older, and has borne a child, and – But she does look so vulnerable. No, more than that, she already carries a wound that has never healed. I'm sure of it, though I can't think what it might be.

'Well, my lady, you honour me,' he found his way to saying.

Dahilis drew him forward until the three of them stood with arms entwining bodies. She kissed Gratillonius and Innilis. 'Goodnight,' she said between laughter and tears. 'Have a splendid night.' She departed.

'Um, uh – ' Gratillonius searched desperately for words.

Innilis raised eyes that had been downcast. 'Do as if I were Dahilis,' she suggested.

'Why, why – ' The Bull awoke. By Venus, she was beautiful! 'Aye, indeed,' Gratillonius exclaimed. 'First let's have a bit of wine, and then maybe you'd like to share my bath, and later, we'll dine and talk – '

– And hours afterwards – he had been as heedful and patient as he was able, until she began astounding him with passion – she whispered through the dark: 'I was afraid. But now I love you too.'

'Me *too*?' he asked.

354

She caught her breath. 'Have we not all of us . . . others . . . we love?'

'Ah, well.' He slid a hand down her flank and laid it to rest. 'I'll inquire no further if you'd liefer I didn't.'

'Oh, dear Grallon.' She kissed him fleetingly, wearily, happily. For a moment, before sleep overtook her, resolution spoke: 'No more am I afraid. I will leave the Herb aside, in hope of your child.'

XXI

1

Summer welled forth in its final great warmth, light, and greenness. Fields stood ripe, sickles laboured, wagons creaked behind oxen. Osismiic villagers brought in the last sheaf, gave it a name and the place of honour at festival, next day burned it and buried the ashes, that no witch might use them to wreak evil and that the God might come back to life at springtime. Soon asters bloomed defiant purple; but it would not be long before the first tinge of yellow was on the birches, and already the storks were leaving, while other migratory birds gathered to make ready in clangourous flocks on hills and at meres.

There was less observance of the season in Ys, but folk were nonetheless aware that another year was passing away. Though business bustled for a term at Goose Fair and the Cornmarket, where the Osismii brought foodstuffs to trade, and at Epona Square, where the horse dealers came, and in flour mills, breweries, bakeries, smoking and pickling establishments: Skippers' Market stood empty, windswept, no further merchant ships awaited. Fishermen drew their boats ashore and settled down to caulk, pitch, mend; most also sought odd jobs in town. Housewives polished lamps and saw to oil supplies. Those who could not afford this increasingly expensive commodity dipped wicks into tallow. Husbands stored away firewood bought from lumbermen. Suffetes who were well-to-do, which not all were by any means, prepared for a round of social events, now that work in the Great Houses would be damping down. Poor people looked to them and to the temples for help during the cold months, not that many in Ys ever knew dire want. The temples themselves made ready for rites immemorially old.

The full moon before autumnal equinox came early that year, in the middle of these happenings. It was the night when Forsquilis went forth alone, as the vision granted to her Sending had enjoined.

She left Ys by Aurochs Gate on the south. None of the sentries there or in the flanking towers called the Brothers challenged her; portals stood open in times of peace. They recognized her, though, cowl thrown back to bare those sharply pure features to the moon, silver coronet around her brows, hair blowing loose; they dipped their pikes in awed salute, and when she had gone they dared not mutter about her mission, whatever it might be.

Wind prematurely whetted and skirling drove clouds in tatters across the sky. The moon seemed to fly among them. It touched their darknesses with ice. Water swirled and snarled as she crossed the shouldering rock between city wall and headland. Beyond, along Pharos Way, rime glimmered on grass; gravel scrunched underfoot, a sound small and lonely and soon lost in the wind. Forsquilis followed the road west. The gap sundering rampart and promontory grew wider as she fared, until the western arc swung north and waves ran unhindered. Cape Rach reached somewhat farther. At its end, the lighthouse fire flickered and streamed like a candle flame. Ocean rolled beyond, around, out past Sena to the edge of the world. The crash and long-drawn rumble of surf on rocks came faintly.

She stopped short of the pharos. Here the road passed through the necropolis. Long had that stood forsaken.

Headstones leaned crazily or lay hidden in weeds, names and remembrances blurred off them by centuries of weather. Tombs bulked and gaped. Some were made like miniature Roman temples, some like the dolmens and passage graves of the Old Folk. All were lichenous and eroded, grey beneath the hurtling moon. Forsquilis sought among them, stumbling over the gravestones, until she found the one she needed. It was the largest, a small mausoleum, the entrance Grecian-pillared; but no one could now make out what friezes had been carven above.

Forsquilis stopped. She raised her arms. The cloak fluttered at her shoulders as if trying to flee. 'O Brennilis who sleeps within,' she called, 'forgive that I trouble your rest. It is the whisper of the Gods that sent me hither upon this night. No other sign has been granted me, save omens unclear and portents darkling, which say that your Ys is again at the end of an age. The Old is dying. Time travails with the New, and we fear Its face which we have not seen. For Ys, Brennilis, your Ys that you saved when you walked in sunlight, the sunlight you have forgotten – for Ys, Brennilis, I, Forsquilis your successor, beg a bed for the night with your dust, that in dream I may behold what must be done so Ys may live after I too am gone from the sun. Brennilis, receive your Sister.'

She went to the door. If ever it had been locked, the lock was long corroded away. Bronze flaked off beneath her fingers. The door groaned and sagged open. Lightlessness waited. Forsquilis went in to the dead.

Rain blew out of hidden heaven and sea. Its noises and its bright grey engulfed the city. Water blinded window-panes, drummed on roofs, swirled and gurgled in streets. No fire seemed able to fend off a raw dankness. It seeped through walls into lungs and marrow.

In what had been the temple of Mars, the Christian pastor Eucherius lay dying. His bed was a straw tick on the floor of the chamber which he had made his cell. A lamp guttered nearby; everywhere else the too-large room was full of the dark. Light touched eyeballs, bridge of nose, grizzled beard stubble. It lost itself in the hollows under his cheekbones. The Chi Rho and fish he had drawn in charcoal on the wall, to see above his feet, were swallowed up in thick, swaying shadow; but they were crude anyhow, barely recognizable. He had been no draughtsman.

He plucked at the blanket. Slime rattled in his lungs and bubbled red on his lips. Bodilis must bring her ear almost to that mouth before she could hear him. 'My lady Queen – ' He stopped and struggled for air. 'You are wise.' Again he must toil to fill what was left of his lungs. 'You are pagan, but wise and virtuous.' He coughed and gasped. 'Aristoteles, Vergilius –

'Maybe you know –

'One hears so many . . . tales of ghosts –

'Do souls . . . on their way . . . to judgement –

'Ever linger a while –

'Only a little while?'

She wiped away the sputum and stroked the thin grey hair. 'I know not,' she answered in the same Latin. 'Who does? But in Ys, many of us believe Gallicenae can be reborn as seals, to lie off Sena waiting for their own dear ones, watching over them. Do you want more water?'

He shook his head. 'No, thank you . . . I feel I am drowning . . . But I . . . must not . . . complain.' Coughing shook him. 'Gratillonius, . . . you have seen . . . enough men die, . . . worse hurt . . . than me.' This time his fight was lengthy. 'If I am being . . . contemptible, . . . please tell me, . . . and I'll try . . . to do better.'

'No, no.' The centurion squeezed the minister's hand, very carefully, so frail it was. 'You are a man, Eucherius.'

He had come in answer to Bodilis's summons, after she had heeded the plea of the deacon, who found the chorepiscopus lying swooned, with blood caking down the front of his coarse robe. It was not certain how long Eucherius had been thus alone. She washed him and gave him a fresh gown and tucked him into bed. Presently he regained awareness and courteously refused the healing Touch that Innilis might possess. Most likely Innilis would have failed regardless, as she did oftener than not in desperate cases. Hot infusions gave some brief strength. A courier was on the way to Audiarna. Gratillonius doubted the chorepiscopus would survive a trip over the mired road for Christian last rites. Meanwhile old deacon Prudentius, exhausted, had perforce tottered off to his rest. Bodilis and Gratillonius kept vigil.

Eucherius twitched a smile. 'You are good too,' he said. 'As for me, . . . it would be very pleasant . . . to see Neapolis again, . . . dreaming before the blue bay, . . . my mother's house, . . . the small crooked streets, . . . a garden where . . . Claudia and I – But God's will be done.'

Of course it shall be done, Gratillonius thought. What else? Ahura-Mazda reigns, and beyond Him, inexorable Time. Well, people babble in their death throes.

'Look after my poor,' Eucherius begged. 'Get Prudentius . . . home to Redonia . . . to die . . . with his kin . . .
and in Christ.'

'We will, we will,' Bodilis promised, weeping most
quietly, keeping sight of it from him.

He scratched at her hand. 'My congregation, . . . they
who thirst for the Word, . . . who shall comfort them
now?'

Gratillonius recalled his own mother at her prayers.
The remembrance overwhelmed him. 'I'll bring in a new
shepherd for your faithful as soon as possible,' he heard
himself declare.

Eucherius lifted his head an inch off the pillow. 'Is that
a promise?'

'It is. Before Mithras, it is.' What else could Gratillonius say, with the deep eyes of Bodilis turned on him?

'Good. Good . . . Also for you . . . Not only your
chance of salvation, . . . my son.' Eucherius cawed.
'Could a . . . totally pagan Ys . . . hope for much alliance
. . . with Rome?'

Startled, Gratillonius thought: But he is not
maundering!

Eucherius sank back. 'May I . . . pray for you two . . .
by name, . . . as I do . . . for all Ys?'

Bodilis knelt on the stone floor and embraced him.
Abruptly a measure of resonance was in his voice: 'Our
Father, Who are in Heaven – '

The cough that seized him shivered every bone. Underneath it was a hideous rattling, gurgling noise. With each
convulsion, blood gouted from his mouth. Bodilis ignored
it, held him close.

He slumped back. Waxen lids fell half over his eyes.
He answered no call or sign; he seemed barely to breathe;
to the touch he was clammy and cold. Bodilis cleansed
him again as best she could. She and Gratillonius stayed

at their post. Eucherius died shortly before his confessor arrived from Audiarna.

3

'The military season draws to a close. A winter campaign would be possible, of course – you have read your histories – but is not really feasible, for either Theodosius or myself. Why dare the unpredictables of weather, supply, and sickness? Instead, by tacit consent, we withdraw to our headquarters and govern the territories we hold, pending spring. After all, in this game the prize is the Empire. Neither of us wants to dissipate it.

'I could almost wish that Gratianus were not a victim of the war. More than vengeance for his fallen colleague, Theodosius has prestige to consider. Else he might have made agreement already. As matters stand, he has given to his eldest son Arcadius the title of Augustus to which I aspire. We shall have to see what God desires.

'He helps those who help themselves. Christ keep me from sinful pride. Yet I cannot but feel that our successes to date show that the ultimate victory of our cause is in His plan for our Mother Rome. While campaigning may have ended for the nonce, we must not relax our efforts on every possible front. To do so would be sacrilegious.

'You have done remarkably well, C. Valerius Gratillonius. I have commended you for it before, and I will not forget it in future. However, as a soldier you know that duty has not ended until the enemy has passed beneath the yoke.

'I thought I had assigned you a minor station on the periphery. I was wrong. You yourself have shown your

importance. Now a great part of my strategy for the coming year turns on you.

'Armorica must remain stable, fending off any barbarians or other invaders but else quiescent. I know better than to call troops from it, but I cannot permit my opponents to try. Moreover, in view of your success against the Scoti, I want you to extend a webwork of defensive cooperation not only north along the Saxon shore, but south as far as the Liger estuary. In these past months, wittingly or unwittingly, you have through your negotiations and shows of force, and the secondary effects of these, drawn an outline of it across the peninsula. Now I order you to begin on the actual structure.

'The Duke of the Armorican Tract has consented to this. Herewith his letter of authorization to you. His agreement was given reluctantly and under pressure. You will understand that no such official enjoys handing a crucial commission to an unknown quantity such as you. I also suspect he is less than enthusiastic about the cause of Magnus Maximus. He is, though, intelligent enough to realize what an opportunity this is for Rome. The attention and strength of his command have been concentrated in the east and the interior, and he feels this must remain so. Terrible though the devastations wrought by pirates have been, an overland invasion of Germans would be worse, as experience has shown. Therefore he has scamped the coast defences. Now at last, God willing, something can be done about them. Do it well, and you will make your mark – '

Gratillonius laid down the letter. While he had it wellnigh memorized, he had thought he would do best to read it aloud to Soren Cartagi. 'I could go on,' he said, 'but certain details are confidential, and surely you see the general drift.'

The speaker of his cult, otherwise head of the Great House of Timbermen, nodded heavily. Outside this conference room of the palace, the day reached bleakly bright. Wind whooped. 'I do,' he said. 'You'd fain leave Ys.'

'I must,' Gratillonius replied. 'To Condate Redonum and elsewhere – a circuit with my soldiers, to carry my warrant and knit the region together as it should always have been.'

'Ah. You'd not be content with couriers as hitherto?'

'Nay, I cannot be. The Romans are unorganized and demoralized. They have responded to my calls for a united front against the barbarians with assent but little action and no vigour. Where it comes to choosing sides in a conflict for the Imperium – And yet Rome must have one master, and he an able man. Can you not see?'

Soren stroked the beard that fringed his massive countenance. 'Well do I see. Ys shall serve the ambitions of your war lord.'

'For the common weal – ' Gratillonius left his chair, prowled the room, stood for a while staring out at the wind, turned about and thrust his gaze against that of Soren. 'Hark,' he said, 'I called you in to talk about this not only because of your position in *my* Temple. You are a leader among the Suffetes. They listen to you closer than to most. Help me, and together we may do as much for Ys as Caesar did.'

'I have wondered how much that truly was,' Soren murmured. He straightened where he sat. 'No matter; too late. But you, the King of Ys, propose to go faring about, abandoning your sacral duties, for two or three months, on behalf of Rome. This has never been.'

Gratillonius gave him a tight grin. 'I do not propose to do it, good sir. I am going to do it. What I have hoped for is your support, your explanation to the Suffetes and public that 'tis for their own welfare.'

'And if that support is not forthcoming?'

Gratillonius shrugged. 'Then I go anyway. How do you plan to stop me? But I should think you'd liefest not rive the state asunder.'

Soren glared. 'Be careful. Be very careful, my lord. 'Tis happened erenow that Ys has had Kings who overreached themselves. Suddenly challengers appeared at the Wood, one after the next in rapid succession, until those Kings fell.' He raised his hand. 'Mistake me not. Here is no threat, simply a warning.'

Gratillonius's temper, never the strongest part of him, flew into flinders. Somehow he kept their heat from igniting him; but he planted fists on hips, loomed over Soren, and ground out of his teeth: 'Enough, sir. 'Tis you who are reckless. Not yet have my Gallicenae called down on me the curse they did on Colconor, whom I slew. Nay, I have spoken with them, and they are willing for me to go. A new age is upon Ys, upon the world.

'Enough of provincial selfishness and dragging of feet. My sword and the swords of my men lie sheathed. We will draw them for Rome, when and as necessity dictates. Bethink you how many blades you can summon on that day.'

Soren's breath rasped. I must not drive him into a corner where all he can do is try to fight his way free, Gratillonius comprehended. Again he turned away to the window and the wind. After a moment he said, quite low:

'Sir, we really should not lie in strife as too often we've done. I know not why you've been hostile to me; myself, I've ever wished for friendship. But in your words, no matter. What does matter is the lives of our Mother cities. They are conjoined. Let us set aside any bitterness, yea, any pride, and seek to serve them.'

It took an hour or more, but he won grudging acceptance.

XXII

1

At equinox all the Nine must be in Ys, attending the Council and carrying out certain rites. They took advantage of it to meet by themselves in the temple of Belisama.

Quinipilis opened proceedings. Through the greenish light from the windows, between the four walls whereon were depicted aspects of the Goddess, the old woman limped to the dais. Her staff and her breathing rattled loud in the stillness. Painfully she climbed up, turned about, leaned on the stick and peered down at her Sisters. In blue robes and high white headdresses, they looked back, each in her own way. Bodilis sat calm and expectant, Lanarvilis alert, Dahilis wide-eyed, half afraid and half defiant. The crisis had aroused some excitement in Maldunilis, but in Fennalis largely the indignation that had frequently seized her these past months. Innilis huddled close to Vindilis, who held her hand. Forsquilis kept a distance aside, her countenance unreadable. She had been very quiet since the last full moon.

'Ishtar-Isis-Belisama, Your presence be with us, Your peace dwell within us, Your wisdom speak through us,' Quinipilis prayed. Ritual response murmured from the benches. When the invocation was finished, she began:

'This is a grave matter, perhaps more than the cursing of Colconor; for it concerns that new King whom we ourselves, under the Gods, did summon to slay him and join with us in holy wedlock. Yet the first thing I would

366

say is this – do not be daunted, my dears. We will find our way.'

'The same way as erstwhile?' asked Fennalis.

'What mean you, mother?' exclaimed Lanarvilis, appalled. 'Not to bring early death on Gratillonius!'

'Nay!' shrilled Dahilis. She curbed herself. 'You, you cannot mean that, Fennalis, you who are ever so kindly and helpful.'

The little plump woman stiffened. 'I did not counsel it,' she declared. 'However, somebody must needs set the thought forth. Else we'll slink around it terrified, as we did when it touched Colconor, far too long.'

Quinipilis stood stoutly above. 'Well, then, let us clear the air,' she directed. 'Why should we even consider ridding Ys – and ourselves – of Gratillonius? He's able, forceful, honourable, and better prepared to cope with the outside world than any other King in living memory. *I* think him Heaven-sent. But say on, unabashed. This is the hour for plain speaking.'

'Understand me,' replied Fennalis, 'I hate him not. In truth he is all you maintain. But his soul is harnessed to Rome. Bodilis, you've told the tale of the Atreides, how a curse may hound generation after generation, bringing woe on whole peoples. Is there a fatal flaw in this King? Think only of his leaving Ys.'

'Not till after Council and festival,' Dahilis said quickly. 'And we agreed!'

'What choice had we, as suddenly as he put it before us?'

'There is naught absolutely requiring his presence throughout the autumn,' Bodilis reminded them. 'A King has always been excused from his Watch in the Wood when a great holy time is on hand, or a great necessity such as war – and who judges the necessity but himself? We can safely assume no challenger will appear. If any does, well, we can house him in the Red Lodge to await Gratillonius's return. He promised us he'd come back before solstice.'

'Nonetheless I'm uneasy,' Lanarvilis admitted. 'What if he perishes on his travels?'

'Ys has met contingencies erenow in her history,' said Bodilis. 'The Key remains here. Not that he'll likely encounter any mischance he can't cope with.'

'Be that as it may, this journey of his is but a single violation of ancient ways,' Fennalis pursued. 'We have heard, secretly between us, how he insulted a stream consecrated to Belisama. Everyone knows how he buried a corpse where its rottenness would drain down into Lir's sea. And – ' She reddened, gulped, ploughed ahead: 'And he made mockery of the sacred marriage.'

'He did not!' Dahilis cried.

'That . . . breach . . . has been healed,' Innilis whispered. 'Has it not?' Her glance strayed downward. No doubt remained that she was with child.

'Indeed he has been filling gaps,' said Maldunilis smugly.

Fennalis flushed deeper. 'Has he?'

'You and I are too old for more children,' Quinipilis stated.

'Just the same – ' Fennalis choked on her words.

Bodilis leaned over to stroke her hand and murmur, 'We know. We feel the hurt to your pride and, aye, your loneliness every night. But Sister mine, remember Wulfgar – my father, who died of my birth as surely as my mother could have done – because she was his daughter. And Wulfgar was sheerly heathen, a sacrificer of horses to Thor. How much more does a civilized man with a stern faith, like Gratillonius, look on incest as a deadly sin? He knows, too, how of old it brought damnation on Grecian Oedipus and plague on his kingdom, innocent of

368

wrong intent though he and his mother had been. Why, in Ys, too, 'tis abhorred.'

Fennalis's features worked. 'The royal marriage is different. The Gods Themselves choose the Gallicenae. They know what They do! Oh, aye, since I am no longer under command of the moon, he may claim lawfulness in shunning me.' She forced a smile. 'And I hope you'll agree I've no large vanity to wound. I was ever homely and dumpy and, once past girlhood, resigned to it.' She paused. 'But what if, in future, when some of us here have passed on . . . what if then the Gods confront Gratillonius with the full meaning of Queenship?'

'They wouldn't!' Dahilis wailed.

A shiver went among the rest. 'Will They, ever?' Innilis asked desperately. 'What would make Them that angry at him?'

'He has already affronted Them,' Fennalis said. Now her tone held pity; she might almost have been speaking to one of the poor families to whom she ministered, telling them that their breadwinner's illness could prove mortal. 'That is why we are gathered – true, my Sisters? We've bespoken the burial and the misuse of Belisama's waters and his forthcoming journey. Can we be too quick to forgive his treatment of us?' Still more gently: 'Dahilis, darling, I'm sorry. I blame not you, as young and loving as you are. But he did, for months, deny his other wives. If he has lately become more dutiful, he has not repented the past, nor done penance for any of his transgressions.' Her voice lifted, ragged. 'Will the Gods bear with that?'

'Aye,' said Quinipilis, 'there is the real question. You've done well, Fennalis, to force it thus out into the open. What shall we do? Disown the King?'

Dahilis's denial was merely the loudest of those that arose from seven pairs of lips and, after a moment, the eighth.

369

Quinipilis nodded. 'Good.' Strictness descended. 'If he will not do expiation – and in the conscience that is his, he cannot – then we must do it for him. But hear me, Gallicenae. We are not ourselves without guilt. *You* are not.'

Innilis caught her breath. Vindilis let go her hand, flung that arm around her waist, and lifted the free hand for attention. Her visage turned from side to side along the tier, eagle-proud. 'You have heard what is between us twain,' she said. 'We will not forsake it. We cannot. I even believe we may not.'

'I think, I hope we have all come to understand, since hearing yestere'en,' answered Bodilis. That had been at a rite of purification for the Nine alone, when they made confession of everything they knew that might stand between them and the Goddess. Thus had Forsquilis ordered. 'We shall keep your secret because we must. Yet is this not itself a faithlessness towards the King our husband?'

'I wonder, too, how many of you besides Innilis have opened your wombs to him,' said Quinipilis. 'Oh, the Herb is yours to use as you see fit, Her gift to Her high priestesses. But to refuse Gratillonius children, as though he were horrible Colconor – '

'I haven't,' piped Maldunilis. ''Tis but he's not futtered me often enough.'

Laughter jerked through the room, less mirthful than startled.

'I have not either,' said Bodilis. 'But after each of us has decided – for herself – 'tis the Goddess Who disposes. Thus far only Dahilis and Innilis – ' She sighed. 'Let us search our souls. Meanwhile, how can we set right that which has gone wrong?'

Silence lengthened. One by one, gazes sought Forsquilis.

370

She rose and, through the deepening twilight, approached the dais. There she helped Quinipilis down and guided the dowager to a seat before taking the high place. A while she stood beneath the Resurrection of Taranis, like an eidolon, before she said, low and slow:

'You know what I did in our need, that I sought the tomb of Brennilis and slept next her bones. You know that hitherto I have kept silence about what dreams came to me; for they were weird and ambiguous, and still am I unsure whether I have seen through to their meaning. But this is what I believe they foretold.

'The Gods are troubled, even as are we mortals. Therefore They will stay Their anger and at Their appointed time make peace with us, that Ys may abide and keep holy Their names.

'This is the sacrifice They require. At the Turning of the Sun, one among the Nine shall not be here as always erenow, but must keep Vigil on Sena. She will receive a hard test. If she endures it well, then shall she be purified, and with her the sacred family, Queens, King, and daughters. Thus did I hear the Word.'

Ere anyone else could speak, Vindilis called: 'I will go!'

Forsquilis shook her head. 'I fear not. For the Word was that she must bear the morrow beneath her heart. I can only think this means she must be heavy with child.'

To and fro went their looks. Winter solstice was but three months hence; and for most of that span, Gratillonius would be gone.

Dahilis swallowed twice or thrice, thereafter said almost merrily, 'Why, that is myself. Of course I'll go.'

'Oh, nay, darling, nay!' protested Fennalis. 'You'll be too near your lying-in. You know how apt we are to be weatherbound yonder, in winter perhaps days on end.'

'Fear not. As close as I can reckon it, my time will be half a month or more after solstice.'

'Hm. I've consulted records. Both Bodilis and you surprised your mother Tambilis, despite your having different fathers. Early births run in that bloodline.'

Dahilis had attained calm. 'The Goddess will care for me.'

Hesitantly, reluctantly, Bodilis said, 'Remember the tradition.'

'What tradition?' Dahilis asked, bewildered.

'You may never have heard. 'Tis a story ancient and obscure. I sought it once in the archives, but too much is missing after centuries, and I could neither confirm nor disconfirm. The story is that Brennilis was born out on Sena. Thereupon a seal gained human voice, to prophesy that any so born thereafter would bring the end of the age which Brennilis was to make begin. It may be a mere folk tale.'

The others hearked back. The law was simply that one and only one from among them must be on the island, save on the high holy days or in periods of peril. She could be any of the Nine; and more than weather worked to keep Vigils out of orderly cycle. There could be strong obligations elsewhere, illness, the frailties of age, advanced pregnancy, evil omens – In spite of every precaution it had happened a few times in the past that a high priestess was dead when her relief arrived; and this called for the same hecatomb against disaster as when a King died in bed.

Sight converged on Innilis. Vindilis held her close, close. She stared out of that shelter and said in a thin tone, 'I've been chosen. Have I not?'

'It seems you have,' answered Forsquilis. Compassion stirred beneath steeliness. 'Take courage. It may be hard, but it shall be glory unto you, and unto your new daughter.'

Innilis blinked back tears. 'Well, I will go. Gladly.'

372

Vindilis's lips brushed her cheek.

'I have a word further,' said Forsquilis as though it hurt to talk. 'In my dreams was a sigil, white-hot from the fire, and it sealed a book with wax made not from honeycomb but from the fat and blood of sacrificed humans.' To horrified exclamations: 'Nay, the grisly rites of old are long behind Ys.' She smiled, briefly and bleakly. 'Moreover, such a seal would not hold in this real world. 'Twas a sign for me.'

She braced herself before continuing: 'I have thought, I have sought, I have prayed and offered; and this is how I read the vision. We must pledge our faith beforehand. We must take the Great Oath – by the Ordeal – that we will indeed hold a Vigil at Midwinter, which never was before, and that none shall stand it but she whom the Gods have marked out. Then shall all again be well with Ys.'

Anew the Nine fell mute. They had undergone the Ordeal when they plighted fealty to each other and to their purpose ere they went forth on Sena and cursed their King. That had not happened for generations earlier. They fasted and thirsted and scourged . . .

Dahilis gripped her belly. Light-boned as she was, the unborn swelled and burdened her. 'Oh, please,' she implored. 'Not me. I could lose her.'

Quinipilis stood up and made a gesture of blessing. 'I daresay 'tis uncalled for in your case, youngster,' she said. 'And in Innilis's. Your situations are patent.' Her wrinkled countenance went from side to side, haughtily. 'As for the rest of us, we can very well endure it again. We *are* the Gallicenae.'

2

His last night in Ys Gratillonius spent with Lanarvilis. This was not by chance. Dahilis was now forbidden him, save for a kiss and a promise, until after she became a mother. The remaining six out of the Nine he had begun visiting in turn, at their homes so that he might at least have Dahilis freely about in the palace during the day. Everybody concerned realized that, for any of numerous reasons, a turn must occasionally be postponed or exchanged. His forthcoming absence was just the first and most obvious example. Still, he had been surprised and somewhat dashed when the message came that it would not be Forsquilis who received him, but Lanarvilis.

He put on civil garb and his best face, to seek her house about sunset. She met him in the atrium sumptuously clad in a low-bosomed scarlet-and-gold gown that flattered her figure, the blonde hair coiled about her head and caught by a garnet-studded silver frontlet. 'Welcome, my lord,' she said, and held out a hand.

He took it, as was Ysan style. 'Thank you, my lady. I regret I could not arrive sooner. Preparations for departure tomorrow sunrise – '

She chuckled. 'I foresaw, and ordered a supper that would take no harm from waiting. Shall we to it? We've much to talk about.'

They went side by side through this most luxuriously appointed of the Queens' dwellings, past drapes of Oriental opulence, big-eyed Egyptian portraits, exquisite Grecian figurines, and – somehow not incongruous – Roman busts, Marius, Caesar, the first Augustus, Hadrianus, they whose workmanship had shored up, enlarged, repaired their state. Although the food and wines served in the triclinium were no Lucullan feast, they were excellent. A boy stood in the background softly playing a lyre.

'My lady is most generous,' said the King after they were settled.

'The Gallicenae desired a worthy sendoff for you,' Lanarvilis answered. 'We discussed it, and the choice fell on me.'

He sipped from his goblet, a taste rich and tart-edged, as cover for his close regard of her. The countenance – green-eyed, slightly wide in the nose and heavy in the mouth, past the freshness of youth, withal by no means bad-looking – was amply mobile but told him nothing. Best might be if he took the initiative. 'You do it elegantly,' he said. 'However, methinks you were elected for more than the table you set.'

Unsurprised, she nodded. 'Can you guess why?'

'Well, you are the closest of the Nine to the mundane affairs of the city. Quinipilis doubtless was once, but her years are upon her. The rest have their special interests. For yours, you occupy yourself with business of the Temple corporation. You are often in conference with Soren Cartagi, who's not only Speaker for Taranis but a power in the economy and politics of Ys. Hannon Baltisi, too, Lir Captain – you've taken a lead in reconciling them with me, or to me. In that it's helped that you have more knowledge of the Roman world than perhaps anyone else among your people. Were you a man, Lanarvilis, I'd call you a statesman.'

'You cannot, simply because I am a woman?' she said in an undertone. Promptly, aloud: 'Your words do me honour, my lord. Aye, the Sisterhood did feel I might best represent them this eventide – not least because I am, as you know, favourable to Rome. Rome has given civilization so much – the Roman peace – '

As her voice trailed away, he added, 'That peace which is falling apart, but which I hope to help restore.'

'True. Therefore 'twas felt we should talk freely, you and I. Tell me, for you've been taciturn about it, what your plans are for your journey.'

'If I've said little,' he replied carefully, ''twas on account of there being little to say. How can I lay plans ere I've learned, in detail, what the actual circumstances are? 'Twould be scant use sending Ysan agents unaccompanied. No matter how honest their intentions, they could never quite see, quite understand.'

She smiled. '*I* do, at any rate to the extent of agreeing 'tis a Roman military man who must go. But can you say somewhat of your aims afterwards?'

He had no hesitation about that, and the meal passed in conversation as good as with Bodilis – not the same, largely down-to-earth, but scarcely less intelligent. The wine flowed more readily than either of them noticed.

– Her bedchamber adjoined a room of blue carpeting, crimson drapes, furniture with inlays of walrus ivory and upholstery of leather. There they went for dessert – honeycakes, spiced fruit, a sweet Falernian to drink – and private talk prior to retiring. They sat together, leaning against the cushions on a couch that had a back, the refreshments on a low table before them. He rested an arm across that back, hand on the warmth and smoothness of her shoulder. She leaned close to him. Several beeswax candles burned; their light picked out the fine lines in her brow and radiating from her eyes, the mesh across the skin beneath her throat; and the flesh under her chin had started to sag; yet she was a handsome woman.

'Your scheme looks sound to me,' she said softly. 'I will

so tell my Sisters, and we'll ask the Gods to favour your enterprises.'

'You can do better than that,' he responded. 'You can work on the secular powers, Suffetes, Guilds, aye, common folk. If Ys is to take the lead in Armorica that duty calls for, and reap the rewards that faithful service calls for, Ys must be whole-hearted about it.'

'What can I . . . we . . . do?'

'Persuade them. Make them see 'tis their destiny. You, Lanarvilis, you could begin with Soren Cartagi – ' He felt her stiffen. 'Why, what's wrong?'

'Oh, naught.' She leaned forward, took up her goblet, drank deep. Staring before her: 'Soren is an honourable man.'

'Did I say otherwise? Look you, I've always regretted it when we've been at odds. I cannot think why. He's learned, able, aye, and a patriot. He should know where the real welfare of Ys lies. For myself, I'm willing to yield on many matters. But if I seek discussion, he soon breaks it off. What is it that makes him clash with me, over and over? Can you, his friend, milden him?'

'I can try.' Again she took a long drink, before turning her head and saying, eye to eye: 'But you do us, your Queens, an injustice. You never trouble to imagine how we already labour for you.'

Caught short, he had no better return than, 'What? Well, I know you pray, and . . . and you tell me 'tis your doing I am here, although – '

'Nay, more than that, and more. But I verge on secrets.' Lanarvilis brought her attention back to the cup. Her laugh was uneven. 'Desist. We've been political quite long enough, and morning comes far too early, and you must be away and I to my penance. Let us be happy while we may.'

'Your penance?' he asked sharply. 'What mean you?'

She bit her lip. 'I misspoke me.'

Concern rose in him. During these past difficult months she had been steadfast, neither toadying nor accusing, just quietly going about her work on behalf of the city and its Gods. Her spirit was a soldier's. 'Dear, tell me. Is aught amiss?'

'Yea!' she flung forth. 'And we must set it aright, we, the Nine. As soon as you are gone . . . certain austerities begin.'

'But what *is* the matter?' he pleaded. 'I should know, that I may help. I am the King.'

Metal rang: 'You are the King. A man. Do you admit me into your mystery of Mithras? Then ask no more about this.'

He took a while to say, unwontedly humble, 'So be it. However, here I am, and here I will be again. Always feel free to call upon me.'

'Oh, Grallon – Gratillonius!' She put down her cup and cast arms about his neck. Her breath was heady with wine. 'Enough, I said. Let's forget all else and be only ourselves. Surely we've earned that much.'

– Very late, as lamps were flickering low, he raised himself on an elbow and looked down at her where she lay half asleep. Drowsiness crept over him too. But the thoughts, the images stole by behind his eyes, before his soul. Of the seven who were fully his wives, might this be the strangest?

Dahilis, of course, was purely loving. Maldunilis enjoyed, in her lazy and slipshod fashion, and was in truth not a bad person. Bodilis was . . . comradely, altogether a woman when they embraced but otherwise a friend who had a great deal to impart; between him and her he felt bonds of loyalty growing like those between him and his father or him and Parnesius or – With Innilis he came to the frontier of enigma. She was sweet, acceptant, sometimes responsive, delighted to be bearing his child . . . and beyond her defences he glimpsed a shadow, a thing which he could not bring himself to ask about because he was afraid of hurting her. Vindilis seemed (though what was a seeming worth?) a little more comprehensible, whatever wounds she bore being encased in armour, out of sight and never bespoken. About anything else she talked with him like man to man; that included their joinings, where they had found ways which suited him sufficiently and left her, well, not disgusted. Forsquilis – He had looked forward to spending this night beside Forsquilis. Whether or not it was true that a King was powerless except among the Nine, Gratillonius must needs keep abstinent on his coming travels, since Ysans as well as legionaries would accompany him. Forsquilis might actually have made him welcome such a rest. He knew she was the deepest into the unknown of all the Gallicenae; but whenever they were alone, that soon ceased to make any difference.

Lanarvilis, though – He lowered his head to brush lips across the down that covered her cheek, as soft as moonlight. She had learned how to take her pleasure with him, as she took it with her home, art collection, food and drink, the spectacles and recreations and social occasions which Ys so abundantly offered. As for her work in administration and statecraft, doubtless she had a strong sense of duty, but doubtless it was also something she enjoyed, perhaps in the same way as he enjoyed making a piece of craftsmanship grow between his hands. Then what was lacking in her life? From time to time Gratillonius had caught a sense of terrible emptiness. This, too, was a thing about which he did not venture to ask.

She stirred beneath his caress. 'You *are* a good man,' she mumbled. 'I'll do my best, for you and your Rome.'

XXIII

1

The Black Months were upon Armorica. As Midwinter drew nigh, day shrank to little more than a glimmer between two huge darknesses, the sun wan and low and oftenest lost in leaden clouds or icy rain. Weather slowed the last stage of journeying, and dusk had fallen when Gratillonius saw Ys again from the heights of Point Vanis. It sheered sharp athwart the tarnished argency of the sea. Beyond, mists drifted past the pharos flame, the sole star aloft.

He reined in to give the headstone of Eppillus a Roman salute. Metal clinked, leather creaked, horses snorted wearily at his back. 'Dress ranks!' he heard Adminius bark. 'We'll enter in style, we will.' With a rattle of shields and stamp of hobnails, the soldiers obeyed, also the Ysan marines who reinforced them. The deputy had extended his authority over those, not overtly as against their own officer, but by sheer weight of example on the march.

If there had been no trouble, quite likely that was thanks to the sight of disciplined troops. Saxon pirates had ended their raiding till spring, but the woods housed Bacaudae the year around – ever more numerous, it was said, and certainly apt to be desperate in this season.

Gratillonius turned downhill. The horse of Bomatin Kusuri came alongside. He had represented Ys before the Imperials of Armorica. Well qualified he was, Mariner delegate to the Council of Suffetes: more than that, a man reasonably young and entirely vigorous, himself a skipper whose trading and occasional slaving voyages had made him the familiar of folk from Thule to Dál Riata. Gratillonius and he got along well.

'Ha!' he said in his bluff fashion. 'Is it a true parade when nobody's out to watch? Well, I'm as glad of that. Best to arrive quietly.'

Gratillonius glanced at him. In the murk he saw only the hulking body, the flamboyant sweep of moustaches; barbarian-bestowed tattoos were shadowed. 'I daresay you're eager for hearth and bed.'

'Well, now, my lord, between the twain of us – mind you, I say naught against my wife, she's a fine woman, though I could wish she'd nag me less to put on her kind of airs – but as long as we are coming in unheralded – Should she ever ask, would you tell her I had work to clear away, and therefore lodged this night in Dragon House?'

'But there's nothing we can't take care of tomorrow.'

'Save for a bit of sport, without getting jawed for it afterwards. We've been going hard, this trek. For safe return, methinks I should make a thank offering to Banba.' That fertility Goddess had, in Ys, become the patroness of harlots. 'Pour Her a libation or two, haw!'

Gratillonius frowned. Lying went against his grain as well as his faith. However, the chance was slight that Bomatin's wife would ever inquire of him, no matter how much she tried to shine by reflection from the King.

'You, my lord, have a choice ready for you – ' The seaman checked himself. 'Forgive me. I meant no disrespect. 'Tis but that we've fared and worked shoulder by shoulder all this while, you never throwing your weight around more than necessary. I've sometimes forgotten you're also the Incarnation of Taranis.'

'I understand,' said Gratillonius, relieved. He would have hated to give a reprimand or, worse, a cut of the

381

vinestaff. Yet if he did not maintain the dignity of the King, could he remain effective as prefect? He had two dozen legionaries to support his governance of a city ancient, proud, and secretive. It was not what he had awaited when he left Isca Silurum, ages agone.

'We did a good job,' Bomatin said. After a silence broken just by clopping hoofs and thudding feet, surf on reefs and cliffs as they neared the water: 'Did we not?'

'The future will tell,' said Gratillonius, which ended talk.

Riding onwards, he found his own mind less on what had happened than on what lay ahead. Immediately ahead. Had he entered by daylight he would have gone straight to Dahilis. No, the dear lass would have come forth to meet him, running as fast as the weight within allowed, laughing and weeping for joy. But she was doubtless asleep, or ought soon to be, and rousing her might be a little risky, now when her time approached . . .

The sentries at High Gate, and up in the Gaul and the Roman, cried hail. 'Quiet,' Gratillonius ordered. 'No sense in a tumult. Everything went well. Tomorrow in the Forum I'll tell the people. Tonight we're wearied and need our rest.'

He left his horse to the military grooms, bade his men farewell as became a commander, and walked off, still in wet cloak and muddied centurion's outfit. Windows gleamed here and there, out of surrounding houses or aloft in towers. Even nowadays, when oil had become costly, Ysans liked to keep late hours; they would burn tallow if they must. Despite gloom rapidly congealing to night, broad Lir Way was easy to walk on, and when he turned off in the direction of Elven Gardens, Dolphin Lane was so known to him that he walked its narrow, wall-enclosed twistiness with never a stumble.

Glass was aglow at the house of Bodilis. He banged the knocker, which was in the form of a fouled anchor, blurred by centuries of hands (and what had each of those callers been seeking?). It was no surprise that she opened the door herself. She usually let her servants go home when they had cleaned up after a supper simple and early. Then she was likely to stay awake far into the night, reading, writing, creating.

What caught at Gratillonius's throat was how beautiful she was. A blue robe, wrapped around and held by a sash, hugged the full but still graceful figure. Her hair fell in soft and lustrous waves past the broad, blunt, alive countenance and eyes that were like Dahilis's. Lamplight and beeswax candlelight from behind could only touch a curve, a tress, the hands that reached forth, but somehow he saw. 'Oh, you, you,' breathed the husky voice, 'welcome home, beloved!'

He embraced her, mouth to mouth, till he heard a slight gasp and realized he was straining her breasts too hard against his coat of mail. He eased his grip, let palms rove across shoulders, back, hips, while the kiss went on.

'Come in,' she said finally, let him by, and closed and barred the door behind them. 'How are you? What have you . . . what have you accomplished, King?'

'I am well.' He glanced down at himself and snorted a laugh. 'Though mired and sweaty and, in general, unfit for polite company . . . Dahilis! How fares she?'

'Excellently.'

'A-a-ah-h-h.'

Bodilis hesitated. 'I took for granted you'd seek her first.'

He felt his face grow warm. 'We arrived later than we foresaw. Best leave her undisturbed. I knew you'd tell me the truth.'

Bodilis laughed, low in her throat. 'And once any fears

for her were allayed – why, you've been long on the road.'

He gave her a crooked grin. 'I have that.'

Her eyelids drooped. ''Tis been long for me too.'

He strode forward. She fended him off, playfully, seductively. 'Nay, wait half a heartbeat! Would you not like refreshment first? You wouldn't? Then let's at least remove your armour and wash you clean. I'll enjoy doing that.'

– They lay on their sides, close together, each with a hand on the haunch of the other. As yet they felt no need to draw up the blankets. Recklessly many lamps illuminated her in gold. Outside, rain had begun, a susurrus against the shutters.

'Aye, on the whole, things have continued as erstwhile in Ys,' she said. 'Well, poor Innilis has been having a bad time, as she did when carrying Hoel's child. Sickness, pains – but no worse than before, if we remember aright, and the first birth is commonly the hardest, and we Sisters have been taking care of her. I think – if you seek her out tomorrow as a friend, simply a friend . . . that will cheer her much.'

'Of course I will.'

'Of course. You are you.' Bodilis's expression intensified. 'She needs every help she can get. This solstice she takes Vigil on Sena.'

'What?' asked Gratillonius, bemused. 'I thought . . . on the quarter days . . . all the Gallicenae were here.'

'Hitherto true. But the age born of Brennilis is dying, and – ' Bodilis laid fingers across his lips. 'Search no further. This is a thing that must be, that Ys may live.'

Chill struck through him. She sensed it, smiled, flowed nearer. ''Tis well, not ill. A duty to carry out, like standing on the Wall. Surely you've overcome worse hazards this trip. Tell me.'

He hung back. She nibbled his earlobe. 'Oh, do, Gratillonius. I'm afire with curiosity.'

He became eager to oblige. It was a line of retreat from that which had no name. And this was Bodilis whom he had sought, Bodilis, because she was the one who could both meet his body's needs and then discourse widely and deeply – more so than he could always follow, but that was itself a rousing challenge – He set Innilis aside.

'The tale goes on and on, like the miles,' he said. 'I've kept a daily record which I want you to read, if you'll overlook my lame language. For now, though – you're not sleepy? Well, let's bring in some wine and lie at ease while we talk. Interrupt me whenever you wish.'

She did, in questions and comments that heightened his own understanding of what he had seen and done; but mostly she led him on. The story came forth of his march to sad Vorgium, which had once been prosperous as Ys; to Condate Redonum, where he privily broached ideas for putting the Frankish laeti in their place; south as far as Portus Namnetum and Condovincum, to consider mutual assistance between the hinterland resources of those neighbouring cities and the navy of Ys; back north to Ingena and thence along the route he had followed earlier, until he branched off it to visit the tribune in charge at Gesocribate – 'On the whole, we reached agreements in principle. 'Twill take years to build the machinery and get it working properly, I know. Still, we've made a fair start.'

'*You* have,' she murmured, and again her caresses went seeking.

Vindilis had moved in with Innilis. None thought the worse of this, or even of their sharing a bed. The younger woman was so often ill and in pain; she should not be left to servants who loved her but were ignorant and clumsy about such matters. In truth, nothing untoward happened, as weak as Innilis had become, beyond kisses, and those grew to be as between mother and child.

A cry in the night or a feverish tossing would wake Vindilis. She then did what she could. All vestals studied the elements of medicine, and priestesses of every grade who showed any gift for it were trained as full physicians. Vindilis practised little. Her hands were cunning enough, but the Touch of the Goddess was not in them, nor had there been comfort in her manner. This last had changed of late.

The worst attack thus far ended a fitful sleep. Vindilis bounded on to a floor cold beneath her feet and bent over the other. Shutters blocked off any light from outside, but she always left a lamp burning when they retired. The untrimmed wick streamed smoke and a purulent, guttering flame. She could just see that Innilis lay hunched, arms and knees drawn against a now swelling belly. Her hair was lank with the sweat that studded a face blotched, yellowish, sunken in around the bones. The reek drowned any woman-fragrance. Sobs and hissings went between cracked lips. Vindilis put a hand on the brow and felt heat, though Innilis shuddered as with chill.

'Darling, darling!' Vindilis hurried to pour water from a jug, lay arm under neck, raise mouth to cup. 'Here, drink.' Innilis gulped and retched. 'Nay, slowly, sip, sip, oh, my poor sweet.'

Eventually she could ease the patient back on to the pillow. She went after her cloak. Both slept nude, for whatever warmth and consolation that might give. 'Don't go, please don't go,' Innilis moaned. 'Stay. Hold my hand. It hurts so.'

'Abide a little minute or two. I go to fetch powder of mandrake I've had brought. 'Twill give you some ease.'

Innilis's eyes widened to ghastly white. 'Nay! No drug. It might hurt the babe.'

Vindilis bit back a curse upon the babe. 'I think not. In any case, you can't go on like this.'

Innilis clutched herself below breasts that were ripening to full loveliness but too sore for fondling. 'Nay, Grallon's child, and, and she and I together on Sena. I can endure. I must.' Her face turned towards a niche where a small image of Belisama was barely visible in shadow. 'Mother of Mercies, help me.'

Vindilis threw the cloak over her shoulders and fastened the brooch. 'Well, you can at least quaff a pellitory infusion. That's never hurt you, and it should cool you off.' She took the lamp. 'I'll need this. Be not afraid in the dark.'

Innilis shook her weary head. 'I am not.' Vindilis suspected she lied. 'Please come back soon.'

'Very soon.' Vindilis kissed her cheek and went out.

A door opened and Innilis's daughter Audris came into the corridor. 'What is the matter?' she asked. 'Is Mama sick again?'

'Aye,' said Vindilis. 'Go back to bed.'

The girl's face screwed up. 'I want to see my Mama!'

This child of Hoel was ten years old, two more than Vindilis's Runa by the same King. So unforeseeably did the Sign come upon a maiden. Runa, though, was already as tall, and bright and lively. Audris had something of her mother's looks, except for being towheaded, but still talked like an infant, seemed unable to learn much, and fell into occasional fits. Hers had been a frightful birth. Vindilis had wondered over and over how her half-sister's next would fare.

'Back, I said!' the high priestess yelled. 'Back to your room or I'll hit you! And stay there!'

Audris gaped at the snarl above the lampflame, whimpered, and fled.

Dawnlight stole down the smokehole in the kitchen. Vindilis stirred up a fire banked under the hob and fed it with dry sticks and chips to hotten it fast. She kept decoctions readymade, but needed warmth to dissolve honey. That would hide the taste of the willow bark she added to the pellitory. It was supposed to endanger the unborn and Innilis would have refused it on that account; but she required a strong febrifuge – and, yea, a pinch of mandrake. Vindilis paced from flames to wall and back, to and fro, to and fro, while the dull light sharpened and the potion heated.

When she returned, Innilis had slipped partway into unconsciousness. 'Here, beloved, here I am, always, always,' Vindilis whispered. She raised the head and urged the liquid down. Thereafter she laid herself in the bed, damp and stinking though it was from sweat, and held Innilis in her arms and crooned lullabies until sleep came.

The lamp was nearly burned dry, but no need to refill. The servants would arrive shortly and throw back the shutters. Vindilis knew she would get no more rest until nightfall. She might as well wash and dress. Not enough hot water was left for bathing, but she preferred it cold.

The most direct way took her through the adjacent room, where Innilis had spent much of her leisure in happier days. A large bronze mirror on the wall caught what light there was and sent it off silver bowls, painted vases, bright draperies, bits of artwork. Another image of the Goddess, standing in a niche, was pretty too, benign, perhaps a trifle vapid; but abruptly, as the light struck ivory, it seemed to leap forth in the terrible majesty that was Hers.

Vindilis caught her breath. She turned, went to the niche, threw herself bruisingly hard prostrate on the floor. 'Ishtar-Isis-Belisama,' she begged, 'spare her. Take whom else You will, how You will, but spare Innilis, and afterwards I will seek only to serve You.'

3

On the road, Gratillonius had promised the legionaries and marines leave for a homecoming feast. Preparations took several days. They included reserving a favourite tavern down in the Fishtail, where prices were low and rowdiness expected; providing it with a couple of pigs to roast and a barrel of better wine than the landlord dispensed; engaging musicians, entertainers, a few strumpets to help out the regulars; inviting friends from the city and environs. This depleted the company fund, but that didn't matter much. Ys furnished the Romans, as well as her own fighters, necessities and services for which they had been wont to pay in Britannia. Furthermore, it gave them a wage, modest but in honest coin. The King had insisted on that, pointing to their proven value as guardians against foes and patrollers against crime. The move was popular with merchants, since it got money out of the city coffers and back into circulation.

On the appointed day, Adminius led the troops forth.

Otherwise he set his rank aside, and the passage was no march but a roaring romp. This was in the afternoon, in order to have daylight for the jugglers, acrobats, dancers, prestidigitators, and dancing animals. The weather was overcast but cold and dry: a blessing, as performances would have proper space in Skippers' Market rather than being crammed into the tavern. 'Did the Nine arrange it for us?' joked Guentius.

'Quiet!' said Budic. 'Don't mock sacred things. You know they never cast spells like that except at the most awful times.'

'What? You, the superpious Christian, defending pagan faith?' Cynan gibed.

Budic's young countenance flushed like a girl's. 'No, of course not. Although it is a decent sort of paganism. Queen Bodilis – But you don't want to insult our comrades, I hope.'

'I was talking Latin,' Guentius retorted. 'Didn't you notice?'

'Some of them know it,' Cynan decided. 'Budic's right. Lay off.'

Cheerfulness prevailed. When the show ended, as the early dusk was falling, men flocked to the inn and settled down to await the meal whose smoke and savour enriched the air. Goblets thumped, dice clattered, women squealed and giggled, voices lifted hoarse in talk and, presently, song.

– 'Ah, 'tis fine to be 'ome again,' sighed Adminius in Ysan. His left hand hoisted a beaker, his right gave the girl Keban a preliminary feeling over.

Herun of the navy raised brows across the table.

'"Home," said you? We're happy to have you amongst us. However, yearn you not for your Britannia?'

Adminius shrugged. 'God knows when we'll get back there, if ever. And frankly, 'tis no great loss. I could end my days 'ere quite contented. Might do so regardless, when I'm discharged.'

'Hm.' The sailor stroked his gingery beard. 'If you truly mean that, you'll be looking about for a wife. I've a sister you might like to meet.'

'Not so fast!' laughed Adminius, while Keban looked miffed.

'Nay, nay. She's young, hardly more than a child. Our parents will want to know any suitor well ere they give consent. For that matter, no girl in Ys may be married against her will, unless a vestal – Um, but a worthy man with Roman connections would be a welcome visitor.'

– Said Maeloch the fisher to his friend Cynan: 'Aye, do come stay with me when ye can get furlough. Ye know the house is small but snug, and though we're not rich, my Betha is a spanking good cook. The boys as well as myself – not to bespeak our neighbours – we'd love to hear ye yarn about your trip. We can promise to keep your whistle well wetted the while.'

'Thank you,' said the soldier. 'It cannot be till after the Midwinter Council. The centurion wants the whole two dozen of us for a guard.'

Maeloch's rough countenance tightened. 'What, looks the King for trouble?'

'Oh, no threat, surely.'

'Better not be. They'd have us, the whole folk, the seamen 'fore all, to reckon with, did they lay finger on our King or little Queen Dahilis.'

Cynan's usual dourness broke in a smile. 'You've grown fond of him, then?'

'With reason, with reason. He's brought honour back to the Key, order back to the holy family; he's rid us of the Scotic pirates and strives to get something real done about the Saxons; he's dealt fair and square with commoners like me, and now, I hear, he means to hold a court every month where anybody can bring a plea; and . . . he's made Dahilis glad, Dahilis who ever talks kindly.'

'Well, 'tis good to hear you say so. As for the Council, I think he just wants his legionaries for an honour guard, same as before, to help overawe opposition there.'

'Aye, even down under the cliffs we hear as how some magnates, Soren Cartagi of the Timbermen foremost, mislike the way he'd link us back to Rome. *I* say, when a storm is rising, break out your sheet anchor and make fast the rode.' Maeloch's fist thudded down on the table. Its thick planks trembled. 'Enough. Let's drink!'

XXIV

1

There was no wind on the night before Solstice Eve, nor was the air unduly cold. A swelling moon frosted thin, feathery clouds, among which a few stars blinked. Ashimmer like polished obsidian, Ocean heaved slowly, as if breathing in sleep. Sounds of surf rolled faint through deserted streets. The pharos light might have been a candle flame.

Then hour by hour a haze began drawing over heaven out of the west. As the moon sank towards it, a ring came aglow up there and stars withdrew from sight. Shadows blurred, lost themselves in the general darkness.

The moon was low beyond hidden Sena when abruptly a clatter and banging arose. It seemed thrice loud and harsh in this quietude. A cat on the prowl squalled and fled. Had the dead swarmed in from the necropolis to rattle their bones through Ys?

'Open, help, open, ow-w-w!'

A maidservant unbarred the door on which the knocker had beaten. Ghostly in nightgown, she peered at the small figure which jittered on the cobbles. After a moment: 'Oh, but 'tis Audris. What are you doing here at this hour, child?'

'Fennalis come quick!' the girl keened. 'Mama sick, Aunt Vin'ilis tol' me get Aunt Fennalis, quick!' She herself wore merely a shift pulled over her head. The paving must have numbed her bare feet.

The high priestess was swiftly awake. Unlike most of

393

her Sisters, she kept an attendant always in her house, because she had become hard of hearing and might not be roused by a belated appeal. Aside from lacking the Touch that Innilis seemed, erratically, to have, Fennalis was the best physician in the city, responsive to the great and the lowly alike.

She paused for no more than sandals, gown, cloak, and medical kit. 'Audris, stay,' she ordered the yammering visitor. 'Blodvin, tuck her into my bed, warm her some milk, sit beside her. If she throws a fit – drools, rolls her eyes, strains backwards – put a towel in her mouth lest she bite her tongue, but panic not.' Fennalis took a lantern that the maid had kindled from the nightfire and trotted forth. Wan light wavered across snub-nosed features, grey bristle of hair.

The way was short but steep to the home of Innilis. Its door stood open. Fennalis passed through. Candles burned everywhere. She set her lantern down and stood panting and wheezing.

Vindilis came into the atrium. She was naked. Blood bespattered her, dripped from her hands. 'At last,' she rasped. Heedless of stains, she gave Fennalis support while she well-nigh dragged the older woman along.

'A thump, a scream. She may have started out of bed to go to the pot. Or mayhap – Her mind has sometimes wandered. I suppose she fell off the edge on to the floor. There she lay, writhing and screaming. I saw the waves going down her belly. Somehow I got her back into bed, and lights lit to see by. The waters gushed forth. They were tinged with red. Blood followed. I've tried to stanch it. Small success.'

They reached the bedroom. Splotches and footprints went crimson across the floor. Sheets, blankets, mattress were soaked. Innilis half sat against a heap of pillows. Her jaws were wide, straining for air, making a Gorgon mask. Eyes stared, blank with pain and terror.

Fennalis regained her breath. She bustled to the bed-side, kissed the brow beneath her, and murmured, 'How goes it, Sister?' while she removed the cloths Vindilis had tucked between the thighs.

'Oh, it hurts, it hurts,' moaned Innilis. Vindilis clenched fists together but kept aside, out of the way.

'Hm. Naturally it would,' said Fennalis. 'I think you did succeed. No issue now to speak of. Blood always looks like more than it is.'

'But too much nonetheless,' Vindilis replied in the same grating monotone as before.

Fennalis nodded. 'To be awaited. The suddenness and all. I daresay injuries from the first birth never healed aright.'

Innilis reached to scrabble after her. 'Help me!' she cried. 'Save me. I don't want to ride in the Wild Hunt!'

'You shan't.'

'Certainly not you.' Vindilis came around to lean over the head of the bed, stroke the face that was bent away from her, drop kisses and tears down into the hair. 'You are a Queen. Whatever happens to us, Belisama takes us home to Her sea, She, the Star of it.'

'Stop that nonsense,' Fennalis snapped. 'We can get this over fast if we go about it rightly. Vindilis, curb yourself. Stand yonder. Help her kneel . . . Now, child, bear down.'

Innilis shrieked. '*Nay!*'

'Yea,' said Fennalis. 'Harken. You're not going to lose it. You've done that already. Your task is to get rid of it.'

'Oh, my babe, the King's babe!'

Fennalis slapped Innilis on the cheek. 'Stop that. Get to work. Vindilis, support her while I unpack my kit.'

– When at last Innilis lay simply weeping, Fennalis made her drink from a vial. To Vindilis the physician said: 'Opium. Scarce as cocks' eggs nowadays, but I've saved out some for special cases. 'Twill ease her, and can do no harm now.'

'Nay.' Vindilis stared at that which lay on the floor, quiet after a brief stirring. 'It can do no harm now.'

'When Innilis is soundly asleep, we'll sponge her off and shift her to the couch in her receiving room. Ease your mind. I don't believe our Sister is in further peril, though belike she'll be slow to regain strength. The servants will be here before dawn.' Fennalis yawned mightily. 'Then at last we twain can go tumble into bed and sleep till noon.'

'Nay,' said Vindilis again. Weariness barely dulled the iron in her voice. 'Not till well afterwards. Have you forgotten?'

2

The state barge daily set forth at sunrise, or as soon thereafter as ebb tide had started opening the sea gate. This time, fetching Maldunilis back, it carried no replacement. For the next three days, all the Nine would be in Ys, attending to rites and Council. Or thus it had been hitherto.

The last feather-clouds departed. By afternoon the sun shone in a sky gone milky; shadows stretched pale from the south. A breeze sprang up, cold, gradually strengthening until it whittered in streets and raised whitecaps on a darkly greenish-grey sea.

Seven of the Nine met at the temple of Belisama. They dismissed the vestals and minor priestesses, save for one who was to stand outside and admit Dahilis when she arrived, and went on into the main chamber of worship.

Chill and dimness lay within, barely lighted by windows whose glass was the hue of underwater; for lamps and candles had been extinguished. They would be rekindled at midnight – would shine from every observant house in the city – to welcome home the returning sun. Grain of stone and mosaic scenes of myth were vague in vision. At the far end, behind the high altar, the images of the triune Goddess towered pallid and stern. Silently, each in her own way, the Gallicenae prayed for mercy.

After a while Dahilis slipped in, clad like the rest in sacral blue and white. Tears gleamed below the tall headdress. Her voice came thin: 'I'm sorry, I beg pardon I'm late, but – but – '

Quinipilis approached her, looked close, and said, 'Come, best we seek our meeting room at once.'

'Nay, I m-m-must make my devotion – '

'You shall, for the whole Sisterhood and people.'

'You don't understand! Listen!'

'Hush. This is no place for news. Come.'

Numbly, Dahilis followed the old woman, while the others trailed after. They went down the corridor to the chamber behind the sanctuary and entered. It was scarcely warmer, but better served by its windows; the Four Aspects on the walls stood forth in vividness.

Several cried out. On the dais, red-robed, Key in view on his breast, Hammer against hip, Gratillonius waited. He had used the rear entrance – not that anyone would have dared refuse him admission after a single look at his countenance.

Vindilis first got her wits back. Her words attacked like a stooping hawk. 'My lord, what is this? Arriving without right is sacrilege. Begone!'

The square, massive visage hardened still further, the powerful body seemed to take stance as if readying for an enemy charge. Rougher than had been his wont, his answer rolled forth. 'I have every right. I am the King of Ys. He Whose avatar I am is Belisama's lover.'

Dahilis stumbled forward to stand under the dais, confronting her Sisters. They could see how her breath laboured, almost how her heart galloped, beneath the child-bulged gown. She raised her palms. 'Hear me,' she beseeched. 'I never intended – But 'tis my fault. Mine alone. When the m-message came to the palace . . . about poor Innilis – I was so shocked I blurted unthinkingly – '

'And I sensed something more behind that, and thundered it out of her,' Gratillonius said. 'She strove to hold back, but she'd already let slip she must go hither at this time, about a matter more grave than the loss of an infant. I said I would come too, my legionaries at my back if need be, and have the truth. That – ' He faltered. For a moment he stood gnawing his lip, then whispered, 'That broke her will.'

'Nay, wait, wait,' exclaimed Quinipilis. She rocked up to hug Dahilis to her ample bosom. 'There, dear, there, 'twas indeed no sin of yours. You were helpless.'

'She was sensible,' declared Fennalis. 'Better give the man his way, and a while to calm down, better that than an open breach, right in the sacred building.'

'True,' growled the centurion. 'She has a wiser head on her, young though she be, than some I could name. Now can the lot of you sit down and we talk this over like reasoning beings?'

'I fear 'tis too deep for reason,' said Bodilis; but she took the lead in urging that they try. To Maldunilis she must utter a stiff 'Be quiet or I'll throw you out' before that Queen controlled her dread of what these events might portend. The rest won sooner to a stoic peacefulness.

'Well.' Seeking to ease things a little, Gratillonius leaned on the long haft of the Hammer. 'I hope you understand my wish is to do my duty as your King. But I have other duties too, as the prefect of Rome . . . and as a man. It grieves me to hear what Innilis has suffered. If I have not hastened to her bedside, 'tis because of this business. To be frank, I am yet unclear about it. I know only that she was supposed to spend the solstice day and night on Sena, but the task has fallen on Dahilis.'

'I will fulfil it, oh, I will,' Dahilis vowed.

Gratillonius's anger burst forth anew. 'Alone, in your condition? Have you seen the sky? Foul weather's on the way, if ever clouds gave signal. You could be trapped out yonder for days, no boat able to live through the waves and reefs. Madness!'

It was as though fire flickered behind ice in the gaze of Forsquilis. 'Nay, Roman,' she said to the man with whom she had made love this past night. Intensity caused her to tremble. ''Tis the command of the Gods. To learn it I have guested the dead; to carry it out we have thirsted, fasted, and scourged; no more may we deny or defy it than you may spit on the sacrifice of your Mithras. Or less – for He would send you alone down to hell, whereas the wrath of our Gods would fall upon all Ys. It is required that a Sister take Vigil at this Midwinter while bearing within her a child. That was to have been Innilis. Now it must needs be Dahilis.'

'You went behind my back.' Gratillonius raised the Hammer. 'Why, why, why?'

'To expiate the sins against Them, among which yours, O King, wax rank,' said Lanarvilis quietly, almost sorrowfully; and she explained.

'But – but that is – See here!' Gratillonius roared. 'If I've erred, I'll make whatever amends you want . . . if they be seemly . . . *I* will!'

Silence answered, save that Forsquilis shook her head.

Dahilis had gone dry-eyed. She sat straight, hands serene in her lap, resoluteness upon her.

'Mithras will protect you! He is just, and He is above – ' Gratillonius stopped. He knew implacability when it stared at him.

He had two dozen soldiers. Most ordinary Ysan men would recoil from assaulting him, he trusted; even some of the marines might hang back. In any event, given speed and determination, his company could fight its way clear and on to safety in Audiarna, bearing Dahilis along –

No. He foresaw what that would do to her. And it would irretrievably wreck the still frail structure of defence he was building. His mission was to save Armorica for Rome, not tear it asunder.

'Forgive me. I meant no insult to the God of Ys.' A while he stood, head bowed, both hands on the butt of the Hammer to upbear his weight, which seemed to have grown boulder-huge. The Key dangled from his neck.

Finally he shook himself, squared his shoulders, and said, 'Very well. So be it. But Dahilis shall take no needless risk.'

'Do you doubt that the Goddess will look after her?' Vindilis challenged. 'Or if not, who shall fathom Her ways? That which has happened may indeed have been Her will making itself manifest.'

'Then do you doubt its fulfilment, whatever we mortals may do?' Gratillonius retorted. 'I ask merely that one or two of you – or somebody – accompany Dahilis, and stand by against . . . troubles such as we have had already.'

'None of us may,' answered Quinipilis. 'Gratillonius, my dear, you're a kind man in your fashion, and I feel what wound is in you. But 'tis a condition of this sacrament, and we are bound to it by the Great Oath, that none among us may betread Sena tomorrow, other than the chosen high priestess and her unborn. And of course nobody else ever may.'

Gratillonius pounced. 'Ha! What of the workmen – *men* – who repaired the storm damage?'

'That was a holy necessity,' Lanarvilis replied. 'First they underwent rites of purification and consecration. Afterwards the entire island was rededicated. Think not we can evade Belisama's commandment by falsely praying over anybody at this late hour.'

His response came as no surprise to himself. It had been rising like a sea tide. '*I* am sanctified,' he said.

Horror hissed around the room.

'I am the King. I am Taranis on earth,' he followed. 'If the King's presence on Sena is unheard of, why, likewise is a Midwinter Vigil.'

'The King – in Ys – must preside over the festival,' Fennalis protested.

Gratillonius fleered. 'Are they backwoodsmen here, to believe their celebrations rekindle the sun? Nay, those are but celebrations. I've asked about them. All I'm supposed to do is take part in a ceremony. Somebody else – a priest or Soren, my Speaker – he can do it as well. Has naught like this ever happened erenow in your history?'

'There have been two or three times,' Bodilis confessed. 'A King was ill, or at the frontier when invasion threatened, or – '

'You see?' Gratillonius cried. He drew breath. 'Fear not,' he said in a level tone. 'I've no wish to profane anything. I'll keep away from the mysteries. But . . . come worst to worst, I am a good man of my hands, a farm boy who has helped birth many an animal, a soldier who knows how to treat many a hurt. The sailors who ferry you there set foot on the wharf, at least. Would you

401

refuse your sacral King what you grant them?' Most softly: 'I am going. I have spoken.'

Bodilis stirred, raised her hands, gazed beyond the walls as her mind felt its way forward. 'Hold, wait,' she said. 'Sisters, a God does dwell in our King. Who can be certain that Belisama wants not him also? . . . I told you, Gratillonius, the matter is too deep for reason. Yet while sunlight never reaches the ocean depths, it illuminates the waves . . . Aye, listen. 'Tis true that outsiders may walk on the wharf. Indeed, the ground below high-water mark is allowable. That law is for the sake of mariners who may be driven on to a lee shore, but does not explicitly ban others.' She met his glance. 'Can we, together, find a compromise?'

Hope blazed in him. 'I think we can.'

The face of Dahilis was like sunrise.

XXV

1

The barge of state was impressive not in size, for its length was a bare sixty feet, but in appearance. The graceful hull was blue with silver trim. At the prow lifted a carven swan's head, at the stern a fishtail, both gilt. A deckhouse amidships, though wooden, was built and painted to resemble a Grecian temple in miniature. While the vessel was oar-driven, she bore a pole for the flying of a flag – heavy silk, gold-fringed, dolphin argent on azure, the annual gift of the Needleworkers' Guild. The crew were navy men, periodically chosen by their captains as an honour.

She departed Ys somewhat late on solstice morning because seas were running heavy, causing a chop in the very basin. When ebb had swung the doors safely wide, a trumpet sounded, men ashore cast off lines, the galley stood out. From quay, wall, towers, folk watched this unprecedented faring in awe.

Beyond the shelter, the craft rocked, pitched, shuddered. Wind drove strong, hollowly hooting, thrumming the stays, making waves roar white-maned along until they burst in a crash and a fountaining on the rocks everywhere about. It harried a wrack low and wolf-grey out of murk rising ever higher in the west. Spindrift flung salt on to lips. Chill slashed.

The galley toiled onwards, picking a way through the safe lanes. Lookouts strained their vision overside, the steersman and his standby poised taut, rowers changed frequently so as to keep at peak strength. Slowly the shining spires of Ys sank away aft, until flying brume swallowed sight first of them and then of the mainland. No birds were aloft except a cormorant that followed afar, a hovering and soaring blackness. As the barge approached Sena, a score or more of seals appeared and accompanied it.

The interior of the deckhouse was a cabin, snug and well-appointed, dim today when windows perforce were shuttered. Gratillonius and Dahilis shared a seat. Most of the time she leaned close and he had an arm about her, bracing her as the vessel rolled and plunged. Whoosh and boom of waves, creak and groan of timbers, occasional shouts of the men filled the room. Yet they could talk. They needed to, for yesterday he had spent the evening on his preparations, whereupon she passed the night at the temple, in purification as well as sleep.

'How much may you tell me of what you shall be doing?' he asked.

''Tis to be a Vigil like any other – in form, at least,' she replied. Earnestly: 'You do understand what that means, do you not? On behalf of Ys, communion with the Goddess, prayers for the people; and, yea, devotion to Lir, since 'tis Taranis Who is with Her everywhere else. At the House of the Goddess I drink Her wine and eat Her bread; more than that I must not say. I then walk to the two Stones that the Old Folk raised near the middle of the island, and perform certain rites. Thence I go to the far western end and give Lir His honours. After that I return to the House for orisons, meditation, another sacred meal, and rest until sunrise. After dawnsong I am free, and soon the barge comes to bring my Sister and take me home.' She squeezed his hand. 'To you. This time, with you.'

'Hm!' He scowled. 'I mistrust the weather.'

404

'Oh, but we're not supposed to endanger ourselves. We do whatever looks safe, and are excused from the rest. The House is stoutly built. Its tower is for refuge when a storm dashes the waters clear across land. I am sure, though, I'm sure the Gods want a full sacrament at this of all Vigils. They will provide.'

Her faith tugged at his heart. He almost wished he could share it. But in the Gods of Ys was too much of the ancient darkness from which They had risen. 'When can I see you?'

She turned her countenance up towards his to give him the gift of her smile, which she thought of as a present to herself. 'Well, the door of the House is in view from the wharf. You'll have sight of me as I go in and out, and I of you. I don't think Belisama will mind if we wave at each other.'

How dear she was. Hair tumbled in a golden cataract past features whose fine bones might be of the Suffetes but whose flared and tip-tilted nose, wide and soft mouth just parted over flawless teeth, fair skin and underlying liveliness were belike from her father Hoel. The great dark-blue eyes she shared with Bodilis; the light that danced within them was her own. Her voice was likewise low: not husky, however; its music, again, uniquely hers. Never before had he known a woman could be so merry and still so loving. He leaned down towards her. The sweetness of tresses and flesh dizzied him.

She blocked his lips with gentle fingers. 'Nay, darling, we mustn't, not till we're back home.' Laughter purred. 'But I don't think She will blame me, either, for looking forward.'

He sighed. 'Suppose we're weatherbound.'

'Then the priestess must carry on the round of services as best she can until she is relieved. I mustn't come to you. We'll make up for that after our girl is born.'

'But what if that happens meanwhile?' he fretted. 'That's why I'm here, you know. Unless worse befall. I will not stand idly by if you need help, Dahilis. I will not. Afterwards let the Gods fight it out with me.'

'Hush!' she said, scandalized. 'You . . . you shouldn't be . . . hostile like that, darling. The Mother loves us. I know She does. And I am not due quite yet. Oh, aye, if bad trouble strikes, of course I may seek your tent. My Sisters and I talked this out last night. This Vigil is not for, for punishment. 'Tis to set things aright, that the Gods may again be free to bestow blessings on Ys.'

He cleared his throat. 'Umf, I meant no offence. Certainly not . . . but the House will be better shelter for us.'

She shook her head violently. 'Nay! A man would desecrate it. 'Twould have to be purified and consecrated anew, as 'twas after the carpenters and masons had finished. Meanwhile the poor dead had to wait in the Twilight.' Dahilis drew a sharp breath. 'The workers were there by divine consent. If you broke in unasked – Nay, I dare not think what vengeance the Gods might take on you. On *you*. Please, beloved, nay, promise me you'll not!'

'Ah, well, we speak of what we trust is unlikely,' he evaded. In haste to change the subject: 'But what's this about the dead? I remember the funeral barge went out more than once while the repair work was going on.'

He could barely hear her whisper through the din: 'That was only their bodies. Later the Ferriers bring their souls to Sena for judgement. On such a night the Queen in the House must stay wakeful till morning to pray for them.'

'Have you?' Instantly he regretted his heedlessness.

She nodded. He couldn't tell whether she had gone pale, but her eyes were more big than ever, staring

406

straight forward. 'Surely. At sundown I have suddenly *known* there would be the landing, and the whisper of the names, and – and been glad to have light around me after I lit lamps on the altar – This is a mystery.'

'I'm sorry,' he mumbled. 'I'd not cause you distress for the world and Heaven.'

She embraced him, carefully chaste but altogether forgiving. Her spirits soon lifted afresh. His did too, somewhat.

2

The barge came in with difficulty through the wild water. Watching on deck, Gratillonius admired the skill of captain and crew. Rowers strained: the master gauged wind and waves, gave hand signals; a stentor bellowed the orders. They caught a billow and rode it. As it crested, the steersman put his helm hard over; larboard oars snapped up out of harm's way while starboard oars brought the hull about; the steersman's partner disengaged the left rudder oar and hauled it free; strokes boomed against rope bumpers suspended from bollards. Immediately sailors leapt off on to the wharf, lines in hand, and made fast. Two aboard ran out a gangplank which their fellows ashore secured.

The captain gave Dahilis the salute of deference. 'Thanks be to Lir that He brought us here in safety, and to Belisama that She gave us you, O Queen, to convey hither,' he said formally. The wind tattered his words.

She inclined her head to him. 'And I thank you on behalf of the Gallicenae and Ys,' she replied likewise, then could not resist laughing: ''Twas a pretty show!'

Gravity returned: 'The hour is late, on this shortest day

407

of the year. I must commence at once. Farewell.'

Gratillonius escorted her to the wharf. Small and alone she looked against the grey-green tumult that battered the island, the dreariness of rock, scrub, and sere grass beyond. Sacral gown and headdress were woollen for winter, as was the cloak she hugged to her, but cold sought inwards. A moment her gaze dwelt on him. 'Fare *you* well,' she said, 'for ever well.'

Turning, she walked off, over the planks and along a short path to the House of the Goddess. From her left hand dangled a bedroll, from her right a bag of other necessities. Despite the burden and even through the garments, he was aware of how dancingly she moved. Her unborn had never dragged her down much. She had often, delightedly, said what a quick and easy delivery should be hers, and what a fine, healthy babe – 'Come, Gratillonius, put your hand here, feel her kick, already she wants out. Oh, she'll make the world remember her!' And only a few days ago, Dahilis had felt the lightening.

She glanced back and waved, as she had promised, before she disappeared in the sombre bulk of the House. Rushing rags of cloud brushed past its towertop. The western half of heaven had become a cavern.

Someone diffidently touched Gratillonius's arm. 'Your pardon, my lord.' The King glanced around and recognized a young man named Herun. 'We have to set up your camp without delay.'

'Oh . . . oh, indeed,' said Gratillonius. 'So you can start back. Trying that after dark would be deadly in this weather, I'm sure.'

'In truth, lord. As 'tis, likeliest the gate will be shut, or too narrowly open to attempt. But given such a tide, we can make Ghost Quay if we've light to see by. It happens often enough.'

Gratillonius must oversee the work and take a hand of

his own, as newly invented as it was. None less than Bomatin Kusuri, Mariner Councillor, had helped him devise his shelter yesterday, and got craftsmen to prepare what extra parts were required. In effect, a Roman army tent went up on the wharf, tethered to bollards and piles. Meant for eight men, it would be less warm for one, though roomier. However, its leather would fend off any blast that did not tear everything loose; a rug would lie beneath; he was well clad, in fisherman's tunic, trousers, boots, with jacket and gloves and ample changes in reserve; he had candles, lantern, oil, tinder, punkwood, flint, steel.

Nevertheless it was a swine of a job to erect the tent. Leather flapped into faces, cords flew abut like slave-drivers' whips. Men said no profane word, but obscenities were plentiful. Afterwards, watching for Dahilis, Gratillonius realized she must have gone out again, inland, while he was thus engaged. He had not seen her greeting to him.

Finally the task was over. He said his appreciative goodbye. The crew embarked, cast loose, fended off, departed. He stood watching the galley dwindle: a brave sight, but how fragile amidst the surges and surfs, like Dahilis beneath the sky.

Having sadly given up on seeing her again for hours, he busied himself settling in. There were things to stow, food such as didn't need cooking, water, wine, bedroll, towels, washbasin, comb, teeth cleansers – the list went on, ending with what he had brought to pass the time. A book could have been too easily blotted, ruined; and he possessed no musical gift whatsoever. He did, though, have waxed tablets and a stylus, for noting down any thoughts that occurred to him about Ys and Armorica. Mainly he had brought pieces of wood, and tools to carve them into ornaments for furniture and toys for his step-daughters. And why not for his own daughter as well, his and Dahilis's? She'd not appreciate more than a rag doll at first, but later she would enjoy, say, a tiny wagon . . .

Gratillonius smiled as he crossed his legs on the rug. He reached for a whetstone. Several of his blades needed sharpening, and no servant of his had quite the right final feather-touch.

Wind gusted, screeched, noisily flapped the doorfolds, which had been tied back to admit light. His pleasure drained from him. He should not be doing work as mechanical as this. It freed his mind to wonder how Dahilis was, alone with her Gods at Midwinter.

3

Gratillonius did not notice her. He and the sailors were struggling to put up his tent. Dahilis wished she could linger till his glance wandered her way. But already she had had to be hasty in the first communion rite. More than half the short day was gone, while clouds drew downward, ever darker, and wind grew still more fierce. She must be back before nightfall was complete, so she could see to kindle fire – on the hearth for herself, in lamps for herself and the Goddess.

'Belisama, Queen and Mother, watch over him,' she whispered, and started forth.

For a space the footpath followed the shoreline. Cast-offs of the tide lay strewn, kelp, shells, dead fish, pieces from the many wrecks that these waters had claimed over the years. Beyond churned and foamed the sea itself, nearly black save where it burst in gigantic whiteness. Growl and roar were like drums beneath the war horn of the wind. Seals swam in the turmoil, They kept turning

410

their heads inland – towards her? The path bent that way, then west again; she lost sight of them.

It hurt to turn her back on the Kindly Ones. It hurt to leave Gratillonius behind. It hurt!

Dahilis halted with a gasp. The pain started at the small of her back and came around to grip her in the belly. It was like the pangs of lightening, but those had been brief and mild. This laid hold of her inmost depths. She barred a cry behind her teeth. Dear Isis, had the birth begun so early?

The cramp passed. A while she stood shivering. Best return, start the fire, wait. If this went on, seek Gratillonius.

Nay. Dead Brennilis, speaking through the mouth of Forsquilis, had warned that the trial would be severe. This was not worse than she, Dahilis, could endure. The pains might well be false. In any event, likelihood was that she could move about freely, most of the time, for hours and hours yet. Let her do so, and win her man forgiveness.

And the Sisterhood and Ys, of course.

She strode on. The wind was now straight in her face. She tasted the salt spray that it flung the length of Sena. It sought to tear the cloak from her shoulders. She could barely hold the garment together; it fluttered and snapped frantically. The cold probed through every opening. Her gown made valiant defence, but the wind flattened it against her and her babe, jeered as it lifted the hem, swirled up from underneath. The low, scudding clouds had given way to a roiling leadenness above, a monstrous gloom ahead. Leafless bushes flicked their twigs above stones and patches of withered grass. Hoot and howl streamed around her.

But there were the two menhirs, where she had helped bring Gratillonius and, later, bring him the aid he needed

411

against the reavers out at sea — A second spasm coiled through her. She waited it out.

Shakily, she approached the Bird and the Beast. She said the words, she danced the sunwise dance, she ate the salt and gave the drop of blood, she asked leave to depart and peace on the Old Folk. It seemed a good omen that the next attack held off until this was all done.

After that, though, she lost count of how many stops she must make on her way west. Belike the wind slowed her, she thought: thrusting, battering, chilling, as if Lir had sent it to keep her away from Him. The flat landscape seemed everywhere the same. As she went on, it grew vague in her sight. The wind was lashing such tears from her eyes. Spray flew ever thicker. Its bitterness caked on her lips. Snow that was half sleet began drifting against her. Horizon and sky were lost.

'Lir,' she appealed, 'Lir, are You really angered that he buried his friend, in the name of their God, above Your sea? You can't be. You are Captain and Helmsman. You understand what manhood is.'

But Lir had nothing of humanity about Him. He was the storm that whelmed ships, the lightless depths that drowned men, the waves that flung them on to rocks for gulls to eat what the eels had not. Well did He nourish great whales, and dolphins to frolic about sailors and seals to watch over them. Well did He raise great shoals of fish and the winds that bore rich cargoes homeward. But He was Ocean, the Son of Chaos, and Ys lived only on sufferance of His, only because it had made itself forever a hostage to His wrath.

Let her appeal and appease — She sank to knees, to all fours, and could not quite hold back a cry. Some births came fast. This, her first, too early at that, this birth ought not to, but, 'Belisama, Mother, help me.'

Dahilis lurched back to her feet. The drift around her

412

grew more white as everything else grew blacker.

Then ahead, at endless last, she spied the tip of the island. Surf ramped beyond it; she heard the boom and long, withdrawing snarl, she could well-nigh feel them through her bones. That was farther out than she must go. She need only descend a few tiers of rock to one that jutted out above high-water mark. Upon it stood an altar, a block of stone, sea-worn until ledges and carven symbols were nearly gone. There she must give Lir His honour. Afterwards she could return to the House of the Goddess.

She picked her way down carefully, half blinded as she was. Wind raved, snow and spindrift flew. Her womb contracted. She bent herself around the anguish. Her heel slipped on wetness. She felt herself toppling, helpless. It seemed to go on and on, while she stood aside and watched. Shock, pain, those too struck somebody remote.

– They waited patiently until she crawled back from wherever she had been. That was a slow battle. Often she slid back downwards. A birth pang would drag her up again. The agony in her right leg resisted this, as the wind had resisted her walking. But when she did break free, it became her friend. It was something other than a confusion of wind, snow, water, darkness, and noise. Her mind clung to it. Don't let go, she begged. If you do, I'll slip away from this, and I mustn't.

Scrabbling, her fingers hoisted her gown. The right foot was bent awry. Fractured ankle. She would dance no more, not soon. How long had she lain unaware? Not long; her head was unhurt, mayhap saved by the cloth wrapped around it, though that had come loose. Nonetheless, thought fumbled through drift of snow and scud. Her garments were drenched, weighting her when she tried to raise herself on her hands. Water sheeted. The tide was coming in swiftly. With the wind behind it, surf would reach around the altar of Lir. It might pull her off to Him, or it might simply kill her and the child.

She must find shelter before the chill reached her womb. Already she felt numbness stealing inwards. She tried to get up on the sound foot and hop. That knee buckled. She fell on the broken ankle. Bright lightnings cast her back into the dark.

It was closing in on the world when she next regained herself. Another cramp pulsed through her. She felt it more keenly than she now felt the broken bones. 'Hold,' she muttered. 'Abide. We'll go to him.' His right name eluded her. It was lengthy, Latin, unmusical. Her tongue remembered how Ysans sometimes rendered it. 'Grallon. Oh, Grallon.'

Dahilis began to crawl.

When she had hitched her way over the terraces, on to the flatland, she could not find the path. Whiteness lay thin upon rock and soil. It flowed along in the air, on the wind, through the deepening dusk. The crash and rush of the sea behind her filled her skull. She must get away from the sea. Somewhere yonder were Grallon and Belisama. 'Be not hasty,' she told her daughter. 'Wait till he can help us.' She knew little else, but she did know that she must creep onwards, each time that the pains allowed.

4

As twilight fell, Gratillonius grew more and more uneasy. Ignoring cold, he sat in the entrance of his tent. It opened towards the building. He did not see her, he did not see her. By every hell of every faith, she ought to be back. Ought she not? The island was small. Any healthy person could walk it from end to end in an hour or so. Allow as

414

much for the return. She did have her duties along the way, but they couldn't be too elaborate, could they? A slight snow had begun, dry flakes borne nearly level out of the west. It hindered vision. He might miss sight of her. He didn't want that.

His woodcarving forgotten, he waited. Thoughts tumbled through him, memories, mother, father, the farm, camp, girls who seemed to have gone unreal, the Wall, Parnesius, combats that no longer mattered – where *was* Dahilis? – Maximus's will to power, the march to Ys, Dahilis, Dahilis, things he needed to do, also among her Sisters – what in Ahriman's name was keeping her? – how he might disengage himself from Ys after his work in Armorica was done, but not from Dahilis, no, he must win her over to Rome, and where *was* she, what was keeping her? The snow streaked denser than before.

Finally he realized he'd better start fire while he could still see. That meant closing the tent against the gusts that had been whirling about in it. The consequent gloom, and his own impatience, cost him several failures before he had ignited the tinder, blown it to life, kindled a punkstick, and brought that to a candle. Then it took a while more to get his lantern going. It was a fine big one, bronze with glass panes, but awkward in the ignition. He'd be stupid not to use it, however, for a naked flame might well die when he reopened the tent flaps.

It did. He blinked at night. Not dark already! He should stand outside and let his eyes adapt. The wind savaged his face. Waves bawled unseen; he felt the wharf tremble to their blows. With the slowness of a torturer, some vision came to him. He discerned the House not as a mass but as an abyss, blacker than black. If Dahilis had entered it while he wasn't looking, she must be asleep in there.

The knowledge struck into him like a swordthrust.

415

'Asleep?' he yelled. 'Can't be!' Not as early as Midwinter nightfall was. She had spoken of an evensong; surely that required lamps. And she would have lighted a hearthfire. But never a glimmer –

He fought himself till the breath sobbed in his gullet. He'd missed sight of her. Shutters and door blocked light. If he went there, she would be aghast. She was supposed to seek him, should necessity come upon her. Stand fast, Gratillonius, stand your watch, keep your post.

Snow hissed. Blindness deepened. He raised his hands. 'Mithras, God of the Law, what shall I do?'

A still small voice replied: Look for the smoke.

Gratillonius's heart stumbled. The smoke of sacrifice, the smoke of the hearth, it rose. However swiftly wind snatched it away from its outlet, firelight from beneath should glimmer on it . . . and on the flying snow . . . but there was no light. None whatsoever.

A faraway part of him recalled moments of commitment to battle. In them had been a certain eerie bliss. You had no more thinking to do, nor hoping nor praying. You only drew sword.

He fetched the lantern and carried it by the lug, as low down as might readily be so that he could pick his way up the path. Wind, snow, night had receded to remoteness; he barely heard the sea. The door of the House bore a knocker formed like a triskele. He thudded it as hard as he was able. 'Dahilis, Dahilis, are you within?' The noise disappeared.

'The sacrilege is mine,' he said, mainly for her sake, and opened the door.

Shadows wavered misshapen around a single room. From the Roman-tiled floor a wooden staircase led up into the tower. But that was for refuge. Here he saw a hearth, an oven, utensils, chair, stool, table, cabinet . . . rug on the floor, lamps and candlesticks on a shelf, hangings to relieve the bleakness of stone walls . . . at the far end, what might be an altar . . . closer by, a single bed, and tossed on to it the rolled sheets and blankets he knew.

'Dahilis!' he roared. Echoes laughed.

So, he thought.

She would need a fire, but he didn't know when he would come back with her. He laid out the nicely stacked kindling and sticks. From a jug he drenched them with lamp oil. Let that soak in, that he might be able to start a blaze immediately when he had brought her here to shelter.

Fire . . . He could be a long while searching. Best that he take several tallow candles to recharge the lantern. He snatched them off their shelf and stuffed them into the pouch at the belt of his Ysan garb. Down with them he put flint, steel, tinder, and punk, just in case – though he'd need some kind of windbreak before trying to start anything burning. Across his left arm he slung a wool blanket, while he took a firm grip on the lantern, ready to keep it level should he trip. Then he set forth.

'Dahilis!' he cried. 'Dahilis!'

The wind whistled, the waves resounded, his voice was lost. As he left the House behind, he glimpsed a seal that had come ashore to lie on the strand. Its gaze followed him till he was gone into his darkness.

He didn't know this damned island at all. There should be a footpath of some kind, but where? Snow had laid enough of a veil over the ground that he couldn't tell by looking. He only knew that it wasn't under the hummocks and tufts of winter grass or the bare, snickering bushes; but those grew sparsely. Besides, she might be anywhere.

It would do no good to run around yelling like a scared pup. Best he weave his way to and fro across the narrow land, guiding himself as best he was able by whatever clues there might be, such as the noise of the waters north and south. At that, he could easily miss her, if she didn't hear him and call an answer. Well, if so, he would work back again. Come daylight he could see farther than by the feeble glow he carried.

But it would be a long night.

–'Dahilis, Dahilis!'

–He came upon a pair of menhirs. Much taller than he, close together, one bluntly pointed and one with a beak-like projection near the top, they must be the Stones about which he had heard words let slip. They might be something towards which she would seek. At least they were things, here in the middle of nothingness. He cast around and around. She was not there. His voice was giving out.

–The snowfall ended in a last, spiteful sleet.

–He could only croak, like a crow with a bad cold.

–When he replaced the candle, fatigue made his hand shake so that he nearly dropped it.

–The wind slackened, but chill strengthened. Heaven was lightless. Gratillonius began to hear surf at the western end of Sena.

–He came upon her quite suddenly. Another shadow he wasn't sure of; a turn for a closer look; he stubbed his toe on a rock; and there she lay. Ice had formed in crackly little patches on her drenched garments. She was huddled around her unborn. Her face was bloodless and peaceful. The lids were not entirely shut, lantern light flicked off eyeballs. As he stooped above, he saw the wrecked ankle. O Mithras! Belisama, why did You let this happen?

He knelt beside her. His hand sought beneath her gown, his ear to her nostrils. Faint, faint . . . but she lived, the weather had not yet killed her . . . Almost as faint was the throb farther down. What, was her daughter trying to be born?

418

You will have to wait your turn, child.

It was less that strength came back to Gratillonius than that he ceased to feel weariness. He got the blanket around Dahilis, both arms under her, thumb and forefinger crooked again at the handle of his lantern. Rising, he began to walk. Meanwhile he, or someone inside him, laid plans. He must know his every move beforehand, for time would be short. His father, in mariner days, had instructed him about death from cold, what the danger signs were, what to do for a victim. An army surgeon on the Wall had similarly lectured to young officers from the South, as winter approached. Dahilis was far gone.

Belisama, Belisama, help her. Surely you love her too.

Did an owl swoop overhead? The merest glimpse –

The House loomed forth. He supported part of her weight on a thigh while he got the door open. As he entered, his light sent shadows bounding hunchbacked around the room. He kicked her stuff off the bed and laid her on the mattress. Wind whined outside, found the door ajar and skirled through. Water dripped from Dahilis's cloak and hair. He had set the lantern on the floor. To start a fire, oil or no, would take longer than he could afford. She must have warmth at once. His fingers flew, stripping the wet garments from her. Dahilis flopped like a jointed doll.

Now, off with his own clothes. The bed was as narrow as a grave, but that was all right; she needed him, the heat of his body, close against her. He grabbed a couple of dry blankets and threw them over both while he found a place for himself. He must cling, and the frame dug painfully into his hip, but no matter, no matter in the least.

His lips touched her cheek. It was like kissing ice.

A change went through her, a shivering, a dewiness on the skin. The breath he could barely sense turned irregu-

419

lar and faintly, faintly, infinitely remotely, laboured. He stamped on the horror that wailed within him and reached under her jaw, seeking the pulse. The jaw fell. He heard sounds and caught smells that were much too familiar.

It was so weak a death struggle that it was almost a surrender. (Belisama, Your will be done.) Gratillonius rolled from the bed, found the floor, bent over her. Again his fingers searched for the pulse in her throat. He couldn't find it. Eyes rolled back and half shut, blank, her face gaped slackly at him. He laid a palm over a breast and caught the slightest of motions. She was still breathing just a little.

The hand went down to her swollen belly. Did he feel a beating, as if against a door? He wasn't sure. He was no physician. Yet he remembered slaughtered beasts and slain barbarians. Caesar himself had made Roman law of what was olden practice: in cases like this, one must try to save the child.

Maybe she wouldn't have wished it, had she known what it was going to cost him. He couldn't ask her.

Time hounded him, closer even than before. The unborn were quick to follow their mothers into death. He had heard of some that were delivered but became defectives, worse than poor Audris. He could stay here and fight for Dahilis's life and almost certainly lose; and then her daughter was best left at peace in the dark. Or he could try for the rescue of her blood, not herself. The odds against that looked long also, but not hopeless. As fast as she was going, he must make his decision *now*.

He took the lantern again and went out, down to his tent, unaware of the wind and the cold.

When he came back, he used the flame to start candles, and thereafter kindled fire. Often he interrupted himself to attend Dahilis. His ministrations had no effect. When he ceased to feel her breathe, he used a bronze mirror he had found in her kit. Of course she had a mirror along, like any woman who wants to please her man.

At first it misted over. Soon that was so little that he crouched holding it in place below her nostrils. When it dried, he flung it clanging across the room.

He would have liked to kiss her farewell, but this was not Dahilis. He dropped a towel over the face. As for that which lay naked, he would not think about what it had been. He hoped he would not think about it. He hoped his farmer and craftsman skills, his rough knowledge of anatomy, would serve. A man could only try.

He had – how long? Three minutes, four, five? No more. Arrayed on the table, which he had dragged to the bedside, lay his small sharp knives.

5

Seas ran high on the morning after solstice, but wind had fallen off and skies were clearing. Dawn was barely a promise when Forsquilis and her companion came down the cliff trail to Ghost Quay and along the path to Scot's Landing. At Maeloch's door she smote the wood with her staff, whose iron finial was in the shape of an owl. The knock, knock, knock sounded loud amidst the clash of waves on rocks.

The door opened. The fisherman stood unclad, battle axe at the ready. 'What the squid-futter – ' he growled, and then saw. The lantern that the other woman bore cast glow across the austere features of the high priestess, hooded in her cloak. Behind them, water gleamed under the first thin light in heaven.

'Oh! My, my lady Queen!' He shifted the axe blade to

cover his loins. 'I thought . . . 'twasn't the Summons – pirates? My lady Forsquilis!'

'We have not met,' she said levelly, 'but you know me by sight and I you by repute. They call you both the boldest and the most knowing among the fishers. I command you to a faring as momentous as any of yours with the dead – or more, because on this hinges the morrow of Ys.'

'What?' Behind his shaggy beard, he gulped. 'My lady, that's plain recklessness. Look.' His free hand gestured at the chopping and leaping.

The eyes beneath the cowl would not let him go. He saw how haggard she was, as if she had been awake this whole night. 'Go we shall, Maeloch,' she said, 'and faster than ever you travelled erenow.'

He thought before he answered: 'I've heard as how Queen Dahilis went out to Vigil yesterday, like none ever did before. And the King at her side. Will you relieve her?'

'One might say that.'

'Why . . . why, I'll go, be sure I will, if little Queen Dahilis needs help. But the others may balk.'

'Are they Ferriers or not?'

Maeloch squinted past the lantern at her who bore it. 'This is Briga, of my household,' Forsquilis explained. 'She goes too.'

She was a sturdy, blonde young woman, clearly an Osismian. Such often came to the city and worked a few years, earning dowries for themselves. Sometimes they got married there, or seduced. Briga's free arm nestled a very new babe against her large bosom. Her countenance declared both fear and a doglike trust in her mistress the witch.

'Make haste!' said Forsquilis's whipcrack voice.

Maeloch mumbled excuses, retreated to get dressed,

422

came forth again to beat on neighbouring doors and bawl men off their pallets. When they saw the Queen, their grumbles quickly ceased, though she stood in place like an eidolon. Enough of them heeded the call to make a crew for *Osprey*, as they did at a Summons. Most of the regular deckhands lived elsewhere.

The smack lay beached under a roof for the winter; but the Ferriers of the Dead kept gear and supplies always aboard their boats, and were swift to fetch rollers and launch this one. She was off soon after the sun had cleared the Bay of Aquitania. The passage went better than the sailors had feared, though amply difficult. The tide was with them and the wind cold but easy, swinging around widdershins until after a while they could raise the sail to help them at their oars. Sundogs danced in a crystalline heaven. Given such brightness, the helmsman readily kept off reefs.

Briga huddled under the bows, miserably seasick, caring for her infant between trips to the rail. Forsquilis sat nearby, impassive. None ventured to address her. A sailor even forgot her when he pissed over the leeward side a short distance off. His ritual apology to Lir reminded him. 'Hoy, my lady, I'm sorry!'

She gave him the phantom of a smile. 'Think you me a vestal?'

He wrung his calloused paws. 'I should've taken the slop bucket aft. But this crossing, we know not why, 'tis got me all muddled . . . We do head straight back home, don't we, my lady?'

Forsquilis nodded. 'I shall abide. The rest of you will return.'

'Ye – ?' He looked down at his feet, braced wide upon the pitching deck. 'But 'tis festival time.'

Her own look went beyond the horizon. 'There are

signs to seek, rites to begin. In another day or two the barge can safely come fetch me.'

He saw that she wanted to be by herself, saluted awkwardly, and went about his duties.

– The rocks around Sena made approach so tricky that perhaps no skipper but Maeloch could have accomplished it today. When at last he brought *Osprey* to the wharf, his men slumped exhausted on their benches.

Forsquilis rose. 'Rest a while,' she said. 'We drove relentlessly west. You can go easier eastwards, homewards. Wait here.'

She sprang ashore, no need for a gangplank, and made for the House of the Goddess. Her cloak rippled blue. Gulls dipped, soared, creaked through the salt wind. Out amidst the skerries, where waves crashed and foam burst, were many seals.

– The door stood open, the windows were unshuttered, the room was bright and barren. On the bed lay a form covered by a blanket. The floor had been scrubbed clean. Gratillonius sat in a chair next the bed. In his arms he rocked a newborn girl. Her crying was loud and furious.

Forsquilis entered, darkening some of the light. Gratillonius looked up. Auburn hair and beard seemed doubly vivid against a face drained and congealed, nothing behind it but weariness. 'I have brought a nurse for her,' said Forsquilis. 'Come down to the boat. I will see to all else.'

XXVI

1

He came awake believing it was Dahilis who roused him. Happiness filled him like sunshine. His heart felt bird-light. Oh, my dear darling!

He opened his eyes. Bodilis withdrew the hand that had been shaking him. Gratillonius remembered. He cried out and sat up in bed.

Dim day entered the chamber through its panes. Bodilis stepped back. She was clad entirely in white, no jewellery, a coif over her hair. 'I'm sorry,' she said low. 'But you must arise. You've well-nigh slept the sun through a round.'

He recalled vaguely that Fennalis had given him a potion after he reached the palace. Earlier than that, sailors had borne a wrapped form on a litter from the quay towards Wayfaring House. Earlier than that he had been at sea, a rough passage . . . His memory was full of jagged gaps where mists and fragments drifted.

'We cannot delay further,' Bodilis urged gently. 'You are the King. The Gods require Their due. And then there is the infant.'

Dahilis's daughter. 'How is she?' grated out of him.

Bodilis smiled a tiny bit. 'Lustily yelling and kicking, the last I saw. Amazing, in view of – ' the smile died – 'the circumstances. But yours is strong blood, and her mother was no weakling. Now do get up, Gratillonius. You have your duties.'

His whole body ached, as if he had spent a night in

425

combat. His mind moved heavily. His spirit wanted to go away, home to Britannia or off to war or anywhere else. But he was the King. He was the prefect of Rome and a centurion of the Second.

Bodilis guided him to a hot bath. While he lay in it she brought him bread and wine. He had no appetite, but partook and gained strength. A massage afterwards by his burly body servant pummelled some sluggishness out of his muscles. Bodilis stood by as attendants arrayed him in crimson robe and royal finery. 'Where are we bound?' he asked.

'To the temple of Belisama,' she replied. 'It was decided to have both sacraments together, inasmuch as the mother is gone and you soon have your Watch to stand.'

'Both?'

'First the naming and hallowing of the child.'

He nodded. Dahilis and Innilis had told him about that while they were expecting theirs. 'I am to do what the mother would have done?'

'This is custom when a Queen dies in childbed.'

He remembered thoughts he had had while he waited in the House of the Goddess and afterwards aboard ship. 'Very well.'

Side by side, he and Bodilis went forth. The day was overcast, a silvery grey deepening towards lead as the unseen sun declined. The air lay quiet and raw. His legionaries stood marshalled to escort him. They saluted. 'Oh, God, sir, I'm sorry,' Adminius said. His lean features worked. 'We all are.'

'Thank you,' said Gratillonius, and walked on.

''Bout face!' Adminius shouted. 'For'ard march!' Hobnails hit paving like a roll of drums.

Traffic stopped when people saw who was coming. Nobody ventured to draw near or even utter a greeting.

Gratillonius and Bodilis moved within a shield-wall of quietness.

'We know almost nothing of what happened,' she said softly. Her arm was tucked in his. 'From what the fishers and the maid Briga and . . . others here in the city . . . had to tell, we can guess at some of it. What do you wish to relate?'

In faint surprise, he noticed that talking didn't hurt. It was merely a task he performed. Most of him was trying to understand what the thing itself meant. He could not yet really realize that he would never see Dahilis again, and that his last sight of her must for ever be – what it had been. 'When she had not returned by nightfall, I went in search. It took hours to find her. She lay with a broken ankle, in labour, unconscious, nearly frozen to death. I carried her back, but I could not *bring* her back. As soon as she died, I did my best to save the child. Any sin, profanation, blasphemy is mine alone. She was entirely innocent.'

Bodilis's grasp tightened. 'We shall purify and dedicate the island over again. As for your deeds, I dare hope – we Sisters have decided we dare believe – the justice of the Gods is satisfied. They need but look into your spirit. And as for the sacrifice They demanded, we believe Dahilis must have made that. It was not what the Nine awaited, and mayhap not what the Three intended, but surely it was an offering precious enough.'

Bitterness seared his gullet. He wanted no part of any such Gods. He refused the load of guilt They would lay on him. Let Mithras be his witness. But he would keep silence, he would duly go through Their rites, for Rome, and because he did not want to wound Bodilis. She must already be inwardly bleeding.

They reached the temple. The soldiers clanked up to form a double line on the stairs. King and high priestess went on in. 'The ceremonies will be brief and simple,' she reassured him. 'It is not like a Bestowal of the Key. A new Queen is presented to the people, and they make merry, only after the soul of the former Queen has crossed over.'

'What?' he asked, startled out of reverie. Before she could dispel his confusion, they were inside.

Vestals were ranked along the aisles. Their clear young voices lifted in a hymn. It chimed through the twilight of the sanctuary. Minor priestesses flanked the altar at the far end. From under her coif Bodilis pulled a gauzy veil across her countenance and went to join her Sisters. They waited behind the altar, beneath the tall strange images of Maiden, Mother, and Hag. Lamps on the marble block threw gleams off a golden basin which rested there. The white vestments everywhere around made the temple ghostly.

Gratillonius paused a moment before he concluded he should advance. He did so at a solemn pace. In front of the altar he halted and stood empty-handed, bareheaded. Neither Hammer nor crown had been laid out for him. Here in the holy place of Belisama, he bore just the Key.

A high priestess came forward to face him across the stone. Veil or no, he recognized Quinipilis. Though she spoke steadily, the youthfulness that had hitherto lingered in her voice was gone. 'King and father, we are met to consecrate your child. Because her mother has departed, yours is the benison. Let her be brought unto us, and do you give her name and First Sign.'

A senior underpriestess approached carrying the infant, which slept, red and wrinkled and how very small. You would not have thought that anything so small was hard to bring into the world. Quinipilis whispered: 'Do you know, Gratillonius? Dahilis was Estar.'

He knew, and knew that generally the first-born of a

428

Queen received the name that she herself had borne as a vestal. But he had known her as Dahilis, and this creature he had cut from her body was all that remained to him of her. Alone with the dead on Sena, he had pondered the question. It had been something to fill the hours.

Quinipilis took the blanket-wrapped babe and held her out. 'Draw a crescent on her forehead,' she directed low. 'Say: "Ishtar-Isis-Belisama, receive this Your servant Estar. Sanctify her, keep her pure, and at the last take her home to Yourself."'

Gratillonius dipped his right forefinger into the water that glimmered in the basin. He traced an arc on the diminutive brow. His voice rang loud: 'Ishtar-Isis-Belisama, receive this Your servant Dahut. Sanctify her, keep her pure, and at the last take her home to Yourself.'

The hymn faltered. Breath rustled and hissed among the priestesses. It was overriden by an angry scream from the awakened child. She struggled to get free of her swaddling.

Gratillonius met the unseen stares of the Gallicenae and growled in an undertone, 'I want her mother uniquely remembered in her. 'Tis lawful, I believe.'

'Ah, aye,' answered Quinipilis. 'Contrary to usage, but . . . the law is silent . . . Be you Dahut.' She returned the babe to the elder, who took it away to soothe.

Gratillonius's intent was clear. Dahilis had taken her sacral name from the spring of the nymph Ahes, to whom she had had a special devotion. The prefix 'D' was an honorific and could be retained. The suffix could not, but '-ut' formed a commemorative ending. Thus did Dahut come to Ys.

The hymn ended. Quinipilis straightened as much as she was able, raised her arms, and cried: 'Let the divine wedding commence!' Echoes flew around the hush.

Wedding? Gratillonius stood hammerstruck. Now?

But of course. How could he have forgotten? He must have wanted to forget. When a Queen died, the Sign came immediately upon a vestal. Eight women stood before him; and Forsquilis was on Sena.

He would not! Dahilis was not even buried yet!

The spectral forms came from behind the altar to surround him. Quinipilis stayed where she was. One of the others moved, stumbling a little, next to Gratillonius.

'Kneel,' the old priestess commanded.

He could go. They were nothing but women here. Outside waited his Romans. Thus easily could he betray his mission. Gratillonius knelt beside his chosen bride.

As if from far away, he heard a prayer. A new hymn swelled. More orisons followed, but they were mercifully short. He and she were bidden to arise. He obeyed the order to lift her veil. At the same time, his wives threw back theirs. The song soared triumphant.

He had seen the homely, timorous face before, but he could not recollect when or where.

'Gratillonius, King of Ys, in homage to the Goddess Who dwells in her, and in honour to the womanhood that is hers, receive your Queen Guilvilis – '

2

There was a modest banquet at the palace, which the Gallicenae shared. Directly afterwards the seven each kissed the new Sister and left. Servants requested her benediction and reverently escorted the pair to a bed-chamber swept, garnished, and lighted by many lamps and wax candles. Celebrations would come later, when the spirit of the former Queen had departed.

Talk had been scant at the table. Gratillonius said

nothing whatsoever. She sat by her husband, eyes down-cast, eating as little and as mechanically as he did. While goodnights went on, Bodilis had drawn Gratillonius aside and whispered in Latin: 'Be kind to her. Poor child, she never wished for this. Nobody imagined it. The ways of the Goddess are a mystery.'

'What is her lineage?' he asked hoarsely.

'Her father was Hoel, of course. Her mother was Morvanalis – full sister to Fennalis, but that makes her no closer than a cousin to Lanarvilis. Morvanalis died a few years after this girl was born. The child was good-natured but dull. I remember how she suffered the teasing of brighter classmates uncomplainingly, and sought her few friends among menials and animals. Everyone took for granted that when she finished her vestalhood – that would have been next year – she would take vows as a minor priestess, unless some man of humble station offered to marry her for the dowry the Temple provides. Instead – Don't blame her, Gratillonius. Treat her gently.' Bodilis's gaze went deep into him. 'I believe you have the strength to do that.'

I believe I shall often be drawing on the strength that is in you, he thought.

Incense sweetened the air in the bridal chamber. The flames gave warmth as well as amber light. Beyond the shutters, a night wind lulled. Guilvilis stood in her white gown at the middle of the floor, hands clasped above her loins, head bowed. It was a small head with rather thin, dull-brown hair and a protruding nosetip. Her figure was tall, bosom low, hips and legs heavy; her movements were awkward.

I have to say something, Gratillonius decided. 'Well.'

She stayed mute. He began to pace, back and forth in front of her, his own hands clenched together behind him.

'Well,' he said, 'fear not. I shan't hurt you. Indeed, tell me what would please you.'

He could barely hear: 'I know not, lord.'

His cheeks heated. Without meaning to, he had asked that which it took an experienced woman to answer, and every vestal was a virgin. He cleared his tightening throat. 'Might you like something in the way of comforts, pleasures, enjoyable tasks, freedom from uncongenial ones? Anything?'

'I know not, lord.'

'Um-mf. It seems . . . nobody told me what your name was before.'

'Sasai, lord.' She had not moved an inch from her passive stance.

'Ah!' It came back to him. 'Aye. You were at the Nymphaeum and guided me to the guardhouse when – '

When Dahilis and I went there to ask a blessing on her babe, and that night we made love.

I will *not* hate this person here.

Gratillonius moved to a nacre-inlaid table where stood cups and carafes. He poured wine for himself without adding water. 'Do you care for drink?' he asked. 'Make free.'

She glanced up, and hastily away. 'Thank you, nay, lord.'

He tossed off the cup in a few draughts that lit fire in his stomach. He'd need help getting to sleep. At least this was not the same room, the same bed where Dahilis and he had taken their joy. 'How came you to pick the name Guilvilis?'

'It . . . oh . . . Queen Lanarvilis said I could. 'Tis from a hamlet in the hills, she said. The house of Suffete Soren owns p-p-property there.'

'Hm,' Gratillonius rubbed his beard, refilled his vessel, drank more slowly. A thawing had begun to spread

432

through him. 'I take it . . . when the Sign appears . . . you tell somebody, and word goes to the – the rest of the Nine – and they meet with you?'

'Aye, lord.' A finger strayed up to touch her gown above the shallow curve of breasts. 'I woke from sleep, from a flash like fire, and, and – ' She swallowed. He saw tears. 'I was so afraid.'

A certain pity touched him. He took another swallow, set the cup down, went to stand before her. His left hand he laid on her shoulder, his right he put beneath her receding chin, to raise her face towards his. 'Be not afraid,' he said. ''Tis the grace of the Goddess.'

'They . . . were good to me – but – Oh, why was it me?' she quavered. 'Naught do I know.'

'You'll learn,' he said. 'Belisama must have known what She was doing.' Inwardly, he wondered. He patted her back. 'Be of brave heart.'

She half moved to put her arms about him, but withdrew them, a jerky, frightened motion. 'My lord is kind. O-o-oh . . .' She gulped, snuffled, somehow kept from sobbing.

He let her go and sought the wine. It gave him the courage he had been needing. His back to her, he said, 'Well, 'tis been a hard day for you, Guilvilis. Shall we to our rest?'

'Aye, lord.'

Still looking away and drinking, he said, after a space: 'You must understand something. I have had a great sorrow. All Ys has, but . . . as for myself . . . take it not amiss – we'll simply sleep this night, and – for a while to come.'

'Aye, lord.'

Perhaps the Goddess had shown him a mercy. This mooncalf would make no demands on him, ever.

He finished his wine and turned about. She had

433

undressed and stood naked at the bedside. There was more paunch than he had seen on most young women, but her complexion was clear, but her buttocks were huge and her legs like tree trunks, down through the ankles to the big feet. Ankles . . . The crescent above her breasts smouldered red.

She ventured the faintest of smiles. 'Whatever the King wants,' she said tonelessly.

'We'll sleep,' he snapped. He went about blowing out the lights as if he were the bride, not the groom. The bed creaked and rustled when she entered it. In the dark he removed his own clothes, left them on the floor, and felt his way.

He lay down and pulled sheet and blanket over him. Wine or no, he feared lying awake through the night. The incense cloyed. He turned on his side. It had been towards her, he suddenly knew – sheer habit. She stirred. He felt her nearby warmth. A scent of clean hair and flesh pierced the sweetness. His hand fell upon hers.

His member awoke. No! he cried, but it swelled and throbbed. No, this isn't decent! Heat boiled in him. She sensed his restlessness and, herself, turned. He made a motion to keep her off. His palm encountered a breast and closed over its softness. The nipple hardened and nudged.

O Dahilis! The Bull shook horns; Its hoofs tore the earth. Blind though he was, Gratillonius knew how Guilvilis rolled over on to her back and spread her legs. He was not Gratillonius who mourned, he was he who cast himself between her thighs, thrust straight through her maidenhead, heard her cry aloud and took delight, hammered and hammered and hammered. Gratillonius stood aside, at his post of duty, hoping that afterwards the Gods of Ys would allow him to sleep.

The funeral barge was fifty feet in length, gold-trimmed black, with a low freeboard and broad flat deck. Stempost and sternpost terminated simply in spirals. A staff amidships bore an evergreen wreath.

When possible, she went out every third day, bearing the dead of Ys from their homes or from Wayfaring House. Often that was not possible, and sometimes their hostellers must lay them to rest in the brine vats. Always, though, in the end, they went to sea.

This morning was bright and calm, sun frosty in the south. Wavelets glittered sapphire and emerald, marble-swirled. They lapped against cliffs, wall, hull. Oars chirked and splashed as the barge passed the gate on an ebbing tide. Gulls dipped and hovered. Seals glided among the reefs.

The dead were laid out shrouded, each on a litter with a stone lashed to the feet. Deckhands went quietly about their work. The loudest noise, and it low, was the ringing of a coxswain's gong, timing the slow stroke of the rowers. Passengers stood aside or sat on well-secured benches. For the most part they were kinfolk who wanted to say a final goodbye, clad in more subdued fashion than was ordinary. Three were ever on hand: a trumpeter, a drummer, and some one of the Gallicenae.

Upon this faring the whole Nine were aboard, and likewise the King, to follow their Sister. They stayed in a group near the bows, mute, looking inward or else far outward.

The barge travelled no great distance, because the bottom dropped rapidly. When the captain deemed they were over the deeps, he signalled. The trumpeter blew a long call, the gongbeat died away, the rowers merely held their vessel steady.

The captain made ritual request of the high priestess in charge. This time she was Quinipilis, who because of frail health had not come along in years. Blue-clad, her headdress tall and white, she trod forward, lifted her hands, and spoke with more strength than anyone had awaited. 'Gods of mystery, Gods of life and death, sea that nourishes Ys, take these our beloved – '

Having finished the invocation, she received a tablet from the captain and read the names aloud. They were in order of death, as were the bodies. At each, sailors lifted that litter and brought it to a chute on the larboard side. 'Farewell,' said the high priestess, and the men tilted their burden. A shape slid down. The water leapt a little and closed again.

–'Without a name.' Innilis caught her breath and reached after Gratillonius's hand. He took hers. 'Farewell.' Still weak, barely able to go through with the parts that had been hers, she sat down again.

–'Dahilis.' He felt his other hand taken, glanced aside, and saw Bodilis. The shape dropped from sight. 'Farewell.' The men carried back its bed.

–A trumpet call flew forth over Ocean. The drum marched underneath. There was a silence, save for the waves and mewing gulls. 'About and home!' the captain ordered. Oars toiled, the gong resumed, the galley turned landward.

–The declining sun changed the waters to molten gold whose light sank into the wall and the towers of Ys and radiated back. Shadows had begun to lengthen. Their intricacy made sculpture of the brutal headlands, made a weaving of mystical signs, while the city glimmered between like a dream.

When the boat had passed through a now narrowing gateway, it found the harbour basin full of mist and blue shadings. High and high overhead, an albatross caught sunlight on his wings. A murmur stirred in the coolness, traffic noises muted to a single sound, the breathing of a woman about to go to sleep.

The barge docked and passengers got off. On the quay, under a proud, time-crumbled façade, stood a few men in robes of office. Among them were Soren Cartagi, Speaker for Taranis, and Hannon Baltisi, Lir Captain. A touch surprised, Gratillonius accompanied his Gallicenae to meet them.

Soren offered salute. 'My lord,' the Suffete said, 'not hitherto have I had opportunity to bespeak my sorrow.'

By immemorial law, neither he nor Hannon were permitted on the barge until their own final journeys. 'Aye,' said the grey skipper, 'she was dear to everybody, but most to you.'

Soren's gaze travelled to Lanarvilis, then back to Gratillonius, and heid steady. His heavy features gave less away than his voice. 'You will have memories, King,' he said. 'They burn you, but may you later warm your hands at them on cold nights.' He cleared his throat. 'Enough. What I – what we here wish to tell you is this. We think the Gods have worked Their will and are at peace with Ys. In a certain measure you've bought that, lord. And you *are* a good King. We'll fight you no more.'

Lanarvilis smiled as though she had foreknown.

Soren lifted a finger. 'Mind you, lord,' he said, 'we may well find you wrongheaded in future and ourselves in opposition to you. We must stand fast for what is right. But 'twill be loyal opposition, for the welfare of Ys.'

Gratillonius took a moment to marshal words. 'I thank you,' he said. 'More than you know, I thank you. We'll go on together.'

Abruptly he realized that he meant it. Despair was for cowards. He still had work to do, battles to wage, dreams to dream. The life that had been in Dahilis flowed on in Dahut. Her tomorrows, which he must make sure of, were his renewal.

His next Watch would begin on the Birthday of Mithras.

XXVII

Maeloch awoke. Night engulfed him, save for fugitive red gleams from the banked hearthfire. The single room of his home was full of chill and odours, woodsmoke, salt, kelp, fish, humanity, sea. Again it knocked on his door, a slow one, two, three.

He sat up. His wife Betha stirred beside him. The straw tick rustled. He heard a child of theirs whimper, terrified.

Knock, knock, knock. 'I come,' he called.

'The Summons?' she breathed.

'Aye, what else?' he replied, lips close to her ear. 'The island's been hallowed anew, I hear. And 'twas a while in the doing; we'll have a load this trip.'

He always kept seagoing clothes where he could find them in the dark. Best not to light a torch at these times. You mustn't linger. Nor did you want to see too well.

'Who has the Vigil?' he muttered as he fumbled. 'Queen Bodilis? Meseems I've heard 'tis she. Pray hard, Queen Bodilis.'

The command had gone on down the row of cabins that was Scot's Landing. Clad, Maeloch gave Betha a quick, rough kiss and went out. The moon was full, the air mild. Light glittered and torrented on small inshore waves, flickered and shimmered across the swells beyond, made flags of the foam on skerries. Only the brightest stars were clear in sight. Orion strode opposite the hulking murk of the cliffs, thence the River of Tiamat flowed across heaven past the North Eye and back into unknownness. Frost glistened on thatched roofs. A breeze wandered from the southeast, winter-cold, not strong, but you could lift sail and get help for your oars on the way to Sena. Well, They

439

made sure before They called the Ferriers of the Dead.

Among the men gathering by moonlight, Maeloch recognized two fellow captains. Three boatloads, then. So many had not crossed over since the battle in summer.

Fishing smacks were soon launched. *Osprey* and the others lay alongside Ghost Quay. Gangplanks thudded forth. The wind and the sea murmured.

Maeloch spied nothing but moonlight on shingle, cliffs, and waves. He heard nothing but the sounds of the night. Yet he felt a streaming across the planks, and saw how hulls settled down into the water. They would bear a full cargo tonight.

The stars wheeled in their silence.

Osprey rode no lower. 'We are ready,' Maeloch said. His breath smoked white. 'All hands aboard.'

The three boats stood out. Sails blundered aloft. The trimming was tricky, and oarsmen must keep their benches, but it gave a little more speed for passengers who had waited long. Maeloch walked around issuing low-voiced orders as needed. Otherwise nobody spoke. The companion craft were like swans afloat.

Moonlight sleeked the coats of seals.

– The boats manoeuvred in among reefs whose treachery the moon betrayed, and made fast at Sena dock. The House of the Goddess loomed black, apart from glimmers of lamplight where the high priestess was praying. The island stretched ashen.

Men who had been securing lines came back aboard and stood aside. Maeloch drew back the hood of his leather jacket, to uncover his head, and took stance near the gangplank. The moon shone, the stars gleamed.

As the souls debarked, *Osprey* rocked ever higher in the water.

Maeloch heard them blow past, breaths in the night, bound for he knew not where. 'I was Dauvinach,' came to him barely . . . 'I was Catellan . . . I was Borsus . . . I was Janatha . . .'

The sea and the wind sighed.

–'I was Rael,' he heard. 'I was Temesa.'

–A whisper went by without a name.

–'I was Dahilis.'

–When it was done, the Ferriers of the Dead cast loose and made for their homes.

Afterword and Notes

Although our aim has been to make the text of this novel self-explanatory, certain historical details may surprise some readers, who may thereupon think we are in error. Other readers may simply wish to learn a little more about the era. Nobody has to look at these notes, but anybody who wishes to is welcome.

A word about nomenclature. In the story we generally give place names the forms they had at the time, rather than use their English versions. This is for the sake of accuracy as well as colour. After all, the boundaries of most cities, territories, etc. were seldom quite identical with those of their modern counterparts, and the societies occupying them were entirely different. There are a few exceptions, such as 'Rome' or the names of famous tribes, where insistence on the ancient rendering would have been pedantic.

As for personal names, the story uses original forms throughout. Most are attested, a few represent conjectures by us. Ysan names are imaginary but not arbitrary; they are supposed to show the Celtic and Semitic roots of the language, plus later Graeco-Roman influences. 'Ys' itself is pronounced, approximately, 'eess', though the vowel is pure, not a diphthong of the English sort. The French 'ice', as in 'justice', comes close.

A discussion of the Breton legend follows the notes at the end of the last book.

1

Mithras (or *Mithra*): A deity of ancient Aryan origin, whose cult reached Rome by way of Persia. Especially popular among soldiers, it became for a time the most important rival of Christianity, with which it had much in common.

The Birthday of Mithras: 25 December. Formerly it had been celebrated on the winter solstice, but precession of the equinoxes caused the latter to move backwards through the calendar. About 274 A.D. the Emperor Aurelian fixed the birthday of Sol Invictus as the 25th, a date which the related Mithraic faith adopted. The Christian Church would not settle on it for the Nativity of Christ until much later; in the fourth century, that event was still considered of secondary importance.

Gaius Valerius Gratillonius: Throughout the lands that the Empire ruled, inhabitants belonging to the upper and middle classes, and often persons more humble, generally imitated Roman nomenclature. Here 'Gaius' is the given name – which, however, men did not much use, if only because the selection was small. 'Valerius' belongs to a Roman *gens*, and indicates that at some time in the past someone of that tribe patronized, adopted, or freed a British ancestor. 'Gratillonius' is the cognomen, the family name, and is a Latinization of a native one (in this case, postulated rather than historically attested, in order to account for the later form 'Grallon'). Admittedly, by the time of our story, the system was breaking down and there were many exceptions to it; but provincials would tend to be conservative.

Borcovicium (also recorded as *Vorcovicium, Vorcovicum,* etc.): Housesteads.

Mail: Heavy infantrymen of this period generally wore coats of mail, not the loricated cuirasses of an earlier day. A centurion was outfitted differently from those under him. The crest on his helmet, detachable for combat, arched side-to-side rather than front-to-back; greaves protected his shins; his sword hung from a baldric, and on the left instead of the right; he did not carry the two javelins, light and heavy, but did bear a twisted vinestaff as emblem of authority and instrument of immediate punishment for infractions.

Cliff: Where nature had not provided such a barrier, a deep ditch paralleled Hadrian's Wall on the north. Another, with earthen ramparts, ran at some distance to the south.

Fifteen feet: Post-Roman quarrying has much brought down what is left of the Wall, but this was its original height, more or less, along most of its length. As for that length, from Wallsend on the Tyne to Bowness on the Solway it is 73 English or about 77 Roman miles.

Eboracum (or *Eburacum*): York.

Other legions in Britain: Besides the Sixth, those permanently stationed there were the Twentieth Valeria Victrix, based at Deva (Chester), and the second Augusta, based at Isca Silurum (Caerleon). Evidence indicates that a vexillation, a detachment, of the latter was called to Housesteads in the emergency of 382 A.D. As elsewhere throughout the Empire in its later days, legionary regulars were outnumbered by auxiliaries from all over, equipped and operating in their native styles.

Duke: At this time the *Dux Britanniarum* commanded the Roman forces in the provinces of Britain, with his seat in York.

Vindolanda: This site is today occupied by the farm Chesterholm.

Tungri: A tribe in the Low Countries.

Basilica: Originally this word meant an administrative centre, civil or military.

Base: Contrary to modern popular impressions, Hadrian's Wall was not intended as a line of defence, and hardly ever served as one. It provided a means of controlling peacetime traffic between Roman Britain and the tribes to the north; in the event of hostilities, it was a base out of which soldiers operated, taking war to the enemy rather than waiting for an attack.

Highlanders: The country of the Picts (a name loosely bestowed by the Romans) lay well to the north of Hadrian's Wall. Another common misconception makes them dwarfish; they were actually a rather tall people.

Warriors from across the water: The Scots were at this time living in what is now Ireland, except perhaps for an enclave on the Argyll coast. As the Empire declined, they came more and more to raid it, much in the style of the Vikings centuries later.

Praetorium: The commandant's house in a legionary fortress. It doubtless had other uses as well.

Principia: The headquarters block, generally comprising three buildings around a courtyard.

Isca Silurum: Caerleon in southeastern Wales.

Hispania Tarraconensis: A Roman province occupying a large piece of Spain, in the northeast and east.

Clean-shaven: To judge by contemporary portraits, many Roman men of this period were, though closely trimmed beards may have been a little more common.

Cunedag: Better known as Cunedda, but that is a later form of the name. His move to northern Wales with a following of his native Votadini (sometimes rendered 'Otadini') is historical; there he drove out the Scots and founded the kingdom of Venedotia, which eventually became Gwynedd. The Roman intention was that this should be a foederate, a closely controlled ally, but when the Empire receded it naturally became independent. Most authorities take for granted that the move was at the instigation of Stilicho, not Maximus. However, this is not certain; and Maximus himself did enter Welsh legend as Maxen Wledig, a prince who did something wonderful though unspecified for that country. Could it have been providing the leadership and organization from which the medieval kingdom developed?

Ordovices: The people occupying northern Wales. Roman practice was to convert native tribes into local units of government, somewhat like Swiss cantons.

Dumnonii: The people occupying, approximately, Cornwall and Devon.

Language: It is not quite certain, but it is not unlikely that there was a single Celtic language, with mutually intelligible dialects, throughout England and southern Scotland.

Stools: Chairs were not in common use. People ordinarily sat on stools, benches, or even floors.

Hivernia (or *Hibernia*): Ireland.

Wine: The Romans favoured wines so sweet and thick that they were best watered.

Mediolanum: Milan.

Augusta Treverorum: Trier.

Arians: Christians following the doctrine of Arius, which the Council of Nicaea had declared heretical.

Silures: The people occupying southern Wales.

Belgae: These folk held a broad territory in the South, ranging approximately from Somerset through Hampshire. They were the last Celts to reach the island, just a couple of centuries before the Roman conquest, and their Continental kin retained the same name. The Belgae claimed a strong Germanic strain in their ancestry.

British soldiers: For reasons uncertain today, auxiliaries of British birth, unlike most such, seem hardly ever to have been stationed in their home country. However, probably this was not so general a rule for regular legionaries.

Aquae Sulis: Bath.

Dacia: Approximately, modern Romania. In the later fourth century, the Empire had almost entirely abandoned this province.

Nervii: A tribe in the Low Countries.

Abonae: A small town on the River Avon (Latin *Abona*) in Somerset, near the meeting of this stream with the Mouth of the Severn (Latin *Sabrina*), which gives on the Bristol Channel and thus the sea.

Armorica: Brittany.

Gesoriacum: Boulogne.

Condate Redonum: Rennes.

Vorgium: Carhaix. In Roman times, until it was sacked, it was the most important city in western Brittany . . . except Ys!

Caledonians: A confederacy in the far North. However, the name was often given generally to the peoples beyond Hadrian's Wall.

Temenos: The hallowed ground before or around a temple.

Parnesius: Kipling makes him a centurion of the Thirtieth Legion, which was stationed in the Rhineland; we have found no confirmation of T. S. Eliot's assertion that it, or a vexillation of it, was on Hadrian's Wall at any time. Rather than leave Parnesius entirely out of the story, we suggest that he actually belonged to the Twentieth.

Serfs: Latin *coloni* (singular *colonus*), tenant farmers and their families whom the 'reforms' of Diocletian had bound to the soil they cultivated, as their descendants would be bound for the next thousand years and more.

Ahura-Mazda: The supreme god of Mithraism.
Pronaos: An entrance hall above or adjoining the inner sanctum of a temple.
Tauroctony: A representation of Mithras slaying the primordial Bull.

2

The history of Ireland from the earliest times through the heroic age, and even the beginnings of the Christian era, is obscure, often totally confused. Such sagas, poems, and chronicles as we have were written down centuries after the events they purport to describe. Taken as a whole, they are full of contradictions as well as anachronisms and outright impossibilities. Moreover, it is clear that the medieval recorders misunderstood much, deliberately changed much else as being too pagan or otherwise unedifying, and supplied numerous inventions of their own. Foreign historians are of small help, because Ireland never came under Roman rule. Archaeology supplies some clues, as well as data about everyday life. One can also extrapolate backwards from the oldest extant documents, notably the Brehon Laws, and from customs and beliefs reported by observers almost until the present day. Anthropology, with parallels to draw from other parts of the world, gives many hints as well.

In general, for this novel we have chosen those interpretations and hypotheses which best fit our story. Various authorities would disagree with us on various points. We will try to discuss briefly the most controversial matters as we go along.

The Irish still have no unanimity on how to spell Gaelic. The basic problem is that this is a language which does not lend itself well to the Roman alphabet. Besides, historical and dialectical variations are great. Our characters speak a forerunner of the language known as Old Irish, which itself is at least as different from modern Gaelic as Old Norse is from modern Danish. For a single example, the medieval and modern 'mac', meaning 'son of', was earlier 'maqq', pronounced approximately 'makw'. We are indebted to Celtologist Alexei Kondratiev for what knowledge of the ancient forms we have, but he must not be held responsible for our mistakes and deliberate modifications. Notably, we use the name 'Niall', although the older version is 'Néll', because its bearer looms so large in Irish history and tradition.

Imbolc: In the modern calendar, 1 February. The pagan festival must have taken place approximately then. Our guess is that it, like others, was determined by the moon. The customs mentioned flourished as late as the early twentieth century. They look very ancient, only slightly Christianized.

Manandan (maqq Leri): Later called Manannan mac Lir; a major Irish god, associated with the sea.

Brigit: Originally an Irish goddess. She appears to have been tripartite, as many Celtic deities were. Her name passed to a Christian saint – nowadays Brighid or Bridget – who was especially popular and whose feast day was 1 February. The spring tide nearest this date bore her name and was believed to be the greatest of the year.

Condacht (or *Olnegmacht*): Connaught, west central Ireland, still a recognized division of the country. We will presently discuss the Fifths.

Mumu: Munster, southwestern Ireland. Like 'Leinster' and 'Ulster', the modern form of the name traces back to the Danes, as does, for that matter, 'Ireland' itself.

Tuath: This word is often rendered 'tribe', but that is somewhat misleading. A tuath, consisting of families with

449

an intricate social ranking, was a political unit occupying a definite territory, but not otherwise especially distinct from others of its kind. Each tuath had a king (*rí*), who owed allegiance to the King of the Fifth, about which arrangement there is a later note. (The ancient form is *tótha*.)

Temir (later *Teamhair*): Now called Tara, this hill is located about 15 miles northwest of Dublin (which, of course, did not exist in our period; early Ireland had no towns). It had been used, if not continuously occupied, at least since megalithic times, and was regarded as especially charged with *mana*. However, tradition says that it was not until a few generations before Niall that a dynasty from Connaught established itself here.

King: The institution of the High King (*Ard-rí*) of Ireland did not exist even in theory until a much later date, and was never really very effective. In ancient times, at best the principal king of a Fifth commanded the allegiance of various lower-ranking kings, each of whom led a tuath or an alliance of several tuaths. (More grades of royalty eventually developed.) The King of a Fifth might, though, have additional powers or claims outside its borders. Allegiance amounted to little more than the payment of tribute – with the overlord expected to give a smaller amount of goods in return – and military service on strictly limited terms. Basically, any king lived off the proceeds of his own holdings, off certain payments from those beneath him, and off whatever he could plunder in wartime. His function was at least as much sacral as political.

Niall maqq Echach ('Echach' is the genitive of 'Eochaid'): Later famous as Niall of the Nine Hostages, ancestor of the Uí Néill dynasties. On the whole, we have followed traditional accounts of his life and exploits. Certain modern scholars maintain that these date him a generation or two too early; a few doubt that he is historical at all. It is true that many contradictions and other puzzles in the medieval chronicles can be resolved by some such theory, and we do not venture to say this is mistaken. Yet perhaps it gives certain annals more weight, at the expense of others, than they deserve. There are authorities who think so. Discounting the fabulous elements that have crept in, the old stories about Niall look plausible enough. The real problems arise with some about his successor Nath Í, which are scarcely to be taken seriously. For that matter, the chronology and the very identity of St Patrick are in confusion. Given all this, we have felt free to choose, from among the different accounts of Niall, those parts that accord with our story. Of course, we have added inventions of our own, beginning with his son Breccan, but these are not incompatible with our sources.

Ollam (or *olave*): The highest grade of any profession considered learned or skilled.

Free tenants: Land was held in ancient Ireland under a system too complicated to describe here. Briefly and incompletely put, however: land was inalienable from the tuath, which held in common the nonarable parts suitable for rough grazing, peat and wood gathering, etc. Farmland and the richer pastures were usually the property of some 'noble' – whether the king, a *flaith*, or a learned man such as a judge, poet, physician, etc. – who, though, basically held the acreage in trust for his family. Otherwise real estate belonged to a sept, who subdivided it from time to time among different members. Land not directly used by the owner(s) was rented out to tenants, who paid in kind and in services, since the early Irish did not coin money. A free tenant (*soer-céli*) supplied all or most of his own stock, paid moderate rent, enjoyed a good social standing, and might often be wealthy. A bond

451

tenant (*doer-céli*), to whom the landlord must furnish 'starting capital', paid a much higher rent and ranked much lower. Both classes had other obligations, but those of the free tenant were lighter, and his rights and privileges under the law were far more. Nevertheless, the bond tenant was in no sense a serf; the relationship was contractual, and either party could terminate it. Indeed, there appears to have been social mobility, with poor men occasionally bettering their lot. Slaves, without rights and set to tasks nobody wanted, were generally captives taken in wars or raids, or children of these.

Mide: Occupying approximately modern Counties Meath, Westmeath, Longford, parts of Kildare and Offaly, it is supposed to have been carved out of Connaught, Leinster, and Ulster by the upstart Tara dynasty. Whether or not it actually existed as such an entity in our period is uncertain, but we assume that it did.

The Lagini: The people of Leinster, southeastern Ireland. Their territory was known as 'Qóiqet Lagin', i.e. 'the Fifth of the Lagini'. The later form is 'Cóiced Laigen'.

The Ulati: The people of Ulster, northeastern Ireland. Their territory was Qóiqet nUlat.

Fifths: According to tradition, Ireland was anciently divided into five parts, the Fifths. Though their inhabitants had much in common with each other, four of these regions had quite distinct histories and, in some particulars, ways of life. Those were Ulster, Leinster, Munster, and Connaught, which retain a meaningful existence to this day. The medieval chronicles state that Mide was formed out of parts of them, mostly Leinster, by a dynasty originating in Connaught. This dynasty took possession of holy Tara and eventually produced the High Kings who theoretically were supreme over all lesser kings throughout Ireland. Boundaries were ill-defined and often variable, not identical with those of the four modern provinces. Thus, at times Munster was divided in two, and Ulster shrank under the impact of the Uí Néill. As we have remarked above, at best the Fifths corresponded only roughly to separate kingdoms, as limited as royal powers were; and the High Kingship, which did not appear until well after Niall's time, was more a legal fiction than a working institution. (Some modern scholars argue that the chronicles must be wrong and that Connaught actually developed out of Mide. It may be so; but as far as possible, we have chosen to follow the traditional accounts.)

Emain Macha: The seat of the Ulster kings, near modern Armagh.

Hill fort sacred to Medb: The ruins of this are now known as Ráth Maeve (a later form of the name 'Medb'). They may or may not be contemporary with the main earthworks on Tara; our guess is that they are older, but were maintained. The attribution to Medb may well be right. She has been identified with the wife of Airt the Lonely, father of Corbmaqq (later called Cormac), but we suspect that originally the dedication was to Medb, tutelary goddess of Mide.

Forest: Unlike the country today, ancient Ireland was thickly wooded.

Boand's River: The Boyne, of which Boand was the goddess.

Great Rath: The remnants of this are now called the Ráth na Ríogh, or Royal Enclosure, but that is pure guesswork. 'Rath' means such an enclosure, surrounded by an earthen wall – usually circular – which was originally topped by a palisade and often ringed by a fosse. It might protect anything from a single farmstead to a whole group of houses.

Pigs: The early Irish kept swine not only for food and leather, but occasionally as pets.

Heads: Like their Continental cousins before the Roman conquest, the Celts of Ireland were head-hunters until they became Christian.

Flaw: No man could be king who had any serious deformity or disability. Some kings abdicated after suffering mutilation in war or accident, rather than risk expulsion.

Hostages: Alliances, subjugations, etc. were cemented by exchange of hostages, generally from leading families – unless a victor took his without giving any in return. As a rule, provided the terms of agreement were observed, they were well treated.

Bodyguards and champion: Besides his retinue of full-time warriors, an Irish king had several bodyguards – the number four is in the annals – who were with him whenever he went forth, as much for his dignity as his protection. For similar reasons, he kept a champion to deal with challenges to single combat, as opposed to war. Incidentally, aggrieved parties could not bring lawsuits against him, but could do so against his steward. In case of adverse judgement, naturally the king put up the compensation. The British monarchy preserves a version of this custom.

Equipment of the warriors: Contrary to Giraldus Cambrensis, the Irish used battle axes before the Viking invasions; but they did not wear armour, except occasionally helmets or greaves.

Royal Guesthouse; King's quarters: It is merely our suggestion that these may correspond to what are now dubbed, respectively, the Forradh and Teach Cormaic. Some scholars question whether Tara was ever actually occupied, proposing instead that it served just for meetings and ceremonies. But not only are there raths, there are traces of actual buildings. Our idea is that, at least after the establishment of a dynasty centred here, a maintenance staff lived permanently on the hill, while aristocrats and their retainers came for short periods during the year.

Mound of the Kings: Today called the Mound of the Hostages, because of a story that a dormitory for hostages stood upon it. This is impossible; it is far too small. Another story says that hostages who died while in captivity were buried here; but excavation has turned up only a few post-Neolithic skeletons. Undeniably, this mound had some kind of sacredness from of old. Archaeology has revealed that it consists of earth heaped over a megalithic passage grave. Our guess is that this led to a reverence for it which grew over the years, until it was the site chosen for consecrating new kings at Tara.

Phallus: The Lia Fáil, Stone of Destiny. It stands on the Teach Cormaic, but was moved there in the eighteenth century; earlier, it seems to have been on or near the Mound of the Hostages. The name 'Phallus of Fergus' was local in recent times, and probably well-founded. Certainly this upright pillar could not have been a stone on which kings stood at their consecrations, as they did throughout early Ireland. The legend that it roared upon contact with a true king is ancient; we have borrowed a modern idea that in fact somebody swung a bullroarer. The 'coronation' stone on top of the mound is our own notion; nothing of the kind is there now.

Rath of the Warriors: Today called Rath of the Synods. More guesswork on our part: if kings stayed on Tara for any length of time at all, their military retinues would have needed some shelter, and this earthwork could have enclosed their barracks.

Dall and Dercha: The names of these two small burial mounds may or may not go back to our period.

Druid (actually the plural, *drui* being the original singular): Unlike their Continental (and probably British) counterparts before the Romans, Irish druids were not

455

priests. Rather, they were repositories of knowledge, tradition, and wisdom, who had undergone a long and arduous education. Some were female; women had a high standing in this society. Druids served as teachers and counsellors. In the earliest times they were also poets, judges, physicians, etc., but these gradually became separate specialists. They were believed to have powers of divination and magic. We might note that they did not collect mistletoe – a plant introduced into Ireland much later – nor pay any special regard to the oak; the trees that the Irish considered powerful were the hazel, yew, and rowan.

Ogamm (later *ogham*): A primitive alphabet, its signs consisting of strokes and dots along a central line. It seems to have been used almost entirely for memorial and magical inscriptions.

The Mórrigu (or *Morrigan*): The goddess of war. She seems to have had three aspects or avatars with different names. It has been suggested more than once that Morgan le Fay of Arthurian legend is a later version of her.

Taking valour: Ancient Irish of the warrior classes often put their sons through a ceremony of 'knighthood' as early as the age of seven.

Poets: A top-ranking poet (*fili*) was an awesome figure; in some respects, he was more powerful than any king. Like a druid, he had survived a relentless course of training and commanded incredible linguistic and mnemonic skills. His words could make or break a reputation; if he was angered and composed a satire, its effects were believed to be physically destructive. Probably the worst crime in old Ireland was to offer violence to a poet, druid, or other learned person. There was a lower class of versifiers, whom we may as well call bards, but they, although respected, were essentially just entertainers.

Senchaide (or *shanachie*): Today, simply a storyteller,

albeit often a delightful one. Very few remain active. In ancient times he was historian and genealogist to a basically illiterate society: he carried the annals of the country in his head.

The Feasting Hall: More guesswork on our part. What is now called the Banquet Hall (Teach Miodhchuarta) is the remnant of a great oblong earthwork, of approximately the dimensions that old stories ascribe to the hall where the Kings of Tara held their feasts. Some modern scholars think this was merely an open-air meeting site – but then why the ramparts? Others say the banks were formerly higher, which they doubtless were, and roofed over – but then why no traces of wood, when these have been identified elsewhere on Tara? Now it is attested in later history that the Irish could and did raise quite impressive temporary buildings, e.g., on one occasion to receive the King of England. Therefore we suggest that anciently they would erect such a hall within the elongated rath, demolishing and rebuilding it every three years for the triennial fair.

The feast: Unlike many peoples, the Irish generally took their principal meal of the day in the evening.

The cookhouse: Because of the fire hazard, cooking was usually done in a separate structure.

Battle-scarred women: Celtic women not uncommonly fought side by side with their men.

Laidchenn's verse: The syllabic prosody and interknit alliterations attempt to suggest one of the numerous early Irish poetic forms. Laidchenn himself figures in the sagas.

Lúg: A primary god of all the Celts, remembered in place names as far off as the south of France (Lyons, which was known to the romans as Lugdunum).

Magimedon: A nickname meaning 'servant (or slave) of Medon', who was presumably a god. Another interpretation is 'master of slaves'.

Carenn (or *Cairinn*): Laidchenn is relating the legends about Niall's early life that have come down to us today. It is not implausible that these would have cropped up almost at once; examples of the same thing are everywhere around in our own era, usually less close to the facts than tales of him may have been. We have modified them only slightly, in order to rationalize the chronology. Our assumption is that listeners, including Niall himself, accepted even the most fantastic parts as being metaphorically if not always literally true; moreover, there could well have been a considerable amount of selective recall and actual self-hypnosis, phenomena which are also common enough today. As for his mother, the medieval account calls her a Saxon princess, but this is most unlikely. On the other hand, if we take her name to be an Irish rendition of 'Carina', she could have been Romano-British – perhaps the daughter of some tribal chieftain, or even a princess.

Succession of kings: Kingship, whether over a tuath or a larger polity, was inherent in a particular family: that is, a particular line of descent on the male side. Otherwise it was elective, and illegitimacy was no barrier.

Marrying the land: Well into Christian times, Irish kings at their inaugurations went through a ceremony of 'marrying the tuath' or 'the realm'. This was purely symbolic; but the earlier pagans doubtless enacted it literally, choosing some maiden to embody the goddess, with whom the new king spent a night. The patron deity of the Tara line, and so presumably of Mide, was Medb. Thus legend says that Niall coupled with her, despite her disguise; and whether or not he believed this happened in fact, he did with her mortal representative.

Dál Riata (or *Dalriada*): A kingdom of eastern Ulster which founded a colony of the same name in Argyll, the first important settlement of Scots in what was to become

Scotland. The date of the founding is quite uncertain. Since the colony enters into the traditional story, we perforce assume that it was already in existence by Niall's time. This is debatable but not impossible.

Gess (later *geas*; plural *gessa*): A kind of taboo; a prohibition laid upon an individual or a class. It might be traditional or might be imposed by one person on another. Sometimes the gessa look very strange. For example, another of those on the King at Tara was that he must never travel widdershins around North Leinster; and the hero Finn mac Cumail (Old Irish form) was forbidden to sleep more than nine nights running at Allen. To break a gess was thought to bring disaster, and would certainly be disgraceful unless one was forced to it by trickery or circumstance, as various legendary figures were.

3

Burdigala: Bordeaux.

(Gallia) Narbonensis: A Roman province incorporating part of southwestern France.

Wine: This was produced in southern Britain under the Romans, and well into medieval times, after which the climate became too severe. With conditions now again milder, some is once more being made.

Fish and Chi Rho: These ancient Christian symbols were still in common use, whereas the crucifix was not yet so, and the cross not often.

Villa: To the Romans, this word meant a farm, not a house – especially a farm of some size.

Solidus: A gold coin, one of the few that had not been debased, therefore valuable and hard to come by.

Saddles: It is not certain whether the Mediterranean

civilizations had yet adopted the Asian invention of stirrups; but improved saddles were already making cavalry more important than it had ever been before.

Cataphracts: Heavy-armoured cavalrymen. Such a corps may have been the historical original of Arthur's knights, half a century or so after our story closes.

Ard: A primitive plough, wheelless, and possessing merely a pointed end. The mouldboard plough appears to have been a Celtic invention, not much employed by the Romans except in areas where heavy soil gave it the advantage. Since no effective horse collar existed, an ox was the usual draught animal.

Curials: The curials, also called decurions, were those men of a city and its hinterland who had a certain amount of property. That is, they corresponded more or less to the middle class of modern Western civilization. They were expected to be active in local government and to meet various public expenses out of their own coffers. The caste system imposed by Diocletian froze them into this station, while the decay of the economy and the inordinate taxes of the state gradually ruined them.

Londinium: London. Its official Roman name, Augusta, was falling out of use.

Senators: In the late Empire, senatorial rank was conferred as often as it was inherited, carried privileges and exemptions rather than obligations, and was frequently attained by corrupt means.

Theatre: Despite the generally moralistic atmosphere of the late Empire, performances – supposedly of classic stories – were apt to be as raw as anything on our contemporary screens.

Navicularius: A shipowner. Such persons were tightly organized into a guild. Theoretically they were born to their status and could not get out of it, but in practice there must have been exceptions.

Dubris: Dover. Rutupiae (Richborough) had supplanted it as a major military base, but being a fort of the Saxon Shore it must have kept a garrison, and it was still an active seaport.

Navigation: The ancient mariners generally avoided sailing in autumn and winter less for fear of storms than because weather was too likely to hide the landmarks and heavens by which they found their way.

(Gallia) Lugdunensis: A Roman province incorporating much of northern and part of central France.

Wives: In contrast to the practice of earlier times, soldiers of the later Empire were allowed to marry during their terms of service. Doubtless this was meant as an inducement to enlist, for conscription was seldom resorted to any more, and when it was, oftenest out of subject peoples. Wives and children lived near the base, husbands joining them when off duty.

Gesocribate: It is not certain whether this town developed into the modern Brest, or was simply near the site of the latter.

Count (Latin *comes*): An official in charge of the defences of a particular area. Best known to English-speaking moderns is the Count of the Saxon Shore, who governed the fortresses along the southeastern coast of Britain.

Foederate (Latin *civitas foederata*): A nation allied with or satellite to Rome. The word was also used for troops recruited from such peoples.

Gratillonius and his men: The army of the late Empire was organized differently in some respects from that of the Republic or Principate. Eight men of a legion formed a *contubernium*, sharing a tent and pack horse; in barracks they also shared two rooms, one for equipment and one for sleeping. Ten such parties made up the usual century (*centuria*), commanded by a centurion: thus numbering 80 rather than the original 100. Six centuries were grouped in three pairs (maniples) to form a cohort, and ten cohorts comprised a legion. The first cohort was larger than the rest, being made up of five double centuries, because it included all the technicians and clerks of headquarters. Hence the legion contained about 5300 infantrymen. In addition there were 120 horsemen – orderlies, scouts, and dispatch carriers rather than cavalry – distributed among the various centuries; there were also higher officers and their staffs, specialists, etc. Altogether a legion was from about 5500 to 6000 strong. As political, economic, and military conditions worsened, the actual total often became less.

The backbone of the legion was its centurions, most of whom had risen from the ranks. The senior centurions (*primi ordines*) were in the first cohort, whose first century was commanded by the chief centurion (*primus pilus*), a trusted and honoured veteran who, after a year, might go on to become camp prefect (*praefectus castrorum*), in charge of the legion's internal organization and operations – or might take some equally responsible post, if he did not simply retire on his savings and a large gratuity given him.

Originally the commandant of the legion was the legate (*legatus*), who was a political appointee of senatorial rank, although he was expected to have served before as a military tribune – staff officer – and so to have learned generalship. Since the reign of Gallienus, the camp prefect had supplanted him. There is no need here to describe other functionaries.

Many legions had existed for hundreds of years, and some had been based at their sites for almost as long. Strangely enough, considering the vital function of the centurions, they were quite commonly assigned and reassigned to different legions, sometimes across the width of the Empire. Probably the government did not want too close bonds of mutual personal loyalty between such career officers and the enlisted men. Gratillonius had not held the rank sufficiently long for this to have happened to him, but likely it would have if Maximus had not entrusted him with a mission that brought him to an unforeseen fate.

Or perhaps it would not have happened. What we have just been describing no longer existed in the eastern part of the Empire. There infantry was largely made up of *limitanei*, reservists who were called on to fight only in the areas where they lived, while the core of the armed forces was the cavalry, composed mostly of Germanic mercenaries. By the end of the fourth century, the strength of a legion was no more than 1500 men, set to garrison and other minor duty.

However, though these transformations were also taking place in the West, they were much slower, and quite likely had scarcely begun in Britain or northwestern Gaul. For one thing, there the principal menaces to Rome – Saxons, Franks, Alemanni, etc. – were not yet horsemen. Military reforms like those enacted at Constantinople were indeed imperative, but the enfeebled government of the West was incapable of doing anything quickly or efficiently.

Thus a soldier such as Gratillonius could have begun his service in a unit in a legion not very different from, say, one of Marcus Aurelius's – aside from the large number of auxiliary troops – and ended it in an army not vastly different from, say, William the Conqueror's.

4

Sails: Roman transport ships did not use oars, except for steering. Warcraft generally did, making sails the auxiliary power. It is worth remarking that the rowers were free men, and rather well paid. Galley slaves did not appear until the Middle Ages.

Pharos: Lighthouse. The beacon was a fire on its top after dark; by day, the tower was a landmark helpful to navigators. The Dover pharos, of which a part still exists, was about 80 feet high.

Dobunni: A tribe occupying, approximately, Gloucestershire, Herefordshire, and some adjacent areas.

Deputy: Second in command of a century, chosen by the centurion himself, hence the Latin name *optio*.

Regnenses: A tribe in Sussex.

Demetae: A tribe in the western part of southern Wales.

Coritani: A tribe occupying, approximately, Lincolnshire and adjacent territories.

Navy: The *classis Britannica* that guarded the coasts around the Channel and the North Sea approaches disappears from history about the middle of the third century. Its former base at Dover, abandoned even earlier, was converted to a fort of the Saxon Shore. However, Dover remained a seaport, and surely the military still needed some ships of their own.

Prefect of the cohort (praefectus cohortis): Commander of a unit of infantry auxiliaries. The word '*praefectus*' was used in a number of different contexts.

Lanterns: These, with panes of glass or thin-scraped horn, were known to the Romans. Some were quite elaborately made.

Hostel (Latin *mansio*): Accommodations for persons travelling on business of the state were maintained at rather frequent intervals along major routes. It seems reasonable to us that the one closest to a small city such as Gesoriacum would be outside rather than inside the walls, to save valuable building space and for the benefit of persons who arrived belatedly. On the other hand, there would probably have been at least one hostel near the centre of any large and important city.

Candles: The Romans had both wax and tallow candles. The latter, at least, were considered much inferior to lamps, if only because of the smell, while the single material available for the former, beeswax, was too expensive for any but the richest people. Nevertheless tallow candles were much used, especially in areas where oil for lamps was scarce and thus costly.

Publican: The publicans of the Bible were not jolly taverners, as many moderns suppose, but tax farmers. Only Jesus, among decent people, could find it in his heart to associate with them. Their circumstances and practices changed as the Empire grew old, but not their spirit.

Tax in kind: This had become especially important as debasement made currency increasingly worthless. Diocletian and Constantine had reformed the coinage, but honest money remained scarce.

Couriers: The Roman postal service must still have been functioning reasonably well in most areas, since we have a considerable volume of correspondence among clergy and other learned men. Graffiti show that literacy was not confined to the upper classes, either. However, in regions as distressed as the northern Gallic littoral now was, the mails had surely deteriorated.

Massilia: Marseilles.

(Civitas) Baiocassium: Bayeux.

Hoofs: Horseshoes had not yet been invented, but a kind of sandals or slippers was sometimes put on the animals when ground was bad.

Standard bearer: The *signifer* wore an animal skin of a sort traditional for his unit. In a small detachment like this, it would make sense to rotate the duty. The standard was not the legionary eagle but a banner.

Rations: Archaeology has revealed that the legions enjoyed a more varied diet, with more meat in it, than historians had thought.

Beans: Broadbeans (fava), the only kind known in Europe before the discovery of America.

Lent: As yet, the formula for calculating the date of Easter had not been finally settled upon, but varied from area to area and was the subject of much controversy. Nor was there agreement on how long a period of abstention should precede it, or on what austerities should be minimally required. For that matter, there was no standardized weekly practice of self-denial, such as the meatless Friday of later centuries. One may presume that even soldiers who were devout would not trouble themselves about that, at least while on duty. However, Easter, the holiest day in the Church calendar, and observances directly related to it, would be of concern. Strictly speaking, therefore, our use of the word 'Lent' is anachronistic – but it conveys, in brief, approximately what Budic had in mind.

Sunday: The week as we know it had not yet been officially taken into the Roman calendar, though of course it was ancient in the East. One may well wonder how many ordinary soldiers were conscious of it, especially when in the field.

Nodens: A Celtic god, especially revered at the Severn mouth, in which flow great tidal bores.

466

Leagues: The Gallic *leuga* equalled 1.59 English or 1.68 Roman mile.

Rhenus: Rhine.

Caletes: A tribe in northeastern Gallia Lugdunensis, occupying approximately Seine-Maritime, Oise, and Somme.

Osismii: A tribe in the far west of Brittany, occupying approximately Finistère and part of Côtes-du-Nord. Place names and other clues seem to show they were not purely Celtic, nor were neighbouring tribes. Rather, Celtic invaders probably imposed an aristocracy which interbred and became identified with the people. Meanwhile the language, too, became largely Celtic. The earlier race was not necessarily descended straight from the megalith builders; there could have been more than one set of newcomers over the centuries. Yet nothing appears to forbid our supposition that the Armoricans *believed* the 'Old Folk' were among their ancestors. An analogous tradition exists in Ireland.

Honestiores: Great landholders, virtual feudal overlords.

Alani: An Iranian-Altaic people, originally living in what is now southern Russia. Under pressure from the Huns, the western branch of them mingled with the Germans and joined these in that great migration into Roman territory which was just getting well under way at the time of our story.

Ingena: Avranches. Today it is Norman rather than Breton, but of course neither of those peoples had yet reached France.

Vorgium (later *Osismiis*): Carhaix. Folk etymology derives the present name from 'Ker-Ahes' ('Stronghold of Ahes', the latter name being given to Dahut in some versions of the Ys legend), but this is false.

Mauretania: approximately, northern Morocco.

Condate Redonum: Rennes.

Veneti: A tribe in south Brittany, occupying approximately Morbihan.

Fanum Martis: Corseul. The tower is still there, in remarkably good condition.

Garomagus: There was a Roman town of some small importance – as we describe later – in the area of modern Douarnenez, but its name is not known. 'Garomagus' is our conjecture, referring to its production of *garum*, a fish sauce which was a major item of Armorican trade.

Passage grave occupied by refugees: A case of this is known. There were probably more.

Ahriman: The supreme lord of evil in the Zoroastrian religion and its Mithraic offshoot, as Ahura-Mazda (or Ormazd) was the lord of good.

Franks in Condate Redonum: Those tribes lumped together as Franks (Latin *Franci*) originated in western Germany and the Netherlands. As yet they had not overrun Gaul, but some had entered and settled in various areas. The laeti at Rennes and their open paganism, including even human sacrifice, just at the time when Gratillonius passed through, are attested.

5

Sena: Île de Sein. Archaeology shows it to have been occupied since prehistoric times, but we suppose that for several centuries it was reserved exclusively for the use of the Gallicenae – as the first-century geographer Pomponius Mela says was the case in his own period.

House: There are traces, now submerged, of what is believed to have been a Roman building at Île de Sein. Was this actually the sanctuary of its priestesses, remodelled under Roman influence?

Stones: These two megaliths are still on the island.

Cernunnos: A major Celtic god, represented as a man with stag's antlers.

Yes, yea, aye: You may have noticed that hitherto no person in the story has used any of these words. This is because Latin and the Celtic languages have no exact equivalent. We suppose that Semitic influence on the evolution of the Ysan tongue, otherwise basically Celtic, produced such words in it, just as the Germanic example would cause the Romance languages to develop them. Latin and Celtic do not employ a simple 'No' either when giving a negative response. However, we have supplied it in rendering the former, in order that that may seem colloquial to the modern reader, and have also provided Ysan with it.

6

Astrology: Belief in this prevailed throughout the late Roman Empire, along with countless other superstitions. Since it appears to have been part of the Mithraic faith, Gratillonius was heterodox in his reservations about it.

Book: The codex may go back as far as the first century. Towards the end of the fourth it had displaced the scroll except for legal and other special purposes. Elaborate illumination of the medieval sort was not yet done, but illustration of a simpler kind was, and it seems quite likely that the binding of some religious manuscripts was ornate and costly.

Twenty miles: Roman miles, of course.

Gobaean Promontory (Promontorium Gobaeum): The Cap Sizun area.

AVC: Anno Urbis Conditae ('V' was habitually used for

'U' in inscriptions), year after the founding of Rome, for which the traditional date corresponded to 753 B.C. The Romans themselves rarely counted time from this baseline, but the reference was not unknown.

SPQR: Senatus Populusque Romanus, 'The Roman Senate and People', proud motto of the Republic, long borne on standards of the legions.

Fortress and maritime station: The remnant of the fortress can still be seen on Pointe de Castelmeur. There must have been more of it extant in Gratillonius's day. The station is rather conjectural.

Key: By Roman times, locks had developed into bolt-and-pin types not too unlike modern sorts. Their keys had corresponding prongs. When a key was inserted, these prongs pushed up the pins, whereupon a sidewise pull drew back the bolt.

7

Fresh-made laurel wreath: The laurel is an evergreen.

Cape Rach: Pointe du Raz (hypothetical reconstruction of the aboriginal name). The *ch* is supposed to be as in modern Scottish or German.

Refusing the crown: While today our knowledge of Mithraism is scanty, this detail is attested.

8

Point Vanis: Pointe du Van (hypothetical reconstruction of the aboriginal name).

Nummus (plural *nummi*): A coin of the late Empire, minuscule and debased. It took more than 14,000 to equal one gold solidus. Archaeology shows that Gresham's Law was as operative in Roman times as it is now.

Thule: It is not certain what the Classical geographers meant by this name. Iceland and Norway are among the more common suggestions. We incline towards the latter.

The sea gate of Ys: Today one would solve the problem of protecting a harbour from overwhelming tides by constructing locks. These, however, were not developed until much later.

Saxons (Saxones): This name did not distinguish any single tribe or kingdom. Rather, it was a general term used by the Romans for all those robbers and invaders who came across the North Sea from the northern Netherlands, the German littoral, Jutland, and possibly regions still more distant.

9

Soap: This appears to have been a Gallic invention, regarded by the Romans more often as a medicinal for the skin than as a cleansing agent.

Basilica: In this period and earlier, the word referred to a building for public business – administration, trials at law, etc.

The layout of the church: Private homes were frequently converted for this purpose, but it is clear that no one in Ys who might be willing to make such a donation possessed a suitable one; so, as happened elsewhere (for example, to the Parthenon), this pagan temple was expropriated by Imperial decree. Normally there would be a baptistry, but in Ys there was no resident bishop, and a chorespiscopus had no authority to administer this sacrament – which was not usually given children anyway. *Vide infra*. Believers who had not received it could enter no farther than the porch or vestibule, and were dismissed before the Communion service began in the sanctuary. Even in the great churches, furniture was basically the same as described here. Such amenities as pews were for a later era.

Redonic: Of the tribe of the Redones, around Rennes.

Audiarna: Audierne, on the River Goyen, some nine English miles east of the Baie des Trépassés. There are traces of Roman occupation. Our Latin name is conjectural, and we assume the name of St Audierne comes from the town rather than vice versa.

Consecrated bread and wine: At this period, only a bishop could consecrate the bread and wine for the Eucharist, or perform several other important functions. This consecration was generally of large quantities at a time, which were then distributed among churches. Eucherius would seldom have to restock. Not only was his congregation tiny, but the majority of it were unbaptized, having only the status of catechumens and therefore unqualified to partake of the Lord's Supper. Baptism was a rite regarded with great awe. It must be done by a bishop or, at least, under the supervision of one; as a rule, this was just once or twice a year, notably at Easter. Most believers received it comparatively late in life, not uncommonly when on their deathbeds – as in the case of Constantine I. After all, it washed away prior sins, but was of no avail against any that might be committed afterwards, which indeed would then be the deadlier.

Eucherius's heresy: It anticipated that of Pelagius, in some small degree; such ideas were in the air.

The appointment of Eucherius: At this time the Church organization that we know today, including the Papacy itself, was still nascent. Originally each congregation had had its own bishop, the priests and deacons being merely his councillors and assistants, but eventually the numbers of the faithful were such as to require something more elaborate, which naturally came to be modelled on the Roman state. The process was under way in the decades around 400 A.D., but as yet there was a great deal of local variation, arbitrariness, and outright irregularity. For example, St Patrick may well have consecrated himself a bishop. The chorepiscopus served most of the functions later assigned the parish priest, but by no means all of them.

Neapolis: Naples.

(Gallia) Aquitania: A Roman province occupying, approximately, the part of France south of the Loire, west of the Allier, and north of the Pyrenees.

Tamesis: The Thames.

The Hooded Three: The *genii cucullati*, a trio of gods (?) in Britain about which we have little more information than some representations and votive inscriptions.

Handclasp: The handshake as we know it seems to be of Germanic origin, but might have appeared independently in Ys, or been observed by travellers and become a custom at home.

Niall and the women: In sleeping with women of various households, the King was not exerting any special prerogative nor giving any offence. Early Irish society gave a great deal of freedom to women other than slaves, includ-

473

ing the right to choose which of several different forms of marriage or cohabitation they wanted. Wives often took lovers, with their husbands' knowledge and consent.

Mag Slecht: In present-day County Cavan. Cromb Cróche (later Crom Cruach) and the twelve attendant divinities were probably pillar stones, sheathed in gold and bronze. There will be more about them later.

Ruirthech: The Liffey.

Clón Tarui: Now Clontarf, a district of Dublin on the north shore of the bay. It became the site of a famous battle in the year 1016.

Public hostel: There were several classes of these in early Ireland, endowed by kings or communities with enough land to support the provision of free food and shelter to all travellers. Such hospitality was required to maintain honour; and, to be sure, it encouraged trade. The inn-keepers were usually men, but sometimes women.

Border of the Lagini: The River Liffey does *not* mark the border of present-day Leinster. It did, though, come to form one frontier of lands subject to the southern Uí Néill. Given the enormous uncertainties about conditions at the time of their great ancestor, we think it reasonable to suppose that Mide extended this far. After all, Niall could scarcely have ravaged Britain as repeatedly and thoroughly as the chronicles say, did he not have at least one port of embarkation on the east coast of Ireland.

Bóru tribute: About this, more later. Imposed of old by Connaught on Leinster, it came to be claimed by the Tara kings, but more often than not they had to collect it by force, and oftener still it went unpaid. In large part this was because it was exorbitant (though one need not take literally the traditional list of cattle and other treasure). King Brian, eleventh-century victor at Clontarf, got the nickname Bóruma – now usually rendered as Boru – because he did succeed in exacting it.

Smoke: Modern experiments have shown that primitive Celtic houses could not have had vent holes as more elaborate halls did. Instead, smoke simply filtered out through the conical thatch roofs, killing vermin on the way.

Horseblanket: The ancient Irish seem to have used merely a pad when riding. It is not certain whether they had saddles by the time of our story, but if they did, the use of these could not have been common.

10

Greenish light: Even the best Roman window glass had such a tinge.

Diocese: A division of the Empire. In our period there were fifteen, of which Britain constituted one. Each was governed by a vicarius, who was responsible to a praetorian prefect. The praetorian prefect of Gaul, residing in Trier, also administered Britain and Iberia. A diocese was subdivided into provinces, whose governors, called praesides, had civil but not military authority.

Triclinium: The dining room in a Roman house. However, the basic layout of an Ysan home was different from that of a typical Roman one.

11

Ishtar: The recorded Carthaginian form of this name is 'Ashtoreth' or something similar, but we assume 'Ishtar' was the older version; and Babylonian immigrants to Ys would have reinforced its use.

Sea level: This has varied considerably in historical time, presumably because of melting and refreezing of polar ice as climate passes through cycles of warmth and cold. In the late fourth century it was at, or not long past, a peak. Western Brittany, where the tidefall is always great, would be especially affected – above all in small bays with steeply shelving bottoms between sheer headlands.

12

Lutetia Parisiorum: Paris.
Draughts: Board games of various sorts were popular in antiquity, though none seem to have been identical with any played nowadays. However, versions of what we now call draughts or chequers go back to Pharaonic Egypt.

13

Noble landowners: A *flaith* was a man who actually owned land, normally by right of inheritance although subject to the claims of his kindred and tuath. He rented out most of it to others, for payment in kind and in services.
Beltene (also spelled *Beltane, Beltine,* etc.): In the modern calendar, 1 May. In pagan times the date may have been set according to the moon, but would have fallen approximately the same. Most lunar calendars count from the new moon, which is the phase most readily identifiable, but we assume that the Northern Celts, at least, wanted a full moon at their great festivals, to help light ceremonies held after dark. They could have added fourteen or fifteen days to the time when they observed the new one – or

they may simply have taken advantage of the fact that the full one is less often completely lost to sight in the wet climate of their homelands. Second only to Samain in importance, Beltene carried with it many beliefs and customs which survived, somewhat Christianized, almost until the present day. We have extrapolated backwards in order to suggest what various features may originally have been like.

Marriage: In ancient Ireland this had several different forms. Among them was not only the usual arrangement negotiated by parents with an eye to advantageous alliance between families, but unions for a limited span, freely entered into by the individuals concerned. While women did not have all the rights of men, on the whole they enjoyed – if freeborn – more liberty than their sex would again, in most of the world, until the twentieth century.

Needfire: Before the invention of matches, kindling a fire was a laborious and ofttimes precarious task, therefore a serious matter. If a hearthfire went out, it was generally easiest to borrow coals from a neighbour to restart it. Deliberately extinguishing it, in order to begin quite afresh, was an act fraught with religious and magical significance.

Rath of Gráinne and Sloping Trenches: These are present-day names of ruined works on Tara which were probably burial rather than dwelling sites. People in Niall's day may already have been telling much the same stories about them that we now hear.

Síd (later *sídhe*): 'Fairy mounds' or, in general, underground habitations of supernatural beings, to whom the same word is applied as a name. They appear to have been originally megalithic tombs, although later they included natural hills. When Christianity had prevailed in Ireland, the síd folk became largely identified with the

Tuatha De Danaan, tribes possessing magical powers who had retreated into these fastnesses after suffering defeat in war, but still came forth on occasion for good or ill. It is clear that those were, mainly, the old gods themselves, slightly disguised. To the pagan Irish, the síd folk were presumably ghosts and other such night-wanderers.

Conaire: The story of this king and his death at the destruction of Dá Derga's hostel appears to be so ancient that it was already a myth among the Irish of Niall's time.

Samain (today usually spelled *Samhain*): In the modern calendar, 1 November. It was the most important and awesome of the Celtic festivals. Many beliefs and practices associated with it continued through the Christian era virtually to the present day.

Diarmait (later *Diarmuid*) and *Gráinne*: A legendary pair of lovers, with whom folklore associates the Rath of Gráinne.

Liger: The Loire.

14

Bare marble: The classical Greeks generally painted their statues and buildings. The Romans did likewise for sculpture, but as for buildings, at least in the later part of their history, they were more apt to make the stone itself the decoration, frequently as a facing on a concrete structure.

Portus Namnetum: Nantes. Condovincum, uphill, was later incorporated.

Shield grip: Celtic and Nordic shields were not held by loops for the arm but simply grasped by a handle. The Romans added a shoulder strap.

Breccan maqq Nélli: Breccan son of Niall, 'Nélli' being the genitive.

Tír innan Oac: The Land of Youth, one of several paradises which Celtic mythology located afar in the western ocean.

Milesians: In Irish legend, the last wave of invaders (prior to the Vikings). A number of tuaths, especially in Connaught, claimed descent from them, and looked down on 'Firbolg' who could not.

Following wind: It is not clear whether Germanic galleys and Irish currachs (or 'curraghs' or 'coracles') could tack at all. Roman square-riggers could get no closer than seven points off the wind, and had the advantage of comparatively deep draught, in that era when the keel was not yet designed to help. Sprit-riggers did better. As for currachs, Tim Severin put leeboards on his *Brendan* but admits this may be an anachronism, since there is no evidence for them until well into the Middle Ages. We therefore suppose that they did not exist in our period. Under sail, doing anything but running straight downwind, crews would have used their oars for lateral resistance to keep on a broad reach, which was probably the best they could achieve; without a wind from astern, they struck their sails and rowed. It must have been likewise for Germanic galleys. Certain archaeologists doubt that those even had sails until just before the Viking era, but we think that at least some had primitive rigs in imitation of the Romans.

Christian Scoti: It appears that there was a significant Christian community in Munster, if not in the rest of Ireland, well before St Patrick.

Wolf: We know that the bad reputation of this animal is undeserved. However, until recent times most people dreaded and hated it, and there is reason to believe that wolves did occasionally attack humans – especially in hard winters when they could get no other food – as well as raid livestock. Firearms have changed that; the wolf is quite able to learn a lesson and teach its young.

15

Maze: Intricate sets of paths had been laid out in northern as well as southern Europe since neolithic times, probably for religious or magical use.

16

Funeral societies: A Roman legionary was expected to belong to a military funeral association, the dues of which were stopped from his pay. When he died it gave him a proper burial.

Sena: Implicit are various topographical differences from today's Île de Sein. It is most unlikely that so low and small an island, constantly battered by waves which storms sometimes dash clear across, would remain for centuries unchanged.

17

Mithraism: Little is known today about the doctrines of this religion. We present those which are reasonably well attested. Their parallels to Christianity were remarked upon at the time, in writings which survive, and are presumably due to common origins of the ideas in question. As for the rites, there is virtually no record, aside from some propagandistic Christian references. Out of these we have taken what looks plausible, and added thereto a good deal of conjecture.

18

Planets: In classical astrology and astronomy, the sun and the moon counted as planets, making – with Mercury, Venus, Mars, Jupiter, and Saturn – seven in all.

Carthaginian abhorrence: It is not certain what the actual attitude of the Carthaginians was towards homosexuality. The Mosaic prohibition suggests that they may have tried to ban it like their fellow Semites the Jews, if only as part of a general reaction against the Graeco-Roman world, but this is perhaps a mistaken idea. However, in any case Ysans who did disapprove – conceivably as a legacy from the Celtic side of their descent – would naturally attribute the same feeling to the founders of their city. As for contemporary Romans, although bisexuality among men, especially in the form of pederasty, had been widespread in the late Republic and the Principate, under the Dominate Christian influence and a generally puritanical mindset eventually drove it underground.

19

'Tene, Mithra,' etc.: The line is adapted from Kipling's poem 'A Song to Mithras' – 'Mithras, also a soldier, keep us true to our vows!'

20

Theatre: Where there was a curtain in a Classical theatre, it was generally deployed from below rather than above, since the building was roofless. The Ysan theatre is unique in several respects, perhaps most notably in allowing women – preferably respectable women – to perform. Among the Greeks and Romans, they only did so in pornographic shows; otherwise female roles were played by boys.

Feast of Lug: Known to the Irish of recent times as Lugnasad, it is now fixed at 1 August, although we are again assuming that originally the date varied. We also suppose that the Continental Celts pronounced the name differently from their insular cousins.

21

C. Valerius Gratillonius: the name 'Gaius' was abbreviated 'C.', a relic of times before the Roman alphabet possessed a letter 'G'.

22

Guilt and expiation: Some modern Christian apologists have maintained disapprovingly, and some neo-pagans have maintained approvingly, that the ancients had little or no concept of sin, few sexual inhibitions, etc. This is utter nonsense, as even a superficial study of their writings, onwards from the oldest Mesopotamian and Egyptian texts, will show. For that matter, anthropologists have found that the concept of any noble savages living anywhere in happy innocence and harmony with nature is equally ludicrous.

Dahilis forbidden to Gratillonius: Present-day medical doctrine allows sexual intercourse, if there are no complications, practically to the end of pregnancy; but this is a very recent idea, as your authors can attest with some ruefulness. In most societies, abstinence has been urged or commanded for expectant mothers during the last several weeks or months. Given the limited capabilities of physicians and rudimentary knowledge of sanitation in the ancient world, this was probably wise then.

Falernian wine: Renowned in Roman times, it came from an area within Campani, which was a region including modern Capua and Naples. Today's Campania, in turn, includes ancient Campani in a larger territory.

23

Black Months: The Breton expression for this time of year may well have ancient origins.

Dál Riata: A kingdom in Ulster, or its colony of the same name, across the North Channel on the shore of what is now Scotland.

Mandrake: Beside its alleged magical properties, mandrake root was anciently used as an emetic, purgative, and narcotic. The *Encyclopaedia Britannica* (11th ed.) observes, '. . . it has fallen into well-earned disrepute.'

Pellitory: Pyrethrum parthenium, Shakespeare's 'fever-few', related to the chrysanthemum.

Money in circulation: The economic depression in the Roman Empire, with more and more trade being in kind, inevitably affected other states. Coins, especially those least debased, tended to accumulate in hoards such as later ages have unearthed. However, a society whose institutions were still basically sound would respond to any stimulus given its businesses.

24

Opium: This was known to the ancients in the form of extract from either the whole plant or the capsule, but apparently used only as an analgesic. The source being Asia Minor, where the opium poppy was native, supply to Western Europe must have cut off as trade declined.

25

Teeth cleansers: The Romans had versions of toothbrushes and dentifrices.
Toys: If Gratillonius appears unsentimental about Innilis's miscarriage, one should remember that attitudes towards such things, and towards infants, were different then. Prior to modern medicine and sanitation, mortality was so high that parents dared not invest much love in a child until it was old enough to have a reasonable chance of living further.
Snow and ice: These are not especially common in Breton winters, which are oftener rainy, but do occur sometimes.
Caesar: The Caesarian section gets its name not because Julius was thus born – he wasn't – but because he re-

established the old Royal Law that when a woman died in late pregnancy, a surgical attempt should be made to save her child. The first recorded operation on a living woman occurred in the sixteenth century, and until recent times the fatality rate was so high that it was a last-choice procedure. Nowadays, of course, it is almost routine.

Bay of Aquitania: Sinus Aquitanicus, the Bay of Biscay.

Wet nurse: For a newborn infant, it would naturally be preferable to have a woman who had herself given birth very recently.

The Birthday of Mithras: As we have stated before, this was fixed at 25 December – but in the Julian calendar, which was already out of step with astronomical time. Hence the date of the full moon following was earlier than a modern ephemeris for the fourth century, using the Gregorian calendar, indicates. Throughout the writing of this book, we have tried to be as accurate as possible about all verifiable details.

Geographical Glossary

These equivalents are for the most part only approximations. For further details, see the Notes.

Abona: The River Avon in Somerset.

Abonae: Sea Mills.

Alba: Scotic name for what is now Scotland, sometimes including England.

Aquae Sulis: Bath.

Armorica: Brittany.

Audiarna: Audierne (hypothetical).

Augusta Trevororum: Trier.

Bay of Aquitania (Sinus Aquitanicus): Bay of Biscay.

Boand's River: The River Boyne.

Borcovicium: Housesteads, at Hadrian's Wall.

Britannia: The Roman part of Britain, essentially England and Wales.

Burdigala: Bordeaux.

Campani: A district of Italy including modern Capua and Naples.

Cape Rach: Pointe du Raz (hypothetical).

Clón Tarui: Clontarf, now a district of Dublin.

Condacht: Connaught.

Condate Redonum: Rennes.

Dacia: Romania.

Dál Riata: A kingdom in Ulster, or its colony on the Argyll coast.

Deva: Chester.

Dubris: Dover.

Eboracum: York.

Emain Macha: Seat of the principal Ulster kings, near present-day Armagh.

Ériu: Ireland.

Falernia: An area in Campani, noted for wine.

Fanum Martis: Corseul.

Gallia: Gaul, including France and parts of Belgium, Germany, and Switzerland.

Gallia Lugdunensis: A province occupying most of northern and part of central France.

Gallia Narbonensis: A province in southwestern France.

Garomagus: A town near present-day Douarnenez (hypothetical).

Gesocribate: Brest (?).

Gesoriacum: Boulogne.

Gobaean Promontory (Promontorium Gobaeum): Cap Sizun.

Hispania Tarraconensis: A province in the northeast and east of Spain.

Hivernia: Roman name of Ireland.

Ingena: Avranches.

Isca Silurum: Caerleon.

Liger: The River Loire.

Londinium: London (in part).

Lugdunensis: See *Gallia Lugdunensis*.

Lutetia Parisiorum: Paris (in part).

Mag Slecht: Cult site in present-day County Cavan.

Massilia: Marseilles.

Mauretania: Northern Morocco.

Mediolanum: Milan.

Mide: A kingdom occupying present-day Counties Meath, Westmeath, and Longford, with parts of Kildare and Offaly.

Mumu: Munster.

Narbonensis: See *Gallia Narbonensis*.

Neapolis: Naples.

Osismiis: Later name of Vorgium (q.v.).

Point Vanis: Pointe du Van (hypothetical).

Portus Namnetum: Nantes (in part).

Qóiqet Lagini: Leinster (in part).

Qóiqet nUlat: Ulster.

Redonum: See Condate Redonum.

Rhenus: The River Rhine.

Ruirthech: The River Liffey.

Rutupiae: Richborough.

Sabrina: The River Severn.

Sena: Île de Sein.

Tamesis: The River Thames.

Tarraconensis: See *Hispania Tarraconensis*.

Temir: Tara.

Treverorum: See *Augusta Treverorum*.

Vindolanda: Chesterholm, at Hadrian's Wall.

Vorgium: Carhaix.

Ys: City-state at the far end of the Gobaean Promontory (legendary).

Dramatis Personae

Where characters are fictional, their names are in Roman lower case; where historical, in Roman capitals; where of doubtful or debatable historicity, in italics. When a full name has not appeared in the text, it is generally not here either, for it was of no great importance even to the bearer.

Adminius: A legionary from Londinium.

Adruval Tyri: Sea Lord of Ys, head of the navy and marines.

Allil: A half-brother of Niall.

Antonia: A sister of Gratillonius.

ARCADIUS, FLAVIUS: Eldest son of Theodosius, his eventual successor as Emperor in the East.

Artorius: The former steward of the Gratillonius estate.

Audris: Daughter of Innilis by Hoel.

AUSONIUS, DECIMUS MAGNUS: Gallo-Roman poet, scholar, teacher, and sometime Imperial officer.

Betha: Wife of Maeloch.

Blodvin: Osismiic maidservant of Fennalis.

Bodilis: A Queen of Ys, daughter of Tambilis by Wulfgar.

Bomatin Kusuri: A Suffete of Ys, a sea captain and Mariner delegate to the Council.

Borsus: An Ysan.

Breccan: Eldest son of Niall.

Brennilis: Leader of the Gallicenae in the time of Julius and Augustus Caesar.

Briga: Osismiic maidservant of Forsquilis.

Brión: A half-brother of Niall.

Budic: A Coritanic legionary.

Carenn: Mother of Niall.

Calloch; A Gaul, former King of Ys, father of Fennalis and Morvanalis.

Camilla: A sister of Gratillonius.

Catellan: An Ysan.

Cathual: Charioteer to Niall.

Claudia: A woman mentioned by Eucherius.

Colconor: A Gaul, King of Ys at the time of Gratillonius's arrival.

Commius: A Romano-Britannic senator.

Cothortin Rosmertai: Lord of Works in Ys, head of the civil service.

Craumthan maqq Fidaci: Brother of Mongfind, successor to King Eochaid maqq Muredach.

CUNEDAG: A prince of the Votadini.

Cynan: A Demetaic legionary.

Dahilis: A Queen of Ys, daughter of Tambilis by Hoel.

Dahut: Daughter of Dahilis and Gratillonius.

Dauvinach: An Ysan.

Docca: A Dumnonic woman, once nurse to Gratillonius.

Donalis: A former Queen of Ys, mother of Quistilis by Wulfgar.

Ethniu: A former concubine of Niall, mother of Breccan.

Elissa: (1) Birthname of Lanarvilis. (2) Daughter of Lanarvilis by Lugaid.

Eochaid maqq Muredach: A former King at Temir, father of Niall.

Eppillus, Quintus Junius: A Dobunnic legionary, Gratillonius's deputy.

Esmunin Sironai: Chief astrologer in Ys.

Estar: Birthname of Dahilis.

Eucherius: Christian minister (chorepiscopus) in Ys at the time of Gratillonius's arrival.

Evar: A maidservant of Innilis.

Ewein: A neighbour of the Gratillonii in Britannia.

Faustina: A sister of Gratillonius.

Féchra: A half-brother of Niall.

Fennalis: A Queen of Ys, daughter of Ochtalis by Calloch.

Fergus: A half-brother of Niall.

Forsquilis: A Queen of Ys, daughter of Karilis by Lugaid.

Gaetulius: A Mauretanian, former King of Ys, father of Maldunilis, Vindilis, and Innilis.

Gladwy: Birthname of Quinipilis.

GRATIANUS, FLAVIUS: Co-Emperor of the West with Valentinianus.

Gratillonius, Gaius Valerius: A Romano-Briton of the Belgic tribe, centurion in the seventh cohort of the Second Legion Augusta, later King of Ys.

Gratillonius, Lucius Valerius: Older brother of the above.

Gratillonius, Marcus Valerius: Father of the two above.

Guennellius: A Britannic curial.

Guentius: A Britannic legionary.

Guilvilis: Name taken by Sasai when she became a Queen of Ys.

Gwynmael: Gamekeeper, later groom on the Gratillonius estate.

Hannon Baltisi: Lir Captain in Ys.

Herun: A seaman in the Ysan navy.

Hoel: A Gaul, former King of Ys, father of Dahilis.

Innilis: A Queen of Ys, daughter of Donalis by Gaetulius.

Iram Eliuni: Lord of Gold in Ys, head of the treasury.

Janatha: An Ysan.

Julia: Mother of Gratillonius.

Karilis: A former Queen of Ys, mother of Forsquilis by Lugaid.

Keban: A prostitute in Ys.

Kerna: Second daughter of Bodilis by Hoel.

Laidchenn maqq Barchedo: An ollam poet who joined the court of Niall.

Lanarvilis: A Queen of Ys, daughter of Fennalis by Wulfgar.

Laurentinus: A Britannic curial.

Lugaid: A Scotian, former King of Ys, father of Forsquilis.

Lugotorix, Sextus Titius: A Gallo-Roman publican.

Lyria: Birthname of Karilis.

Maclavius: A Britannic legionary and Mithraist.

Maeloch: An Ysan fisher captain and Ferrier of the Dead.

Maldunilis: A Queen of Ys, daughter of Quistilis by Gaetulius.

MAXIMUS, MAGNUS CLEMENS: Commander of Roman forces in Britannia, later co-Emperor.

Mongfind: Stepmother of Niall, said to have been a witch.

Morvanalis: A former Queen of Ys, mother of Guilvilis by Hoel.

Nemain maqq Aedo: Chief druid to Niall.

NIALL MAQQ ECHACH: King of Temir, overlord of Mide in Eriu.

Ochtalis: A former Queen of Ys, mother of Morvanalis and Fennalis by Calloch.

Parnesius: A Romano-Britannic centurion, friend of Gratillonius.

Pertinax: A Romano-Britannic centurion, friend of Parnesius.

Prudentius: A Redonian, deacon to Eucherius.

Quinipilis: A Queen of Ys, daughter of Redorix, mother unspecified.

Quistilis: A former Queen of Ys, mother of Maldunilis by Wulfgar.

Rael: A prostitute in Ys.

Redorix: A Gaul, former King of Ys, father of Quinipilis.

Runa: (1) Birthname of Vindilis. (2) Daughter of Vindilis by Hoel.

Sasai: Daughter of Morvanalis by Calloch; later Guilvilis.

Semuramát: Third daughter of Bodilis by Hoel.

Silis: A prostitute in Ys.

Soren Cartagi: Speaker for Taranis in Ys, Timbermen delegate to the Council.

Taenus Himilco: An Ysan landholder.

Talavair: (1) Birthname of Bodilis. (2) First daughter of Bodilis by Hoel.

Tambilis: A former Queen of Ys, mother of Bodilis by Wulfgar and Dahilis by Hoel.

Tasciovanus: A Britannic curial.

Temesa: Maidservant of Quinipilis.

THEODOSIUS, FLAVIUS (known to history as the Great): Emperor in the East; eventually, briefly, sole Roman Emperor.

Uail maqq Carbri: A henchman of Niall.

Una: Daughter of Ewein and first love of Gratillonius.

Usun: An Ysan fisherman, Maeloch's mate on *Osprey*.

VALENTINIANUS, FLAVIUS: Half-brother of Gratianus and co-Emperor of the West with him.

Vallilis: A former Queen of Ys, mother of Tambilis by Wulfgar.

Verica: A Britannic legionary and Mithraist.

Vindilis: A Queen of Ys, daughter of Quinipilis by Gaetulius.

Wulfgar: A Saxon, former King of Ys, father of Tambilis, Quistilis, Karilis, Lanarvilis, and Bodilis.

Zeugit: An Ysan, landlord of the Green Whale.

Fantasy authors in paperback from Grafton Books

Raymond E Feist

Magician	£3.50	☐
Silverthorn	£2.95	☐

Richard Ford

Quest for the Faradawn	£2.50	☐
Melvaig's Vision	£2.50	☐

Robert Holdstock

Mythago Wood	£2.50	☐

Michael Shea

Nifft the Lean	£2.50	☐
A Quest for Simbilis	£1.95	☐

Tim Powers

The Anubis Gates	£2.95	☐

Patricia Kennealy

The Copper Crown	£2.95	☐

Fritz Leiber
'Swords' Series

Swords and Deviltry	£2.50	☐
Swords against Death	£2.50	☐
Swords in the Mist	£2.50	☐
Swords against Wizardry	£2.50	☐
The Swords of Lankhmar	£2.50	☐
Swords and Ice Magic	£2.50	☐

To order direct from the publisher just tick the titles you want
and fill in the order form.

All these books are available at your local bookshop or newsagent, or can be ordered direct from the publisher.

To order direct from the publishers just tick the titles you want and fill in the form below.

Name _____

Address _____

_____

Send to:
Grafton Cash Sales
PO Box 11, Falmouth, Cornwall TR10 9EN.

Please enclose remittance to the value of the cover price plus:

UK 60p for the first book, 25p for the second book plus 15p per copy for each additional book ordered to a maximum charge of £1.90.

BFPO 60p for the first book, 25p for the second book plus 15p per copy for the next 7 books, thereafter 9p per book.

Overseas including Eire £1.25 for the first book, 75p for second book and 28p for each additional book.

Grafton Books reserve the right to show new retail prices on covers, which may differ from those previously advertised in the text or elsewhere.